the *Makeover* horse

Ocala Horse Girls
Book 5

Natalie Keller Reinert

Also by Natalie Keller Reinert

Ocala Horse Girls
The Project Horse
The Sweetheart Horse
The Regift Horse
The Hollywood Horse

The Florida Equestrian Collection
The Eventing Series
Briar Hill Farm
Grabbing Mane
Show Barn Blues
Alex & Alexander: A Horse Racing Saga
Sea Horse Ranch: A Beach Read Series

The Hidden Horses of New York: A Novel

Catoctin Creek: Small Town Romance
The Settle Down Society: Romantic Comedy
Sorry I Kissed You: A Rock Star Romance

Learn more at nataliekreinert.com

Chapter One

I WOULD HAVE liked a moment to sit and stare out over the steering wheel. Take in the surroundings. Understand that I've really done it, really upended my entire life and embarked on a crazy new career that makes absolutely no sense, on paper or otherwise. This early-summer afternoon in Florida looks custom-made for a fresh start, at least. Blue skies, fluffy cumulous clouds, and a ninety-percent chance of a total mental breakdown.

But my new employers are waiting for me, and they look so expectant, so pleased to see me, that I can't bear to disappoint them by sitting here and bursting into tears—of relief, of horror, of shock, of joy, all commingled into one sob-fest—so I plaster a smile on my face, pop open my truck door, and let the outdoors into the cab for the first time since I filled up the gas tank at the Okahumpka service plaza on the turnpike.

Sixty miles from the closest ocean, and three hundred miles from West Palm Beach, but there's no doubt that we're still in Florida. It's humid as hell.

"Mackenzie!" Basil Han, jumper trainer and friend from my bad old days in Wellington, clasps his hands endearingly. He's of Chinese descent and when the wind blows from behind him, a curtain of alluringly smooth, dark hair falls over his eyes; he smooths it back with one hand, a gesture I remember. "You're here!"

"I am," I say.

Basil's girlfriend, pretty and round-faced, gives me the most welcoming smile I've ever seen in my life. "It's so great to meet you at last!" she exclaims. "I mean, I feel like I know you already."

"I feel like I know you, too," I say, unable to resist her gorgeous smile. I've spent hours on the phone with Basil and Kayla, working out the logistics of this job offer, where I'll stay and when I'll start and what I can bring with me. It's complicated, running away from your past. I had to make sure everything was in apple-pie order before I started this journey in earnest. I slide down from the truck cab and my knees nearly buckle when my paddock boots hit the ground. "Woo, I'm exhausted," I say, laughing sheepishly. "I hope you didn't want me to start work this afternoon, because that was a long freaking drive."

"Oh, no," Kayla says, looking alarmed at the idea. "Settle in today and tonight."

"You can start running our lives tomorrow," Basil offers.

"That's the goal, right?" I put my hands to the small of my back and stretch. "Hope I don't let you down."

"You'll be amazing at it," Kayla says. "You know how to take care of horses already, and everything you haven't done yet, we'll teach you! We're not high-maintenance, I promise."

Basil just smiles, and I know he's amused at Kayla's gross underestimation of their needs around here. They're training high-class show horses out of a rented barn in the wilds of north-central Florida, shipping horses about an hour to the big horse shows in Ocala with regularity all summer—and for weeks at a time in winter. They needed a barn manager with experience running a stable full of high-performance horses. But thanks to this remote location, they got me instead.

"I just hope I can keep up with you," I say, wishing I wouldn't be this honest. It's a fault of mine. I run my hands over my dark brown hair, pressing down as if I can combat the constant flyaways from my taut ponytail. "I mean...you know—"

"You're going to be fine," Basil says firmly, giving me a little head-shake. Basil also knows all about anxiety. I'd known him as a tense young man back on the Wellington circuit, but when I first got him on the phone to talk about the job, I got a calm, measured version of the Basil I used to know. He told me leaving the hustle and bustle of south Florida did wonders for his brain. And he has assured me moving to this remote farm he's rented in the wilds of north-central Florida, far from the madding crowd, will do wonders for me, too.

Well, I need wonders, so I'm hoping he's right. I've kind of risked everything on his promises.

There's no turning back now. Especially since I'm so far from everything I've ever known.

"What did you think of the drive in?" Kayla asks. "Pretty countryside, right?"

"Gorgeous," I agree, "just a little farther from civilization than I expected." I've never seen so few houses per mile, not in Florida. Except for, maybe, driving across the Everglades on the appropriately named Alligator Alley.

"It's far from town, but I think you'll be comfortable," Basil says. He gives me a reassuring smile. Basil is a handsome, kind, intelligent amalgam of cultures, South Floridian by way of England by way of Hong Kong. He's a thoughtful horseman and, I can only assume, a wonderful boyfriend. Kayla is a lucky girl. He continues, "Kayla and I try to go to the price club and stock up on pantry stuff once a month, so you're never far from a box of crackers or extra toilet paper." He grins. "And of course, even out here, we've got high-speed internet and Amazon Prime."

"Don't look so nervous!" Kayla coos, when Amazon Prime fails to ease my expression. She gives me a big, warm hug.

Surprised but touched, I try really hard not to stiffen up in her arms. I can at least *try* not to behave like a wooden cutout of a person. But it's not easy. I haven't been big on human contact over the past few years. Maybe it's just that I've been around too many of them, living in the ant farm that is south Florida, or maybe it's my rat-bastard ex-husband reminding me that he was cozy with way too many other people while I was spending late nights at the show-grounds, jumping under the lights as if that might prove I was worth something.

I feel like, because of his behavior, I've touched a lot of people by association that I'd prefer not to have ever even been near.

Anyway. That's my trauma, in a nutshell. Best packed up and forgotten now that I'm finally here in...what's this place called again? Alachua. I make a stab at saying it aloud, placing the emphasis on the wrong syllable.

"Ah-*latch*-chew-ah," Kayla corrects me. "It means 'land with lots of sinkholes,' apparently."

"Oh." I don't know how to react to this. Surely there should have been a sinkhole disclaimer in the employment contract? But then again, this is Florida. That risk is built in.

"They're all really old," she says reassuringly. "I'll show you ours sometime."

"Your very own sinkhole?"

"That's the dream, right?" Kayla laughs. "It's in the far back corner, that way." She points past the long, low, white-painted barn we're standing in front of. "It's pretty cool, actually."

"You're not afraid of new ones opening up, right?"

All I need is to move to north Florida for a fresh start, only to promptly find myself sucked deep into the bedrock.

Kayla shrugs. "I mean, it doesn't seem to happen very often?"

"You can't have good grass without limestone," Basil says, with surprising authority, "and you can't have limestone without some sinkholes."

"Just look at that grass," Kayla adds.

She's not kidding. Despite the sudden knowledge that the ground beneath me is riddled with subterranean passages held up with all the strength of a stick of sidewalk chalk, I can appreciate that this is one of the most beautiful places I've ever been.

We're surrounded by large grassy pastures, glowing vibrant green with the onset of the summer rainy season. Live oaks line the distant perimeter fences, their upper boughs tangled together, their lower ones scooping all the way to the ground in some spots. A few solitary oaks dot the fields, the sandy patches beneath them showing that horses appreciate their shade and shelter. The fences are no-climb wire with a top board, just like the fences in Ocala. A flock of cattle egrets pokes through the grass in one field, their white feathers gleaming bright beneath the June sun. It is hot and humid, and the air smells of green things growing just as fast as they can.

Somehow—despite the wringer the past decade has put me through, with experiences which might make anyone look for a totally new state and climate to start afresh—when I look around and take in those massive live oaks and these rolling fields with their grass green as envy beneath a huge blue sky, dotted with fluffy cotton-ball cumulus clouds, I'm reminded of how much I love Florida. What an infinite variety of beauty my home-state possesses! These pastures are as Floridian as the tropical paradise I woke up in this morning, as the coconut and queen palms of West Palm Beach, the turquoise streak of the Gulf Stream rushing just off the sandy beaches, or the bird-filled flatness of the northern Everglades that rushed past my truck for the first hour of the drive north.

Some places dwell in a person's blood, no matter how bizarrely the media portrays them. And so yes, La Florida, although truly a land of a million mosquitoes and meth-heads, thou art my soul's home.

"You have lucky horses," I say, looking back at them. "That's really gorgeous grass, for sure."

"Speaking of which," Kayla says, glancing at the long, sleek trailer behind my Ford F-350. "We're dying to meet Thomas. Basil says you're a little obsessed with this guy. I love that!"

I make a grimace to cover up my true feelings, which are of such deep and utter devotion that they're embarrassing. Should a person love so deeply? Absolutely not. I am probably going to get hurt. I am absolutely going to get hurt. The question is, how long do I have with him before something happens that breaks my heart? Five years? Ten? Twenty? Surely no more than that.

"You're going to love him," I say, shrugging away my existential dread with the practice of many years, "but he's best if he just waits and has a look through the windows first."

"If you say so. Let's get your bags inside."

"Thomas, be good!" I call as I sling my hiking backpack over my shoulder and heft a suitcase with my free hand. My phone rattles from its side-pocket and hits the ground; I scoop it up and shove it in my purse. "We'll be right back, sweetie."

There's no answer from Thomas.

That's normal for him, though.

We walk into the center aisle of the barn, a concrete-block affair with two wings that stretch out on either side, each side lined with stalls facing a long aisle. It's old-fashioned, but comfortable. The rafters are a little low and the translucent panels in the metal roof are dim with age, so the aisle seems midnight-dark compared with the brilliant June sunlight we've just left outside. Kayla flips a light switch and the overhead fluorescents stutter to life, revealing an aisle badly in need of sweeping and stall fronts desperate for a good dusting.

I have very little practical horse-keeping experience, but at least my fancy Wellington stables taught me that everything should be perfectly clean at all times. My fingers are already itching to get to work.

Kayla gives me a sheepish smile while Basil says, "As you can see, we're pretty much hopeless at keeping this place up ourselves."

"That's why we need you," Kayla says. "We were crazy to think we could do this without a good barn manager."

"I hope I can be that for you," I say awkwardly. I should be an apprentice, honestly. Barn Manager is too big a title for my skills. But I didn't come up here under false pretenses, either. They know what they've hired.

I walk a few paces up the aisle to our right, looking at the dusty stalls. There are about twelve horses on this end, most of them leaning over their nylon stall guards to see what we're up to; the sliding doors, with bars to keep horses from reaching into the aisle, are slid back out of the way. It's nicer this way, if you're certain your aisle is wide enough to walk a horse down the center without getting nipped by inquisitive neighbors. The stall bars always give me an uneasy feeling, like I'm keeping these lovely, freedom-loving creatures in jail cells. Even if it's just for the day, when it's too hot to turn them out.

"Hello, boys!" Kayla calls to the horses. "We've brought you a new friend!"

Two horses whinny and a third reaches a hoof out, sliding his metal shoe across the concrete aisle with a screeching sound.

"Ugh, really?" Kayla asks, shaking her head. She turns back to me and says, "Sorry about Killian. He loves to do that."

"It's fine," I assure her, while fastening a beady-eyed glare on Killian, a red chestnut with a bold white star between his eyes. He does not look repentant. "As long as he doesn't do it at midnight."

"Well, he's out at midnight during the summer," Kayla says. "In winter, no promises. Basil, have you got the apartment key?"

"Right here." Basil is fumbling in his pocket. I look around, wondering where the apartments are. I was promised a barn apartment, which I'd assumed would be upstairs, but as soon as I drove up, I realized there doesn't seem to be an upstairs. So then I assumed it was around the back, but looking across the aisle to the riding arena behind the barn, I can tell there's nothing out back, either. So...where...?

I watch Basil turn to the first door on the right, just off the center aisle—what I just figured was a tack or feed room.

"It's right off the barn aisle?" I squeak, dismayed.

"Well—uh—" Basil begins and then leaves off. He pushes

8

the door open. A small apartment waits within, huddling just off the barn aisle like a shy dog.

This is where I've agreed to live for the next year?

Oh, my.

Oh, this is not what I expected at all.

"It's really cozy," Kayla says eagerly, following Basil into darkness worthy of an Egyptian tomb. "Let me just open the blinds and show you." And the closed blinds on a window facing directly into the barn aisle zip up, revealing her smiling face.

My heart flutters in my chest and my breath is suddenly shallow, starving my lungs. I feel light-headed.

This is a mistake. I've made a huge mistake. I can't live in a repurposed tack room right off a barn aisle in the middle of a field somewhere in the North American sinkhole capital. I just left the keys to a sixteen-hundred square-foot riverfront condo with the doorman, what, four hours ago? Five? I can get those back.

Of course I can't.

Those keys belong to my ex-husband now. And Shelly. And what, I'm supposed to get them out of *Shelly's* clutches? About as easy as getting my dirtbag husband back from her—in other words, a no-go. And I don't really want it. She wanted the condo looking over the sailboats and yachts cruising endlessly along the intracoastal waterway. She got it.

And everything that comes with it.

Kayla sticks her head out of the door, beckoning to me. "Come on, Mackenzie. I promise it's not that bad."

"It's really not!" Basil shouts from somewhere in the depths behind her. And then more light floods out behind Kayla. "I've got the back windows open, too! Sorry we didn't do that before. Now there's lots of light."

"We were riding all morning," Kayla explains, stepping back to make room for me. "And we didn't think to stop and actually open up the place for you. That's our bad."

"It's fine," I say weakly, in no hurry to alienate the two of them. I'm here now. I made this commitment. And Basil didn't have to hire crusty old me, not when there are plenty of fresh-faced young college grads longing for apprentice-barn-manager jobs which include a tack room apartment, and Kayla doesn't have to be so sweet to the new divorcee who is clearly just using her farm as an escape route and probably won't stay past her first contract.

I owe these two a lot for taking me in. I can be graceful about living in a cubbyhole off the barn aisle.

So, as Kayla steps out of the doorway, I follow her in...and I am pleasantly surprised by what waits for me on the other side of the gray steel door.

It's *not* a tack room, as I expected. Thank goodness.

Instead, this is a full apartment. The barn aisle door opens into a small living room that's pleasant enough. Yes, the kitchen linoleum is stained, and the living room carpet is best not discussed, and the sad gray couch sags weirdly in the center, but there's a thrift-store coffee table to rest my chamomile tea on in the evening while I watch *Parks and Rec* on the TV against the opposite wall. Through a doorway, I find a tiny kitchen with three cabinets (only three! It's fine. I don't need a walk-in pantry), a small fridge which seems to crouch against the wall next to a window overlooking the riding arena, along with a sink and a miniature oven.

"Whoops," Basil says as he backs into the doorway to the right of the oven. "Watch out for the kitchen table."

I've already tripped over the chair that's wedged into the corner of the kitchen, but it's fine. "Two chairs, so I can have company," I joke, shoving it back under the tiny table. "Just kidding, there's no way I'm having company out here." I'd have to invite over the neighbor's cows that I spotted on the drive in.

"You never know," Kayla chirps from behind me. "Check out the bedroom!"

"Ah, the bedroom," I say, surveying the little room. It's just big enough for a queen-size bed, which has a sag in the center just like the sofa back in the living room. Put two people in that bed, and they'd be face to face, nose to nose, and utterly incapable of climbing out without help. "Trust me, this is only for me."

Yes, I'll be living right off the barn aisle—but there's no one here to bother me. Kayla and Basil don't have boarders or students. It will be the three of us and the horses. I can live with this.

I push past the dresser and open the final door to my right, aware I've made a complete circle. The bathroom doesn't have a window, because it would look onto the barn aisle and that would be weird, but at least it's a decent size, with closet racks along the left and a full bathtub with a shower along the right. A large mirror reflects both my exhausted face and the bedroom window behind me. Determinedly avoiding meeting my own gaze, I look at the window and notice the sky is growing thick with gray-bottomed clouds.

Thunder rumbles in the distance. Then again, not so distant.

"Looks like it's time for our three o'clock thunderstorm," Basil observes, looking out the window. "They've been like clockwork so far this summer."

"Well, thanks for the tour," I say, tossing my bags on the bed. "But I guess now it's time to meet Thomas."

Chapter Two

THOMAS SHUFFLES IN the trailer as I slip through the back door. I know he's hot and sweaty from waiting out here, the sun beating on the metal roof. He's ready to get out, but I know him well enough to understand he needed this adjustment time. We've only been together three months, but it feels like we've been through a lot together. I move slowly, careful not to startle him and risk getting myself crushed in this tin can.

"Hello, love," I say gently, stroking his neck. "Are you doing okay?"

Thomas snuffles at my chest with his long nose, then snorts, blowing dark snot and road dirt all over my designer riding shirt that I'd put on with such care early this morning, anxious to make a good impression.

Well, the first impression came and went without horse snot. That's going to have to be enough.

"Let's go see your new home, pal," I say, using a handful of hay to swipe away the worst of the mess. Then I drop the chest bar and lead Thomas to the back ramp of the trailer. This horse trailer is enormous—a four-horse "head to head" with a center side-ramp and a back ramp, allowing all kinds of configurations for happy horse travel. It also has a living quarters section in front, with a full bed, a tiny kitchenette, and a travel shower/toilet I have never used, but enjoy knowing is available to me, just in case. There's nothing quite like having a back-up apartment when the life you used to know has crumbled around you.

This ridiculously high-end horse trailer, along with the gleaming red F-350 I use to haul it, are my prizes from the divorce. They're the last things I bought with his money and the first things I insisted on keeping, even if ultimately that meant allowing Ryan to keep the condo, with its view overlooking the river and the Atlantic Ocean just a short distance away—a perfect trophy case for his newest trophy wife. Which is what I assume Shelly will be, once he's had a few months to forget how thoroughly the last wife took him to the cleaners.

Yes, he got the condo, but I got security on wheels *and* managed to snag a decent hunk of formerly shared stock assets, too. I'll be eternally grateful for my bulldog attorney on that count. The investments are socked away while I make my new life on my own, just acting as a cushion in case I fall so hard that I'm one jump from living under a bridge...or back in my father's house. And while I love my daddy, he's the reason I ended up with a control-freak like Ryan in the first place. Going home isn't an option.

So, I had to make sure to bring my own parachute on this plane ride. When your whole life needs a makeover, you don't go back to the salon that made you feel terrible in the first place.

"Here we go, pal," I say. "Into the great unknown."

Thomas struts along beside me with his head held high, ears

pricked. We stop at the top of the ramp and I give him a minute. He gazes out at the broad pastures, the towering oak trees, and the blue sky—which is rapidly transitioning to a landscape full of ominously tall and gray-bellied clouds. "Buddy," I tell him, jiggling the lead-rope under his chin. "Could we possibly speed this up?"

Kayla and Basil walk over to the ramp to take in the evergreen spectacle of yet another new horse. "Oooh," Kayla says admiringly. "He's a cutie!"

"Look at the chest on him," Basil says in more professional tones. "I can see what attracted you to him."

"I just felt like it was time to get back to Thoroughbreds," I confess, looking at Thomas. As usual, I get a thrill of pleasure from knowing this gorgeous, spirited horse is mine. Yes, he's basically a green-bean baby compared to the well-trained European imports I've been riding for the past ten years. But I had off-track Thoroughbreds as a teenager, and I did just fine. Now that I am on my own again, and off my ex's never-ending spigot of fun money (or guilt money, as I came to find out) it just seemed to make sense to go back to my roots and adopt a retiring racehorse.

"Are you going to do the Thoroughbred Makeover with him?" Kayla asks. "I know you said you'd been accepted...is he coming along okay?"

"It's still the plan. Which means we go to Kentucky in what —four months?" I gulp a little. "That seems soon, all of a sudden." As a month, as a season, as a mood, October can't be more different from June...and yet there it is, waiting at the end of summer like a monster under a bridge.

"But you've been riding him since February, right?" Basil reminds me, as reasonable and calm as a person can be. "So you're ready to start taking him to shows. Has he been anywhere yet?"

"He's been off the farm once or twice, but not a lot," I admit. "That's how I know he likes to stay on the trailer and get his bearings before I take him off."

Beside me, Thomas lets out a long breath, then sticks out his tongue a little before making a chewing motion with his jaw. "Lick-and-chew," the universal horse sign language for "my brain is now present and I'm ready to learn."

It's so important to watch for that presence when working with hot-blooded Thoroughbreds. So many of these race-bred horses will lose their cool in a volcanic fashion if they are pushed before they're ready to receive new information. It's not their fault. They're just so intelligent and so anxious to work, it can be hard to keep them within their own limits.

Thomas doesn't believe he has any limits. This can be a blessing and a curse. On one hand, I could wish for a little more natural caution from my ex-racehorse. On the other, I'm kind of jealous of him. He does what he wants, and never mind the consequences. Thomas has never stopped at a jump or balked at a request. Even though on several occasions, it would have been in our best interest if he had.

Now he stretches out his neck and nods his head up and down, his signal to get going.

"He's ready to come down now," I tell Kayla and Basil, so they step back, giving my horse ample room in case he comes off the trailer sideways, or on his hind legs, or simply bolts for the horizon. All completely reasonable assumptions to make, of course.

But Thomas strolls down the ramp with the easy nonchalance of a horse who has been around the world and can't be impressed anymore.

I'm so proud of him I could burst. "Good boy!" I tell him, clapping him on the neck...then catching myself and turning to a slow stroke along his withers, instead. I heard a trainer say that horses have no natural response to being patted, but they understand a stroke or a scratch, and I've been trying to break myself of pats. It's harder than I expected.

"Wow," Kayla says admiringly. "I wish my mare unloaded like that."

"Well, you *do* have a mare," Basil points out. "So...I mean..."

"Shut up," she laughs. "Someday, a mare will happen to you!"

"I've had three mares," I say, giving Thomas another moment to look around at the foot of the ramp. A humid breeze lifts his black forelock, revealing the small white star beneath. Thomas is a dark bay, his espresso-colored coat so dark he could be mistaken for black, but his two white hind socks and his tiny shining star relieve his darkness with a gleaming brightness that I like to pretend are signs of hope.

They're the universe's way of promising that I'm going to come out of this awful black place I've been for so long, so much brighter and stronger, mounted on my dark and magical Thoroughbred.

"Three mares," I go on, "all of them more persnickety than the last. But you know what? Once we got to know each other, we were good partners. Mares will do anything for you."

"That's what they say," Kayla sighs, "but Feather still seems to be on the fence about me sometimes."

"Well, every day is a new day for them." Thomas follows me as I start towards the barn. Thunder, sharp and near, makes a crackling rattle across the sky, and he dances sideways a little, snorting. "There's my racehorse," I tell him fondly. Over my shoulder I say, "You have to make him feel special all the time."

"An emotionally needy Thoroughbred," Basil says dryly. "What a surprise."

"They say horses reflect their owners," Kayla adds, grinning.

"I never said I wasn't needy," I say. "Lucky for me, maybe money can't buy friends, but it sure can buy horses."

WITH MY HORSE settled into his stall just next to my bedroom (admittedly, kind of a cute concept), Kayla and Basil show me around the rest of the barn.

Across from my apartment, the tack room and feed room sit side by side. The feed room is dominated by two huge chest freezers relieved of their former duties to serve as rodent-proof grain bins, with a little room left for stacks of feed buckets and a shelving unit dedicated to supplements, minerals, and various potions. In the tack room, two walls are hung with saddles and bridles, while the concrete floor is stacked with tack trunks and rubber storage totes. A second plastic shelving unit holds saddle pads, bins of polo wraps, and drawers full of horse boots. There's a desk shoved against one wall, the dusty surface scattered with cords, notepads, an iPad in a heavily scuffed, heavy-duty case, and a large coffeemaker.

The coffeemaker is key. I know there's no way I'll survive as a groom without bucketloads of caffeine. I eye it, admiring the sheer volume of its gargantuan pot.

"You can use the washer and dryer in here for your clothes," Kayla says, gesturing to a commercial-sized set of laundry machines against the opposite wall. "Just might want to wipe out the horse hair with a paper towel before doing your sheets or anything nice. If you have anything nice. I don't." She grins again.

All of my clothes are nice, actually, but I don't mention that. "It's fine," I say, smiling to show I'm a good sport. "I expect to be covered in horse hair at all hours."

"Well, Basil and I certainly are," Kayla agrees, laughing. "And we are just fine. If you really want to be *clean*-clean, there's a laundromat in High Springs."

I have no idea where High Springs is. I might have driven through it on the way here. The town with the Winn-Dixie and, perhaps more importantly, a Winn-Dixie liquor store? My eyes were so fuzzy from driving, I missed the town name. "Sure," I agree vaguely. "High Springs."

They point out the racks reserved for my saddles, which are still in the trailer along with the rest of my equestrian gear, my luggage, and all my worldly goods, and then we go next door to a sliver of floor space that Kayla calls the barn office. It's half the size of the tack room, with a window air-conditioner unit currently getting the hell beat out of it by the pouring rain. Basil throws himself into a desk chair and gestures to a spare one for me, while Kayla settles onto a love-seat, which I suspect is the brother of my sagging gray sofa. There's no room for anything else, but an imposing tiger cat stalks in and settles onto the desk with an air of possession.

"This is Mocha," Kayla explains. "He came with the farm. And there's another barn cat, too, Shadow. She's very secretive, so you might not see her too much."

"Hello, Mocha," I say gravely, giving the barn cat the respect he deserves.

Mocha gazes at me for a moment, then closes his green eyes. A rusty purr rattles from his throat.

"He likes you," Kayla says.

"Want to go over hours and responsibilities now, or would

you rather settle in first?" Basil asks.

"Let's do it now," I say, dropping my elbows onto the desk and leaning over it. "I can settle in tonight. Let me see what my punishment is for uprooting my life and moving to the wilds of Al-*latch*-chew-uh."

Kayla grins. "You're getting it already!"

"I've lived in Florida most of my life. You'd think I'd know it already. But I *can* say Immokalee fives times fast, can you?"

Kayla widens her eyes. "Um, no? Say that again?"

"Imm-MOCK-a-lee," I repeat.

"Is *that* how you pronounce it? I had no idea."

"South Florida I've got," I say. "North Florida is a whole new ball-game."

"You'll like it here," Kayla promises. "We're so close to Ocala, but it's so quiet. No traffic, no constant construction from giant new hotels at equestrian centers—"

"Where we spend half our winter, anyway," Basil reminds her, grinning.

"I mean, yes, we will be at Legends Equestrian Center a lot in the winter season. And we'll do the summer circuit, too. But most of the time, we just live out here in the quiet, letting summer do its thing." Kayla says this dreamily, as if we won't be busy from sunup to sundown working horses, mucking stalls, and doing general farm work with the sweat rolling down our backs and into our underwear. She seems to have a very romanticized view of her own life.

I like that about her. Basil seems to be more open and happy than the serious young rider I knew back in Wellington, too.

However you say it, Alachua has been good to him. And I'm willing to give this place a chance and see if it can be good for me, too.

After all, isolation is exactly what I was going for.

"Let's talk chores," I say. "I assume I'm doing everything from morning feed to night-check?"

"That's the plan," Basil agrees, and he flips open a binder, turning it around so I can see the breadth of responsibilities I'm about to take on for the two of them.

"Oh, my," I whisper.

I'm about to be a busy little farm-girl.

THOMAS'S TRAINING DIARY

June 8

Well, it's Day One. We made it to Alachua! Thomas was such a good traveler. I'm proud of my boy. Thomas the Tank Engine rides again!

Kayla and Basil suggested I plan on riding him in the evenings after feed time, weather permitting. I think they're right—it would be impossible to get up at five and ride him in the morning, even if it's cooler then, because all the other horses would want to come inside and eat breakfast. They'll start shouting and galloping and being nuisances. I don't want to start my time here by waking up my bosses an hour earlier than they want. I have to play by their rules. We can make it work.

They also said to just let them know ahead of time when I need a weekend day off to take Thomas to a show. So I guess that will be happening!! I didn't tell them that at the last two shows we attempted, he just alternated between standing still and blowing his stack, and I never even got on him. It's going to take time to settle him into horse shows versus horse racing. And anyway, Thomas is just like me...he needs some time in the countryside to unravel his brain.

It's going to be fine. I'll ride him tomorrow, and we'll just keep progressing the way were back in south Florida. Slowly, but all we have to do in Kentucky is jump a little course and do a dressage test. So slowly should be just fine.

Four months!

Ahhh!!

Chapter Three

"WHAT DO YOU think? Is it going to work out?" Casey's voice, coming out of my laptop, is the closest thing to a security blanket I've got. I just wish I could see my best friend, too.

I sigh at the blank screen on my laptop. I'd hoped the wi-fi in the barn would be strong enough to allow video calls. After a shower and a bowl of ramen from the supply of packets I keep in the horse trailer kitchenette, I wrote in my training journal for the night, then tried to turn on the TV...and got nothing but snowy feeds from a station in Gainesville. The streaming services wouldn't load at all. When I texted Basil to let him know that the TV wasn't receiving any streaming channels, he'd said to go to the barn office, check the router, and hit the big, round button to reset it if the light was blinking. Easy enough, right?

But when I opened the door of my apartment, I was confronted with total darkness. I'd done night-check of the horses in their paddocks with a residual afterglow still burning in the western sky, but that had vanished. A profound and disconcerting darkness had fallen over the farm. We had lights, obviously, but I hadn't memorized where the switches were, I didn't particularly want to shine a flashlight around the silent barn aisle. Shining a spotlight into the darkness is how you find out how many large and many-legged neighbors you're sharing your space with.

I'd stood there in the doorway for a minute, testing soft, full-of-noodles me against the vast darkness. I felt very small. By craning my neck and peering through the center aisle, I could see the porch light at Basil and Kayla's manufactured home in the distance but other than that, the starlight picked out only the treetops along the fence-lines.

No, I knew I couldn't go out there. It was too dark, too lonesome. And more than a little threatening. Who knew *what* was out there?

I'd gone slinking back into my apartment and slammed the door shut in my haste to keep that darkness at bay. With the lock turned and the blinds closed, I could at least *pretend* I wasn't alone in a sea of grass and grazing horses.

I mean, obviously that was what I'd thought I'd wanted, but the reality was pretty terrifying.

So, I'd called Casey. My best friend back in south Florida, Casey had moved from a West Palm Beach townhouse to a farm that is fairly isolated by South Florida standards, and lived to tell the tale. Of course, she has a boyfriend. And a dog. Those have to help.

But my plan is to learn to survive without crutches, and while I might consider a dog, I'm definitely not getting a boyfriend. Hardest of passes; thanks but no thanks.

"It's going to work out," I tell my blank screen. "It has to."

Casey chuckles, and I can picture her grin even if I can't see her face. "You're a force of nature, Mack-truck. I have faith in you. Although I will repeat, once again, that you can come to our farm if you decide Alachua isn't for you."

"Did you already know how to pronounce it?"

"Of course I did. This state hasn't thought of a name I can't pronounce. Did you drive through Micanopy on the way there?"

"I didn't, but it sounds familiar."

"It's spelled like 'my canopy,' but obviously that's not how it's said."

"Can we get back to my thing, pronunciation goddess? It's freaking *dark* out there."

"I was so scared when we first moved to the farm, too," Casey says. "But you really get used to it! You can see more than you'd think in the dark. And the predators are afraid of you."

"The *predators*?"

"Yeah, you know, bobcats and panthers and coyotes, things like that."

"There aren't panthers in north Florida. They all live in the Everglades."

"That's what they *want* you to think."

"Who is they? The panthers?"

"Fish and Wildlife," Casey says gravely. "There's a whole conspiracy about Florida panthers. The truth is, they're everywhere. Some people say they're living all the way up to Georgia now."

"Casey," I say, "I am beginning to regret this call."

"Sorry," she replies meekly. "Gossip is different when you live in the country."

"I guess it's better than who is sleeping with who."

"Oh, we get that, too," she laughs. "Anyway, like I said, the predators are afraid of you. And of the horses."

I hadn't even thought about the horses. "Are you saying

Thomas is outside in a pasture surrounded by panther-infested forests right now?"

"No..." Casey is noncommittal.

"Ugh, Casey! I called you for reassurance. Tell me this was the right decision."

"You have made the right decision," Casey says promptly. "Ryan is a horrible nightmare-man and Shelly deserves him, as much as I hate saying anything negative about a fellow woman in this patriarchy of doom we live in. She's definitely gone over to the dark side."

"Thank you," I say, picking up my cooling mug of Sleepytime tea. "That helps."

"Thomas is an amazing horse," she goes on, warming to her task, "and you two will have a great summer prepping for the Thoroughbred Makeover and he will win grand champion in Kentucky this fall and everyone will say 'oh my god, Mackenzie, I love your plaid breeches.'"

"Thank you," I sigh, feeling soothed already. "I do love those breeches."

"They're going to be make you an equestrian fashion icon someday," Casey says. "Sooner rather than later."

"That's the dream!" I've been ordering custom breeches and tops for myself for a few years now, and if I ever get up the courage, I'm going to start my own clothing company. Well, the courage and the money. But we're not there yet. Baby steps. First, I have to prove to myself I can live on my own, without a doorman and twelve stories and several square miles of concrete jungle to protect me from the ravenous panthers that apparently roam the state I call home.

"You are a strong, independent woman who don't need no man," Casey continues, evidently getting lost in the compliment train.

I smile, sipping at my tea, and then freeze.

Because I just heard a sound in the barn aisle.

Something's out there!

"Panther," I whisper.

"What?" Casey asks, her voice confused. "I mean, wait. I know you don't need a man but you're not a cougar. Is that what you meant? Mack, you're not even old enough to be a cougar!"

I hear a scuffling noise outside. Footsteps. Not a panther, but a person. *Right outside my door.* I look at the heavy steel door and wonder why it has to open directly into my living room, three feet from my sofa. Why didn't they put the kitchen here instead? This is too close to the outside world for relaxation.

"Casey," I hiss, "there is something outside. A person. Outside my door. Casey. Casey. *Casey*—"

"Okay, shhhh, maybe it's your new boss checking something in the barn—"

The door handle turns, ever-so-gently, then stills as the lock catches.

"Someone is trying to open the DOOR!" I scream-whisper, my face close to my laptop screen. And then I hear something so terrifying, I nearly knock the whole thing off the coffee table as I rear back in panic.

My phone is ringing.

My phone is *making noise.*

My phone has been on silent since the day it came in the mail. I don't even know how to turn the sound back on. Who would have their ringer on? Who would be that crazy?

"What is that noise?" Casey demands.

"My *phone* is ringing," I whisper, descending into full horror-movie terror. I stare at the phone as if it might leap off the table and try to bludgeon me to death.

"What? Phones don't ring." Casey also belongs to the silent-phone generation. "Did it maybe fall on the floor and break?"

"It just started ringing all by itself," I hiss, shoving a pillow on top of my haunted phone. Abruptly, it stops ringing. Probably lost the signal it needs to work. Great, now I have no phone coverage.

All the better to be murdered with.

I need the internet to work, dammit. I need the internet to work so I can live-stream my imminent demise. Because I'm going down. This is the end. I have to leave a record of my destruction, or what was it all for?

There's another rattle on my door and I hear breathing—*breathing!*—on the other side.

"Casey, call the cops and tell them my new address so they can forward the call to the local sheriff," I mutter, but then the breathing sound stops. I hear a muffled voice outside, suspiciously seeming to say a lot of curse words. And then footsteps walking away.

"Wait. They're leaving. I hear them walking away." I hope and pray and wish and manifest that they don't steal anything. The tack room door is locked, right? Did I lock it? Was it in my monumental list of responsibilities to lock the tack room door? *Probably.* Why can't I remember?

"I'm already looking up the Alachua County Sheriff's direct number," Casey says. "Quicker response this way—"

"No, seriously." I think of how embarrassing it would be to have a deputy out on my first night, with no one even here. Maybe it was...a late delivery? I look at my laptop clock. It's nine forty-five. No one is delivering things to barns at nine forty-five, right? Amazon, is that you?

A door slams in the barn aisle, making me jump "Casey, they went into another room," I moan. "I don't know which. The tack room? Maybe?"

"I think you need the cops," she says. Her voice is quavering now. "I'm telling Brandon. He'll know what to do."

I don't try to stop her, although I'm not sure what her husband is going to do about it. They are five hours away; he can't exactly drive up here and save me.

Suddenly, a voicemail notification chimes from beneath the couch cushion.

"The hell..." I murmur, picking up the pillow and retrieving my phone.

Voicemail, the screen reads, *from Kayla - Boss Lady*.

"Oh," I say. "Um, Casey, is it still a thing that if you mark a contact in your phone as a VIP, it will ring after the second call?"

There's a moment of silence, then Casey says, meekly, "Brandon says yes, that's a thing."

"Oh. Um. The phone call was from my new boss."

"Better listen to the voicemail then."

"Dammit." I hit the button to play the voicemail.

Kayla's voice is high-pitched with concern. "Mackenzie? I'm sorry it's so late. But I just saw Landon's truck go past the house and I realized we didn't tell you about him. I thought he was coming next week. Don't freak out, okay? You know what? I'm coming over. Stay put."

I stare at my phone as the voicemail ends. *Landon?*

And then there's a gentle knock at my door.

"MACKENZIE!" Casey is hyperventilating. "DO NOT ANSWER THE DOOR!"

"Okay, but now I think it's only Kayla," I say. "Did you hear her message?"

Knock-knock.

"No, I didn't hear it—I was talking to Brandon, and he says to call the cops, no matter what. Is there still someone out there? Do you think he might have a machete? Brandon said something about a machete murderer—"

"Good grief, Casey, calm down." Suddenly, I am the collected one. "Kayla called me. Her message said there's someone coming out here, and then she said she's coming down to talk to me. Let me go, okay?"

"DO NOT HANG UP THIS CALL!"

"Okay, okay." I get up and put my mouth close to the apartment door. "Who's there?" I call.

"It's Kayla," comes the reassuring voice. "I'm so sorry to bother you."

"It's Kayla," I shout over my shoulder.

"OKAY!" Casey shouts back, her voice tinny on the laptop speaker.

I open the door and allow in a confused-looking Kayla. "My friend Casey is on a voice-call," I explain. "From my laptop."

"Hi," Casey shouts, a disembodied voice. "I'm here to make sure there are no murders!"

"Oh, hi," Kayla says, bemused. She waves to the laptop. "I guess no video, huh? I can show you how to reset the router and that should fix it."

"I was going to," I say, "but then I realized it was as dark as Satan's butthole out there, and *then* someone tried to open my door."

"Right." Kayla looks embarrassed. "I feel so bad about that. Landon Kincaid came home early. And we forgot to mention him earlier. There was so much stuff in Basil's Big Binder of Everything..."

She has that right. Basil spent two hours going over the contents of his binder, which detail the needs of every horse, machine, and blade of grass on this property. It was so big that I accidentally called it the Big Binder of Everything and Kayla announced that had to be the official name. We were not making fun of him, either. The boy is nothing if not meticulous, and I can respect that; keeping a horse farm happy is not for the faint of heart. But overlooking a late-night intruder named—what? Landon Kincaid?—is not a small omission for a woman living on her own in the wilderness for the first time. So my voice is a little testier than I'd like when I reply, "Yeah, seems like you left out a pretty big detail."

"He wasn't sure he was coming back," Kayla says, "and I thought maybe it wouldn't come up at all—"

"Kayla," I interrupt. "Straight answer. Please?"

She nods. "Sorry. I get off track sometimes. Jules says I can be like talking to a pinwheel in a hurricane. And Jules is— never mind. Sorry. So, Landon is a farrier. He rents the other apartment."

"*What?*" Casey and I burst out in unison.

"Yeah." Kayla looks miserable. "Like I said, I thought he wasn't coming back. But...he did. That's his truck out front."

"So...you're saying I have a neighbor? Twelve feet away from my front door? And it's a dude?" I struggle to keep my voice even. But, this is *so* not what I planned.

"A farrier," Kayla corrects me, as if this automatically makes things better. "Like, a seriously accomplished farrier. He's worked at the Winter Equestrian Festival, so you've probably seen him. And he's gone with the U.S. dressage team to the

World Equestrian Games. He's very professional."

"So what's he doing in the back of beyond?" Casey demands from the laptop. "Shouldn't he be on the summer circuit up north? Or in Ocala?"

"He needed space for some rehab horses," Kayla says, wringing her hands a little as she stares at my hostile laptop. "He's working on some experimental techniques with some really tough neglect cases. And he wanted them to have a lot of turnout space. That's expensive further south. We rented him some pasture and stalls...and the other apartment. But then he went up to Kentucky, and we thought he was staying! We didn't know he'd be back! I'm so sorry, Mackenzie. But on the other hand," she says, brightening up, "you won't be alone out here in the dark barn anymore! I know you're safe already, but won't you feel safer with a big, strong farrier living across the aisle?"

The answer to that is...hard to work out. I shrug in lieu of an answer. I don't really want a neighbor.

But I also don't know that living alone out here is the bright idea I thought it was back in West Palm Beach, when I was stacked into a high-rise with humans all around me.

"Do you want to meet him?"

I look at Kayla. "What? Now?"

"Well, yeah. You're both up. You're dressed." She looks at my t-shirt and boxer shorts as if they're actual clothing—maybe out here in the hinterlands they are. "And better now than at seven o'clock in the morning when you're bringing horses in and half-awake, right?"

"Uh, right." I feel like I'm being tugged into something I'm not ready for.

Kayla's already heading for the door. She flings it open and her face lights up. "Landon Kincaid!" she exclaims. "Speak of the devil!"

"Well, Kayla," says a deep voice with the faintest hint of a southern drawl. "I hope I didn't surprise you by coming back so late."

"Not me," Kayla laughs, "but your new neighbor."

"New neighbor? I forgot my key and remembered Basil said he kept a spare one in the kitchen of the other apartment," that deep voice rumbles. There's something alluring about it, like honey-coated thunder. (I'm very embarrassed that I thought that just now.) "It took me a minute to tell that door was locked, too. Did I almost break in on someone? Sorry about that, buddy. I jimmied my way into my place and found my spare key, so it won't happen again."

"I didn't know you rattled the door!" Kayla gasps and steps into the barn aisle, leaving me standing in the doorway. "You must have scared poor Mackenzie here to death!"

Landon Kincaid stares at me, like he's never seen a woman in a t-shirt and boxer shorts standing in a horse barn at ten o'clock at night before.

But to be fair, I'm staring right back at him like I've never seen a six-foot-plus, broad-shouldered red-bearded Viking of a man in a horse barn at ten o'clock at night before.

Because I haven't.

And I don't know what to think about it, now that I have.

Chapter Four

"SORRY ABOUT SCARING you, neighbor," the red Viking standing across the barn aisle says to me, in a voice about as deep and rumbling as you'd expect from someone who looks ready to board a long-ship and pillage the villages of the North Sea. "I guess Kayla here forgot to tell me she was renting out the other apartment."

And he gives Kayla a sidelong look.

Kayla snorts and punches him in the arm, a gesture that appears to affect him like a gnat landing on an oak tree. "*You* said you weren't sure you'd be back. Something about Kentucky bluegrass being the cure-all for everything a horse could have wrong with him?"

"We-e-ll," he drawls, grinning and showing off a set of straight white teeth beneath his auburn beard, "I guess it's good for horses, but not always so good for the man. So I called up Basil and told him I was on my way back. You know he forgets stuff."

"So, there were the predictable problems back home?"

"I wouldn't call that place my home," he says, shrugging. "Home is where my horse trailer is. And that's parked out front."

"Any horses in it?" Kayla peers into the dark night as if she expects a groom to lead in a tired, travel-worn horse.

"They're coming in a few days, riding down on a Sallee van. I packed my rig full of hay."

"Oh!" Kayla claps her hands like a child. "Kentucky hay! I hope you brought enough to share."

"Now, no one said anything about sharing—"

"Guys?" I interrupt, lifting my brows as they both turn curious gazes on me. "Am I done here? Because I left my friend on the phone in there, and—"

"Sorry!" Kayla exclaims. "So sorry. We all need to get to bed, anyway. Landon, don't make any racket out here. Be a good neighbor."

He snorts at that, hand on his door as he prepares to retreat into his apartment for the night. "Sure, like the good neighbor over here that's gonna be making a racket at seven a.m., bringing in horses right past my bedroom."

Somehow I don't like to think of walking horses past the wall when that giant will be sleeping just on the other side of the cinder blocks. He doesn't look like he wakes up cheerful.

"I'll walk them in from the other side," I say impulsively. "We'll be as quiet as we can."

"Oh, don't worry about it," he says. "Maybe I'll come out and help ya."

"That won't be necessary." I can't help the prim note that comes into my voice. "I have everything under control."

Landon lifts his eyebrows like he doubts it, and then says a courtly goodnight to the both of us. Kayla gives him another weak punch in the arm, then lets him shuffle back to his apartment. I hear the lock click into place.

Kayla looks back at me and shrugs. "I'm *really* sorry about all this, but I promise he's a good guy. He won't give you any trouble. This'll be a good thing in the end, seriously."

"Let's just hope I don't wake him up," I sigh, easing myself back towards my apartment door. Suddenly, I'm exhausted. The weight of the long day, from leaving my condo forever to driving up the middle of Florida in hellacious tourist season traffic with my horse in tow, to Basil's exhausting binder and then this insane late-night arrival, is settling firmly around my shoulders. The very act of standing upright is beginning to feel like too big an ask.

"You need your bed," Kayla says. "I'll go."

Then she does something that surprises me. She crosses the concrete aisle between us, holds out her arms, and pulls me in for a quick, comforting hug.

My second hug in six hours. Clearly, I'm showing I'm in need of something.

"Goodnight," she says, her hands on my back and her mouth closer to my ear than I ever would have expected from one of my new bosses. "We're really glad you're here."

A moment later, I'm back on the sofa and Casey's voice warbles from the speakers. "*What* the hell just happened? Can we get on video, please?"

I stare at the blank screen on my laptop and sigh. "Well, I forgot to reset the router, so not yet."

MY EYES FLUTTER open sometime in the middle of the night, and I stare at a blue glow shining on the ceiling directly above me. Without my glasses on, it's a luminous blur that seems to hover just over my head. I close my eyes again tight, trying to stop my heart from running away, but both it and my imagination are galloping for the worst-case scenario.

This is not a haunted barn apartment, I tell myself, wishing I had the wherewithal to say it out loud.

But if I do, that might alert the ghost that I'm awake.

And *then* what?

I'm no ghost whisperer. I don't know what spirits from the beyond want. I have never watched a show about paranormal investigation. They're too scary!

I really shouldn't have left West Palm. I should have taken the licks the Wellington community wanted to mete out to me, the divorced trophy wife who couldn't afford her posh coach and barn anymore, and found a place to work down there. I could have found a trainer to take me on as a stall cleaner, right?

Okay, probably not. The trainers back there only ever saw me as a white woman in couture riding clothes who showed up in a massive, shiny red truck, fueling an expectation that I would be a new client ready to pay them a few hundred dollars per hour for riding lessons, not a potential employee who wants to work for fifteen bucks an hour under the table. Getting away from the social constructs of south Florida's complex equestrian community was definitely necessary in order to forge a new, quieter life for myself.

But now I've got a freaking ghost in my bedroom, so how's that working out for you, Miss Quiet Life?

I open my eyes tentatively. The ghost is still there. Hasn't moved. That might be a good sign. Slowly, gently, I reach a hand from beneath the thin sheet and grasp my glasses on the wobbly nightstand, hissing in a sharp breath when the legs shake and make a faint rattling sound on the linoleum. But the ghost doesn't move.

I slide the glasses onto my nose.

And look at the patch of moonlight above me.

What the hell? How is there moonlight over my head? The laws of physics don't apply out here in the north Florida wilderness? A land of open pastures, ancient trees, and midnight Vikings?

Okay, Landon didn't arrive at midnight, but his unexpected appearance kept me up late and I really wanted a proper night's sleep before I start my backbreaking new job in the morning.

First Landon, now a fake ghost. Good grief. I have to figure out what's causing that stupid light on my ceiling. I can live with it if I know what it's from.

Annoyed, I throw back the sheet and hop out of bed, nearly yelping as my sensitive feet hit the hard, cold linoleum floor. I will mourn the loss of my thick shag throw rugs later. Or better yet, I'll order a new one. I can borrow a little spending money from my emergency accounts. My feet are thirty-three years old and they deserve a little softness.

The window is only two feet from my bed; I snap up the blinds and the light overhead disappears. What the—

I look out the window.

Outside, a world draped in blue light distracts me from everything else in my life.

The moon is huge and round, hanging overhead like a blue imitation of the sun at noon. It's so bright, only stars near the horizon can find enough darkness to show their glimmer, tiny pricks of white light just above the dark outlines of the trees surrounding the property. Closer, the blue moonlight shows me everything as it snoozes through the night: the jumping course set up in the white-sand arena just a dozen feet beyond my window, the footing glowing as if it's a bioluminescent desert; the lines of fencing marching away over the back pastures; horses, their blazes and stars and socks picked out as if they're dancers beneath a black light, grazing and sleeping in the fields.

It's so beautiful I feel a tiny prick of heat in first my left eye, then my right, and before I can catch myself, the tears begin to roll down my cheeks.

I remember moonlit nights like this from childhood. For a brief moment when I was a kid, we had a little farm, just two acres, barely room for a barn and a horse. My second mare, Sassy, was an ex-racehorse who loved moonlit nights as much as I did. I would ride her around the paddock next to the house, where my mother could see me from the living room window. My mother was hands-off, to say the least; she never questioned why I felt the need to be out on summer nights when the moon was full. She just made sure I was safe and left me to it.

And then there was the summer I spent riding with an Olympic medalist in Virginia, the golden moon rising over the rolling fields there like a huge gleaming coin, while the other students and I sat on the porch of her gracious old house and drank lemonade and talked about the horses we'd ridden that day, and the great things we'd do someday, as if jumping courses on horseback was some kind of world-changing life's calling.

At the dramatically lit condo where I lived for the past eight years, I can only remember one magnificent moonlit night like this, with the ocean gleaming silver-gold. That was due to a massive power outage after a hurricane, and it was so humid and miserable that experiencing the moonrise is the only pleasant memory I can access from that entire period. Lord knew Ryan didn't enjoy the moonlight that night; he was too busy bitching about the power grid.

But the moon has always been a part of me, something that reaches out and touches my soul, and I remember feeling privileged to see the moon glowing like a sorceress queen over that dark ocean, even if the price was no air conditioning, no elevators, and flushing the toilets with water scooped from the bathtub I'd filled before the storm struck.

And, well, Ryan.

I feel like I could stand here all night, watching the moon sail through the sky and light up the farm with her magical glow. But of course, it's late and I have an early morning, so I get back to business. Even knowing that the luminous pool of light over my head wasn't a ghost, just my old friend the moon, I still want to know what caused it, so I put the blinds back down and do a quick investigation. It only takes a moment to realize there's a missing slat at the top of the blinds, and a puddle from the summer rains has pooled just outside my window. When the moon is directly overhead, the light reflects upwards, slides through that hole in the blinds, and lights the ceiling above my bed.

Fine. Dandy. Goodnight, moon.

I climb back into bed, take off my glasses, and close my eyes. But of course, there's no falling back asleep now. My mind is racing, worry about my new job interspersed with anxiety about the sounds an empty barn makes at night, like squeaking and scuffling—are there mice playing in my kitchen cabinets, or are they up in the rafters where barn mice belong? And then there's the unsettling reminder that I'm not alone in an empty barn...there's a man about twenty feet away, in an apartment which I assume is a mirror image of this one.

Unsettling...but also a little relaxing, if those two things can exist side by side. I don't want to rely on a man to keep me safe. Heaven knows that hasn't worked out for me in the past.

But it's also just a little calming to know I'm not alone out here.

Especially when a lot of squeaking in what sounds like the ceiling above my kitchen is followed by a thud, one long squeak, and the yowl of a cat.

Oh good god. It's Wild Kingdom out here.

I'm never going to fall asleep.

Chapter Five

THOMAS HAS A nose like black silk, whiskers like a kitten's, and a little white spot beneath his chin that I am fairly certain only I know about. I like to give it a soft poke while I'm working with him, like just now, when I'm haltering him to bring him in for breakfast.

He looks a little wild-eyed this morning, and there's sand coating his short coat, which tells me he must have galloped around in that beguiling moonlight and gotten himself sweaty, before rolling in some nice, soft, sandy wallow another horse had set up for him. There are also sticks caught up in his black tail, and a tiny scrape above his left eye. He was turned out alone last night, but even without another horse to get into trouble with, Thomas seems to have achieved some mischief. I glance around the paddock, looking for the source of the scrape, and spot it at the back of the paddock.

I'm pretty sure that lower fence rail wasn't hanging at such a disreputable angle when I turned him out last night. Luckily, it doesn't look like he cracked it—just knocked the end loose from its post.

Probably with his big, beautiful head, during one of those rolling sessions.

"Goober-boy, what did you do?" I chide him, slipping his leather track halter over his nose and flinging the crown-piece behind his pricked ears. It's a heavy piece of tack: reinforced leather, triple-stitched for strength, with strong brass fittings and a scratched brass name-plated engraved with his racing name. ATOMIC TOM.

I thought it was a silly name the first time I saw it, but his racing owners, friends of my riding coach back in Wellington, said they named him for a band they saw in New York City when they were young and foolish. "In our thirties," the wife added, winking at her husband. "We were just kids!"

I liked them, so I promised I'd keep the horse's name as a tribute to them and their generosity—they sold me the horse at a rock-bottom price. But I wasn't about to call him Atomic Tom every day, so I renamed him Thomas around the barn. And sometimes I call him Thomas the Tank Engine, because obviously, right?

Now, Thomas struts alongside me as we walk across the damp grass, his ears pricked and his eyes round enough to show the whites around his dark irises. The morning is foggy and almost cool—as close to cool as we can get in June, I figure— and the sky overhead is a shade halfway between pink and gray. The live oaks are shrouded in mist, looming in the distance like hulking giants lurking along the fence-lines. I've seen enough calendar photos to know that north Florida fogs are legendary things, so I'm glad I don't have to drive anywhere to get to work this morning. Nope, in this life, I simply have to roll out of bed by seven, pull on some work clothes, and head out to get the horses in for their breakfasts.

In another half-hour or so, Basil and Kayla should be down to get started with their rides. Not every horse is ridden every day, but even so, most days I will have to be responsible for twelve horses who will need tacking up and cooling down after their rides. It seems a little intimidating, if I'm being perfectly honest. When you add in feeding them their breakfasts, lunches, and dinners, and mucking stalls in between all of that? Oh, and turnout/bringing in? It's a lot of work for one person. Basil even admitted as much while he was going through his Big Binder of Everything yesterday.

I'm not sure if it's a good sign when your boss admits they're giving you too much work, or a bad sign.

Kayla, looking guilty over the schedule Basil was proposing, quickly promised to pitch in as much as she can, but I know she'll be busy riding all day. I assured her it was fine, that I'd known what I was getting into. I do remember Basil's work ethic from Wellington, and it's pretty formidable.

The important thing to remember about these two isn't that they'll be working me to the bone, but that they gave me a chance. And that's something no one else has been willing to do. For that alone, I'll do my best to get through everything in a day without complaining. Or crying.

Too much.

Thomas steps lightly once we're in the barn aisle, snatching up his hooves after each step as if he's walking on eggshells. I frown at his movement before deciding I can chalk it up to the concrete aisle. He's not used to pavement. At the racetrack, he walked on a clay shed-row. At the boarding stable in Wellington, he walked on expensive equine pavers. He probably feels like he's been barefoot at the beach all day and now he's walking across the hot parking lot on the way back to the car. I'm sure he'll adjust.

"Into your house you go," I murmur, turning into the first

stall on the right—it's the one closest to my apartment door, which is nice. When he's inside, he'll be about twenty feet from me. I can open my front door and see him through the stall bars. Or leaning over his stall guard, which would be nicer. I snap up the stall guard webbing so I don't have to shut the barred stall door while Thomas digs into his breakfast, hitting the feed bucket so hard it rattles against the wall.

The sound seems to draw Landon from his apartment. By the time I have Thomas's halter and lead-rope hung on its hook and am turning to get the next horse in, Landon is standing in the barn aisle, holding an enormous steel coffee tumbler and wearing heavy jeans and a denim work shirt. The size of him takes me aback for a moment. It's like a huge statue has been dropped in the middle of the barn. A statue with flaming copper hair on top.

But it's just my unwanted neighbor. And he looks awfully over-dressed for a hot Florida day. Those jeans alone make me itchy.

I almost ask him what he's up to today, but stop myself. He just lives here. That doesn't mean we have to be friends. I didn't move all the way to Middle of Nowhere, Florida, so that some granite-chinned Viking with poor clothing choices can take up any of my valuable time.

"Morning," I say, walking past him with a brisk stride, to indicate how very busy I am.

"Hey, wait," he says as I'm halfway out of the barn.

I glance back at him. "What? I'm in a hurry. Kayla and Basil —"

"You don't want to leave your horse's stall door open like that," he says, nodding down the aisle towards Thomas's stall.

I shake my head. Seriously, dude? Are we new to stabling

horses with a stall guard? "It's fine," I say. "The stall guard is up. He's not going anywhere."

I've only taken one step out of the barn when he calls after me, "This barn aisle is kind of narrow, so during feeding time it's best to keep the doors closed!"

Oh my god. This guy is really going to show up, drink his coffee, and tell me how to do my job? Absolutely not.

I sigh gustily for his benefit.

The pair of horses in the next paddock wait for me with pricked ears, one of them pawing impatiently at the damp sand. She's already made a fairly deep hole. Note to self: bring Kayla's mare Feather in before everyone else or she'll dig a new well in the paddock.

As I'm slipping the halter over Miss Excavator's ears, I hear a rumble from within the barn that can only be one thing. No way. No way! Did he *really* just shut my horse's stall door? After I said it was fine?

That man needs to mind his own business. I came out here to be alone, to enjoy solitude for once in my freaking life, and somehow I've ended up with a nosy neighbor who is messing around in the barn behind my back? I can't stand it when people correct my work after I've told them to leave it alone. Ryan did that constantly, and look how well that ended up.

Well, it wasn't just the constant corrections that made me leave, of course. There was the whole Other Woman part. I should remember to send Shelly a thank-you note.

But dammit, I deserve a reset without another man following me around, correcting my so-called mistakes and undermining my authority. I deserve a chance to just be me, without anyone else's views or opinions interrupting my thoughts. I want to muck stalls in a quiet barn, do night-check under a quiet sky full of stars—hey, I'll get used to the scary wide-openness of it all—and relax in a quiet apartment with no one around to tear me down.

I'll figure out Landon. I didn't come all this way to let another know-it-all man break me down.

"Okay, silly ponies." Feather, who is a chestnut mare with a rather wild look in her eye, nudges me hard. "Got it, Feather. That makes your friend here Mara...right?"

The dark bay next to Feather nods her head, which is a helpful trick.

"Great, you two. Kayla said yesterday that I can lead you two in together and you won't kill anyone, especially me, so let's go."

With the horses stationed on either side of me, I get them to walk through the open gate one at a time, with Feather waiting for me on the other side. (Feather made it very clear she went through the gate first, not Mara.) It's a trick that involves a little skill; luckily I learned it as a kid and haven't lost my touch. The mares have clearly been doing this every morning for a while. No one freaks out, and no one gets kicked. They trail happily after me as we walk to the barn, their nostrils fluttering with interest when Thomas pokes his head through his stall window to watch them arriving.

"Oh, you already like Thomas, don't you?" I laugh.

Feather snorts, sliding her dirty nose along my thigh and leaving a trail of black, sandy boogers to adorn my breeches.

It's a little tougher navigating the barn aisle with two horses than I expected, and with a stir of irritation in my empty belly, I realize it's because the aisle is narrower than most—just like Landon said. I guess the barn *is* kind of old, and things like twenty-foot aisles didn't come into vogue until after it was built. In this situation, there isn't much room to have one horse stand back while I put the other horse into a stall.

Mara's stall comes up first, so naturally it seems like I should put Mara away first. But holding back Feather with my free hand pressing hard against her chest, while letting Mara slide into her stall alone, is easier said than done. Feather is pretty sure she should get her breakfast before Mara. There's a lot of shoving and swearing while I fight Feather off, all but bodily push Mara into her stall, then slide the stall door shut before Feather can dart in after her and get World War III started.

Thomas pushes his nose against the stall bars while I maneuver the mares, flicking his ears back and forth and rumbling deep in his chest, like a randy stallion.

I'm surprised at his behavior, but I guess he made friends over the fence last night, and the girls made him some flirty promises. "They didn't mean it," I tell him, once everyone is in their place and their halters are hung with care on their hooks. "Finish your breakfast."

I look around for Landon as I walk back out to get the next pair of horses, hoping he isn't around to see how studdish Thomas is acting. Because if he does, he'll absolutely tell me he was right to close my horse's door...and I don't want to hear about how smart he is.

I really don't care.

And I also don't want to think about the potential trouble if Thomas had been able to lean out of his stall and get frisky with those mares while I was trying to maneuver them into their stalls one at a time.

Now I'm bringing in horses one by one, anyway, even if it takes more time.

By the time the final gelding is packed away in his stall and munching at his breakfast, I hear a truck outside and realize Basil and Kayla must be here to start riding. I'm supposed to have the first horse in the cross-ties by now, grooming in preparation for their schooling session.

Crap, where did the morning go?

Suddenly, Landon is back in the barn aisle. He's ditched the coffee mug and has a saddle over one arm, a bridle over the other. I watch him set them next to the set of cross-ties hanging next to the tack room. "What are you doing?" I demand, not bothering to keep the irritation out of my tone. "I need those cross-ties to tack up!"

He pauses in the tack room door and glances back at me. "I'm getting your tack out to save you some time," he says, in the measured tones of a tired mother dealing with a cranky toddler. And then he disappears into the tack room.

He's doing *what* now?

Did I ask for his help?

I sigh hard, then suck in another breath and sigh *harder,* like I'm doing Lion's Breath in a yoga studio, somewhere back in my old life of white cushions and spa music and a husband who undermined everything I tried to do for myself. *Lots of love in, lots of rage out,* I used to think to myself while I listened to my earnest yoga instructor talk about positive vibes and gratitude and all that jazz. Her words come back to me, her voice urgent as she encourages me, again and again: *Let that stuff go, Mackenzie!*

It's harder than it sounds. Maybe harder than it should be. I might be the kind of person who holds onto grievances. Nice on the outside, but fueled by a special blend of spite and I'll-show-them on the inside.

Meanwhile, I hear Kayla laughing at something Basil is

saying, reminding me that work has to be done, right now. As much as this situation sucks, I can't fight back against Landon's help now. His unasked-for, unwanted, but apparently very necessary help.

I sigh and flip open the latch on Feather's stall. She's in the first set to be ridden, according to the white board next to the feed room door, and she already has her nose against the bars, ready to come out and do her dance for Kayla.

Chapter Six

LANDON'S HELP ALLOWS me me get the first two horses ready with just a minimum of delay for Basil and Kayla. The two of them don't seem to mind that the horses aren't standing saddled and waiting, but their inherent niceness isn't the point. I know I need to do better. That means getting up earlier tomorrow, for sure. I underestimated how much time it would take me to get the horses in and breakfasted.

Luckily, the two of them aren't in a huge rush to get started. Kayla pauses in the tack room to make a pot of coffee for all of us, then makes a point of reminding me there's a cabinet stuffed with sweeteners and syrups and all kinds of goodies to make fancy coffee if I feel like I need it, since there's no Starbucks for miles and she knows that sometimes a person just wants a six-hundred-calorie cup of coffee to feel like a functioning human.

"But we are out of beans after this pot," she murmurs, poking her head into the cabinet. "So I'll have to grab some later today or we won't have caffeine tomorrow, and that would not be good, right?"

"That would not be good," I agree, happy that Kayla and I are on the same page regarding coffee. The instant packets I keep in my horse trailer are for emergencies only.

"Well, you know, there is always tea," Basil suggests, popping into the office with what feels like unnecessary energy for so early in the morning. "A nice English Breakfast has caffeine in it, but not so much that it will scatter your brains like coffee."

"Don't listen to him," Kayla sighs. "He can be *that way* about tea, if you know what I mean."

"Oh, I know," I say, smirking. "One of *those*."

Basil holds up his hands as if to show his tea-fueled innocence and purity in a world run by coffee-mad women, then grabs a pair of black riding gloves from the desk and leaves the office again.

Kayla gives me a happy grin. "If you want to pick on Basil with me, that would be great."

"It would be my honor," I assure her, secretly delighted. I know Basil just well enough to feel comfortable teasing him. Things are already looking up.

But the morning can't be all fun and games with Kayla. I have a zillion things to do and I'm determined not to fall behind again. As soon as my bosses have their horses out in the arena, I'm rushing down the aisle and ducking into stalls, pulling each feed bin to hose out and set in the morning sunlight to dry so that they won't attract flies between now and noon, when I feed lunch. We might be out in the Middle of Nowhere, Florida, but a lot of Basil's horse-keeping practices are on par with the most elegant stables in Wellington. No complaints here—I love a clean barn—but it's going to take time to get the schedule down pat.

It's hot out already. The fog is burning off quickly, and the sun is gearing up for a big day of making everyone feel like ants under a magnifying glass. I feel sweat prickling at my hairline and dampening my sports bra. Being damp is part of being Floridian, I remind myself, and head back into the barn for a second armload of feed bins. Thomas lets me takeaway his empty bin reluctantly; I know he'd lick it all day if given the option. "No emotional support feed bin for you, buddy," I tell him. "Eat your hay like a smart boy."

Thomas sighs and takes a bite of his hay.

"Good pony," I say, sliding his door shut again. Maybe when Landon leaves, I'll open it and let him enjoy leaning over his stall guard. I can't leave my horse standing behind bars all day, like a criminal.

I've got six feed bins heaped up against my chest, and am rounding the corner to the wash-racks at the end of the barn when I see Landon walking out to his truck.

It's one of those huge farrier trucks with the custom cap on the back. Without seeing inside, I already know that the rear is fully furnished with racks of horseshoes, a portable forge, anvils, and an astonishing array of hammers and files and nippers and heaven knows what else. Farriers are like the machinists of the stable; sometimes I swear they have the ability to turn our horses into cyborgs with all their shoes and pads and fillers. A good farrier can be the most important person in a horse's training program; a bad farrier can ruin the season's prospects for an entire stable of horses in just one visit.

Landon is apparently one of the very best farriers in the business, which I find both intriguing and annoying. Intriguing, because I have plenty of experience struggling with hooves and it would be nice to have a true expert take a look at Thomas's feet. Annoying, because, well, it's *Landon*. Maybe I don't know the man very well at all, but from what I've experienced so far, he's a know-it-all who has no concept of minding his own business. I mean, really, just stepping in and helping me this morning, without asking?

I know it *sounds* like something a nice guy would do but, really, do we need men doing our jobs for us, like we can't handle our own responsibilities? I don't, thanks very much. I need less of that.

While I dump the feed bins on the concrete pad of the wash-rack, I keep an eye on Landon. He sets that enormous coffee tumbler of his on the truck roof, unlocks the door—he *locked* the doors last night? Who did he think was breaking in? *Me?* —and climbs into the truck cab. The door slams shut. Then the engine growls to life with that satisfying diesel grumble, and I watch with fascination as he puts the truck into reverse and starts to back away from the barn.

The coffee mug he has left on the roof wobbles dangerously.

So does my lower lip, as I try not to grin. Look who is so smart now!

Okay, it's not nice to let someone forget their coffee, especially when that someone has just made my morning a lot less stressful than it should have been. He did tack up a whole horse for me so that Kayla and Basil could stay on schedule.

But, I didn't ask him to do that.

And also, I'm not always the best of people! I can be the first to admit that. Here's the thing: I've had a lot of problems to deal with lately, and I've been pushed around by a lot of awful, bossy people, so maybe I am just looking for someone else to step up and steal my run of rotten luck.

So, I don't wave my arms and tell Landon he forgot his coffee.

Get him, Universe. Get anyone but me.

(Again, my capacity to care about anyone but myself is just a little capped right now.)

And so when Landon finally turns the wheel to reverse into the farm lane and the coffee tumbler topples at last, tossing his morning brew all over the windshield, I am fully aware that my bursting into laughter is both the wrong response *and* the only one I've got available to me.

Landon puts the truck into park and gets out, surveying the mess of coffee with a resigned expression, and then he looks down the stretch of grass between us and gives me a truly demonic glare. Coupled with his bulk and that fiery head of hair, he gives off extreme murder vibes.

Or he would, if I were the least bit scared of him.

Somehow, his staring at me like I willed his coffee to its death is even more hilarious than the tumbler falling over in the first place.

However, after a few moments, the intensity and duration of his glare actually do begin to make me nervous.

He's looking at me like a guy who can really hold a grudge.

Like maybe if I hold on to spite for just a little fuel to get through my days, Landon Kincaid could hold on to spite for a full tank of diesel, to power through his whole life. And right now, he's focusing all of that perfectly primed resentment on me.

His neighbor.

My skin begins to tingle with the force of that gaze raking over me, and I drop eye contact, turning back to my work. I'll just get busy with my chores until he heads out and we forget all about this. Yeah. It'll blow over.

I duck down to scrub out a particularly messy feed bin and when I straighten again, Landon is standing two feet away. That look is still on his face. I just manage to bite back a scream, but I know he sees me jump. *Dammit.*

With supreme effort, I fasten a disdainful expression on my face and drawl, "What do you want now?"

"I want to know why you watched me back up with my coffee mug on the roof of my truck," he says, folding his arms across his chest, "and didn't even try to stop me."

He really has a very wide chest. I'm momentarily mesmerized by the size of him. He looks like he could shoe a Clydesdale without breaking a sweat. A *naughty* Clydesdale, no less.

He clears his throat and I flick my gaze up to his eyes.

They're extremely blue. We're talking Baldwin blue, here. And I know because once I saw Alec Baldwin at a party my husband's firm threw at a polo match, and that man's eyes are *really* that blue.

Landon Kincaid has got that same deep, electrifying, Caribbean-Sea-in-a-storm shade of blue going for him.

And there's something snapping about them right now that makes me think there's lightning in that storm.

"What could I do?" I squeak.

He lifts an eyebrow. "You could have waved your arm, shouted, maybe?"

"Over coffee?"

"Yes, over coffee!"

"This is a *lot* of fuss over a spilled cup of coffee," I complain, refusing to drop my gaze, even though I feel like I'm staring down a Category Five hurricane.

"I *helped* you this morning," he reminds me.

Resentment curdles in my stomach, mixing uncomfortably with my frazzled nerves. "You did, but I didn't *ask*—"

"No buts," he interrupts, cutting me off. "I won't make that mistake again. You're on your own now, kid."

"I'm not a kid," I tell him, aware I sound like a child for saying it. I draw myself up, wishing I could be a foot taller. Then I'd almost be able to look him directly in the eye, instead of lifting my chin like a toddler staring up at a Shire. "Now, you're just being rude. It was a cup of coffee! What was I supposed to do, run you down waving my arms and screaming that you were about to spill it?"

"That's exactly what you'd have done for Kayla," he says.

I have the uncomfortable realization that he's probably right. But only because Kayla and I discovered we were caffeine soul sisters about twenty minutes ago, and that kind of thing matters to women like us.

"You're being ridiculous," I say. "Can I get back to work now? Go get yourself another cup of coffee and forget it. Next time you leave it on your roof, I'll come running with my arms waving. I didn't realize that was my responsibility before, but now I know. Okay?"

He lets those blue eyes rest on me for another long moment, his expression still hard. It's like I've disappointed him, and the worst part is that I feel like I *care*.

Caring what men think of me is definitely one of the things I want to leave behind in my old life. Other than riding coaches helping me with my position, I really don't want to hear a peep of criticism from anyone with a penis. Let's just say I've already had enough to last me a lifetime, and most of it wasn't worth the wind that created the words.

"Fine," Landon says at last, and he stomps away. He goes back towards his truck, which is still running in the distance, driver's side door hanging open. I watch him scoop up the coffee mug from the ground and head into the barn.

"See?" I mutter, turning back to my work. "All you had to do was get another cup of coffee. Simple." And I decide that as soon as I'm finished hosing out these feed bins and have them flipped over to drip dry, I'm going to get myself a cup. *With* some nice vanilla syrup, and a little creamer, too. I'm working hard for my living now. I need the extra calories for energy. Non-fat, non-sugar, you're out the door.

My mouth is absolutely watering by the time I make it back to the office. I can just taste that coffee. It's going to be so—

I stop short and stare at the empty coffee pot, remembering the absurd size of Landon's steel tumbler.

That bastard didn't go into his apartment to get more coffee.

He came back in here and took all of *mine.*

WELL, THIS IS war. That's all there is to it. You take my caffeine, you have entered the Thunderdome. I check the time and bring out the next horse on the list to be tacked up, a doe-eyed gray gelding named Prince—what a silly, but adorable name!—who watches me with flicking ears as I quickly maneuver around him with a curry-comb and a body brush. It's easy to groom a horse on autopilot, which is perfect, because I need all of my brain for Landon-destruction thoughts.

A man does not simply *steal all my coffee.*

Because Kayla wasn't kidding when she said there were no more coffee beans. Believe me, I checked—*exhaustively*. I went through all the cabinets twice. I already know don't have any coffee in my apartment yet. Back in the condo, I left behind a pantry stocked full of essentials for kitchen and home—except for one thing, which I stole with a smirk, and I can't wait for the inevitable realization of what's missing after Ryan brings Shelly over to gloat about the gorgeous love-nest they now have, one hundred percent Mackenzie-free at last. I probably should have spent less time cackling over my theft and more time throwing some boxes of crackers and a bag of coffee beans into my luggage, but I didn't and here we are.

Caffeine-free and probably already spiraling towards a headache.

Prince is fully saddled and waiting in the cross-ties, and I'm working on Kayla's next horse, a tall bay Thoroughbred named Galaxy, when I realize there's only one way to get back at Landon *and* prevent a caffeine withdrawal migraine from wrecking my first day on the job.

I'll just break into his apartment and steal his coffee.

Yes, I think, a smile spreading across my face as I comb the tangles from Galaxy's black tail. I'll steal *all* his coffee!

Or maybe just...half of it.

To confuse him.

He'll think, "Didn't I have more coffee than this?" And he'll look around, wondering. He'll think, "No, she couldn't have."

But he'll never know for sure.

And it will haunt him.

I cackle. Diabolical!

"That was a scary laugh."

I look up, startled, and drop Galaxy's tail. There's a man standing in the aisle. Not a Viking like Landon, thank goodness—one of him is *more* than enough. This is a good-looking guy of normal size and height, wearing breeches and a navy-blue quarter-zip shirt, with a farm logo embroidered in white on the chest, above the words *Briar Hill Farm*.

"Oh," I say, remembering Basil's business partner. "You must be Peter Morrison!"

"And you must be...the new groom?" He chuckles and takes

off his US Eventing Association cap, running a hand through his dark, coppery hair. "Sorry, I'm terrible with names. It comes with the sleep deprivation."

"Of being a horseman?" I ask with a smile, stepping forward to shake his hand.

"A horseman, a husband, a father of a toddler," he says with a rueful smile in return. "If just over eighteen months counts as a toddler."

"I think it does," I say, "although I don't have any kids, so I'm not really the best judge." His hand is strong and calloused. It's the opposite of Ryan's hand, and I think for a single silly moment that if I ever allowed another man to enter my life, I'd want him to have a hand like this. There's a ring though, and talk of a baby at home, so this one's taken. Naturally. "Were you riding a horse this morning?" I ask, realizing why he must be here, in boots and breeches, at prime riding time. "Should I be tacking someone up for you?"

"Oh, I've got it," he assures me. "I wasn't planning on coming over, but I woke up to *two* missing shoes on horses who were apparently intent on not working today, so I had a little time open up in my schedule. I'll ask Basil who needs my attention with an extra ride. I'm kind of the tune-up guy," he adds, looking over the white board with its list of horses for the day. "Basil does the daily work and I come by to polish it up and check his progress."

"Lucky Basil," I say, wondering if that's hard on his ego—I've yet to meet a man who enjoys having input from someone else on his horses. Then again, I'm not much better.

A horse appears at the far end of the barn aisle, and that's my cue to hustle to work, halter in hand. Basil hands me the reins and I walk his horse to the wash-rack for his shower while Basil heads down to meet Pete.

Kayla walks her mare, Feather, over to the wash-racks while I'm still hosing down Basil's horse. She puts her horse into the other wash-rack and unravels the second hose.

"I can get to her in a second," I offer, rushing to get the last of the sweat off Basil's gelding, but Kayla waves a hand.

"No, no, we'll all pitch in and get through the day together," she says cheerfully, and squints up at the sun. The fog is long gone. "In summer, it's a matter of surviving the heat and the humidity, and in winter, it's all about getting the work done before the sun sets stupid early. There's always a deadline we can't reach. So don't feel like you have to do everything all alone. We're in this together."

"That's probably the nicest thing anyone has said to me in a long time," I admit.

"Well, I mean it. And Basil feels the same way, even if he gets rushed and tense sometimes. It's just his way; he's an anxious little guy." She laughs softly.

"I remember that about him."

"Oh, right, you knew him in Wellington! He must have been incredibly tense there," Kayla says, flicking up Feather's tail to get the sweat rinsed out from between the mare's hind legs. Feather lifts first one hind leg and then the other in warning, but Kayla must know her horse pretty well, because she ignores the threat and the mare settles, sighing with disappointment.

"He was wound pretty tightly." I pick up a sweat scraper. "Listen, you should know something...Landon took all the coffee. There's none left."

Kayla sighs heavily. "That man."

"He's a little weird," I venture, hoping she's up for some

Landon-bashing. "You want to talk about tightly wound..."

"Oh, he's a nice guy. You'll love him after a while," Kayla laughs. "Everyone does."

I doubt it. I scrape the excess water off my horse in silence, disappointed she doesn't want to commiserate about what a big, weird grump he is. I don't *want* to love him after a while.

I want to make him so crazy that he stops messing with me. According to Ryan, I'm really good at making men crazy. So, this should be pretty easy.

Starting with the Great Coffee Heist.

Chapter Seven

WITH THREE HORSES in the ring, everyone's attention is thoroughly taken up with trying not to run into one another. It's not the biggest riding arena in the world.

The riders' complete concentration on their riding is the perfect situation for me, because I can feel the tension building beneath my forehead and I know there's only one answer.

And no, Basil's lightweight English Breakfast tea is not going to do the job.

Running a barn all by myself is going to take the real deal, caffeine squeezed from beans, not leaves. Also, there is a principle here. I must show Landon I am a force to be reckoned with, by sneaking into his apartment, leaving no trace, and hoping that he remembers how much coffee he had left, so it's utterly confounding to him that he's now completely out.

Hey, it's psychological warfare—it doesn't have to sound logical.

Getting into his apartment is the first hurdle...or it would be, if Basil's Big Binder of Everything didn't include a note about where to find the spare keys to every lock on the property. I'm only supposed to know about this set of keys as my job essentially encompasses the title "Property Manager"—if Basil and Kayla are away at a horse show and I'm here running the place alone, I have to be able to access every corner of the farm. So the "In Case of Emergency" section tells me that if I need access to a locked door, all I have to do is look inside a little box hidden beneath a hose in the wash-rack and... yup, here it is. The loop of keys jangles as I pull it free. There are a lot of keys.

This could take a few minutes.

I hazard a glance out the center aisle, towards the arena, as the riders trot past in opposite directions. Eyes are straight ahead, chins are set with the grim determination of another day in the saddle. Horseback riding is hilarious because we all look miserable as hell while we're doing the thing we supposedly love more than anything else in the world. Show me a smiling rider and I'll show you an equestrian who just isn't working hard enough. Or she's learned to fake a smile with such terrifying precision, she deserves a ribbon for her expression alone.

The three riders in the ring are still dead focused on their horses, and that's perfect for me. I kneel down next to Landon's apartment door, the better to hear the lock with, and start trying keys.

It's not the most finessed way to break into an apartment, but listen—I'm not a professional burglar and I'm not going to apologize for that. I'm just a woman who wants a cup of coffee and to instill confusion in the brain of her neighbor. I have simple needs.

I try five keys to no avail, but the sixth key is the magic key. I know this because it has a little taped-on label that reads "South Apartment" in Basil's tidy handwriting. Maybe I should have just looked at the keys before I started shoving them into the lock. Whatever—the key turns and the door swings open, admitting one Mackenzie. I'm in now.

I've broken and entered.

Not even sorry.

The apartment looks just like mine, only slightly more lived-in. There are a few pieces of mail discarded on the thrift store coffee table, and a few fat books about horseshoeing on the sofa, a tired brown cousin to the one in my living room. There's a hoodie thrown over a chair in the kitchen, which makes me pause for a moment...then I remember he was in Kentucky. I suppose a summer evening might cool off enough for a light jacket up there. Certainly not in Florida, though.

The kitchen is tidy, even dusty, which makes sense considering he hasn't been in town for a while. The only thing which has seen any recent use is the Mr. Coffee, gleaming on the counter with nearly half a pot of coffee still waiting in its glass carafe. Perfect! And also truly maddening, because he could have walked right back in here and refilled that huge coffee tumbler of his, but instead he chose to use up everything left in the tack room pot, just to get at me.

Does he even know what a mistake that was?

I pour as much of the coffee as I can into my tumbler without risking a spill from overflow, then root around in one of his three cabinets in search of where he keeps his coffee beans. I find a container of coffee grounds that are disappointingly grocery store-brand, but I guess that's not a huge surprise. He doesn't look like a gourmet coffee guy. I unscrew the lid and dump the grounds into the spare mug I've brought with me from the barn office.

The entire time, I resist glancing over my shoulder into the bedroom, even though the door is half open and I'm very curious about whether he's the sort who makes his bed in the morning. I don't know why I even care. It's just that Ryan never made his bed, ever. I guess I would like to confirm my long-held suspicion that Ryan is the worst person in the world, and that having a messy bed is part of how he won that title. Maybe that it should have been a giveaway in the first place, ten years ago when we first met, that this guy was going to be nothing but trouble.

And not the fun kind.

Finally, with the empty coffee can returned to the cabinet and my mission all but accomplished, I let myself peek into the bedroom. It was just killing me not to.

The bed is made. I nod in appreciation.

Not made *neatly*, mind you. It didn't take a lot of work, there are no edges or anything. But he pulled a duvet up to the pillows, anyway. There's some civilization at work here.

And then I hear hoofbeats on the concrete outside. I hop up, racing to grab my coffee from the kitchen counter and get the hell out of this apartment.

I've locked the door behind me, and am hustling to stow the keys back in their hiding place, before I remember that I left my stolen coffee grounds on Landon's kitchen counter.

IT TURNS OUT the rider who came back in early was Pete, which makes it all the more frustrating that I left those coffee grounds sitting out. He probably wouldn't have noticed I was in Landon's apartment at all; even if he knows who lives where in this barn, he has an absent-minded air to him, as if he pays so much attention to the horses and their behavior that he barely sees the world around him. I try to help him untack his horse, but I only get in the way, and after Pete stumbles over me for the third time, I withdraw and let him do his thing alone. He takes the horse out to bathe, giving me the opportunity to check Basil's binder and find that to stay on schedule for the day, I'd better start prepping lunch. It feels like I only just fed the horses their breakfast, but somehow it's already almost eleven o'clock and once I've washed down the horses they're riding now, we'll be at the midday break.

Well, it's a midday break for the horses. I'll be skipping out stalls with a manure fork and wheelbarrow to make sure that the full stall-cleaning this afternoon doesn't take hours, running laundry in the tack room, and working my way through whatever weekly tasks I can fit in before it's time for the late afternoon rides.

Oh, and dodging lightning bolts—my phone buzzes with a friendly reminder from the National Weather Service that there's a good chance of strong thunderstorms in the area this afternoon.

"What else is new?" I murmur, giving Thomas a pat on the nose as I rush past his stall.

I'm feeling more energetic now that I've got Landon's cold coffee, heavily doctored with syrup and milk to cover up the cheap taste, and I have no regrets about breaking into his apartment to steal it—although I wish I knew if he plans on coming back here for lunch, because I'd really like to get back in there and finish the job by taking those coffee grounds, too. Leaving them on the counter is too obvious, a calling card that I was there, while the mystery of the empty pot and the container back in its cabinet would be a nice conundrum for him to ponder when he might otherwise be using his brain to come up with ways to annoy me.

I resolve to let the right answer come to me, a gift from the universe, while I do my job and keep an eye on where the others in the barn are. The right opportunity will arise if I'm patient and aware.

With their horses ridden, bathed, and put away, Kayla and Basil help me feed lunch. Pete is on a horse in the arena, working diligently on the horse's lateral movements at the walk. "Isn't he hot?" I ask, looking out the aisle doorway at the horse and rider. Both are evidently deep in concentration.

"It's his thing," Kayla says, shrugging. "He's in his own world. Don't worry—he'll put the horse up himself before he leaves. Basil and I are going to head to the house for lunch. Then I'm going to town to get some groceries. It's too hot to ride right after lunch. Do you need anything?"

I think of my empty cabinets. The supply of ramen and pasta from my horse trailer kitchen will only last a few days, with the amount of physical work I'm doing. "I should go tonight," I say. "I didn't bring any real food with me."

"Oh, there's no reason for both of us to drive in. I know you want to ride your horse, so I'll grab you some staples and you can just Venmo me or whatever." She takes my phone from my hand and types in the grocery store's web address. "Check their sales and text me what you want."

"Thanks," I say, astonished. "That's so nice of you."

Kayla laughs. "There will be plenty of times when I'll ask you to run into town and get me something, trust me. This is just a light day. Enjoy it, okay? I know Basil's got a list of things to be done, but settle in. Unpack your stuff. Take a nap, for heaven's sake. We'll be back at three to do the rest of the horses."

"Weather permitting?" I ask as she walks away.

"Well, yeah," Kayla agrees, shrugging. "You know how

Florida is."

Finally alone—well, almost, if you don't count Pete out in the arena—I take the opportunity to dig out the keys and run back into Landon's apartment, snagging the coffee grounds. I'm locking up again, congratulating myself on the heist, when my phone buzzes. It startles me so badly that I drop the mug, which shatters on the concrete.

"For god's sake!" I shout.

"Are you okay in there?"

It's Pete. I've distracted the dressage maestro. "Fine!" I call back, hoping he stays in the arena. "Everything is fine!"

I have just enough time to sweep up the shattered bits of mug, and most of the coffee grounds, before Pete walks his sweaty horse back into the barn. I'll have to trust the breeze to blow away the rest. I dump the shovel of debris into the trash can by the feed room door and offer to help Pete with untacking. I assume he will do things himself, but it's polite to ask.

To my surprise, he hands me the reins. "Thank you," he says. "I better get home and meet Landon. He just texted to say he was on his way to my farm."

"Landon's your farrier?" I ask, starting on the horse's noseband.

"When he's in Florida," Pete says. "And if he'd been here two weeks ago, I wouldn't have two horses who need shoes tacked back on today. Wait until he does your horse. The man is magical with a hoof."

Thomas has very difficult feet. I should be thrilled that the world's best farrier is in my barn.

I'm not.

I mean, just today he has butted in on my morning work,

we've gotten into a fight about coffee, and I've broken into his apartment. I don't feel like we're on the road to a good professional relationship in general, let alone with my horse's hooves.

I'm trying to think of a polite response for Pete, something that doesn't give away what I really think of our magical farrier friend, when I look up and realize I'm alone. I hear a truck door slam out front. He's already leaving.

Okay, Pete's a bit of an odd duck. But I like him.

I like everyone here, really.

Well, except for you know who.

AFTER THE HORSES eat their lunch and begin nosing through their afternoon hay, I head back to my apartment and boil up some water for ramen. I stare idly out the kitchen window while the electric burner clicks its way to full heat, making a mental note that cooking anything on this tiny stovetop will probably take a lot of creativity and loose adherence to instruction times. The apartment might be clean, but it's decidedly run-down, and nothing is really running to factory specs any more.

I'm still gazing out at the empty arena and the green fields beyond when I notice that the midday clouds are thickening up. Looks like those strong thunderstorms are starting to materialize already, or at least getting their ducks in a row for some monsoon action. The breeze picks up, shaking the long grass lining the arena fence. Mowing and weed-eating are in the binder, too, but they're a very low priority compared to getting horses ridden every day.

With the clouds and breeze, I suppose the weather might be almost bearable for a few minutes. Maybe after I eat lunch, I'll have enough time to get on Thomas. He's not ready for a tough workout or anything, but it would be great to hack him around the arena and let him get a feel for the place. I'm supposed to ride later, but I know we'll get eaten by mosquitoes.

What began as an idle thought quickly solidifies into determination. While the soup is simmering, I head into the bedroom and dig around in my suitcase for my favorite summer-weight riding breeches and a sun-shirt with mesh panels under the arms and down the sides. Ryan used to make jokes about how much money I spent on riding clothes that are designed with a bare minimum of actual fabric, and yet cover me up from head to toe. "Wish you'd spend that much on a bikini and show me some skin," he'd say, thinking he was funny.

Such an idiot. Like I would be a better wife if I was constantly getting bad moles burned off at the dermatologist. When I started designing my own riding outfits, covering up from the sun in the most comfortable and stylish way possible was my number one aim.

Satisfied that the only parts of me left uncovered are my hands and my face, I sit down at the rickety kitchen table and slurp down my ramen. It's really too hot to be eating soup for lunch, especially at a fast pace. I'm already sweating when I head out into the barn, scoop up my saddle and bridle from the tack room, and halter Thomas.

"Ready for a little ride, buddy?" I ask him, and he nudges at my pockets for treats, knowing I've always got something for him. For Thomas, I have all the treats and all the time in the world.

But right now we have to hurry, because it's already thundering in the distance.

"Even if we get fifteen minutes, even if we only get *ten*, that's fine," I tell him as I walk him out to the arena. "We just need a little time to walk around the arena so you can get to know the place, okay?"

Thomas snorts loudly at everything in the arena: every set of jump standards, every ground pole, every puddle. He looks at the mounting block in one corner and snorts for so long I'm somewhat concerned he's going to hyperventilate. Then he walks up to it and shoves it hard with his nose, and I know he's going to be just fine. Thomas *loves* knocking things over. He's basically a bulldozer in horse form.

"Okay, goofus," I tell him, pushing the mounting block back into place. "Let's do this thing."

Once I'm on his back, shoving my feet into the stirrups as he walks away with his usual impatience before I've had a chance to find my seat, everything about life feels settled and safe. Kind of ironic, when you consider how many things can go wrong on horseback. But like sliding tired feet into a pair of well-worn slippers after a long, hard day, the familiarity and comfort of sitting on the horse you know best is the most reassuring and relaxing feeling in the world.

Even if that horse is snorting and blowing at every jump standard, ground pole, and puddle in the arena, because now he's seeing these things from the *other* direction, and of course it's all different this way.

So I snug up on the reins, just to make sure he can't spook out from under me, and make sure my heels are down as far as those suckers will go. With the wind picking up and the thunder growling ever more closely, I'm sort of begging for a big reaction from my ex-racehorse here.

But it isn't the weather that finally coaxes a leap out of Thomas, one that's *almost* enough to unseat me. Once I've got my butt firmly back in the saddle, I look around to see what set him off...and there is the problem, standing in the barn aisle doorway, arms crossed over his chest in what I'm starting to think is his normal stance.

"Oh, hi, Landon," I say nonchalantly, turning Thomas in a circle to get his attention back on me. "How was your morning?"

"Long and hot," he says, eyeing Thomas's hooves. "How about yours?"

"Kind of the same," I reply, shrugging. "Can I help you with something?"

Thunder growls, close enough that I know I should go inside. But Landon triggers something rebellious in me, and I keep circling Thomas, determined to stay outside until he goes away and leaves me with the barn aisle to myself again.

"Yes," Landon says. "You can tell me where my coffee has gone."

"You're still worried about coffee?" I ask, laughing, but I'm aware my voice is pitched just a little too high. Luckily, he doesn't know me that well. Ryan would have caught the guilty tone there in a heartbeat.

"I'm worried that we have a thief on the property," Landon says. "Because someone has broken into my apartment and messed with my kitchen."

Wind whips across the arena and tugs at his auburn hair, tossing it back from his forehead. His blue eyes bore into me, twenty-five feet away and yet still capable of flinging that menacing glare straight into my soul.

Maybe I shouldn't have broken into his apartment, after all.

Maybe this guy isn't like Ryan—easy to mess with, satisfying to screw around with.

Maybe I misjudged this entire situation.

Lightning crackles through the clouds and thunder echoes all around us, shaking the air. Thomas spooks hard and this time I go with him, letting him trot away from the far end of the ring where we've been circling and back to the gate at the other end. I hop off and jog him up to the barn, getting him inside just before another flash and bang lets us know that the storm is really, truly arriving.

"Well, that was fun," I tell him leading him up the aisle to the cross-ties. When I get there, Landon has beaten me to his halter.

He holds it up with one brawny hand, keeping it just out of reach, and demands, "How'd you get in there?"

Chapter Eight

I STARE AT him for a moment, wondering if I should be worried. And then I decide that's ridiculous. Kayla basically told me he's a big teddy bear. Basil seems to like him, and Pete trusts him with his horses. He's used to being intimidating because he's a big guy with muscles to spare, but being intimidating and actually being dangerous are two very different things. If horses have taught me anything, it's that scaring people into doing what you want is fun and easy when you're big and strong.

For those of us who are smaller, being smart and conniving will have to suffice.

And part of wisdom is knowing when to give in. So I just hold out my hand, as if I'm certain he will drop my horse's halter into it without a fight, and say, "I used a *key*, Landon."

For a moment, he just glowers down at me. And then a smile creeps across his face, spreading from his mouth to those lagoon-blue eyes of his. Landon shakes his head and hands me the halter. "You used a key," he repeats.

I unbuckle Thomas's noseband. "I wanted coffee, and you took mine," I tell him matter-of-factly. "So I took yours. It's not like you were drinking it. I'm not sure how I'm in the wrong here."

"Not sure—" he guffaws, crossing his arms over his chest again. But this time he's not doing it to be intimidating. He just has big, heavy arms and it must be more comfortable to hold them up than let them hang at his sides all the time. "So it's going to be like that around here? I should expect frequent surprise inspections and theft of my personal belongings?"

"I hardly think coffee grounds count as personal belongings —" I bluster, making him laugh harder.

"You're a Wellington girl, alright," he says, wiping at his eyes.

"What's *that* supposed to mean?" I demand. I slip Thomas's halter over his ears and buckle it in place while he side-steps, nervous from the storm crashing over the farm as well as how noisy the supposed Best Farrier in Florida is being. His hoof catches the side of my boot and I suppress a yelp as I shove him off my little toe. "Can you calm down, please? You're upsetting my horse."

Landon obliges, quieting down and taking a step back. "Sorry about that. As for the Wellington bit...oh, I don't mean anything by it. You know, south Florida girls just have a reputation for...you know. Being a little difficult."

"I'm not a girl," I say coolly. "I am thirty-three and a third years old."

"So you're a bit like playing a record?"

There's an innuendo in there, but it's probably not worth unpacking. "Yeah," I say. "Like that." I set the saddle on a rack along the wall and pick up a towel from my grooming kit to rub away the sweat marks—no bathing is possible now. The rain is coming down like a hurricane, and lightning is flashing on and off as if someone's screwing with the barn lights. "I know you're saying that I'm probably rich and spoiled and have to get my own way," I tell him, rubbing away at Thomas's back while the horse leans into the pressure, enjoying himself.

"No, I'm not—"

"And I just want you to know," I interrupt, "that I am all of those things."

Landon rubs his mouth with one calloused hand. "You're a pistol, aren't you?"

"Fully loaded," I assure him. "And the safety is off."

"I'm not sure there ever was a safety," he says.

Oh, no.

Now he looks admiring.

I have to shut this down, because if there was ever a result I did not intend, it was *intriguing* this guy. Why are men like this? Why do they interpret hostility as interest? "Can you leave me alone to finish up my horse?" I ask curtly. "If you want your coffee grounds, by the way, they're gone. I dropped the cup they were in and spilled them everywhere."

"That's fine," Landon says, still watching me with far too much interest. He rubs his hand along his chin again. I wonder if his hands are as rough and calloused as Pete's, and then I wonder why I would think about the way his hands feel. Possibly I just need a nap, like Kayla suggested. "I'll just drink some of yours tomorrow."

I shrug. "Kayla is going to the store to buy more. So I guess we'll all survive the coffee crisis."

"You know, if you'd just told me—"

"Fine!" I shout. Thomas shifts uneasily and Landon looks taken aback. "Fine," I repeat, adjusting my tone to a more horse-friendly volume. "I should have told you about the coffee. I shouldn't have laughed at you. Fine, fine, fine, fine. I'm sorry. Are you happy now? Will you please just leave me alone?"

He's already beating a retreat, so I guess my apology was worthwhile. "Thank you," he says, raising his voice to be heard over the pouring rain. "And tomorrow, before my horses get here, I want to look at your horse's hooves."

"His hooves are fine!" I shout after him. "We had a very good farrier in Wellington!"

"I don't think so!" Landon calls over his shoulder. "I'll show you what I mean tomorrow!"

I huff an aggravated sigh and finish rubbing Thomas's back dry. Then I step back and look at him. My horse twists his head in the cross-ties to eyeball me, wondering what's going on.

I can't see anything desperately wrong with his hooves. They look okay. Sure, they're a little flat and could have thicker walls, but he's an ex-racehorse in Florida during rainy season. He's going to have a long toe and shelly walls. We're going to need extra trims and sometimes he'll need time off for an abscess. That's just life.

"He's not looking at your hooves tomorrow," I promise Thomas, digging a treat from my breeches pocket and letting him lip it off my palm. "Your feet are just fine."

THE THUNDERSTORMS RAGE overhead until after four o'clock, which sets off a chain reaction of late rides, feeding, and turn-out. We don't finish up with work until after eight, as the clouds clear in the west and the sun begins its lengthy and dramatic final descent towards the horizon. A flock of ibis land in the paddocks and begin digging through the puddles with their long, orange beaks. Their white feathers take on a rosy hue as the sunset intensifies, while the towering cloud tops in the east catching the last of the sunlight and turn cotton-candy pink. Occasionally, one of the clouds will flicker and rumble, but the storms are far enough away now to let us turn out the horses in safety.

I'm glad I rode Thomas before the storms hit, or I wouldn't have had a chance to get on him at all today.

"That was an unfortunate end to your first day," Basil says as I walk in from turning out the last horse. "Sorry it went on for so long."

"Oh, that's just summer in Florida for you," I say, pretending I'm not exhausted, overheated, and ready to collapse into a little puddle in the barn aisle. I pick up a broom, but he puts out his hand to stop me.

"Honestly, there's no point," he says. "Those horses are coming back inside in less than twelve hours and no one is going to see the place between now and then, anyway. Go inside, have a shower and dinner, and go to bed. Or watch TV. The router is working now, right?"

"Yup, it's fixed," I say, although I'm too tired to bother calling Casey tonight. And that's a shame, because there's so much to tell her. This day has been so bizarre, I almost feel like I dreamed it.

"There's a broken mug in the trash," Kayla says, frowning as she pulls the full trash bag out of the bin.

Nope, didn't dream it.

"Sorry," I say. "That was me."

"As long as no one's hurt, it's fine. We have plenty of mugs." She knots up the bag. "I'll put this in the dumpster at the end of the driveway," she says. "Basil, you ready to head home?"

He glances back at me. "Remember, no sweeping," he says.

Ordinarily, I don't like a man telling me what to do, but there's a reason I decided I could happily work for Basil, and he's showing it to me right now. Such a thoughtful person. "No sweeping," I agree. "Goodnight, guys."

"Goodnight," Kayla calls. "Great first day, Mackenzie! Thank you!"

With them gone, the empty barn aisle stares back at me as if daring me to sweep it. The mess of a day's worth of riding, feeding, stall cleaning, and horses tramping in and out to pasture is truly appalling. But I really am wiped out, and Basil's right about no one else seeing it.

"Going in so soon?" Landon asks, popping out of his apartment like a jack-in-the-box. Was he watching me through the living room window overlooking the barn aisle?

Creep.

"I'm going to eat whatever Kayla bought for me at the store and go to bed," I tell him. "I haven't even had time to look. I just know she went in with groceries and came out again without them."

"You really trust her, huh?" He folds his arms and leans against the door-frame.

"She seems like a person I can trust." I shrug. "It's just food, anyway."

"Just food! Girl, food is *important*."

"I'm not having this discussion with you."

"Let me make you dinner," Landon says.

I stare at him. I'm almost tempted, which says a lot about how very tired I am. Because if there's one thing I do not need in my life, it's more time spent in the company of domineering, pushy people. "No," I say flatly, and I close the door between us.

WATCHING VLOGS ABOUT riders prepping for last year's

Thoroughbred Makeover while I heat up a skillet of frozen chicken and vegetables is just the therapy I need to get over such an exhausting first day of work. It's so inspiring to see other riders take a Thoroughbred from racehorse to sport-horse in a matter of months. I know I can do it with Thomas, even though we only have four months until the Makeover itself. I've been keeping up with his training faithfully through all the drama of my divorce.

In fact, the divorce is *why* I bought Thomas. I just felt like I needed a project that would carry me through to the next phase of my life. Otherwise, I really would have felt like a failure. Deep down, of course, I know I was not the problem with my marriage. Ryan was. But sometimes the truth can't stop perception from feeling like reality, and there are plenty of people in this world who think I am the reason Ryan cheated, and that I am the person who gave up instead of fixing my broken marriage.

Those people are idiots, of course, but they still exist and their opinions are still out in the world, damaging my reputation and causing gossip that escalates every time I leave a room south of Orlando.

I carry a bowlful of supper to the sofa and set up my laptop on the coffee table to watch another rider illustrate how she got her retired racehorse going as a jumper in under three months, grateful for the working internet. The food makes me sleepy and my eyelids are heavy, so I set an alarm for nine o'clock so I won't pass out on the couch before I do night-check.

When it finally blares to life, I snap upright and drop the bowl, but thankfully it's made of sterner stuff than that mug I broke earlier and it survives the fall.

"Would have been just great if I broke my only bowl," I mutter, scooping it up and heading to the kitchen. "You'll be fine until morning," I tell it, and I put the entire pan of leftovers into the fridge—I don't have any storage containers. Then I slide my sore feet into my paddock boots, trying to ignore how sad that makes them, and head out into the humid night with a big flashlight.

It turns out I don't need the flashlight—the moon is rising above the storm clouds and in between flickers of distant lightning, a glow of moonlight shows me the horses grazing peacefully in their paddocks. The air is heavy and warm again, so I walk slowly along the fence line, trying not to get sweaty before bed. I don't really feel like taking another shower now; I just want to tumble into my bed and stay there forever, or at least until seven o'clock.

I pause at Thomas's paddock and look at the dark outline of my horse grazing away. He's standing close to the back fence, and I can see two more horses on the other side, keeping their bodies aligned with his. Feather and Mara. Maybe, when his quarantine period is over, those will be his pasture mates. They seem to like each other at a distance already.

"Goodnight, ponies," I call, smiling when I see Thomas's star glinting through the moonlight as he looks at me. Then there's a quick flash of lightning that illuminates everything in electric blue, and my smile fades as it lights up not one, but two horseshoes in the sand near the gate.

THOMAS THE TANK Engine's Training Diary
June 9
The first ride couldn't have gone better, so why did he have to go and lose two shoes?? There's work we can do at the walk

while I get a new farrier to come out, but of course, Landon is here. Never fear, right?

Yeah, Landon will be all over this. He's such a disaster. I know there are two million farriers in the Ocala area, but somehow I end up with Mister Personality in my barn, who will insist I have been doing everything wrong with my horse. I just know it.

All I asked for was a job where I could work on my own and become a better horsewoman and not have a man standing over me saying I'm doing everything wrong, and what do I get? Landon freaking Kincaid. What kind of name is that, anyway? Sounds like he's a soap opera character. I guess amnesia, alien abduction, and murder are all part of a day's work for this guy. He better leave me out of his drama.

Are there soap operas set in Kentucky? There probably should be. Rich people, horses, and bourbon. Sounds like a fun time to me. Or for him. He should go back there and be with his own kind!

Anyway. It was a good ride. He needs a few days to look around, just some light work with gentle contact, and then by the end of the week, he should be ready to do some thinking. We have four months. That's all the time in the world, right?

Oh god.

Chapter Nine

"I JUST HAVE one special favor to ask of you today," Kayla says, leaning into the stall I'm skipping out. She's holding Feather's reins, and the mare is bumping her nose into Kayla's shoulder over and over, while Kayla ignores her with such ease that it's obvious this behavior is pretty common. Feather isn't the kind of horse you can just boss around. I'm sure Kayla has picked her battles and decided the nose-bumping thing is the least of her problems. "If you don't mind!"

"Whatever you need, boss," I say cheerfully. I could use a distraction. All morning, I've been thinking endlessly about the Thoroughbred Makeover, counting the days left to us, and how much work we have to accomplish in that time, and how my horse lost two shoes last night. Plus, it's only day two of full-time barn work and I'm already so sore I can barely lift this manure fork. I plaster on a smile and lean on the fork, waiting for Kayla to add more work to my day.

Whatever it is, I'm pretty sure I will survive.

After all, I came here to toughen up and forge a more meaningful life, and I knew it would hurt to get started.

Did I know it would hurt this much? Well...that's why they make industrial-sized price club bottles of painkillers.

"Great!" Kayla says brightly. "Can you please bed four stalls in the other wing of the barn? There should be buckets already in them. Just rinse those out and refill them after you've put the shavings down." She smiles. "Easy-peasy, right?"

Bedding stalls means using a snow shovel to dig into a huge pile of shavings living in steamy conditions beneath a blue tarp, and a wheelbarrow to tote them up the aisle and into the stalls, but sure. Let's call it easy-peasy. "No worries," I say. "I'll do it after we feed lunch."

"Oh, and Basil and I have to leave by eleven-thirty to get to an appointment in Gainesville," Kayla adds. "So it's just you to feed lunch. And we might not get to some of the afternoon rides. We'll keep you posted."

"That's fine." Maybe they'll get back too late to ride anyone. I could use an easy day. A girl can dream, right?

Kayla jiggles Feather's reins, and the mare stops bumping her shoulder for a moment. "That's enough, madam," she murmurs, then looking back at me, she says, "Thank you so much! I am *so* glad you're here! We never would have made it to this appointment if you weren't here to help out."

"Well, that's great. Have fun at your...appointment." Whatever it is. Must be something boring, like seeing their accountant. Are they making enough money to keep the business going? They'd better be. I have my whole future riding on this job.

Kayla leads Feather away and I get back to scooping up manure, blowing a wisp of hair off my lips as I work. The morning is hot, which should go without saying, and I'm sweating from every centimeter of skin on my body. Fortunately, I'm from south Florida, so this is just part of life. It's weirder when I'm *not* sweaty. When I would help at the boarding stables down there, the grooms would look at me with concern, as if they were afraid the red-cheeked white woman might pass out in the aisle and add extra work to their day. I was just trying to keep horses happy, the way I'd learned to as a kid, but most of the barns I boarded at on Ryan's budget were staffed by crews of men who didn't want or appreciate the help of children or women.

Especially women who drove a luxury car and wore thousand-dollar custom-made riding boots for her riding lessons.

Well, I admit the car was ostentatious and I much prefer my truck, but I won't apologize for those boots. I still have them, and I'll give up food and water before I'll let those boots go.

As soon as I'm finished with this stall, I hustle down the aisle to get started on the ones that need bedding. I try not to chew too hard on the fact that I'm doing this favor for Kayla, but it's really for Landon. His horses are on their way south today. They're the only new horses due in.

This is a frustrating development. I'm not here to take care of Landon's horses. Why did Kayla volunteer my services to prep his stalls? And what else will she expect me to do with them? Maybe I'll be feeding and grooming for him, too! Maybe I should just handle all their rehab, take them out for hand-grazing, and soak their sore little toes in Epsom salts?

"You *are* the hired help," I remind myself. "There's no need to get all outraged over this."

Sure, there's no need. But it's happening, anyway.

I flip up the huge tarp covering the shavings pile. The shavings live in a three-sided shed at the far end of the barn. The shed sits in broad sunlight, and the tarp has been holding in all the moisture of a truckload of pine shavings as it slowly steams in the summer heat. My glasses fog up immediately, and the air takes on the tang and aroma of a lumber-yard, a cloyingly sweet perfume that clings to the back of my throat and clogs my sinuses.

Ah, shavings. I know buying a truckload of pine shavings is cheaper than buying a pallet of the bagged stuff, but it's *so* much easier to toss a few bags of shavings in a stall, rip them open, and do the little dance-shuffle to get them all out of the bag. I look at my wheelbarrow, then back at the shavings pile, then down at the shovel in my hand. This is going to warrant an extra dose of Advil at lunchtime, I can already tell.

"Okay," I say. "Three loads per stall should do it. You've got this, Mackenzie. You're the barn manager of the year. The groom of the century. It's just four stalls."

And since that's the most hype I can manage, I dig the shovel into the shavings pile, ignoring the protest in my shoulders and hips.

BY LUNCHTIME, I'VE managed to get the four stalls bedded with three wheelbarrow-loads each worth of shavings, with the bedding swept neatly away from the door and the front of the stall where the horses eat their grain and hay, and I've rinsed out the water buckets. There were only three giant spiders living in them, which, for eight buckets, is a pretty good average. And I only screamed at the first one, so yes, I'm feeling pretty impressed with myself.

Basil and Kayla take off after their second horses as promised, leaving me to feed lunch alone. The barn is already fairly silent while they're riding, but there's a new quiet that descends with no one around at all. The horses eat noisily enough, then they turn back to their hay, a much quieter affair.

A barn cat ripples through the aisle like a gray-and-white ghost, her striped tail held high as she disappears into the feed room for some rodent recon. That must be Shadow. Kayla said no one here has ever touched her.

I'd like to be the first person in history to stroke Shadow, but her piercing green gaze from behind the supplement buckets lets me know that event won't happen today, so I unravel the hose wound up at the far end of the barn and start filling the water buckets for Landon's horses.

While the buckets slowly fill, I plan out my ride on Thomas. Since my darling, lovely horse chose to pull *both* his shoes last night, there isn't much work I can do without risking sore feet. Fortunately, the training plan was always to simply hack him gently around the arena for two or three days before we start proper work. And since the temperature is a fairly dramatic ninety-two degrees plus sixty-percent humidity at the moment, it's actually too hot to do more than walk him under saddle. Combining ninety-two and sixty makes a sum of one hundred fifty-two, which is *all* the way into the dangerous red color blocks on the horse heat index chart hanging on the tack room door.

Giving my horse heat stroke is not high on my list of fun things to do.

I could wait and see if a storm rolls through just long enough to cool things off. But the storms could also stick around until late, like they did last night. Add in the potential for late hours this evening if Kayla and Basil decide they want to ride everyone after they get back...nope, it's got to be the midday hack if I want to be absolutely sure we get a ride in.

"And I still have to figure out how to get his shoes tacked back on," I mutter, moving to the next stall's water buckets. The water roars noisily into the empty bucket, foaming up around the bottom. "It's going to be a problem finding a farrier and getting him out here with Landon around all the time."

"A big problem," a deep voice says from behind me. "What if he finds out?"

Somehow, I hold myself together and don't jump out of my skin. But it's an effort. I don't turn around. He'd see the mortified expression on my face and he'd probably laugh his ass off at me.

"So, you're back," I say, keeping my tone level. It's an effort, believe me.

"Yeah. I like to come back for lunch," Landon says. I can hear the amusement in his voice.

At least he isn't mad? Although, I can't say I enjoy being laughed at, either.

"Must be nice having a lunch break," I say pointedly, turning off the hose with the little knob at the end. "Excuse me, please. I have to get to the next stall. Of *yours.*"

Landon remains in the stall a moment after I leave, and I feel my shoulders tensing. He's going over my work. If he has a problem with the way I've bedded these stalls...

"You have a lunch break, too," he says, finally following after me. "Aren't you going to take it?"

"And when would I do your stalls?" I snap.

We stare at each other for a moment. I'm uncomfortably aware of two things: I was just rude to a paying customer of the farm where I work, and his eyes are just the most ridiculous blue I've ever seen on any man. They should be illegal. I should write a letter to the authorities.

"I didn't ask you to do my stalls," Landon says quietly. "Do you want me to talk to Kayla about it?"

"No." That would be beyond embarrassing. "I'm managing just fine."

"I can finish doing the water."

"I'm almost done." I gesture to the last bucket.

"Then you can take your lunch, right?" He sounds like a teacher reasoning with a difficult child. "Go inside and cool off. You look hot."

"No, I'm going to hack out my horse," I inform him. "I have the Thoroughbred Makeover in four months. I can't mess around."

"But it's a million degrees," Landon points out. "And he's missing his front shoes. Is this really the best time?"

"How do you know he's missing his front shoes?" I demand, whirling around with the hose still in hand. I only get him a little bit wet before I catch myself and shove it back into the bucket. Not apologizing for it, either. Nope. "Were you poking around my horse?"

"I was in the tack room when you brought him in for breakfast," Landon says. "I could hear that he didn't have shoes on."

"Why were you in the—*oh*."

He doesn't have any coffee in his apartment, so he made some in the tack room.

"Yeah," Landon replies. " 'Oh.' "

"Well," I say after a beat, "thanks for leaving me something in the carafe this time, I guess."

And at this, Landon laughs so hard I think he's going to pop a vein or something. He bends over, his hands on his knees. It's ridiculously over the top. "Sure," he wheezes, trying to recover himself while I stare in annoyance. "No problem, sweetheart."

"Don't call me sweetheart."

I leave him in the stall to collect himself and drag the hose back into the aisle. I'm carefully coiling it back around its hook when Landon comes out, wiping his eyes. "Enjoy your lunch," I say.

"I'm going to tack your horse's shoes on first." He goes past me, heading towards his truck. "Let me get my things."

"No, that's fine." I'm not going to be reliant on this guy. Or feel like I owe him anything. That's not the plan. I call after him as Landon opens the back hatch of his truck. "He can hack around without shoes!"

"I *want* to do your horse's hooves," Landon insists. He sounds quite firm about it, even if his voice is muffled as he leans into the back of his truck.

"I said no," I retort. "Thank you for the offer, but no."

There's a pause. I heap the final coil of hose into place. A lizard wiggles out from beneath the hose holder and blinks at me, turning his little green head to get a better view of my face. "Okay, you're cute," I mutter.

The lizard skedaddles as Landon comes rattling up with his metal shoeing box, kicked along by one foot. The wheels spin on the concrete floor. He stops it with a boot and matches my gaze, blink for blink.

"Well?" I ask after a moment's contemplation, during which time I wonder if he's actually wearing tinted contact lenses.

Landon smiles and says, in the courtliest tones possible, "May I please have permission to fix your horse's feet, madam?"

I have to bite back a treacherous smile of my own. Who *is* this crazy man? I'm tempted to give in, but of course, that's his whole scheme. I can't even remember now why I didn't want him working on Thomas's hooves, but in the spirit of remaining true to myself, I stiffly reply, "Absolutely not, kind sir, but your request is noted and appreciated."

Landon lets out an exasperated sigh before exclaiming, "Mackenzie! For god's sake! Let me spend fifteen minutes making your poor horse more comfortable!"

"What makes you think my horse is uncomfortable?" Those are fighting words.

"Do you want me to list the signs? From five minutes of observation, I can tell you: he steps short in front, he shifts his weight constantly when he's standing on the concrete, he—"

"Okay, fine, he might be a little stiff from the trip up here—"

"Mackenzie," Landon interrupts, his voice dropping to dangerously low levels. It's enough to shut me up, although I resent him all the more for silencing me. "Can you push past whatever you have against me and put your horse first, please?"

There's a lot I would like to say to that, starting with how I find it really distasteful when a man suggests that just because I don't like him, I am in the wrong, and following that up with a commentary on how his giant ego doesn't make him the best farrier in the world, just the most annoying one. But something stops me. The knowledgeable horsewoman within, I suppose, who has just been given two signs her horse is sore and knows both of them have been right in front of her for weeks now.

Thomas *has* been stepping a little short, and he *did* shift his weight constantly when standing on the concrete yesterday.

So I sigh and say, with a bitterness burning in my stomach, "Yes."

Landon sighs, too, like I've taken a load off his shoulders. "Thank you," he says. "Does he stand in the cross-ties for the farrier, or will I need you to hold him?"

I END UP holding Thomas for Landon, which is annoying,

because it means I have to stare down at Landon's impressive frame while he bends over Thomas's front hooves, contorting himself into awkward poses while he trims, levels, examines his work, and then seems to start all over again.

He asked for fifteen minutes, but the shoeing session stretches to three-quarters of an hour, the sweat rolling down my back just from standing, while Landon's shirt slowly soaks through. Only Thomas looks comfortable, sighing contentedly as I play with his nose to distract him, and Landon takes the pressure off his sore feet one at a time.

Finally, Landon steps back and sets Thomas's left front, the second one he worked on, back on the ground. The symmetry and shape of the hoof is textbook. The difference from Thomas's previous hoof-shape is so stark, I have to glance up and confirm we're still working on the same horse.

Thomas blinks at me with his dark, gentle eyes. Yup. This is my kid.

"Where did all his extra toe go?" I ask, staring back down at his hooves. The farrier my farm used back in south Florida assured me that Thomas's extra-long toes, a common fault in former racehorses, would take years to correct.

"It's on the floor," Landon grunts, pointing at the long, curved hoof trimmings littering the barn aisle floor. "Shame Basil and Kayla don't have a dog, because that thing would be thrilled to chew on these all afternoon."

"And throw it up on their couch later," I agree, nudging a chunk of Thomas's hoof—or a former chunk, I suppose—with the toe of my paddock boot. "I've seen my share of barn dogs, thanks."

"Why don't *you* have a dog?" Landon asks, putting his nail clinchers back into the shoeing box. "Woman living on her own ought to have a dog to watch out for her. Or at least bark enough to tell her when to call the cops."

"If I'd had a barking dog on that first night, I'd have called the cops on *you*," I say smugly, not bothering to share that I'd told Casey to do that exact thing.

"True enough." He grins, his blue eyes dancing with amusement, and I feel momentarily mesmerized by his gaze.

There should be laws against things like this. He should have to wear brown contact lenses to lessen his sheer presence. Magnetism should not be allowed in public. It's too dangerous.

Makes people think things they shouldn't.

"Well, your horse is ready to ride," Landon says. "Why don't you take him out, and I'll sweep up this mess? It's getting late."

I check my phone and sigh at the time. It's already one o'clock. My stomach is growling, but I have to ride Thomas. If the bosses should suddenly come back and want to ride, we'll be out here past dark again and I'll have missed my chance.

Why does it seem like I moved to a farm and it immediately got much harder to get any riding done?

"Thanks," I say, making up my mind. The ride cannot wait. "Ordinarily, I wouldn't let you clean up, because that's my job, but since you offered and time's getting on..."

"Go get your stuff and get on your horse," Landon says calmly, scooping up his shoeing box and starting back towards his truck.

I watch his muscles flex as he hefts the heavy box, dangling with all those steel instruments and spare horseshoes.

Those muscles are almost as bad as his beautiful eyes.

Landon glances over his shoulder. "Still standing there? Go, or I'm taking back my offer to clean up!"

Fortunately, for a handsome man, he always manages to

break any spells his body casts by opening his mouth and making a lot of noise. Grumbling about men who can't ever seem to stop barking orders, I head for the tack room.

Chapter Ten

I CAN'T EVEN count the ways that Thomas feels better with his new shoeing job. Honestly, he should feel a little off *now* because he's adjusting to a new trim and new shape for his front hooves. And yet, what should feel like a strange adjustment actually feels incredibly open and correct. Which leaves me with only one logical conclusion.

Thomas has actually been slightly lame for as long as I've been riding him.

Okay, that might be dramatic, and the way it makes my heart and stomach twist up in little knots of anxiety is definitely not good for keeping him relaxed and cool, which is a necessity if I'm going to be riding him in the middle of the day. Thomas can read bodies with the same ease I can read a book I've half-memorized from constant repetition, and as soon as my heart-rate picks up, so does his head, his tail, and his speed.

As he power-walks around the arena, looking around at the empty fields with bright eyes—oops, *not* empty, because there is a family of Sandhill cranes stalking through the farthest pasture, looking like prehistoric creatures as they stand six feet above the grass—I try to settle my seat in the saddle and slow his gait by resisting the swing of his back. But every time I get him to settle into a more sedate walk, he only holds it for a few strides before pushing back into his long, energetic, pre-race walk. Thomas feels like he's heading for the starting gate.

And while it's nice that he feels so good, I'm trying to get this horse to chill out, not think about his racing days.

After a few spins around the ring, I decide to slow him with lots of changes of direction and small circles. That seems to help settle him. His stiff neck finds an arch, and he begins to reach for the bit.

"Such a good boy," I croon, wiping sweat from my brow before it can trickle into my eyes. My glasses are sliding down my nose, and my lower back is so wet I feel like the seam of my riding breeches is going to rub me raw. Note to self: seamless is godliness. If I ever get to mass-produce riding clothes, I'll make sure they're comfortable enough for even the most sweaty Floridian.

Also, I'm going to have to find a better time of day to ride. It's barely even cloudy today, in total contrast to yesterday's thick midday cumulus, and when I check the radar for any helpful storms, it just shows a few showers off the Atlantic beaches.

It might actually end up a dry afternoon, meaning I could have ridden in the evening if I'd just waited.

But how am I supposed to know what the weather will do? This is *Florida,* for heaven's sake. It's not some logical place up on the continent where weather follows established rules.

After twenty minutes of riding in the relentless sun, I take a sweaty Thomas back into the barn. "Bath-time, buddy," I tell him, sliding the tack from his wet back.

Thomas, a hardy Florida-bred who grew up in this heat, gives my shirt sleeve a playful nip. He probably feels good enough to put in a full ride. But it's my job as the adult in this relationship to tell him when it's not safe to work hard.

"Remember that," I say as I lead him down to the wash-rack. "I'm the adult here."

I find it helps to say that out loud. Not just for Thomas, but for me. Well, probably mostly for me.

I've always been the adult, which is probably how I ended up playing the subservient little female to the first guy who swept me off my feet. Not to be too civilian-psychologist about it, but I'm pretty sure there's a correlation between growing up the only daughter of a woman who preferred her tennis club to home, and a man who could barely feed and clothe himself suitably for his job at a large financial institution (which kind of frowned upon management in mismatched shoes and or forgetting their ties), and marrying a man who was more than happy to make every decision for me.

Some people run towards their talents, and some people run from them.

By adulthood, I could only see my gift for organization and leadership as a definite downer, a result of my ineffectual parents, and Ryan must have recognized the makings of a subservient housewife were strong in me. I suppose I had to have shown him, in those first few encounters at the polo club lounge—where I was wiping up the bar at one end and he was holding it up at the other—that I was looking for a man who was the exact opposite of my father. Someone who used his money to make a girl comfortable and safe, instead of giving her free rein to figure out what to do with it once the household bills were paid.

No, it was not a conventional childhood, but I will give my

parents credit for this: they never said a word when I spent a sizable chunk of my father's annual salary on horses, riding lessons, show entries, and every saddle pad a girl could ever want. I still have a bin of barely used saddle pads in my horse trailer that date back to those constant purchases. Bad day? Buy a saddle pad. Really bad day? Make sure it's trimmed with Swarovski crystals. That'll dull the pain of feeling like an orphan in your own home, surrounded by luxury that you'd trade in a heartbeat for the ability to just *relax,* feel like someone else is at the helm for once.

But that's all behind me now. Both being the caregiver and being the one taken care of. I'm choosing to walk the middle line, a straight line from A to C without a halt at X. It's the course that my largely absent mother, a dressage rider in her youth, probably would have chosen for me if she'd given me much thought. I like to think so, anyway. There must have been a time when she was interested in my riding career, but I probably missed it because I was at the barn riding, or at home making sure my dad left for work on time.

As for caregiving, I hope horses count as a good use of that talent.

Because my goal is to become a barn manager by trade, and lavish all the love and order I once used to keep my father getting up and going to work each day on the horses which, to be honest, need me so much more than he ever did.

Thomas puts up his lip to catch some of the water from the hose, and I can't help but laugh at my big, silly horse as he slurps away.

Taking care of horses is satisfying in a way that can't be explained, and I'm thrilled that I finally have the chance to do it all the time, instead of being called away to do a hundred other things that Ryan felt were more important ways to spend my time.

I might ache from head to toe and be sweating more than I ever thought possible, but at least now I have a chance at happiness.

"Just one thing," Landon says, coming around the corner of the barn aisle so quickly that I nearly leap out of my skin.

"What the hell?" I snap, putting a hand on the post of the wash-rack railing. "You scared me to death!"

"Well," he says, surveying me, "You're still alive."

"No dad jokes," I warn him.

"Fine, fine. I just wanted to tell you something. I noticed when you were riding that your noseband is a bit low."

I stare at him, the water flowing unimpeded from the upturned hose. It runs down my arm and soaks the long sleeve of my sun-shirt. This is a favorite one, patterned with tropical drinks. One of which I could use right about now. "My noseband is a bit low?" I repeat, hoping he'll notice that I'm using my dangerous tone.

The *here come my claws* tone that even Ryan knew was worth heeding.

"Well, just a hole or two, but it can make a real difference. The nerve endings in the face are especially close to the skin, and right where the noseband sits—" He moves closer to Thomas and touches my horse's face around his chin, then slides his hand back beneath his jaw. Thomas moves his head up immediately, even though Landon's touch is clearly feather light. "You see, he can feel anything on his face when he's barely even touched. So it's really important to fit the noseband to each horse, every time. Even just getting some extra forelock or mane caught under the crown piece can adjust where the noseband is sitting...uh, are you okay?"

Apparently my best *I'm going to kill you* look just makes me look like a dyspeptic puppy to Landon, because he's peering at me with curiosity and concern intermingled in his lagoon-colored eyes.

Ah, the hell with it. I switch off the hose and slide my hand along Thomas's jaw as well. "Where would you say it should sit?" I ask. "You can tell me right after you explain which vet school you went to, because clearly you left that out when we first met."

He chuckles. "You know, I'm not here to school you on everything I think you should know. I just wanted to help, but if you'd rather I backed off..."

"I'd rather you backed off," I tell him. Thomas pulls away from my touch, and I can't help but notice it's exactly where the noseband was sitting. Dammit.

"Well, I'll try." Landon backs out of the wash-rack, ducking the cross-ties. "But I should warn you..."

"What?" I grit out as he trails off, because he's clearly trying to get me to ask, and succeeding in the most maddening way possible.

"I like to help people," Landon says, shrugging as if he can't believe how great he is, either. "And I know a *lot* about horses and physiology."

"So you're saying you'll never stop giving me tips I don't ask for and advice I don't want, is that it?"

"That's it," he says cheerfully. "Now you're catching on."

And wisely noting that my hand is once again resting on the water spigot, while the hose is trained directly at him, Landon heads back into the barn. I hear a whistle echo down the aisle as he trills a happy little tune. I think it's the theme to

"Animaniacs."

"That man," I say to Thomas, "is *insufferable.*"

Thomas nips at my shoulder and says nothing.

And that's why horses are better than men. The silence. Can you hear it? It's delightful.

SILENCE NEVER LASTS for long, especially in a barn full of fit horses. When I walk Thomas back into the barn, there's a lot of hopeful nickering and neighing from the local jokesters who think they're going to get extra hay or grain from the gullible human. None of them know that Basil wrote me a *very* thorough schedule, though, or that I am just anxious enough about doing my job perfectly to quail at the idea of deviating from it.

"Nope," I tell the crowd. "It's time for *my* lunch. Tell Barn Daddy if you have a problem with that."

The pan of chicken and veggies comes out of the fridge and goes back on the stovetop. Eventually, I'll have to make myself drive to town and get provisions for myself, but for now, the idea of folding my sore limbs into my truck and rattling off to the closest Winn-Dixie or Publix or Piggly Wiggly—whatever they have out here in the back of beyond—sounds like a terrible idea, best put off as long as possible.

I watch the unenthusiastic burner for a moment, then sigh and turn it off again. This will take forever, time I don't have to waste. Cold chicken and veg it is. I'm too hot to be eating a cooked lunch, anyway. I take the pan to the table and sit down heavily.

If there was anyone to see me forking food directly out of a cold saucepan, I would have spooned a portion into a bowl. But, here's the main advantage of living alone: I can do whatever I want. And right now, I'm hungry enough to see no value in dumping food from one receptacle into another. Plus, who wants to do extra cleaning up? Work smarter, ladies. Eat from your cooking pot like a cave woman. I should be writing this stuff down for a motivational book on moving to the countryside and giving up all creature comforts in favor of looking after large, expensive animals.

I flick through my phone while I'm eating, liking all of Casey's recent posts about farm life and her gorgeous Australian shepherd—maybe I *should* get a dog? I'll have to ask Kayla about that—and doing my best to avoid seeing posts from any of my old acquaintances back in Wellington. In this world, you're only as visible as your social media activity. All I need to do is hit like on something by accident, and it will be open season on my inbox, as everyone pretends to be curious about my new life...when I know what they *really* want is to hear how terrible things are now that I've left the protective bubble of our tropical equestrian paradise.

The half-hour I've allowed for my lunch break ticks to a close too soon, and I sigh as I get up, feeling all the bubbles in my joints pop at once. My phone buzzes with a text: Kayla, saying they'll be back in an hour and they'd like to jump Killian and Franz. Back to work.

The outdoor arena glimmers in the heat a few feet from my kitchen window. At least a few clouds are starting to break up the endless blue of the sky. Hopefully, they'll continue to multiply, offering some shade for my horses and riders.

I smile to myself as I head to the door and slide on my boots, because I'm already thinking of them as *mine*. I'm such a freaking mom.

I swing open the apartment door and my fond smile fades

immediately.

"What are you doing?" I demand.

Landon glances back at me but continues pushing a loaded wheelbarrow into one of the stalls I bedded earlier. "Nothing," he says.

"No, seriously!" I slam my door closed and stalk after him, my boot heels snapping on the pavement. "What was wrong with those stalls?"

"You did a very nice start," Landon says, grunting as he empties the wheelbarrow into the center of the perfectly level, carefully swept stall I set up for him. This man has no gratitude at all. "But I like my stalls filled a bit more. From wall to wall." He nods at the three-foot section of floor along the front wall, which I swept clean of shavings the way I'd been shown in Wellington.

"The front shavings get wasted," I inform him, seething. "Because they're under the water buckets and horses dribble water all over them. And their hay goes on the floor, so with the shavings swept back, they aren't *eating* any shavings. And they can't even put their hooves there because the buckets are in the way, so *why* would you put shavings there?"

"I like shavings to cover the entire floor," Landon says calmly, ignoring all of my excellent points. He backs the wheelbarrow out. "Now, don't be mad. Everyone has their own way of doing things."

But not everyone does things the right way, I think furiously. Aloud, I say as calmly as I can, "The stalls were perfect the way that I did them."

"Now, Mackenzie, there's not just one right way of doing things," he says, setting the wheelbarrow down. His reasonable tone makes me want to throw something. Not necessarily *at* him, but pitching a bucket down the barn aisle just to watch it bounce would feel really good right now.

"There's one correct way to do lots of things," I counter, still working to speak in the most even tone I can muster. "My way is the most cost-efficient without compromising safety."

"Ah." Landon is smiling as if he's caught me in a silly mistake. "But cost-efficiency and horses rarely go together. Common mistake, Mackenzie. Common mistake."

And he picks up the handles of the wheelbarrow and trundles off towards the far end of the barn and the shavings shed, leaving me to stand and clench my fists in his wake.

That man.

That man.

That *man!*

I whirl around, turning my back on Landon. I have actual work to do.

In the tack room, I gather the equipment I'll need for Killian and Franz. Saddle pads and saddles, breastplates and bridles, boots for front and back legs. There's a note in the binder about only using Franz's specific pair of tendon boots, and it takes me a few minutes to find them. By the time I come out of the tack room, boots in hand, Landon has finished bedding up his stalls and is putting the wheelbarrow back in its place in the empty stall where we store the week's hay.

He glances over at me and smiles.

Why is he always smiling at me like this? It's obnoxious.

He needs to just do his work and stop acting like he's having the best time doing it. I *know* he's only putting on this bright, sunshiny face to annoy me. I shouldn't have let him get to me about those stalls. I should have just shrugged and been like, "Whatever, dude, do more work if you want." But no, I had to defend my work as if it mattered. As if saving four loads of shavings from going beneath his horses' hooves was somehow worth getting hot and bothered over. Why can't I just let it go?

I'll tell you why, a bossy voice in my brain mutters. *Because if your work doesn't matter, what the hell are you doing with your life?*

Well, thanks, brain, but that's not a question I really want to ask myself right now. And thanks, Landon, for even putting that idea into my head. I'm going to ignore him. That's the only way. I don't have time to argue, and I definitely don't have time to second-guess my life decisions, all because he thinks shavings should go under the water buckets (which is so wrong I can't even begin the argument...*stop*).

Seriously, I have *actual* work to do. I get Franz out of his stall and cross-tie the dark bay gelding next to the tack room, where I've set up everything I'll need just outside the door. Fewer steps, quicker job. Plus, this barn has a "door shut when the A/C is running" policy, which I fully respect. So it's better to have everything in place—*ugh*.

I left the brush box in the tack room. There's always something.

Sighing, I tell Franz to stand still and go back into the tack room. Franz contentedly takes a mouthful of cross-tie into his mouth and begins to chew. He's one of those horses. Always has to have something in his mouth.

I'm pulling out a brush-box when my phone does its extra-long emergency buzz, vibrating against my thigh with so much ferocity that it startles me. It sets off a surge of panic in my chest, a tingling in my fingers. This buzz means someone from my In Case of Emergency contacts is calling. It could only be my father, my mother (unlikely), Kayla or Basil, or...

I stare at my phone in chagrin. His name, plastered across the screen, feels like a slap in the face.

Argh! *Why* didn't I take Ryan off my ICE list? I never want to see his stupid name on my phone again, and now he's distracting me from my work.

The phone buzzes again, sounding like an angry bee. He's not going anywhere. I know Ryan. He'll hit redial for hours if he wants. So I hit Talk with a feeling of dread, knowing it's better to just get this call out of the way. As I lift the phone to my ear, I hear Franz shifting, scraping a hoof along the cement. I hit the speakerphone button instead of giving Ryan my full attention and move to the doorway. Franz looks back at me with pricked ears, his mouth still full of cross-tie.

Ryan's voice explodes from my phone.

"WHERE IS THE TOILET PAPER?"

The nervous bubble in my stomach pops and disappears. Oh my god, I'd forgotten about the toilet paper! I put my hand to my mouth and choke back a gasp of hysterical laughter. Franz drops his cross-tie and stares at me in astonishment. That nearly sends me over the top, but I manage to hold it together.

"Excuse me? I am at work," I say, as haughtily as I can. "Can you please keep things professional?"

"DAMMIT!" Ryan explodes. "WHERE IS IT?"

I let myself smile.

The slow, satisfied smile of a woman who has stolen all her ex-husband's toilet paper.

And taken the paper towels, tissues, and makeup wipes stowed around the condo too.

After all, the makeup removal wipes were how I found out Shelly was sleeping with him to begin with. It felt like a nice, full circle moment when I dropped that offending box, left so innocently on the bathroom counter when I came back from a weekend horse show on the west coast of Florida, into my bathroom box to go down to the waiting horse trailer.

And it feels that way now, too.

I don't even wear makeup around horses, but those wipes are a trophy and I'll keep them until they're all used up or dried out to nothing, whichever comes first.

"Ryan," I say, once he leaves off shouting for a moment. "Listen to me very carefully. There is no toilet paper. Whatever has happened in that condo cannot be fixed by anything in that condo. Unless you want to destroy those godawful towels your mother bought us for Christmas two years ago."

He's still shouting when I hang up the phone, remove his number from my emergency contacts list, and finally mute it so he can't get my attention until I'm willing to give it to him. I should have done that a long time ago...but I suspect my subconscious was waiting for the satisfaction of this phone call. I knew he'd move back into the condo within days of my leaving, and I knew he'd expect it to be fully stocked with essentials as it always has been...and I hope, with all my black, revenge-loving heart, that Shelly is the one in the bathroom right now.

Phone in pocket, satisfaction at an all-time high, I pick up the curry comb and start rubbing down Franz. The horse turns his head to watch me, then pricks his ears at something behind me. I don't even have to look over my shoulder to know who has his attention. Of course it's Landon, strolling up in that nonchalant way of his.

He slouches against the tack room door and watches me groom.

"Don't you have work to do?" I ask him, still leaning into the horse with the curry comb. I'd like to throw it at him, but, I really do need to get this job finished on time.

"I'm waiting on my horses to arrive," he says. "And now I feel like I better watch you for any telltale signs that I'm next in your crosshairs. Did you *really* empty your husband's house of toilet paper?"

"I emptied my *former condo* of toilet paper when I moved out," I say, smirking. It still feels so good. Like winning a huge jumper class that someone told me was way too stacked with top riders for me to compete with, or getting the last nitro cold brew at Starbucks before the barista says the keg is tapped out. "And my ex-husband didn't think to check the roll before he sat down...or his girlfriend didn't. Either way, the doorman will probably solve the problem for him, but at least I put a big scare into their day."

"Good for you," Landon says.

I glance at him to see if he's being sarcastic, but no. His gaze is admiring. I feel an absurd little lift in my chest, as if his opinion of me matters.

"Thanks," I say shortly, looking back at my work. This horse has a tiny scar on his hip, and he flinches a little when I touch it, but it seems more psychological than physical. I flick the brush around it, careful to avoid the half-dollar-sized circle of black, glossy skin. "It probably sounds a little petty, but I feel really good about it."

"Petty revenge has its place," Landon says thoughtfully. "I once snuck into a tack room and changed all the right-hand stirrup leathers to be one hole shorter than the left. It drove the trainer out of his mind, trying to figure out why he was so unbalanced on every single horse."

I snort with laughter. "Did you *really*? That's genius! Evil genius, but still."

"He had it coming," Landon muses. "I didn't care for the way he rode with his stirrups even; figured he could use the balance lesson as a little hint that maybe he wasn't the god of riding he thought he was."

"And did it help with that?"

"Oh, of course not." He gives me a rueful grin, his eyes glittering with humor. "But I loved watching him struggle, anyway."

"Yeah, I feel that! It won't change anything, but I wish I could see—" I trail off. Because I don't actually want to picture Ryan or his girlfriend at all, let alone the two of them in the condo overlooking the water, searching for toilet paper or otherwise. I don't want to picture any of it.

This is my life now, and I want to love it without interference from my past.

"They're dead to me now, anyway," I say, switching to the horse's opposite side. I glance at Landon from across the horse's back and see him watching me with an intensity I didn't expect.

As if I've intrigued him with my little revenge stunt, and now he wants to know more about me.

Oh, no, Landon. We won't be having *any* of that.

THOMAS THE TANK Engine's Training Diary
June 10

Our third ride at the farm was a good one. I have to admit it, even if I didn't really want things to go this well. Landon did a complete makeover on Thomas's front hooves. They don't even look like the same horse anymore. I'm in shock and half-tempted to call up my old farrier and ask him what the hell he was thinking to leave all that toe on.

For our ride we did about twenty minutes of walking with lots of circles and changes of direction. Nothing exciting, but it was really hot. His bend to the left is coming along, but we have to do some counter-bends back and forth on a circle before he really starts to bend from the spine and not the neck. Note to self: watch some videos on shoulder-in. I'm not sure I'm asking correctly.

I'm excited to see how he does at the trot and canter with these new feet of his. I didn't want Landon to work on them, but that was really silly and selfish of me. Nothing is more important than Thomas's comfort. I have to remind myself of that.

Chapter Eleven

THE HORSE VAN arrives while Basil and Kayla are in the arena, with me hanging out nearby on jump crew duty. It's blazingly hot and everyone seems really regretful that this jump school has to happen, but there's a summer show series they've committed to along with Pete Morrison, so Ocala is happening this weekend whether they ride today or not.

Apparently Basil prefers being over-prepared, while Kayla would rather wing it. They argue about this extensively while they're warming up their horses and trotting them through a grid of cavaletti, but voices are never raised. It seems like this is an argument they have over and over, like an old married couple kind of thing.

I had those with Ryan, but they were really angry, every time. At least, for the last five or six years, they were. I'm not sure when it went from friendly fire to outright despising one another's arguments, or if we were ever that friendly to begin with.

And it doesn't matter, I remind myself, and hop up to put a fence pole back up after Kayla's horse Killian raps it with a hind leg.

"Ugh," she groans. "Come on, bud. We gotta do better than

that."

"You need more pace going around the turn," Basil informs her. "Lift your hands and give him leg."

"Fine," she says, "although I'd prefer to just give him pep talks and pretend I'm perfect." Then she points towards the barn. We can all hear diesel growling. A horse whinnies, and a few in the barn answer. "The van just pulled up. Mackenzie, can you go help Landon get his horses down and put away? They'll probably all need showers."

"What about the jumps?" I ask, hoping to avoid being Landon's groom as well as hers. So much so, apparently, that I'd prefer to stay in the sunny arena and risk heat stroke.

"I just won't knock down any more rails," Kayla says, looking at Basil. "I promise."

Basil grins at her. "More leg."

She snorts and nudges Killian back into a canter.

I figure Kayla thinks she's doing me a favor by getting me out of the hot sun, so I wave like all is well and jog back to the rail, slipping through the fence and entering the barn through the center instead of going all the way down to the gate and walking up the main aisle. The van is stopped right out front, with the ramp already dropped, and I can see four horses peering over their chest bars, wide-eyed with curiosity about their new home.

Landon is suddenly right next to me, his shirt covered in hay. I jump before I can stop myself from showing any reaction. So my voice is irritated when I demand, "Where did *you* come from?"

"I was putting hay in their stalls," he replies, ignoring my tone. "Are you here to help me?"

"Kayla sent me in," I say flatly, so that he knows helping him was not my choice.

"I appreciate it," he replies, still acting like all is sweetness and light between us. "These guys are going to be exhausted and miserable. I want to give them all liniment baths."

Of course he does. Because just what I want, at three thirty in the afternoon, is to face four more hours of work while soaked to the skin and smelling of witch hazel and rubbing alcohol.

"And they don't stand in cross-ties," he adds. "They're all fresh off the racetrack. So one of us will have to hold the lead-rope while the other one bathes them."

Well, of course they don't stand in cross-ties! Why would Landon fill this end of the barn with nice, quiet, reasonably trained horses? Generally, I don't have a thing against fresh racehorses, but right now, they feel like an imposition. After all, I don't actually work for him...but the way Kayla keeps adding his tasks to my list of chores, it seems likely I'll be handling these horses in addition to the string I was hired to care for.

A burly man in a cowboy hat is already unloading the first horse, so I step up and take the lead-rope as the horse's hooves hit the sandy driveway. The bay horse is already pretty tall, and since he's putting on a pretty impressive giraffe impression, this means his head is miles above mine. I shake the lead-rope to let him know he's actually under my control, despite appearances, and walk into the barn as the horse side-steps and prances just behind me.

"Come on, goofy," I tell him. "Let's get you cleaned up." He really is drenched in sweat and where his coat isn't wet, the hair looks dull, his skin wrinkling loosely with dehydration.

"Wait for me before you start!" Landon calls after me. I roll my eyes. Does he really think I can't turn a hose on a horse without it getting loose? Please. I hose off horses without help every single day. Even scary ex-racehorses like Thomas.

The horse walks gingerly on the concrete, snorting at every stall we pass, while the horses inside plunge in circles and whinny frantically like this is their long-lost Cousin Bob and they need to know where he's been and everything that has happened while he's been gone, *immediately.*

"You don't know this horse," I announce to the barn at large. "This is a new horse!"

"Well, he might know some of them," Landon says from behind me. "I mean, they could have been raised on the same farm or known each other at the racetrack. Thoroughbreds get around, and half these horses are Thoroughbreds."

"Why are you following me? Shouldn't you be putting your horses away?" I turn the corner, bringing the hot horse back into the sunlight. He snorts abruptly, as if the sun makes him sneeze. Do horses have that reaction?

"I showed the shipper where to put them," Landon says, gathering up the hose from its cradle. "So we can get going with the baths."

"I can start on my own," I assure him, turning the horse into the wash-rack. "You go make sure everyone is where you want them and there aren't any cuts or scrapes you need to take up with the shipping company."

Landon hesitates. "If you're sure."

"I'm sure!" Anything to make him go away. He'll probably find fault with everything I do if he stands here and watches me, and then I'll lose my temper, and then Kayla and Basil will be disappointed in me, and then I don't know, I'll just die of embarrassment or something.

Landon glances up the aisle, clearly tempted to go check on his other horses. "Fine, I will," he says at last. "Just—don't tie him in the cross-ties."

"I have worked with ex-racehorses before, Landon," I say, barely avoiding a snarl. "Now *go!*"

To my huge relief, he listens and scurries back up the aisle.

"Now, you stand here and watch the horses in the arena," I tell the Thoroughbred, "and I'll get this layer of sweat off you so you can start feeling like a normal horse again." The horse has already spotted the end of the ring visible from the wash-rack and now he's staring, ears pricked, as Kayla canters around before disappearing again behind the barn. "Yup," I say to him. "In a minute, another horse will show up. Like magic!"

It's like putting a toddler in front of a television—buys you a little time to get some work done, but not much. I flip on the hose and start hosing him down while he tries to swivel and get a better look at the arena. With my left hand, I shake the lead-rope to try to keep his attention from wandering too far away from me.

"I get it, I do," I say, watching the sweat slide off his shoulders and barrel. "New place, straight into the shower. It's a lot to ask of a horse. But you're going to be fine. I have no idea why you're here, but I'm sure it's all above-board, and the way things have been going, I suspect I'm going to be taking care of you most of the time, too. I guess you're my job now. So, let's start off on the right foot—WHOA!" I can't but shout the last part as the Thoroughbred bolts forward, rushing from the wash-rack like he's been bitten on the butt and he's not going to wait around to see what did the chomping. The lead-rope flies through my fingers and then there's nothing in my hand but empty space.

Thoroughbreds are diverse creatures in that they can be both unstoppable forces and immovable objects, depending on their mindset, but this one has decided to be the former. To really own it and be one with it. He thunders towards the arena, ears pricked, in search of the magical horses there.

And wow, his movement is *terrible*. "Oh no," I mutter, dropping the hose and taking off after him. "You're lame as hell, aren't you?"

Of course he's lame. All four of them are probably lame. They're rehab cases being nursed by one of the best farriers in the horse business. I assume they're with Landon because no one else knew how to fix their problems.

Now, I can only hope that by running off, this particular rehab case doesn't get himself sidelined for life. Because while it isn't my fault the horse is on the loose, it's definitely on me that I was alone with him when Landon was ready to help me bathe him. If Landon had his way, the horse would probably not be galloping away while three-legged lame.

In the arena, Kayla and Basil have halted their horses while they watch the unsound juggernaut racing along the outer railing. The horses under saddle snort and spin, flagging their tails with excitement, and I know it's a matter of time before they start hopping up and down and, possibly, take off to join the loose horse.

Then what? I'm responsible for *three* runaway horses? That's all I need.

"Grain!" Kayla shouts when she sees me coming. "Turn around and get grain!" She lets Killian wheel in place, her seat defensive in case he takes off. "Quick, quick, quick!" she adds, as if I can't tell that time is of the essence.

I execute a quick rollback and head into the barn, feet

pelting the concrete. The horses inside are staring through the bars or have their heads out their windows, watching the excitement with pricked ears. I wonder if they're rooting for Cousin Bob out there to stay loose forever and gallop off into the sunset, or if they are waiting to see how we catch him. Whose side are they on, anyway?

Landon bursts from the feed room with a bucket of grain— at least, I think that's what happens, because the door catches me in the shoulder and I hit the aisle with a howl of pain. At first, I don't even realize I made the sound, but then it becomes terribly clear that I've done myself some damage. "Owww," I mumble, writhing a little to get my hand on my left shoulder. "Oh, man, *ow*."

Landon was already two strides down the aisle, but he stops and runs back to me, dropping to his knees by my side. "Are you okay?" he demands hoarsely. His blue eyes are dark, the pupils wide with panic. For a moment, they're all I can see, all I can focus on.

But wait, why am I staring into his eyes? I have a loose horse to catch and I'm sprawled across the barn aisle, clutching my arm like a baby. I go to push myself upright and the pain stops me dead.

"No," I reply, gritting my teeth. "I don't think I am."

"Oh." Landon looks up and down the aisle as if he's hoping EMTs will materialize and rescue him from this moment. "Oh, god."

"Go get the horse," I wheeze, fighting a second wave of pain that threatens to cut off my breathing. "I'll be fine here."

Hoofbeats thunder past the barn and the horses on the arena side of the barn run in frantic little circles around their stalls. A few whinnies hover through the humid air as they try to communicate with Cousin Bob out there. Maybe they're telling him that one of the humans is down and now's the time to stop doing circles and just hit the road. Not sure where he'll find greener pastures, though. This place has gorgeous grass.

Landon continues to hesitate by my side. "Are you sure—"

"Your *horse,* man!" I shout, and Landon narrows his eyes, considering me a moment longer. Then he leaps up and hustles off, his large frame making impressive time. The bucket of grain shakes in his hand, making that tantalizing sound every horse knows means meal-time is on the way. There's a general roar of whinnies and neighs.

It sounds like they're cheering Landon on. "Go get him, man!" Horses don't know which side they're on. No, that's not true. Horses are on the side of food, always.

Left alone on the concrete, I take a few deep breaths, trying to convince my body that it isn't damaged and I can get myself up to help catch the horse. But getting knocked down by a steel door seems to have sidelined me from this chase. Maybe this is all part of getting into barn management at age thirty-three instead of twenty-three, I don't know, but I have to settle, for the moment, for flopping myself back down on the floor and just letting the coolness of the pavement soak into my hot skin.

Simple pleasures, right? Take them where you can find them.

Chapter Twelve

"WELL, THE GOOD news is that it's just a dislocated shoulder," Kayla says cheerfully, opening the back door of Basil's truck. "It's not a big deal! Could have been so much worse."

I look at the sling holding up my left arm and then back at Kayla, half-expecting some degree of sarcasm in her expression. She's serious, though. There's no pessimism allowed in Kayla's barn—that's something I've been realizing through all our interactions so far, and it became painfully apparent during the truck ride to the local emergency room.

Well, to be fair, everything was painful on that truck ride.

Basil slides into the driver's seat and looks back at me over the center console. I pause midway through struggling with my seat-belt, embarrassed, and he frowns at me. "Kayla, can you snap her seat-belt, please?"

"Oh, right!" Kayla leans over me and for a moment, we're far more intimate than I usually get with my bosses. "Sorry," she mutters, her face close to my chest. "There—got it! Are you comfortable?"

I have enough extra-strength Motrin in my system to say, "Yes," and mean it.

But I know things won't stay that way.

Two weeks—that's how long the ER doctor gave me before my dislocated shoulder will be all healed up. Fortunately, I only have to wear this stupid sling for a few days, but still, the restrictions on heavy lifting and hard work, like mucking stalls and stacking hay bales and getting into any sort of interaction with a difficult horse, are for *two whole weeks,* which means I'm essentially on disability from a job that I've only had for two and a half days.

I don't think I'll get fired, because I've already moved here and it would be a real pain to move me out, find a new groom, and move that person in. But this can't look good to my new employers. They've just lost half a day's riding to bring me to the emergency room and be told I can barely do any of my chores for the next two weeks.

"Ugh," Basil says, looking down at the dashboard. "We need gas. Two trips to Gainesville in one day is a lot."

Oh, and I've just cost them a fortune in filling up the truck's gas tank, too.

What a winner.

"Stop for gas at that station on the corner by the exotic tree farm, and I'll run inside and get us some fried chicken for dinner," Kayla says. "With the potato wedges you like."

"Oh, that's a deal!" Basil grins at me in the rear-view mirror. "I hate to say that your getting hurt is working out for everyone, but this place makes insane fried chicken and potato wedges. So, you know, silver linings and all that."

"It's gas station fried chicken?" I venture, feeling like I shouldn't be questioning their dinner choices, but still very concerned at the prospect of eating food that comes out of a gas station.

"Yes, but it's like a country store," Kayla promises. "It's not like we're just running into a 7-Eleven or something."

No, it's so much more shabby than a 7-Eleven. The corner gas station sits at a lonely crossroads near the farm, catty-corner to a vast field of potted trees and bamboo. The parking lot is half-full with an assortment of pickup trucks with weird cages in their beds. "Those are for hunting dogs," Kayla explains as she helps me out of the truck—I've elected to go inside and inspect the premises before I consent to eat any of the fried chicken, even though Basil and Kayla look healthy enough. "They take them out to the woods and hunt wild hogs."

And sure enough, a few of the cages house sleeping hound dogs, who glance up at us with unsuspicious eyes before they settle back into the afternoon naps. Resting up, I guess, for a big night of hog-hunting.

"What do they do with the hogs?" I ask as Kayla opens the gas station door, which has been completely wallpapered over with vinyl banners advertising Bud Lite. I guess it's possible someone once questioned whether this gas station carried Bud Lite and the owners wanted to make sure that mistake never happened again. A strong smell of fried food blasts through the open doors on the breeze of escaping air conditioning.

"Eat 'em, I guess." Kayla laughs. "I honestly don't know! But the hogs are invasive and they tear up pastures, so I don't care *what* they do as long as I don't have a bunch of giant wild hogs in the fields."

I mentally add 'bunch of giant wild hogs' to my list of things to worry about and follow her to the counter at the back, passing displays bursting with more beef jerky and energy drinks than I've ever seen in my life. A sallow-faced woman with stringy hair is taking chicken out of the fryer, and the sight of that perfectly golden, crispy skin makes my mouth water immediately. All of my qualms vanish in an instant. Yes, I'm about to eat gas station food. And if I die, I die. This chicken looks like it will be worth the early grave.

"Hiya," Kayla says cheerfully as the woman glares over the sneeze guard at her. "Can I get the family box with potato wedges and, um, mac and cheese? I think. What do you think, Mackenzie? Mac and cheese or fried okra?"

Health is not on the menu tonight, so I tell Kayla to go for the mac and cheese. Pasta plus potatoes equals perfection, even if it means the big breeches come out to play tomorrow.

The woman nods and scribbles our order on a ticket. "Five minutes," she croaks.

Kayla heads for the front register and joins a line of men in Wranglers and plaid shirts who are buying, you guessed it, beef jerky and energy drinks. Behind us, the fry cook hollers a cheerful hello to the next person to walk up to her. It's a markedly different greeting from the surly glower Kayla received. "I guess you're not on a first-name basis," I murmur to Kayla.

"Oh, no," she says. "We're not locals and everyone here knows it. This is a pretty close-knit community."

"By close-knit, do you mean everyone's related *and* married?"

She snorts. "Mackenzie, you're too funny."

The guy in front of us turns around and lets his eyes travel from our faces to our feet and then back again, taking in Kayla's riding breeches and my paddock boots before drawling, "Y'all girls from Ocala?"

I draw back a little, aware that replying I'm actually from West Palm Beach is *not* the right answer. South Florida and north Florida are as different, politically and culturally, as Manhattan and Mayberry. But Kayla simply says, chipper as ever, "Yup, but we came up here to get away from all that Yankee money."

The guy shifts his pork rinds from one hand to the other before saying, "Well, I don't blame ya." Then he turns around again and steps up to the counter to pay.

Outside, once our fried chicken family box has been acquired, I climb into the truck and wait for the doors to close before I ask, "Kayla, did you just play the Civil War card to get out of an awkward conversation?"

Basil laughs. "Oh, Florida. What happened?"

"It was nothing," Kayla insists. "They just like using the word 'Yankee' as an insult. It's easier to play along. Do *you* want to feel like an outsider in a place like that?"

I glance out the window, gazing at the trucks with their sleeping hounds. There are gun racks in the cabs, and decals pledging allegiance to a number of flags, not all of them in current use. "No," I admit. "I guess not."

"They're mostly nice enough," Kayla says. "But you know how guys can be. Sometimes they think it's funny to make a woman uncomfortable."

I snort. "Sometimes! Try always."

There's a pause. Kayla and Basil exchange glances.

I realize I've made things awkward. Oh, the irony. "I mean—not *you*, Basil. You've always been great. But you're one in a million. Kayla, help me out here." I force a laugh.

Kayla gives a little shrug. "I mean, you won't catch me saying Basil's anything but one in a million." There's an implied *but...* to her tone even though she doesn't go on.

But...you're being a little icky right now, I think she'd like to say.

She's not wrong. Tarring everyone with the same brush is exactly the sort of thing Ryan would do. How long have I been doing it? Once again, I curse that man.

"Sorry," I mumble. "I think it's the extra-strength Motrin talking."

It's nearly dark when we get back to the farm, tortured all the way by the delicious scent of that box stuffed full of fried chicken and potato wedges, and I expect to have to struggle through evening feeding and turnout before we can get to it. My stomach grumbles as Basil turns at the mailbox and drives up the long farm lane; I'm grateful for the bumps in the road because the truck's suspension covers up the sound of my hunger. It seems ungrateful of me to be starving for the dinner Kayla's bought when they all have extra work to do tonight because I couldn't avoid getting hit by a door...and that only happened because I'd let a horse get loose.

So when I see horses out in the paddocks as we drive up to the barn, my heart lifts. And then sinks again, with the realization that yes, my work for the evening is complete.

But that means Landon has gone and done it.

Okay, he probably owes me the favor, since he's the one who swung the door into my arm and dislocated it in the first place. But I'm the one who let his horse get loose, so...who owes who, here?

All I see are entanglements forming where I wanted to have none.

"Fried chicken," Kayla sings as we walk into the barn.

Landon pops out of one of the stalls on his side of the aisle, a huge smile plastered on his face. "Oh, you're joking! You brought back dinner?"

"Well, we went all the way to town," Kayla says, shrugging. "We'd be silly not to take the opportunity to let someone else do our cooking tonight. How did evening chores go?"

"Everyone's fed up and outdoors for the night," Landon says. He looks past Kayla and our eyes meet. "Are you okay? I don't like the look of that sling."

"It's just dislocated," I mutter, dropping my gaze to the ground. I probably look like a sulky child, but you know what? That's fine. Better I look like a kid than a woman who needs his help. He strikes me as someone who is far too interested in playing the savior. And I can't forget the way he looked at me earlier today. Like I was a puzzle he wanted to solve. Talk about getting far too mixed up with a man! Landon getting interested in me is the last thing I want or need in my life.

The idea that I had in the truck floats back to me, a little unwanted breeze of a thought: I've been judging all men by the actions of my ex-husband, and I need to stop.

"Dislocated!" Landon takes a step forward, his hands raising like he wants to do an examination of his own, but he stops himself. "I'll make it up to you," he vows, and it's a little too serious a declaration for my liking.

"Everything's fine," I say, even though I have no idea how I'm going to do my job like this.

"Yup, she's going to be fine!" Kayla sings blithely. "And we'll all work together to get the barn done while she's resting that arm up. It's no big deal. It's the same work Basil and I were doing before the two of you got here. Right, Bas? Hey, help me pull out the folding table from the horse trailer and let's have a barn aisle dinner. It'll be fun!" She hands me the bag from the gas station and I grasp it with my free hand. Sensing chicken is near, my stomach rumbles like a rocket launch. Kayla grins at me. "I heard that, Missy."

Basil and Landon exchange amused glances, then follow Kayla out of the barn. I'm left standing in the aisle, watching them obey Kayla without question, and it occurs to me that despite being a woman working around two men, she's fully in control here.

Neither of them argue with her, or tell her that her ideas are stupid, or simply ignore her and do something else entirely without a word.

Instead, they follow her lead, and smile while they're doing it.

Is it something about Kayla, or is it something about them?

Within five minutes, there's a folding table with chairs set up in the barn aisle and Kayla is tossing out paper plates while Basil unwraps the box of fried chicken and sets out the plastic cups full of potato wedges and a gooey, yellow macaroni-and-cheese which looks like it was made with about six blocks of Velveeta. Landon disappears into his apartment and returns with a jug of Publix sweet tea, which gets applause from everyone, even me—you can't beat Publix sweet tea with a plate of fried chicken—and for a moment I feel small for not having anything to add to the feast.

Then, I remember that I do have something for the table. Small, maybe, but still as Floridian as sweet tea and fried chicken. I hold up a finger, asking everyone to wait, and run into my apartment. I didn't accord much space for kitchen utensils. But I did bring one precious little couple that didn't deserve to spend the rest of their lives with Ryan and Shelly.

"The Publix Pilgrims!" Kayla claps her hands as I bring out the little salt-and-pepper shakers, shaped like a loving Pilgrim couple. "I love it! Okay. We're having a June Thanksgiving, everyone. Oh, I'm so glad you're here, Mackenzie. You just *get* us."

"What are the Publix Pilgrims?" Landon asks, picking up the lady Pilgrim and eyeing her painted face with suspicions. "I've never heard of them."

"Oh, talk about Yankees," Kayla chortles, and Landon makes a face.

"I'm no Yankee, woman," he says in his most thundery voice, but we can all tell it's just for show.

Even me. I'm starting to figure this guy out, I guess, because I burst out laughing at the same time as Kayla.

"The Publix Pilgrims," I say, holding up the husband Pilgrim, "are Florida traditions. Every year Publix makes a sweet commercial about the two of them being separated during the Thanksgiving dinner preparations and then being reunited on the dinner table."

"And everyone cries," Basil adds drily, spooning macaroni onto his plate. "Publix commercials are traditional tearjerkers."

"They're the worst," Kayla agrees. "Just you wait for the holiday season. You'll be sobbing with the rest of us."

"So," Landon says skeptically, "I am expected to cry about salt and pepper shakers?"

"They're animated," I explain. "So they look alive."

"I don't cry at cartoons," Landon says. He puts down the lady Pilgrim. "Sorry to disappoint you."

"I'll bet you cried at *Bambi*," I say, shaking pepper on my macaroni. "Only a heartless villain wouldn't cry at that."

"I've never seen it."

Gasps echo around the table.

I smile to myself. There's something very satisfying about making Landon the subject of the moment. At least it isn't me.

"How can you never have seen *Bambi*?" Kayla demands, flabbergasted. "It's a classic!"

"Maybe because it makes everyone cry?" Landon asks pointedly.

"It's part of the experience!"

"Someday, we will make you watch it," I declare. "Won't we, Kayla?"

"Oh, you better believe it!"

"Challenge accepted," Landon says with great satisfaction, before biting into a chicken thigh. "Oh, lord," he mutters around a mouthful. "Heaven on a plate."

"That's high praise, coming from a Kentucky boy," Kayla says.

"Where in Kentucky are you from?" I ask.

Landon scowls down at his plate and shrugs.

Kayla grins. "Landon's so secretive. He won't tell us a thing about where he's from, will you, Landon?"

"Nothing to tell," Landon says shortly.

"I'll bet there's plenty to tell," she teases. "You're probably the secret son of the governor's secret family, aren't you?"

Landon takes a bite of chicken and gazes into the distance, not playing.

For a moment, I'm interested. Landon's clearly hiding something. A bad break-up? A criminal record?

Then, I bite into the chicken and lose all interest in Landon, or Kentucky, or crying over cartoons, or anything else but this perfect, amazing, sensational...gas station chicken.

Let the world be a mysterious, twirling place. Just leave me alone to eat this fried chicken in peace. Thanksgiving in November never tasted this good.

Chapter Thirteen

THUNDER ROLLS IN the distance as we clean up from our June Thanksgiving dinner, and a helpful wind blows through the aisle, making it tough for the mosquitoes whining around our ears to get a good grip on our skin. Still, I slap at a few on my bad shoulder and groan every time. Guess it's just about time for another Motrin.

Kayla and Basil head home, promising to be down early in the morning to help feed breakfast. I'm embarrassed all over again as they drive back to their house in the distance. How could I have been so stupid? Letting that horse loose, running into a door...now I'm just making everyone's life harder.

Ryan would laugh and say he'd told me so. He's already told me I couldn't possibly make it as a groom, and that barn manager was so far beyond my means, I was crazy to even consider it. We'd had this conversation three years ago, when the PR agency I was working for folded and I was left jobless for the first time since college. By then, Ryan had been telling me to quit my stupid girl-job and let him handle the finances for years...as long as we'd been married, actually. I gave in, but only because I didn't want to start working at another agency. Not at age thirty, competing against a fresh crop of college grads almost ten years younger than me and with a firmer grasp on everything new in social media—the trends in marketing, at this point, seemed to change every ninety days, and I was feeling old just trying to keep up.

At first, I'd resisted him, even taking on a little equestrian PR work. That was how I met Casey, who was out pushing a new horse show management company and hired me for some freelance work. But between gigs, my interest in picking up my laptop again just kept drying up. I wanted to work *with* horses, not type up press releases about people showing them. I wanted to work with my hands.

Ryan made me settle for spending extra time at the boarding stable where I kept my show horses, Wally and Riviera, although I knew the trainer and grooms thought it was weird I spent so much non-riding time hanging around the barn, picking up rakes and shovels and pitching in where my help was neither wanted nor needed.

After it became clear I'd have to sell Wally and Riviera if I wanted to be free of Ryan, I'd pined for a while without a horse. When the opportunity to buy Thomas from his racing owners came up, I worked out a boarding/work swap arrangement, but my trainer made it clear this wasn't going to last forever. She didn't want other students getting ideas.

By the time I found this job and decided to call Basil about it, I'd been helping around barns for several years. But I'd never been responsible for a whole barn until this week.

And just as Ryan would have predicted, I have already made a spectacular mess of it.

Landon slams the horse trailer door shut and comes back to the barn with the wind tousling his hair, tossing it over his eyes. "Decent storm coming up for nighttime like this," he observes, joining me in the aisle and turning to gaze over the paddocks. The trees in the distance toss with the oncoming storm. "Hopefully, it just gets the horses wet and doesn't do any damage."

I glance at him. "Do you think we should bring them in?"

"Not now. We'd end up turning them out again at midnight." He glances at my arm in its sling. "And they'd be spooky with all this wind. Better to just go to bed and hope for the best. You can't bring them in from every storm."

I bite down on the inside of my cheek. It feels like things are going from bad to worse, like now I am putting the horses in danger because I can't be trusted to turn them out one-handed at midnight. "I don't know how tomorrow's going to work with this stupid sling," I say bitterly.

"Well, I'll be here," Landon says comfortably. "Obviously, I'll be helping you. I just have to rearrange a few appointments. But it's all fixable."

"Are you always so optimistic?" I feel the very opposite. And I don't like the way he said, *obviously, I'll be helping you.* Is he planning on rearranging his entire schedule to help me do my job? That sounds terrible on so many levels.

"I don't think so." He puts his hands in his pockets and we stand in silence for a moment, watching the lightning flicker through the clouds. I wait for him to continue, feeling there's something else he wants to get out. At the very least, I suppose I owe him the courtesy of being a good audience. "No," he says eventually. "I wouldn't say I'm even usually optimistic? I guess only when I can tell things are going to work out. And this is just fine, Mackenzie. Two weeks is nothing. You'll be fine by the time two weeks is up. This is a little hiccup, that's all."

"I shouldn't have let your horse get loose," I mutter, my own failure relentlessly bubbling up.

Thunder rumbles deep and long. It's the growl of a mature storm, most of its lightning high in the atmosphere as it rains itself to sleep.

"Those horses have been boxed up in stalls for weeks," Landon says, absolving me. "They were all looking for an excuse to run. Every single one of them has been dealing with chronic hoof abscesses and seedy toe, and their owner sent them to me as a last resort. He should have sent them to me as a *first* resort. If that's a thing." He shakes his head. "You know what I mean. Locking a horse up and hoping for the best isn't how you fix problems."

"How are you going to fix them?" I ask. A cold wind whips through the barn aisle, and the smell of rain comes with it. I hear the downpour approaching, marching across the pastures. The horses look up, dim shadows in the blue dusk, and watch the rain heading their way.

"Step back, so your sling stays dry," he cautions me, placing his hand on my good arm as if to push me out of the doorway.

Something in his touch makes my heart beat faster. Heat, a tingle in my skin that races from my arm to my chest and down to my toes.

I haven't been touched, skin on skin, by anyone besides a doctor in a long time. That's all it is.

"Thanks," I say, pulling my arm back and retreating into the barn. I feel the absence of his touch and rub my hand over the place where his hand was.

A few feet away, he rubs at his hand with a preoccupied expression.

"Well, I'm going inside," I announce, just as Landon says, "With soaking, good trimming, and common sense."

"What?" My brow furrows; I stare at him in confusion. "Soaking *what?*"

For half a second, I think he means my arm. The good one that still feels the echo of his touch. But that doesn't make any sense.

"The horses," Landon says. "You asked how I was going to fix their feet. I have some proprietary soaks I'm developing, to kill the bacteria in seedy toe. And most of hoof management is just having half a brain in your skull, although sometimes I think that's too much to ask of some of these racetrack farriers."

"Oh, right." My cheeks suddenly feel warm. I force myself back onto the same page with an effort. Clearly, it wasn't too hard for him to distance himself from the heat in his touch. That's good to know. I wouldn't want things to get...out of hand.

The rain reaches the barn at last, pouring down on the metal roof with a roar that immediately wipes out our chance at any further conversation. It's the perfect excuse to escape into my apartment without saying another word, just waving to him and spinning around, flinging open my door, and slamming it behind me before I have time to find any more ways to embarrass myself tonight.

I ALREADY WROTE in my training diary, so I settle onto the sofa, determined to watch YouTube videos about retraining racehorses until my eyes are too heavy to take anymore. More than anything, though, I simply let my eyes glaze over as the trainers urge their horses on, listening to the rain pound on the roof and slide down my bedroom window. There is something charming abut a rain-storm without lightning. It's not something a south Floridian experiences very often, and I find it's like expecting a brownie to have walnuts in it, then happily realizing I've been mistaken.

(Brownies should not have walnuts in them, ever.)

As the weather calms and the roar of rain settles, I head to bed and turn out my light—only to hear a dripping sound coming from the kitchen. With a sigh, I fling back my sheet and shuffle out to investigate. Of course, it would be too much to ask that the roof not leak. In Florida. In rainy season.

Drip. Drip. Drip. The water falls calmly from a seam in the ceiling panels into the kitchen sink.

"Well, bless me," I murmur. "A self-draining leak. Finally, some good luck."

And I slide the dish sponge beneath the drip, silencing it.

Pleased with such an easy fix, I climb back beneath the top sheet—but now my eyes stay open. My brain apparently feels free to roam around and examine all the stupid things I did today, including but not limited to: several moments dedicated to staring into Landon's blue eyes, letting Landon make me feel safe and comfortable with his words, and feeling Landon's touch on my arm burn like a blazing fire.

For some reason, all of these moments stand out more than, say, when Landon flung the door open and dislocated my shoulder, or when I stupidly lost control of his horse, or when the doctor said, "Now, don't scream," and shoved my arm back into place...and no, I did not scream.

I'm tougher than I look.

Tougher than Ryan ever *dreamed.*

Landon, on the other hand, now has a pretty good idea of how tough I am. Was he impressed?

Does it matter?

"It would be nice if he had some respect for me," I tell

myself. With the sheet pulled up to my chin, I can feel my words pushing against the fabric. It gives them a feeling of oomph, as if they're more than just air. I decide to set myself a tidy little intention, something to think about as I drift off to sleep. "I am tougher, stronger, and smarter than anyone ever knew," I announce to the night. "Everyone respects and admires me."

I like the sound of that last line so much that I repeat it.

The luminous reflection of moonlight slowly arranges itself above my bed, telling me the clouds are clearing. I watch the eerie light shimmer overhead, imagining any number of futures playing out against that blurry circle of blue, fixating on the scenes that show me alone and victorious with my retired racehorse, returning from our big show in Kentucky with a blue ribbon and a full-time job assured as a barn manager. *Everyone respects and admires me,* I think, again and again.

I squeeze my eyes shut when Landon appears in the picture, smiling as he puts a hand on my back, as he gives Thomas an apple. I don't know what he's doing there, and I don't know why he's so insistent on being a part of my meditation, but for now, I guess, I will blame the Motrin.

Chapter Fourteen

MY ALARM GETS me up before seven o'clock, and with some effort, I make it into the barn aisle early. Dawn is still lazily breaking across the fields, the sun making golden patterns against the concrete block of the barn walls as it lurches over the horizon, the live oaks catching its rays and breaking them up into abstract paintings that stretch across the pastures. There's a fine mist hovering just above the ground, and the horses move through it like ghosts, their ears pricked and facing towards me as they realize someone is standing in the barn aisle.

The morning is golden and clean-washed, but I'm feeling a little dreary and dirty. Last night I was too tired to attempt showering with one arm bound up. Now, with a ball cap pulled over my hair and an extra layer of deodorant to guard against any errant smells, I figure I'm presentable enough for a barn, but not much else. I suppose I chose my life's work wisely. Couldn't have gone to work like this at the PR agency.

At least my clothes are nice. I dressed carefully in the dim apartment, as if I was heading to a horse show instead of just out to do barn chores. My quarter-zip sun-shirt has a purple geometric pattern of horseshoes and flowers scattered over the fabric, and my navy-blue riding breeches have a matching purple trim at the pockets and on the knee patches. I feel better with coordinated clothing, like I can control the colors I'm wearing, if nothing else. Finding the patterns and colors that complement each other is half the fun of designing clothes.

Despite my attempt to get up long before him, Landon appears early too. He pokes his head into the feed room while I'm slowly throwing grain into buckets. "Doing okay in here?" he asks gently.

"Just fine," I reply cooly. I have been planning to keep him at a distance today. But the sound of his voice makes me betray myself pretty near immediately. I find myself looking up and meeting his eyes, my pulse quickening as his gaze locks onto mine.

His morning face is still a little crumpled from bed, and I imagine him sleeping with his face shoved into his pillow, the fabric creasing his skin. Something about him makes me believe he sleeps with the same energy and effort he puts into shoeing horses or opening feed room doors. Like he is a force of nature, driven by the same winds as our daily thunderstorms, unable to draw back even if he wanted to.

He lifts his eyebrows. "How can I help you this morning?" he asks. "Bringing horses in? Tossing feed? Throwing hay?"

I have never really thought about how many quick, fast arm motions this job requires until just now, when he lists my chores with a series of action verbs. I might as well be a professional baseball player, for all the ways I need two arms. Even setting up the morning feed is pretty difficult. "Um," I say, glancing at the buckets spread around me.

"Do you want me to set up feed?" he asks, coming into the feed room. He holds out one large paw for the scoop. "Here, let me."

I study him for a moment. Landon looks back at me, genuinely concerned. I think he believes he broke me. It's kind of touching, actually.

But I don't need him to do everything for me. I just need a little extra time to figure out how to do things for myself.

"I can do it," I say. "I just didn't realize how much balance it takes, turning back and forth from the feed bins to the buckets. I almost fell over the first time I scooped and twirled." And I crack a smile, hoping he will, too. He's watching me so very seriously.

"Oh, jeez," Landon says, still very serious. "Better let me do it, then."

"No, no, I'm figuring it out." I wave my good hand at him. A few pellets from the scoop fling out and rattle on the floor. "I'm just going a little slowly. I can do it."

"Okay, then I'll bring the horses in," he replies, hand bracing on the door-frame, ready to get to it. "Then I'll help you drop feed, okay?"

"Perfect, thank you." The words fall from my mouth with surprising ease. I didn't want his help; I got up early to avoid it. But now that he's here and offering assistance with such concern and charm, I find that his help isn't unwanted at all...I even appreciate it.

"Of course," Landon says.

He stays in the doorway.

I turn away, bending over to get another scoop of grain. When I look up, I find him still watching me. Confused, I ask, "Did you need something?"

Landon grins, the concern falling from his features. "I was just watching to make sure you really could do this without falling. Otherwise, I might need to strap you into a riding helmet. In case you crash to the floor."

Oh, okay—*now* he wants to be funny! Way to sneak in and get my guard down, buddy. I roll my eyes at him, gesturing towards the aisle with the feed scoop. "Go get those horses in and leave me alone."

Landon salutes and disappears.

Digging the scoop into the feed bin for the last bucket in the line-up, I allow myself to smirk at the interaction we just had. Caring and concerned, laced with sarcasm? Not bad, Landon. I might be coming around to this guy, after all. He's definitely nothing like my ex—a major plus in his column. For example, I don't get the impression he is standing around waiting for me to screw up so that he can look good, or that he thinks he knows more than me about all things forever until the end of time. He hasn't corrected me on anything, actually. Even though he added shavings to those stalls, he didn't tell me I'd bedded them wrong. He simply pointed out that *he* liked them with more bedding than most people.

I'm still annoyed about the shavings incident, but maybe... maybe I'm not mad about it anymore.

He's actually been respectful of my equestrian knowledge. He wasn't really a fan of my insisting on bathing that horse alone, but he did let me try it. And he hasn't said 'I told you so' about how that whole situation turned out. Although admittedly that could be because he is the one who dislocated my shoulder. I mean, seriously, who flings open a door like that? He could have hit anyone. He could have broken someone's nose.

But he also apologized, and he's here to help and make up for it.

A man who says he is sorry, a man who admits he can be wrong, a man who can disagree with me but still treat me like an equal who has a right to her opinion...this seems like alien behavior to me after the last eight years I've had, but, honestly, a girl could get used to this.

Not that I want to do anything crazy, like date him, but maybe living in the same barn as him, working with him while I heal up from this little mishap, *isn't* actually the end of the world.

And with that thought, I put the finishing touches of vitamin and electrolyte supplements atop each mound of grain, shaking the buckets gently so that the powders settle into the mix. There, feed is ready, and the first hooves are clip-clopping down the aisle as Landon gets the horses in. Thomas pokes his head into the feed room, his eyes bright, and Landon calls out, "Hi, Mom!"

I laugh and give Thomas a kiss on the nose before Landon makes a few clucking noises and urges the horse to keep moving towards his stall. I'm still shaking my head over how cute that was when Kayla pops her head into the feed room.

"You're early!" I exclaim, startled. I thought I had at least another hour before Kayla came down.

"I wanted to be sure you survived the night," she says cheerfully. She looks at my line-up of buckets. "You did! Look at you!"

"Was there ever any doubt?"

"You never know," Kayla says. "You might have run off in the night to find a job where we won't beat you up so much. Want me to help you dump grain and then go get the rest of the horses with Landon and Bas?"

"That would be amazing," I say, relieved. "You guys are being great about this."

"Oh, we all get hurt sometimes," Kayla says. She scoops a few buckets up. "One day, you'll be out riding my horses for me because I did something stupid. It's the nature of the game."

"You'd put me on your horses?" I follow her out of the feed room with two buckets clenched in one hand. Their metal hands dig into my fingers. "But I'm the groom." Or the barn manager, but that still sounds too important, beyond my skill level. Maybe someday. "You don't put grooms on horses like these. If I learned anything in Wellington, it's that."

"Oh, titles don't mean anything." Kayla's tone is careless. She shrugs and continues, "You can ride, can't you? I've seen your pictures online."

She added me on social media right after they gave me the job. I have been very careful to only post intensely positive quotes and very flattering riding photos since that friend request came through.

"I mean, of course I can ride," I say. "But that doesn't mean —"

"This isn't some big, fancy stable where we worry about coloring inside the lines," Kayla says. "We're a family. All of us. You, me, Basil, Landon. We watch out for each other. Okay?"

I glance up the aisle. Landon is striding into the barn, with leggy Killian walking at his side. It's crazy how much smaller that big chestnut horse seems with a man of Landon's size and breadth next to him. Landon reminds me of a Clydesdale, the horses everyone loves to call "gentle giants" because for all their super size and strength, they are usually calm when other horses are anxious, steadfast in times of trouble, and more interested in making friends than using their power to push others around.

If we're going to be a family, and he's included in that definition, and I guess I can live with it. A gentle giant is a fine thing to have in the family. For one thing, that means there's always someone who can handle the really heavy hay bales.

And for another, it would be nice to have a man around I can trust. Call it a novelty, but I haven't trusted a man with only two legs in a long, long time.

"Okay." I agree with Kayla, but I'm smiling at Landon as he leads the horse up at the aisle, and he's smiling back at me, smiling like I'm the best thing he's seen all day.

Chapter Fifteen

"I HAVEN'T RIDDEN Thomas in *forever*," I moan, staring at the tack room calendar. "We're falling behind!"

What was painfully obvious when I flicked through my training diary this morning is becoming agonizing to look at on a calendar—half a week has gone by without working on Thomas's training, and there are such a precious few weeks to go until the Thoroughbred Makeover. What felt like forever back in January, when I was still just dreaming of what I might do with my life once I was really and truly divorced from Ryan, has dissolved into a few quick months which will flip past in a flurry of storms and heat. It's ten times harder to ride in summer than in spring, and yet the bulk of our work has to be done: Thomas needs to learn more balance in his transitions, not to bolt into the canter, how to jump a full course and not just trot individual lines and gymnastics...

"It has been three days," Landon says, in an annoyingly reasonable tone. He is sitting on a tack trunk, stirring up a few powders in a bucket of warm water. It's some witch's brew he's concocting to soak his rehab horses' hooves in. He says if it works the way he expects, he's going to package the blend up and sell it, so he has a notebook at his side where he keeps tabs on the horses' progress, the time of day he soaks them, the weather and ground conditions—everything. It's actually pretty impressive, even if it looks more like alchemy than science.

And it's very nice for him that he's moving forward with his project, but since I'm stuck on the ground with just one working arm, I'm fairly limited in what I can do with Thomas. My schedule is falling apart around me. I knew it would be important to build in extra time on the training calendar in case of setbacks to a horse's health, physical or mental, but I had no business being the one to get hurt when I have this enormous, self-imposed deadline looming over my head.

"Three days is forever when you only have four months," I tell Landon, tapping the calendar with a fingernail. "We have work to do! We should be working on our trot to canter transitions right now! He still bolts into a hand-gallop every time. I need two hands to fix that, so even if I get on with my sling, I can't get anything done that we actually *need*."

The really annoying part is that I really could have had the entire weekend to work on Thomas whenever I wanted, with no interruptions outside of morning and evening feeding and stall-cleaning. Kayla and Basil left for Ocala on Friday afternoon, and they won't be back until Sunday evening. They took four horses with them, giving the rest of the herd the weekend off to stay outside and relax. There wouldn't have been any worry about trying to dodge storms and heat with afternoon or late evening rides. I could have gotten on first thing this morning, while the weather is nice and *somewhat* cool. But no.

I am sitting here with my left arm in a sling, being tragic.

"You can watch me convince Berry to put her feet in a

bucket," Landon suggests, hopping down from the tack trunk with his bucket of magic powders in hand. "She thinks that if her feet get wet, she'll die."

"Maybe she's right," I grumble, but I follow him out of the tack room.

I have nothing else to do. The horses are out, the aisle is clean, and the temperature is a sizzling ninety-two degrees. When I was packing my things for this new life, I didn't consider the possibilities of being laid-up with an injury, and I have nothing to occupy myself in my apartment besides streaming TV shows or watching still more retired racehorse training videos. And surprisingly, I feel all tapped out in that particular area right now. I want to see something *real* go down.

Suddenly, I'm very interested in how Landon is going to get his mare's fore-hooves into a bucket of warm water which smells suspiciously of bitter herbs, and then keep them there for twenty minutes. This might be the entertainment I've been looking for.

Landon unsnaps Berry's stall guard and slips a halter on the gray mare's slim head, then brings her into the aisle. She steps carefully on the concrete, lame in front just like the other horses he's had shipped in from Kentucky. He cross-ties her in front of the stall while his other horses watch with companionable interest.

"Tell me her story again?" I ask, leaning against a wall. I'm next to the open door of Steel Cat, the gelding that ran away from me on day one; he nuzzles my sling with interest. No hard feelings here. I give him a friendly scratch beneath his chin.

Landon is running a hand along Berry's neck while she wriggles her hindquarters, swishing her tail to let us know she's not comfortable with this arrangement. "She was the slowest runner in a slow string of horses at Kentucky Downs," he says. "And her trainer kept running short of money to pay for services. Her stall was wet and dirty because he couldn't pay a groom regularly, or get fresh straw in when he should've, which built up bacteria in her hooves, and since she wasn't getting her shoes done regularly, that just meant more cracks and room for bacteria. She's full of trouble in her front feet. The hinds aren't so bad, luckily. If her hind feet were bad, I don't know if she'd be standing here with us." The unspoken inference is that this pretty, unlucky mare would be dead, either sold for meat or simply euthanized for uselessness.

"I hope her former trainer is in jail," I say huffily, although I know he's not. It takes a lot more than inflicting seedy toe on a horse to land a person in prison. "What a piece of crap."

"Honestly? He's a nice enough guy," Landon says, shrugging. "Just got in over his head and not particularly knowledgeable. Sometimes you wonder how some of these people get it in their heads to be racehorse trainers. I guess the exam for a license should be a lot tougher."

"So, what did you pay for this beauty?" I ask.

Berry turns a white-rimmed eye on me and snorts, but I wasn't trying to be offensive. She's actually a pretty mare, if you like flea-bitten grays. I don't have anything against them myself.

"Oh, I took her off his hands as a favor," Landon says. "If he could prove he gave the horse a safe retirement home, he didn't have to lose his license."

"But shouldn't he have lost it?" I argue.

"Doesn't make a difference to Berry here." Landon's voice is matter-of-fact. "If he was gonna lose it anyway, he might have sold her to the kill-buyer, just to get some cash out of her. That would have been worse for ya, huh, mare?"

I say nothing, but my fists clench until I can feel my fingernails digging into my palms.

Landon picks up the strong-smelling bucket and edges it close to her front hooves. Berry takes a step back immediately, and when she feels the cross-ties restricting her movement, she lifts her head sharply. "Easy, easy," he says, unsnapping the left tie from her halter so she has room to move back. "Just a tie, baby, nothing's permanent."

"Let me help you," I say, pushing away from the wall. "I have a free hand."

"Do not get hurt," Landon warns, but he hands me Berry's lead-rope and I clip it onto the bottom ring of her halter. I'll act as half the cross-ties to help her get used to being tied in the aisle. Usually, all they need to get used to it is a little relief from pressure when they decide to twist or back up. I taught Thomas to cross-tie the first month at my old coach's barn. He only broke two sets of cross-ties, which I considered pretty good since I was doing the work alone. With a helper, no cross-ties have to be harmed in the making of a retired racehorse.

"So she was a free mare, huh?" I ask as Landon lifts one hoof and slowly edges the bucket into place. "That's pretty good for a test subject."

"Free is just another word for 'monumental vet bills,'" Landon grunts, setting the mare's hoof down in the bucket. She looks down and blows through her nostrils, alarmed, then snaps the hoof straight back up. Landon's quick, though, and he grabs the bucket before she can overturn it and spill his precious potion. "Not that these guys have slapped me with anything dramatic I didn't know about, but this entire research process is being funded out of my own pocket."

I raise an eyebrow. "No sponsors? Why don't you get one of the big hoof supplement brands to back you?"

"Because it's a new product that I am developing myself, and it's not for sale," Landon explains patiently, like I haven't been following the conversation at all. "No one's going to fund a commercial venture unless they're getting a piece of it."

"Oh, I guess that's true." Berry snorts as Landon picks up her hoof again, and I run my fingers beneath her chin to distract her. It works; she flops her lower lip up and down trying to catch my fingertips, and forgets that Landon is putting her foot in a terrifying metal bucket. "Silly filly," I tell her. "Only enough brain cells to understand one thing at a time."

"You can restart her when her feet are fixed," Landon says. "Wouldn't it be great to teach her to jump? I think she'd make a pretty hunter."

I look down at the top of his head. He's essentially kneeling at my feet right now, bent over at the waist while he holds Berry's foreleg with one hand and the bucket with the other. The vapors from the hoof solution make my eyes water, but it's his suggestion that makes me blink.

"You think *I* should ride this little turkey?" I ask him. "Have you even seen me ride? I could be terrible. You shouldn't go making crazy suggestions until you know what you're really getting yourself into."

"Oh, you're not terrible," Landon says. Berry shifts her weight, and he eases the pressure he's putting on her cannon bone ever so slightly, so that she doesn't feel trapped. The Thoroughbred brain doesn't like to be told to stand still. "I've seen you riding Thomas, and Kayla already said you'd be riding horses for her if she needs the help. I assume you can ride if she's letting you on her horses."

"Well…" I smile to myself. It's nice to hear someone say I can ride well. Really, it's the biggest compliment I could ask for. I don't need to feel smart or pretty, not at this point in my life. I just need to be pretty capable in the saddle, and getting better all the time. "Okay, I can ride a horse without breaking it," I allow.

"That's rare."

"I wouldn't say it's rare. You don't have to exaggerate to make me feel good. I'm an okay rider. That's enough."

Landon shakes his head, clearly determined to make his point. "Consider how many people in this world ride horses with any regularity. Then realize that you're one of the better ones. Let's say even if you're not ready to ride in the Olympics, you're in, oh, the top seventy-fifth percentile. Hell, even in the top fiftieth would make you rare amongst *all* the people on earth. Not that many people get to ride horses. So, yeah. You're rare. How does that feel?"

"You're right. I never looked at it like that before." I'm just impressed enough with his reasoning to forget to amuse Berry with my fingertips, and she latches her attention onto something in the distance. I turn my head to look down the aisle and see one of the horses turned out for the day ambling along a pasture fence in the distance.

Startled by the horse, or maybe just anxious and looking for an excuse to act out, Berry throws up her head and takes a step backwards, slapping her heel against the side of the bucket as she does. Landon slides it away before she can drag it onto its side.

"Whoops!" I go with the mare, then ease her back into place. "I'm so sorry. I am just not used to being complimented. Threw me off my game."

Landon looks up at me and lifts an eyebrow questioningly. "Well, that's unfortunate," he says softly.

It's the voice he would use on a nervous horse, to settle Berry here as she objects to having her hoof soaked. It's a voice reserved for confused and wounded things.

And I can feel its calming effects on my own psyche, even though a moment ago I would have sworn that I am no longer either of those things.

"Let's get you on Thomas later," Landon says after a few moments of quiet pass between us. "I'll stay at his head to make sure you're safe and don't go flying around the ring with one rein, okay?"

"Really? I'm sure you have things to do—"

"I don't," Landon interrupts smoothly. He runs his thumb along Berry's knee as she stands quietly at last, finally giving in to our strange human need to hold her foot in a bucket. "Soaking hooves and helping you, that's my whole plan for the day."

"But—"

"No buts," he says. "I broke it, I bought it, right?"

Chapter Sixteen

I DON'T KNOW about *buying* me, but he definitely assisted with breaking me. And he's been making it up to me steadily ever since. There's really no way I could have comfortably gotten through chores alone over the past few days, especially since Kayla and Basil went to Ocala for the weekend, leaving me with all the stalls, turn-out, and feeding to contend with.

We don't have to feed lunch while the horses are outside, which means we can work right through the noon hour on Landon's soaking regime. We've got Steel Cat in the aisle, who flicks his tail anxiously and overturns three buckets in a row, when Landon looks up from his work and asks, "Did you just hear thunder?"

"I was hoping it was horses running around," I say. The rumble was so distant it was more like a shudder in the air than an actual sound. But when I pull out my phone to check the radar, I find a long list of notifications piling up on the screen, all of them screaming about severe thunderstorm warnings for the area. Although heavy storms are the order of the day, every day, from now until September, a severe thunderstorm warning is enough to get me on edge. In south Florida, that can mean crazy lightning, howling winds, even a tornado. It's probably no different here. Is this barn tornado-proof? It's cement block, so probably. I glance up at the old rafters overhead, wondering how sturdy they are after a couple of decades of storms, droughts, and hurricanes.

"Big warnings," I say, holding up my screen for Landon to see.

He winces. "I need three more minutes for this hoof."

"Can you do it alone? I think I need to bring the horses in." Another rumble of thunder punctuates my words, undoubtedly closer this time. It has moved from a suggestion of sound to an actual sound.

"Let me finish and put this fella away, and I'll be right behind you," Landon says, holding up his phone. The timer on the screen is steadily ticking down the seconds until the soak time is complete. There's no doubt that Landon is being scientific about his product trials. I kind of wish I could be that precise with my sketches and ideas for riding clothes. Imagine if there was a way to experiment and record the results for a particular pattern, instead of just hoping other riders will appreciate my taste.

Maybe there is? I start to consider it...and then I take a few steps out of the barn, turn back to see the northwest sky, and forget all about trial runs of breeches and riding shirts. The sky is ominous, a cloud of deepest smoke ringed with white fringes —that special flare for doom which I see regularly before a severe storm in south Florida. Lightning flashes behind the white ruffled edges like a strobe light half-hidden by a curtain, and the thunder begins to hum in a long, unending rumble.

Seeing how quickly this storm is coming up, I change my trajectory and bolt for the farther pastures while Thomas stands by his gate and stares after me with astonishment written all over his long face. But it will make more sense to leave the horses close to the barn for last, I figure. If the storm catches up with me, I'll have less distance to run with a horse at my side.

The problem, I realize as I skid up to the pasture gate, is that there are four horses in this field, and only one of me. It would be workable if I had two hands, but with just one, I'm going to have to be pretty quick and clever to halter a single horse and get him through the gate without the others crowding out after him.

As I finesse the halter over Crunchy's poll, a sharp burst of cool wind teases my sweaty neck. I hazard a glance behind me and see the darkness drawing closer, the fleecy white lining above its blue-black underbelly looking weirdly like sheepskin on a jumping boot. A thin finger of lightning flicks in the distance, then a second, fatter one that pulses for a long second before vanishing. I hear a squeak and it takes me a moment to realize it came from me.

The thunder changes from a rumble to a crackle, urging me to stop staring and get a move on.

Crunchy tosses his head and backs away from me just before I have the buckle secured. The halter swings loose. The other horses in the paddock bounce backwards as well, their wide eyes fastened on me as if I'm the scariest part of their day, not the storm hurtling towards us.

"Come on, you dorks," I snap. "You're acting like dummies."

Crunchy turns and bucks, sending sand flying into my face.

"That's not helpful!" I shout, and reach for the next closest horse. I figure Crunchy can wait if that's how he's going to be about it.

But Virgo has the same idea and backs up just like Crunchy.

Then Toddy and Arlo do the same thing.

They're all lined up now, but they're four feet from the gate and giving me the crazy eyes. Their forelocks fly up between their ears, blown by the wind that's now whistling around the barn eaves and picking up handfuls of coarse white sand.

"You guys are *idiots*!" I inform them. I want to cry with frustration. How am I supposed to get these dumbbloods— yeah, I said it!—into the barn before this storm swoops in? The lightning flashes again, much nearer now, and the thunder that follows it seems to shake the air in front of my eyes. "Dammit, come *on*!"

"They're too spooked to pay attention to you," says a calm voice from behind me. "Just open the gate and let them head inside. They know where to go."

I look back at Landon, standing with his hand on the gate. The wind is tossing his red hair, making him look almost as wild as the horses staring at us. "I can't just let them run in! If someone gets hurt, Kayla will kill me." I don't even mention what Basil might do. He's so small and quiet...the sort of person you have to watch out for.

"It's my idea," Landon says. "So blame me."

And he flings open the gate, swinging it wide to give the horses plenty of room. I take a step back, flattening myself against the fence, as the horses stare at the open gateway, trying to decide if he's serious.

"Go on, go inside!" he shouts, his voice blending with the thunder ramming through the air as the ground quakes beneath our feet. The horses don't need to be told twice. They take off, bucking and squealing, and race past us towards the barn. Landon pulls me out of the paddock as Crunchy veers our way, tucking me close against his chest with one strong arm. "Get by, horse!" he yells, waving his free arm, and Crunchy snorts, pins his ears, and heads after the other horses.

I stay pressed against Landon's hard chest for a second longer, and when he releases me, the air seems crackling and dangerous, as if the world is charged with electricity. For a moment, I think we're in the firing line for a bolt of lightning, but then I realize the storm hasn't arrived yet. It's just the abrupt absence of Landon that makes everything seem so menacing.

I don't even have time to analyze the feeling, though; he's already running away from me, opening up the next pasture gate, and the next—I lurch after him, cursing my bad balance, and start flinging open the individual paddock gates facing the barn. Thomas is the last horse I get to, and he looks at me quizzically as I open his gate. Then he moves to my side.

"Oh, Thomas," I gasp, my heart lurching with love for my horse. "Come on, silly."

I break into a jog and Thomas trots alongside me as if I'm leading him, his nostrils blowing nervously.

Back in the barn, horses are everywhere. You'd think they might go right into their own stalls but no, they've elected to go crazy instead, arguing over a loose hay bale left in the aisle for the dinner feeding, nipping and squealing at each other, stealing the dry-erase pens right off the board and flinging them across the aisle. Thomas and I both stop short when we arrive into this chaos, and my horse looks every bit as aghast as I am.

Then Landon comes up the middle of the aisle with a swinging lead-rope, shouting. "Get up, get on, go in your stalls, get—get—*get*!"

The horses scramble to do his bidding. Most of them even

choose the correct stalls, although a few just duck for the nearest safe place.

Thomas trots into his stall, then turns and stares at me, blowing.

"You're a good boy," I assure him, sliding the door shut—this is no time for the casual closure of a stall guard—and turn to help Landon sort out the horses who have gone into the same stalls. Crunchy is still standing in the aisle, a black dry-erase marker hanging from his mouth like a cigar. "And you're a very *bad* boy," I tell him, snatching the marker from between his teeth.

"He just wants to be barn manager," Landon jokes, leading Virgo from the stall across from the tack room and setting the horse free to trot into his own stall a few doors down. "He's going to set the training calendar for tomorrow."

"Let me see," I say, pushing Crunchy towards his open stall door. "I think that calendar is going to be a big-fat *zero* for no rides, Crunchy-boy."

"Well, one ride." Landon shuts a stall door and suddenly the horses are all where they belong. Thunder roars outside. He waits for it to finish vibrating the rafters, then says, "Don't forget about Thomas. He's had three days off already, I think you said? Three too many, right?"

I watch Landon walk up the aisle to me as rain sweeps across the fields behind him, pelting on the roof with a frantic fury. Suddenly, I remember being pressed against his chest, the hard assurance of him, the casual strength in his massive arm as he held me out of the way of that wayward warmblood looking for trouble, and despite the cool wind whipping up the aisle, I feel hot all over.

Oh, no.

One week into my independence from men, and I'm already in a state of complete and total attraction to the one who lives across the aisle from me.

Chapter Seventeen

SOMEHOW, I MANAGE to retreat into my apartment for a late lunch on my own—despite Landon's entreaty that I come over to his place and eat with him. Still eating out of the provisions Kayla brought me, I stick my head into the fridge and forage until I find bread and mayo and sliced American cheese.

I make myself a grilled cheese that takes forever to brown on the temperamental stovetop, and all the while the rain rattles deafeningly against the window and the lightning flashes like a strobe light and the leak in the roof drips with a rhythmic patter into the sink.

This hapless combination of discordant and consistent would probably drive me insane except that I'm already doing that to myself as I stand over this frying pan, because I'm thinking about Landon.

Not necessarily his excellent achievements in the scientific method, either.

No, embarrassingly, stupidly, I find that I'm completely caught up in thinking about his lagoon-blue eyes, his broad shoulders, his taut muscles, his hard chest. Things I know about intimately now that he's felt the need to protect me from a loose horse as a storm blew in. I mean, I was pressed against that chest for barely thirty seconds, but it was enough. It was *enough*.

And, as if all that physical prowess isn't enough, he's getting into my head with his *personality,* too. Generous, funny, kind, naturally good with animals—the kind of man I just finished convincing myself doesn't really exist. Or, if such a man does exist, that man is not available for me. Not in this lifetime. Because if men like that revealed themselves to me, or were attracted to me, then why would I ever have married *Ryan*?

It wouldn't have made any sense. And I don't want the past eight years of my life to make no sense. I don't mind admitting that things might have gone wrong; I certainly can't deny that he's not the person I thought he was when we met, or when we were married. But to think that I made a mistake and simply should have waited around for a better option...no. Come on.

I can't have wasted all that time with a better guy waiting for me in the wings. I did the best I could with the guy I got.

It didn't work out.

There's no sense thinking it could be different in another go. Ryan started out nice—I swear he did—and ended up cruel. Who is to say Landon wouldn't do the exact same thing? Who is to say that about any of them?

"Men are dogs," I say to my sandwich, plopping it onto a plate. "Although, I really like dogs. So, apologies to dogs."

Maybe, if I adopted three or four dogs, I would stop thinking about the way Landon felt with my body pressed against his, the strength in his arm, the safety in his grasp.

Maybe I better adopt five or six dogs, just to be safe.

RIGHT AROUND FOUR o'clock, there's a gentle knock at

my door. I rouse myself from the half-nap I've been drifting through, lulled by the patter of rain as the storm tapers off and the oddly satisfying drip-drip-drip of the leak in the kitchen. Once the thunder wound down, the leak stopped sounding like it was beating a hole through my skull and turned into a lullaby, instead. And while this old sofa sags in the middle and isn't the best for sitting on, it turns out it's pretty great for napping.

I struggle to my feet, wishing I had my left hand free to help push me from the soft cushions, and open the door. This sling is the worst.

Landon smiles at me as soon as I open the door.

His firm jaw and sparkling eyes send a sensation like a wash of cool water over my shoulders and down my spine, and I just barely resist the physical urge to shiver. "Hey," I say cautiously, testing my voice to make sure I won't squeak or croak. "I was just taking a nap."

"Oh! I'm sorry." He takes a step back, as if he can undo waking me up.

"No, it's fine. It's already four...time to think about feeding dinner and all that. Plus, now that the horses have been in, we have to do stalls. Ugh. Did you want to get to it early, or..."

"Actually," Landon says, looking up and down the aisle, then back at me. His smile flashes again. "It's nice and cloudy out. Let's get you on your horse for that ride."

"Oh! Okay. Um..." I blink and look down at myself. My nice, tidy riding outfit of the day has become wrinkled and sandy with the chaos of barn chores and our storm fiasco, but the colors still match and I love riding in these particular breeches, one of the last pairs I ordered before the divorce put an end to my bespoke clothing days. "I guess we can do that, if we're quick."

"I'll get Thomas out and start getting him ready," Landon offers. "Come out when you're set, okay?"

"Yes," I say. "Sure. Thanks."

In the bathroom, I splash water on my face and try to rub away the lines the couch cushions have made on my cheek. They're not going anywhere. Resigned to pillow-face, I study my hair in the mirror, wishing for a way to get my hair into a neat braid, but talk about impossible with one hand! I have to settle for the same messy ponytail I've been tolerating for the past three days, though I tug it a little so it dangles over my right shoulder.

The flip of hair gives my face a flirty look. Not that it matters. In fact, I shouldn't look even remotely like I'm trying to dress up for Landon or be cute for Landon. I toss the ponytail over my shoulder again and for a moment I consider changing into something less Instagrammable. But that would take forever, and he's probably ready to saddle up Thomas by now. And anyway, maybe he'll take my picture for my Insta and I can post a crazy riding update: *here I am in the wilds of north Florida with my arm in a sling but we're still prepping for #TBMakeover!!*

I accept my cuteness as part of the job and slide on my paddock boots before heading back into the barn aisle.

Thomas, standing in the cross-ties by the tack room, pricks his ears at me and his nostrils flutter with a silent nicker of greeting. He's so cute. I think I'm cute? Forget it. Thomas is the best, cutest thing in the world. Instantly, my horse takes up all the space in my brain, shoving Landon right out—mostly, anyway—and I give my horse a one-handed hug around the neck. "Best boy," I croon. "So proud of you for coming in like a gentleman today."

"Which saddle is yours?" Landon calls from the tack room.

"Far right, by the window," I reply, stepping back as Thomas shifts to look into the tack room. I start into the tack room to make sure he finds it okay amongst the vast forest of saddles populating the interior. "The brown Bates, it has a blue saddle pad thrown over it—"

Landon comes out of the tack room with my saddle draped over one arm and we both stop short before we run into each other. I'm staring up at him, heart hammering against my ribs. He gazes back down at me—or is *gaze* too strong a word? Maybe it's a little too swoony?

No, he's definitely gazing. This is a gaze.

I feel locked in place, like I couldn't look away even if I were to try, with all my might.

But why try, why do anything at all, when I can drown myself in Landon's oceanic blue eyes?

"*This* saddle?" Landon asks, in a husky voice that makes me want to curl my fingernails into my palms—no, actually, I'm doing it.

"That's the one," I reply. My voice is kind of breathy, like I have forgotten how to talk normally. Or draw a breath.

"Nice saddle," he says, still matching my gaze. Still gazing, himself.

"Thanks," I say, and then I feel a silly grin lurching into place. "It was really expensive."

Suddenly, I remember that I bought it with one of the gift cards I started buying and squirreling away for myself when I knew Ryan and I were cruising for a divorce, and I can't help but laugh.

Landon's smile curves in reply, like he'd laugh along with me if he only knew the joke, and then he flicks his gaze towards the horse standing behind me. Our little moment of—whatever that was—is over, and I miss the warmth of his attention already.

"Let me grab a fresh saddle pad," I say, and duck past him into the tack room. I grab the first pad from the pile on the shelf next to the saddle racks, a baby pad of thin, white cotton that has seen its share of horses and washing machines. Landon steps out of my way as I return to the aisle and toss the pad over Thomas's back.

"The saddle fits him really well," Landon remarks, tugging the saddle pad up into the saddle's gullet so that the fabric can't pull against Thomas's shark-fin withers.

"I had it fit by an expert from the saddle-maker's," I say, remembering the petite woman with dark eyes who took exact measurements of Thomas's back and made sure the saddle's padding echoed his shape. The whole thing was fascinating—and it was very satisfying to do that for my horse. Especially since now I wouldn't have the money for such a service. "But it will probably need to be fitted again before we head to Kentucky. His back will have changed shape, more muscle and everything from all the dressage. They can adjust the wool flocking."

"What divisions will you do in Kentucky?" Landon asks. He goes back into the tack room and comes out with Thomas's snaffle bridle—also expensive, also fit by an expert. I got everything as pristine as I could for Thomas, all thanks to those gift cards. No regrets. "You get to enter two, right?"

"We're doing dressage and show jumping. How did you know? Have you entered it?"

"I've heard about it," Landon says. "A show just for retired racehorses, two divisions allowed, Kentucky Horse Park. Have I got all that right?"

"Exactly." I rub Thomas on his neck, finding the place beneath his mane that is always itchy. "Just for *newly* retired racehorses, who haven't done anything else in their life yet. It's a big deal just to get the horse there, but of course, I'm hoping for a pretty ribbon, too."

"Well, sure. Everyone wants a pretty ribbon."

"Even you?" I tease, my fingernails digging into Thomas's short coat. He leans against me, stretching out his nose to show how much he's enjoying the scratching session, and Landon has to move with him so that he can adjust the bridle.

"Especially me," Landon says, grinning at me. He fastens Thomas's noseband by feel, not even looking at the leather. "If all my horses weren't broke-down nags, maybe I'd enter the makeover, too. Like I said earlier, I think Berry would make a nice hunter, and Steel Cat has jumper written all over him."

"You can do it next year. Even with one of your broke-down nags, if you really fix their feet, and you stick to the riding schedule to make sure the horse stays eligible. That would be a really nice comeback story. Good for your brand."

"My brand," Landon repeats.

"If you're going to sell a product, you need a brand," I say. "I don't want to brag or anything, but I've worked in PR like, a little bit."

"Well, maybe I'll look into it," Landon says. "You know I'm always thinking about my brand. Now, for this very non-broke-down horse, let's get you out there and back in the saddle. I have to make sure my silly mistake doesn't cost you that pretty ribbon you want to so badly."

"It was my mistake that led to me getting hurt," I remind

him as we walk out to the arena, paddock boots splashing in the puddles. I know he opened the door, but I don't want him to beat himself up over it, when I caused the entire situation.

"It was no one's mistake," Landon says. "It was just one of those things."

I feel grateful to him for saying it. Maybe I should be nicer to myself and accept that sometimes, even *often,* horses do things that we can't help and it all goes wrong.

Maybe it really wasn't my fault, or anyone's fault, and it just was a thing that happened?

Can I make myself learn to live in a world where everything isn't my fault? That would be nice.

Seems fake, but, I mean, I also didn't know, a year ago, that I'd be living in north Florida on a horse farm, being assisted into the saddle by a gorgeous farrier who so far seems to have a heart of gold. So it can be hard to sort out fact from fiction when life is changing in such unexpected ways.

He was right about insisting I ride this afternoon, too. The air is humid and warm, of course, but at least the sun is hidden behind clouds. With any luck, they'll stick around until sunset. A growling rumble in the distance lets us know there are still storms around, but they're too far away to be worried about. We have the time and space right now to enjoy a ride.

Landon arranges Thomas at the mounting block and I slowly ease myself into the saddle, feeling very wobbly without the use of my left hand to press into his neck for balance. Thomas shifts, probably nervous because I feel different, and Landon puts a calming hand on his neck. "Stand still for your mother," he chides the horse. "She's had a rough couple of days."

I laugh lightly, settling into the saddle. My boots find the stirrups without trouble and I can't help but sigh with pleasure. This is where I belong, on horseback. And not just on any horse, but on my lovely Thomas. I run my hand along his withers and beneath his mane. "What a good boy," I tell him.

Landon smiles up at me, diverting my attention from my horse with an ease that I know I'll be thinking about later. "You look happy," he says.

"I *am* happy," I say. "Thank you for helping me. This is the best I've felt in a few days."

"Good, let's keep you that way. I'm going to lead Thomas around the arena. You just sit up there and let yourself feel his motion."

"Oh, are you a riding instructor now?" I ask, highly amused.

"I could be a riding instructor." He clucks to Thomas. "You don't know."

"I've been here a week and haven't seen you on a horse yet, so I don't even know if you can ride, let alone teach."

"Hey, we already pointed out that all my horses are broke-down nags, remember? Cut me some slack."

"That's true. Maybe we should take you to a trail-riding place and rent you a horse."

"So you're not even going to *offer* me a ride on Thomas. Noted."

"I'm really bad at sharing," I tell him. "Fun fact about me: I've literally never shared a dessert with anyone."

"No sharing desserts, no sharing horses..." He glances up at me, eyes dancing with laughter. "What else?"

"Everything. It's all off the table."

"I'll bet you share with the people you really like."

"It's never come up."

"Well, I guess I'll just have to test you with dessert sometime.

Something you won't be able to resist sharing."

"You won't get any."

"There will only be one plate," he says, and then quickly, as if calculated, Landon diverts his gaze from mine and leaves me gaping at the back of his head as he walks Thomas forward.

My balance is off from looking down, and Thomas shifts uncomfortably. I bring my focus back to the arena in front of us, between his ears and a few strides ahead, and try to center myself, to think only of his four legs hitting the ground, one at a time. But even my mindfulness work doesn't stop me from feeling fully, dizzyingly aware of Landon's calm presence, his steady hand on my horse's bridle. There is an intimacy to being led on horseback which I'm pretty sure I never noticed before. He's very much in charge of my safety right now. Landon could let go of the reins, or be rough with my horse and cause a problem, and so for this thing to work, I have to trust him to do the right thing for me.

That's a very big ask. I have to resist the urge to snatch the reins from his hand. With a few deep breaths, I manage to splay my fingers across Thomas's withers, opening them wide so that they can't clench and demand. They can only receive.

The arena is dotted with puddles, and as Thomas steps through a smallish one, I remember something about my horse that Landon doesn't know. He has...a little splashing game. It's nothing too serious for a rider; he doesn't drop down and roll or anything. He just has a lot of love for stomping in water.

There's a great big puddle of a lake on the other side of the arena, which I should probably warn Landon about, but...well, let's just see what happens. Most likely, he'll lead Thomas around it and nothing will happen. The anticipation is enough to take my mind off the mental image of Landon presenting me with a single plate, a delicate dessert to share.

"So, what should I be working on, coach?" I ask as we amble around the short end of the arena. I'm keeping my eyes up, towards the horizon, and the view is stunning. Low clouds, ragged and white, scoot beneath the gray tail of the distant storms, and a cool breeze arrives to ruffle the puddles. I'm not sure the rain is actually over for the day.

He looks over my position while I hold my breath and try to sit upright in the saddle, shoulders back and chin up, in a parody of perfect equitation. "Breathing," he decides after a moment, and I let out the air in my lungs with a big *woosh* of breath.

"Thank goodness you said so! I was wondering what I was doing wrong."

Landon laughs. "Fine, maybe I'm no riding instructor, but I'm pretty sure oxygen is an integral part of good equitation."

"Over-rated," I inform him. "I jump my best rounds while holding my breath."

"Are they really your best, or is that just what you tell your trainer?"

I grin, remembering the way my childhood coach, Lauren, would yell at me to breathe. "I'll tell you what I told my trainer. I started holding my breath over fences when I was fifteen and it's worked out for me so far."

"For ten whole years?"

"For *eighteen*—oh!" I laugh along with him. "Yes, for ten whole years. Thank you for noticing I am still only in my twenties."

"You could easily be in your twenties," Landon says, leading Thomas towards that big puddle. "Except for your brain."

"My brain?"

"Yeah. You have one."

"Oh! That's—that's a nice thing to say."

"I know." I can see his ears move; he's grinning.

We've reached the point of no return, lake-wise, and I steel myself for the moment Landon takes a step into this great big puddle—it takes up nearly half this side of the arena, with the jumps popping out of it like cypress trees in a flooded swamp. He's wearing waterproof boots, but nothing prepares him for Thomas's enthusiastic stomping. My silly horse swings his forelegs up high with each step, then brings his hooves crashing down in the water.

Landon gets soaked immediately and I'm hit with plenty of spray as well. I bend over his neck, convulsed with laughter, while Landon whoops and yells at Thomas to knock it off. But there's nothing he can do. There's nothing anyone can do to make this Thoroughbred live with *less* zest for life, and for him, puddles are the peak of perfection.

We're both *very* wet by the time we make it to the other side of the puddle, and Thomas is walking more quickly, a satisfied bounce to his stride.

"Wow, I really feel his motion!" I announce as blithely as possible. "This is such a forward walk!"

Landon stops the horse and looks up at me. "Madam, did you know he'd do that?"

I snort at the *madam* and shrug, indicating my innocence. "How could I know?"

"Because he's your horse and you live in Florida and I have reason to believe you've already encountered quite a few giant lakes with him?"

"Yes," I laugh, giving in without a fight. "I knew."

"Unbelievable." Landon shakes his head, but there's a grin

overtaking his face that he just can't resist. "You're pretty sassy, you know that?"

"I am," I chortle. "I'm so, so sassy."

"Lucky for you," Landon says, turning to walk Thomas forward again, "I like that in a woman."

And just like that, I stop laughing and start feeling hot all over again.

Now, though, I have to wonder if he knows exactly what he's doing.

Chapter Eighteen

YOU KNOW BETTER.

You KNOW better.

I look at myself in the mirror, then splash my face with cold water.

It doesn't help.

I've felt warm ever since our little lead-line ride, and at this point, I think a cold shower is my only option. I need to cool down my overheated lady-brain, because I am not thinking clearly. And it must be the heat, because it's not as if Landon has propositioned me or anything like that. He just...he only... he *simply* invited me to go to town with him for dinner.

And I'm very tempted to accept the invitation.

What's wrong with that? What's wrong with going to town with Landon for dinner? *Nothing,* says half my brain, while the other half insists that getting further involved with Landon, that having anything more than a little light workplace friendship, is a huge mistake that goes directly against my purposes in moving to this remote farm in the first place. I came here to get away from controlling, grasping, unacceptable-in-all-ways men, my contrary half of my brain continues bossily, and immediately jumping into this all-day, all-evening friendship with Landon is not the way to go about that. I need, my half-brain insists, a full detox from relationships of every kind, bad friendships and bad romances alike, not a work husband who tantalizes me with suggestive talk of desserts and completely unwarranted compliments.

Jeez, the other half of my brain sighs. *When you put it like that.*

So, that means no dinner out, I suppose.

And yet...I really want to go out to dinner.

It doesn't have to be because of *him.* I mean, I haven't even been off the farm yet. I've been here over a week, and now my senses are starting to wonder when this vacation from humanity is over, as if I have been at a spa on a tropical island instead of mucking stalls and scrubbing water buckets. Some senses don't seem to know what the other ones are up to, is what I mean. All they know is, it's time to go back home. Or at least go back out amongst other people, to eat food which wasn't badly prepared in a pan on a faulty stovetop.

Don't I deserve that much?

I do. And neither side of my brain can deny that.

I smirk at myself and leave the tiny bathroom, flicking out the light on the way. Since when do things work out the way I planned?

"But this time, it could be different," I say aloud. I've started talking to myself over the past week...honestly, I probably started back in West Palm, living alone in the condo. If I did back then, I didn't really notice at the time, maybe because so much sound permeated the sliding glass doors to the balcony. Boat sounds, airplane sounds, traffic sounds. Thunder from over the ocean, and illegal fireworks from along the beach. Laughter from drunk vacationers renting the neighboring condo on Airbnb. There was an all-hours buzz when living amongst so many other people; here, of course, that is replaced by the humming of insects, the drip of the ceiling leak, and the astonishing late-night screeching of the tree crickets.

Anyway, somewhere along the line, I started breaking the silence of living alone by talking to myself, and since I don't plan on living with anyone else ever again, that shouldn't be a problem now or in the future. I just need to be amongst other people every so often, so that I remember how to behave and don't completely leap off the crazy-lady deep end.

And with that logic, I decide, we can go to dinner. It won't be a problem. He's just a means to an end.

I slide on my boots at the door and head out to feed the horses their dinner. Landon's already in the aisle. He smiles at me.

My defenses waver and wobble.

Do better, Mackenzie.

"WHOA," I GASP, as we pull into the parking lot of a brightly lit retro diner. These are the most lights I have seen in a week, and after the miles of country dusk that we've driven to get here, they seem to blast the dark clouds into oblivion. "Where the hell are we?"

"Dinner," Landon replies, parking in the pink glow of a huge, neon-strip flamingo. The neon theme continues around the retro silver trim of the restaurant before giving way to hanging light bulbs strung above a large garden.

Wait, that's not a garden.

"*Mini* golf?" I say blankly.

"You don't like mini golf?"

"Of course, I do. I'm not a monster. I'm just confused—what

kind of restaurant is this? I thought we were in Back of Beyond, Florida. Not, like, Orlando." This place would look right at home on International Drive, the strip of themed restaurants and hotels in the middle of that tourist haven.

Landon smirks and unlocks the truck doors. "Trust me," he says, "we're not in Orlando."

Well, obviously. He insisted on doing the driving and took us to High Springs, a town about twenty minutes from the farm where he promised me a Winn-Dixie for filling my empty fridge and a few restaurants where we can eat beforehand, to make sure we don't go absolutely wild and buy everything in sight on our grocery run.

Judging by the size of the towns I'd passed on the drive north last week, I was expecting a run-of-the-mill country restaurant, smelling unappetizingly of fried pork chops wilting under hot lamps, or an overheated pizza joint with a few wobbly tables under some flickering lights. A gleaming diner with a mini-golf course is almost too much for my country-fried eyeballs to take in after so long on the farm.

"High Springs is a funny little town," Landon says, hopping out of the truck. He walks around and opens my door while I'm still fumbling with my seat-belt. "The springs and parks around here attract a lot of cave divers and hikers. They need something to do at night. And the granola crowd needs something to eat. The vegan menu at this place is pretty good."

"They allow vegans up here?" I joke, sliding out of the truck. Landon puts a steadying hand on my good shoulder and I stop myself from leaning into him.

"They allow all kinds," he says. "Even horse girls."

"Well, they probably shouldn't. We're very unpredictable."

"I always approach with my hand flat," Landon says, leading

me towards the restaurant. "In case they bite by accident."

"It's never by accident," I say.

He glances over his shoulder at me, his eyes twinkling beneath the string lights. "A good nip never did a man any harm."

I smile back at him, trying to ignore the screaming in my brain: *What does that mean? What does he mean? Is he flirting with you? Mackenzie, he's flirting with you!*

"No, he's not," I mutter, forgetting I'm not alone.

"What?"

"Nothing," I say quickly. Okay, talking to myself might have some repercussions if I can't control it in public.

The weather is nice enough to eat outside, even if it's a bit sticky. In Florida, stickiness is expected. We find ourselves at a patio table, where we're immediately visited by a chunky orange cat who looks as if dumpster diving is not his only means of survival. The cat rubs against my paddock boot—no, we did not shower or dress up for dinner, because that might have made this like a date, plus if I showered, I'd be ready for bed in no time flat—and then purrs like a rusty motorboat.

"You're *not* coming home with me," I tell the cat.

Landon leans back and surveys the kitty. "Always room for another barn cat," he suggests.

A waitress arrives with two ice waters just in time to hear Landon. She shakes her head and says, in a sharp country accent, "Vicious here already *has* a job. He's not fielding new offers."

"Vicious?" I ask incredulously, and run my knuckles over the cat's soft head. He gazes up at me worshipfully.

The waitress laughs. "You should see him with a mouse!"

"That's exactly why we should steal him," Landon whispers

loudly.

The waitress rests a hand on one jutting hip and surveys him for a moment. "You gonna be one of *those,* funny guy?"

He shakes his head meekly. "No, ma'am."

"Good." She grins, forgiving him easily, as I suspect most people do. "Now, what can I get y'all to eat?"

My heart longs for a massive burger with a mountain of French fries, but years of conditioning to watch my figure take control and I dutifully order a salad. Landon orders a Reuben and fries. "And you can't have any of my fries," he says as the waitress takes our menus and leaves.

"Not *any?* That seems ungentlemanly."

"A hardworking girl like you should be eating more than a salad," he says. "You're about to learn a valuable lesson about protein."

"Fries don't have protein," I argue.

"You know what I mean. Fries accompany meat. They help with the right carb to protein ratio. The golden ratio, if you will."

"I had no idea they taught food chemistry at farrier school," I gibe. "Did you do a semester abroad studying poetry, too?"

"Maybe I can't *quote* Tennyson," Landon says, leaning back in his chair. "But I can say I've read him."

"And?"

"Less punctuation than I'd like. I'm more of a thriller man, myself."

"Dick Francis," I guess. "All the racetrack murders a man can handle."

"For a start. When I was a teenager, I liked knowing there were other people living in the same crazy world I was, so I got kinda hooked on his stuff."

I raise my eyebrows and lean forward, leaning my good arm on the table. "What crazy world is that?"

He shrugs. "Not the mob, if that's what you're thinking."

"Well, I wasn't *before*."

"Repeat after me," Landon says. "There is no such thing as the mob."

"Isn't that what a mobster would say?"

"I guess you'll have to trust me," he says.

We stare at each other. I feel like I'm daring him to say something else. Anything else. A hint about his background, maybe, or else a question about mine. But instead, we just lock eyes and breath for breath, blink for blink. Neither of us seems willing or capable of more than just assessing the other person —for what?

For a lot of things, I guess. For compatibility, in all its forms.

I stare into his ridiculously blue eyes and imagine I can see his whole personality bared to me. Humor, kindness, gentleness. A person who can be relied on. How can all that be carried in the iris of a person's eye? Or is it about more than the eye itself—maybe I see the story of Landon's soul and values in the soft lines creasing at each corner, as if he spends a lot of time laughing; in the unhurried way he blinks, as if he has nothing urgent in his life to drag him away from the people and things he cares most about; in the smoothness of the skin beneath his eyes, as if he has no anxieties or regrets to keep him awake at night.

That must be nice.

I blink slowly, trying to remember what Ryan's eyes would say to me. But right now, the image in my mind of my husband of eight years is oddly blurry, hard to conjure up. Something is delaying the transmission.

Someone.

This has to stop.

I sit upright so quickly my chair rattles backwards, and I take advantage of the momentum to thrust myself to my feet. The chair topples backwards with a clatter that sends Vicious scurrying for cover, and for a moment, despite Jimmy Buffett warbling about Margaritaville over the speakers, it's the only sound on the patio. The other diners turn and look at me with concern.

"I'm fine," I say, holding up my free hand. "The sling is unrelated."

"Mackenzie? Are you okay?" Landon is sliding his own chair back, ready to stand up and help me. I already know what his steadying hands would feel like on my skin and so I can feel his touch, even with this table between us.

I want it.

A deep blush spreads across my face. I hope it just looks reddish from the glow of the neon flamingo hanging over the restaurant. Please, please, don't let Landon see how embarrassed I am. Please, please, let me stop caring about what he thinks of me at all...

This has to stop!

"I want a beer," I gabble, looking towards the bar across the patio. A few sunburned locals over there are bending the elbow, watching NASCAR and laughing loudly at each other's jokes. "Do you want a beer? Can I get you something?"

Landon runs a hand through his hair and sighs. "Yeah, I guess so," he says. "Something light. Coors is fine."

"Great," I say. "Great. I'll just go and get that."

"Okay," Landon replies, watching me closely. "Be careful. Don't knock over any more chairs."

I realize I'm making things weird and scoot across the patio, weaving through the half-empty tables and a wide, unlit fire-pit to the open side of the bar. "A Coors Light," I say to the bearded guy behind the bar. "And a Sierra Nevada."

He nods and dips his hand into the fridge behind him. "You got a tab with the kitchen?"

"No," I decide. "I'll pay." I dig out a silver credit card and slide it across the bar.

"Oooh," the bartender says, in that overly friendly way of a man who has been drinking on the job since his shift began three hours ago. "Getting you those airline miles."

I look at the card as he taps it against the reader, realizing that my days of platinum SkyMiles cards are probably numbered. Eventually, the credit bureaus will notice my personal net worth is now significantly less than it was when I was married. But even if the credit limits shrink, I keep the miles that have already added up.

It feels good to think about those miles, the way they can take me across the globe, leaving tracks behind me like the dotted line of a map in an Indiana Jones movie.

They could serve as a little escape route, maybe. Or just a safety valve, to release some steam, if things get too intense back at the farm.

I resist the urge to glance over my shoulder, but I can feel Landon's gaze on my back.

And I know that I shouldn't be able to *feel* something like that...but, it's there. Reminding me that somehow, despite all the miles I've put between myself and the man who tried to control me, I am still susceptible to the pull of a charismatic person.

"Yup," I agree as I take back the card. "Getting those miles."

* * *

"TELL ME ABOUT your horse," Landon says.

We've been eating in relative silence since the server put our food down. There's nothing quite like the hunger of a person who has worked in a barn all day. But now I put down my fork —I've already eaten all the chicken on my salad and the lettuce is just filling me with regret—and stare at him across the table.

Landon lifts an eyebrow. "Did I say something wrong?"

"No, of course not," I say, flustered. "I just...I don't know why this is so strange to me, but..."

Ryan never once asked about my horses. I could have just had a five-figure vet bill and dark smudges under my eyes from a sleepless night at the equine hospital and he wouldn't have asked about the horse. He'd have asked why the hell the horse cost him so much money, but that wasn't the same thing.

"Did you think we were going to talk about politics?" Landon asked, amused. "I suppose there's a lot to say about the weather."

"No, stop," I laugh, feeling ridiculous, but not ridiculed. If that makes sense. "I will tell you about my horse. Thomas is a six-year-old off-track Thoroughbred. I got him last year and we've been working towards the Thoroughbred Makeover since day one."

"Fascinating," Landon quips. "Be sure to leave out any interesting details."

"What do you want to know?"

"What would you tell a journalist, if you won your makeover thing?"

That's almost too scary to consider. If I *won*, if I spoke to a *journalist*? "I don't think about that," I tell him.

"You don't think about winning?"

"No! I don't want to get in my head about winning when just getting him there will be hard enough."

"There's a way to hold the idea of winning in your head, and being prepared to do it. That isn't the same as setting yourself up for disappointment," Landon says. "If you don't believe you can win, you probably can't."

"Are you a self-help guru, too, master farrier?"

He eyes me for a moment before saying, "I just don't like to see people run themselves down, that's all."

I look at my plate, the limp lettuce dripping with oil.

I should have gotten a burger. Heavy on the cheese and bacon. A pile of fries to douse in ketchup and, you know what, mayonnaise too, even if everyone thinks that's disgusting.

"Thomas is...special," I say slowly, thinking about my words. "If anyone believes we can win together, it's him."

"You should believe your horse," Landon says. "He sounds smart as hell."

Chapter Nineteen

I CALL CASEY as soon as I get the apartment door locked behind me and can get my laptop flipped open.

"Hey," she says, watching me as I gingerly set myself down on the sofa. "How's the arm?"

I texted her about the injury on the way home from the doctor the day it happened, but nothing since. That's weird in itself, I know—we're close friends, or we were, so why don't I know what to say to her since I moved away to work with horses full-time? Casey would get it more than anyone else. Oh, why pretend? I know that I'm not texting her because every text would be about Landon.

"It still hurts some," I admit, "but I have a nice fat pill to pop before bed so I can get some sleep."

"That's the dream." Casey caresses the head of a silky Australian shepherd who has just nosed his way into her lap. In the background, I see Brandon in her kitchen, making dinner.

"You're eating late," I observe.

"It stormed here from like, two until seven," Casey sighs. "I helped the girls get the horses fed and turned out. We were in the barn until nine."

"We had big storms today, too." I stop myself from getting

into it. I didn't call her to talk about the weather. It's June in Florida; we know the weather outside is frightful. With a gulp, I say what's on my mind: "Casey, I went to dinner with him tonight."

Her eyes widen; she leans forward, short hair slipping in front of her ears and falling down her cheekbones. "Not the farrier!" she gasps.

"Yup."

"Oh, my god. Mackenzie! That's huge."

"No. I needed some groceries and a break from the farm. He felt bad about the shoulder thing and wanted to drive me. It just made sense to get dinner since we were going all the way to town." Making it a grocery run adds a layer of innocence. We were just being practical. Saving gas.

"Listen to you, saying 'all the way to town' after a week in the boonies." Casey snorts. "But seriously, I thought he was a pain in the ass, always acting like he knows best?"

"He is, but he's also really knowledgeable and he likes sharing what he knows. He helped me ride Thomas today, too."

"Oh," Casey says, eyes rounding again. "Well, now we're getting serious."

"No," I say. "Come on. Let's not make this into something it isn't."

"If it isn't anything, why are you calling me?"

"Because you're my best friend? I thought?"

She smirks. "Okay, bestie, then I'm mad at you, because it has been radio silence since you got hurt. All I get is a text saying you dislocated your shoulder, and it's going to be fine in two weeks? Was I supposed to wait two weeks for an update?"

"No, it's just been..." I falter. It's just been what? I don't even know what I'm feeling, so how can I put it into words that

Casey will understand? "It's been a lot," I say at last. "Casey, I'm struggling a little with this whole situation."

"Ah." Casey pushes her hair behind her ears and rearranges her face to look serious. "If you're feeling any regrets, just remember, you were miserable down here and it wasn't going to get any better. Big change is hard, but—"

"I don't have any regrets," I blurt. "I'm just worried that it's not going to be like I thought."

"Well, it probably isn't," she says sensibly. "But why do you feel that way?"

Because of Landon. "Over-active imagination, I guess," I reply, copping out of being honest with her.

"Have you been riding?"

"I rode today."

"Well, that's good," she says, smiling encouragingly, like a kindergarten teacher praising my shapes. "You always feel better when you ride, right? How did it go with the arm? Did you like, stick to a round pen or something? Don't tell me you rode that green bean with one hand!"

"Someone led me," I mumble.

"Someone *led* you?" Casey rubs her dog's ears and gives me a thoughtful look. "Like who?"

"Landon." The syllables squeeze their way out.

Casey shakes her head. "He led you around the arena? He gave you a pony ride on your own horse. That is what you're saying to me."

"Don't make it something it's not. It's Landon's fault I got hurt in the first place—"

"I thought you said it was your fault for letting a horse get loose—"

"It was *his* horse, dammit!"

185

Casey blinks at me. "Okay, okay. I'm sorry."

I'm embarrassed by my outburst. "No, I am. That was uncalled for. I'm just tired."

"Of course you are," Casey says comfortingly. "It's very late for us. Why don't you just get yourself into bed and take your fun pill and have a nice night's sleep, and text me tomorrow, okay?"

"Yeah, okay," I mumble.

"And dream about Landon."

I shake my head at her. "You have to stop."

"I'm sorry," Casey sighs, but she's not sorry; she's really holding back laughter. "I'll stop, really!"

"I'm hanging up now."

"Bye, Mackenzie! Be good! Don't do anything I wouldn't—"

I close the laptop, shaking my head. Don't do anything Casey wouldn't do? I'm already copying her life the best that I can. She's not the first woman in south Florida to run away from her real life to play with ponies. She's just the first woman I've known who was so successful at it. Sure, there were some missteps along the way, but now Casey has a great life on a gorgeous horse farm. Of course, I'd like to follow in her footsteps.

I sigh and look around my tired little apartment. Somehow, my path seems very different from hers.

THOMAS THE TANK *Engine's Training Diary*

June...oh, whatever...

Thomas had three days off while I recovered from my shoulder accident and I was getting freaked out about his missing work, but honestly? He did really well. Splashing Landon with water was kind of the highlight. If there was a division for silly splish-splash tricks at the Makeover, he'd be a shoo-in for first.

Sometimes I wonder why the Makeover is this huge, important goal that keeps me awake at night. Kayla and Basil are at a horse show this weekend. In the middle of June, in Florida, they are riding in air-conditioned indoor arenas and facing top competition. What I mean is, there are plenty of other options for Thomas and me. We could skip the Makeover and pick an easier goal for our first year together. We could just show locally and then go to Ocala this winter. Or in fall. Whenever we want. Florida has horse shows literally all the time.

The Makeover is just this huge, looming presence in my life. It's probably too stressful. I know I would wake up in the middle of the night less often if I wasn't still trying to get there.

But I can't imagine pulling out of it, either. Why is that? Maybe it's just because the Makeover isn't about winning or losing...it's about getting there. It's about taking a horse who has only known one way of life and giving him the education he needs to take the next step on a new version. We get less than a year to train them for the Makeover. But everything he learns this year will be valuable for the rest of his life.

Oh, my god, is the Makeover about Thomas, or is it about me?

Ugh. I'm going to bed.

Chapter Twenty

THE NEXT MORNING comes too soon—well, it feels too soon, but actually I have overslept. The rattle of buckets in the aisle makes my eyes fly open. *Loose horses!* I think, and then, as I throw back my sheet, I realize that I'd hear horseshoes on the aisle if the horses were out there, making a mess. Nope. I check my phone and realize it's past seven-thirty, and I forgot to set my alarm last night.

Which means Landon is out there, feeding breakfast alone.

"It's not your job," I groan, staggering out of bed. "Please stop doing my job for me, Landon. Please, please, please. Why won't you just wake me up and yell at me for oversleeping like a normal—"

Rap, rap, rap rings out from my door.

Still standing in my bedroom, I stare into the living room as if I can see around the corner and right through the steel door. Is he actually going to yell at me? Look, maybe I was thinking it, but if he really does—

A gruff voice, muffled by metal, floats through the door. "Mackenzie? You okay in there?"

I look down at my t-shirt and boxer shorts, run a hand through my mussed hair, and sigh.

He's just checking on me. Not yelling. Reluctantly, I walk over to the door.

"Hey, Landon," I say as I open up. "I'm really sorry, I forgot to set—"

Landon, looming on the threshold, looks down at me and starts laughing.

"What?" I cross my arms over my chest and scowl up at him. It's too early for this much hilarity. "What are you laughing at?"

"You're a mess," he chuckles. "You were still asleep? Thank goodness. I was afraid maybe you slipped and fell in the shower last night. I was mad at myself for not checking on you, and then I realized I don't have your phone number. I didn't want to wake you if that was all it was, but...well...I couldn't get the idea out of my head, so..."

He shrugs for punctuation.

I stare at him until he stops laughing. Then I demand, incredulous, "You thought I fell in the shower? What am I, on my deathbed?"

"Well, you said you lose your balance easily with your arm in that sling," he says reasonably.

That's true. I did say that. At the time, I was turning in rapid half-circles, bending at the waist and straightening again quickly, but I *did* say that. And for some reason, he registered it as a valid concern about my ability to stay upright. Softening, I say, "Okay, well, um, thanks. I didn't. I just stayed up too late and forgot to set my alarm."

"Sorry I kept you out so late," he says, a grin sliding into place.

I'm starting to think a friendly grin is his habitual expression. I can't remember the last time I saw a man smile as much as Landon.

"I needed the change of scenery—and the groceries—so you're forgiven. This time." I add a smile of my own.

"Okay, well...can I get your phone number, please? So I can set my mind at ease when I have crazy thoughts like that?"

"You want to text me every night to make sure I don't fall in the shower?"

"Or you can text me, if that's easier."

I really think he's serious. He *looks* serious. The grin has slipped somewhat, and a small line has found its way between his brows.

"I'm not really in the habit of falling in the shower," I say, "but fine. Let me get my phone and I'll send you a message so you have my number."

I come back with my phone and wait for him to say his number aloud. This is such a normal ritual in every social setting I've been in, I don't feel like I have to tell him the routine.

But Landon doesn't say anything.

My eyes lift curiously from my phone screen to his face, and I realize that he's looking down.

Not at his phone, but at my chest.

Hello? I feel something between shock and stimulus, an all-over tingle that buzzes from my toes to the tip of my nose. With an effort, I clear my throat, and Landon's chin comes up immediately, his gaze meeting my astonished one.

"Uh," he fumbles. His cheeks seem to turn fire-engine red all at once, faster than anyone should be able to blush. "Your shirt..."

And it's my turn to blush. I glance down, and wonder why in god's name I put this shirt on last night.

White, with a peeling decal of a jumping horse on it, the shirt had been my favorite when I was a teenager. Now it's too tight, too thin, and full of holes, but I still pull it on when I want to get that buzzy horse show high going, the one that makes me feel like a kid with my whole life ahead of me. I guess working on my training diary before bed put me in that headspace, or maybe...I'm remembering now what I wrote...I felt like I needed to get into that headspace, because I stopped writing about Thomas and started writing about myself.

Something stupid about needing the Thoroughbred Makeover for myself, not for Thomas? And then, as I brushed my teeth, I'd looked at myself in the mirror and thought: *the last thing I need to do is make this about me, not my horse.* I'd dug out the t-shirt as a sort of talisman, to conjure up my teenage self. I'd even flexed in the mirror! But this shirt is not fit for anyone else's eyes.

Especially not my farrier/coworker/neighbor across the barn aisle.

Judging by how hot my cheeks are, my blush must match Landon's. Without another thought in my brain besides escape, I take a quick step backwards and slam the door shut, then stare at it, as if the door's the one at fault here.

Then I rip off the shirt so violently that the tatty fabric just gives up, shredding in my hands. I look at it for a moment, the remains of the jumping horse decal that used to be so inspirational. I was easier to impress back then, I guess.

"Goodbye, jumper shirt," I sigh, tossing it into the trash bin as I walk back to my bedroom to find something more suitable for work.

I HEAD BACK outside wearing one of my brightest outfits.

It's dominated by a sun-shirt in rich cornflower blue with floral-patterned sleeves. The flowers are yellow, blue, and purple; my riding tights are the same purple as the flowers. The pockets and belt loops are trimmed with the floral pattern. I'm still waiting for socks to come in the same pattern; the manufacturer I ordered from is notoriously slow, but the quality is supposed to be impressive. I think they've been on a ship from China for about eight months now.

Landon walks in two horses, giving me a nod as he passes, and I think he won't mention my costume change. But once he's closed the doors on the horses, he strolls back up to me and says, "Look at you now."

I don't know what that means, so I decide to take it as a compliment and preen a little, cupping my hand at my chin. "You like it? I call this design Chelsea, like the flower show."

"You name your outfits?"

"I *designed* it," I say haughtily.

He lifts an eyebrow. "You're a clothing designer, too? A fashion mogul?"

"Not really," I say, dropping the act. "I have a few riding outfits I've designed. This one, the purple one from yesterday." I let my words trail off, hoping he'll make a remark about how pretty the purple outfit was. But it doesn't seem to register with him. Sighing a little, I go on, "Eventually I'm hoping to start a little company of my own, but I'll need more seed money than what I've got at the moment. It seemed to make some sense to wear my own designs for a little while, though, in case they start some buzz."

"Any luck yet?"

I shrug. "It's a crowded space. I probably should have ordered the clothes before I got out of my marriage, and set up a store I could promote with my Instagram or something. But you know...I wanted to do one thing on my own. Maybe that was stupid."

Landon gives me a thoughtful look. "I don't think that's stupid," he says eventually. "Making your dreams come true with other people's money isn't everything it's cracked up to be."

"It's probably the number one way to actually start a business, though," I counter.

"Well then," he says, "start your business the number two way. Number two ain't bad."

"Better than last, I suppose."

"Now you're thinking." He glances down at my outfit again, and I feel my blush creeping back to my cheeks. Landon has now seen me practically topless. What's he thinking right now?

Abruptly, he wheels away and heads for the barn door. "Gotta finish getting in horses," he says.

I watch him walk into the sunny morning, a silhouette against the vibrant pastures.

Personally, I'm too embarrassed to ever move again, but good on him for getting back to work.

"Thomas is waiting for you at the gate," he calls out. "I left him for you."

"Thank you!" Thomas will make me feel better. Thomas has never seen me in a see-through shirt, and even if he did, he wouldn't be weirded out by it. Horses are better than people, Reason Number 1,045: you cannot be embarrassed by them, and they're never embarrassed by you.

My cute little horse is waiting at the gate for me with pricked ears, his white spot gleaming. That's the *only* part of him that is gleaming. The rest is coated in gray-white sand, because someone has been rolling in the mud for what appears to be the better part of his fourteen hours spent outside.

I slip the halter strap behind his ears and sand cascades down on my face, getting in my eyes.

"You're a monster," I inform him.

Thomas responds by rubbing his face hard on my chest, probably because he's itchy from being *completely covered in sand,* and the halter buckle catches on the zipper of my shirt. When I hear the sound of ripping fabric, I don't panic, don't jump backwards. I just nod to myself in resignation. Of *course* he has ripped the chest of my shirt wide open.

Horses will destroy your life, Reason Number 62,549: they act like they love you, but you're really just a scratching post that dispenses feed.

Clutching both sides of my poor, mangled Chelsea shirt together, I walk Thomas into the barn. And, before Landon even has time to wonder why I'm flashing him for the second time this morning, I go straight back into my apartment and slam the door.

I'll come back out after coffee. Things always look less ridiculous after coffee, right?

Chapter Twenty-One

LANDON WISELY DOES not say anything about my double-flashing situation, and the day proceeds at a more normal pace. Horses eat their breakfast and then go back outside. The aisle is swept, and then, since the trainers are away, the mice can play. Or rather, they can sit around and drink coffee, which is how adults play when they're at work with no supervision.

I decide to make it a sharing session.

"So, where in Kentucky are you from?" I ask Landon with practiced casualness, slouching into a canvas chair in the tack room. My tumbler is full of hot, sweet coffee and the air conditioner is running full-blast, blowing cold air straight onto my face. It's a proven combination for summer refreshment.

Landon's filling his own tumbler, his back to me. But I see his shoulders stiffen, as if my question is immediately too intimate.

"Just some small town," he says, adding creamer from the cabinet of coffee fixings.

"I've been to Kentucky before. Try me."

"You wouldn't know it." Landon turns, mug in hand. "Barely a wide spot on the road. Not worth talking about."

He looks down at his coffee.

Something in me stirs. Casey has said before that I have a naughty little habit of digging when people don't want to volunteer information. I can't say why, but when I feel like someone's keeping something from me, all I want is to pry it out of them. It made my marriage very contentious, even when things seemed to be going well. I ask, "Is it close to somewhere I'd know? Louisville? Lexington?"

His face shifts subtly. "Not really," he says.

He's lying.

Look, I know all about lying men. I was married to one. And I lived in a world where socialites buy million-dollar horses just to have an excuse to sleep with their trainer. Lying is a language I am *fluent* in, thanks very much.

And I don't appreciate it from him. Not when we've been getting along the past couple of days. Not when he helped with my horse's hooves or led me around the arena or took me to dinner. Not when he lives right across the barn aisle from me and could be *anyone*.

Who else has he been lying to? He could be a murderer! Kayla and Basil have no idea who this guy really is, do they? Just a secretive farrier who wants to live in the wilds of north Florida so he can perfect his hoof care product line. Oh-ho-ho, a likely story! I draw my knees up to my chest, balancing my heels against the edge of the chair-seat. The canvas stretches in a taut line beneath me. He's just like Ryan and all the rest of them, pretending to be nice until they've got a woman locked down, right where they want them. If he had nothing to hide, he'd have plenty to say.

"You know what I think?" I demand, suddenly furious with all men, and Landon in particular. "I think you're not even from Kentucky."

To my extreme irritation, Landon laughs.

He laughs and his eyes crinkle up at the corners, adorable crows-feet framing his beautiful blue eyes.

I hate him.

A beautiful liar is the very worst kind.

"Don't laugh at me!" I scold. "You're lying to me. You think I can't tell? I'm from West Palm *Beach*. Those crazy people *invented* lying about their past."

His laughter fades into a chuckle. "That's a good point," he says. "In fact, I think I've seen you in the background of some *Real Housewives* shots."

"You've never seen *Real Housewives*."

"How do you know that?"

"Because I can tell when you're lying." And because there's nothing about this man that would find entertainment in the orchestrated arguments of taut, breakable millionaires. What if I have been in the background of a *Real Housewives* shot? I probably have been. What difference does it make? He's trying to change the subject. I tell him, "You're just being deflective now."

He's still amused. "Is that a word?"

"Close enough."

Landon sighs and the smile falls away from his face, like he has finally realized that I'm not going to play with his cute little "You've never heard of it," roundabouts. "If I told you where I'm from, I'd probably have to tell you a lot of other stuff, too," he says. "And it's just not anything I feel like getting into right now. So why don't we just leave it with Kentucky for now?"

"If you apologize for lying," I say, crossing my arms over my chest.

It won't be good enough for me to suddenly start trusting him, but I'd appreciate the apology.

"Fine," Landon says. "I apologize for lying."

"And being a pain in the neck about a simple question," I continue.

"Hey!"

I shrug. "All of this could have been avoided, but you chose lying."

"Fine. Sorry I was a pain in the neck about a simple question. Is that good? Can we be good now?"

I consider him for a moment. He gives me a puppy-dog look. It's so at odds with his height and broad shoulders that I can't help bursting into a rebellious peal of laughter. Can I like him, even if I don't trust him? I suppose so.

"Dork," I say, letting my feet fall from the chair. "We're good now."

But we aren't, not really. Because now I know for sure that he has a secret. And people are welcome to have secrets, of course, but when it's about their past and they are a large man sharing a roof with me out in the dark, empty countryside, I can't let that go unnoticed.

AFTER COFFEE, LANDON decides that he can give me a riding lesson in the round pen. He announces this with no input or, indeed, requests on my part. "I'll put Thomas on the lunge line so that I can whoa him down if you need me to," he says. "Sound good?"

I consider the idea for a moment. "Actually, yeah. It sounds fun," I decide. I'm used to the sling and doing things one-handed at this point.

The round pen is just forty feet in diameter, with high

wooden walls so that a horse can't get any ideas about jumping out. It's not something Kayla or Basil seem to use in their training program; the door hinges whine and resist when Landon pulls it open, and the footing is mostly covered with grass. But there aren't any holes or loose boards, so it seems safe enough to trot around for a while.

Thomas snorts and blows as I ride him in, eyeing the high walls with suspicion. "You've been in a round pen before, sir," I remind him, patting his neck. "We restarted you in one of these things, down in Wellington."

"Did you do his transition from racing yourself?" Landon asks, positioning himself in the center of the round pen.

"I did. That's part of the Thoroughbred Makeover—doing the work yourself. I rode a few off-track Thoroughbreds back when I was a kid, and I always liked them. When I wanted a project for myself and this cute pony turned up, I knew it was time to see what I remembered."

"Pretty bold of you."

I shrug at his compliment. I wouldn't say I feel *bold*. I just feel like a horse girl. These are the things we do—we find ex-racehorses and figure if we could do it when we were teenagers, we can do it now. "He's a quiet horse," I say. "I got him from some friends, too, so it wasn't like I just picked up a horse without knowing his history."

Thomas walks quickly along the circumference of the pen, his head still high and his breath coming hard and fast. He's trying to see out, as if he's offended we've closed him off from the outside world.

"And you started him in..."

"Winter," I say. "Six months ago."

"Oh, well, that's pretty good. He's ready to show now, isn't he?"

"At a local show, for sure. I need to talk to Kayla about that, actually." Since I started working and discovered the scope of the job, I have been a little worried I won't be able to find a couple Saturdays free to take Thomas to a show in the area. He needs to get experience at horse shows or our trip to Kentucky will be way too much for his little brain to handle. It often takes a few trailer rides off the farm before ex-racehorses understand that a horse show is not the same as a horse race. "The last time Thomas heard a loudspeaker was when we were trail-riding close to a show in Wellington," I recall.

"How did that go?"

"Well, we beat everyone else back to the barn."

He laughs.

"So, we definitely need some schooling show experience before October. Preferably a few shows."

"We can find you some shows."

I wonder why he says *we*. Does he think he's part of my team now? Did I somehow miss the part where I asked him to be my training assistant? But Landon does this, doesn't he? He just insinuates himself into things. He just started helping with the barn work. He just pulled out his tools and tacked Thomas's shoes back on. He just decided he would help me ride while my arm is in a sling.

It's like he can't stop himself from being helpful. I probably shouldn't find it annoying; I'm sure it's a pain and a half to live with.

Thomas feels more settled in the round pen now, but he's still walking awfully fast, so I nudge him into a trot. Sometimes it's easier to just let him move out rather than trying to mold him into the perfect warm-up. Once he's gotten his wiggles out, he finds it easier to focus on our work. Some days, that takes ten minutes. Some days, it takes three-quarters of an hour. That's the joy of a hot-blooded Thoroughbred, but I wouldn't want him any other way.

As his pace quickens, sand flings up against the fence boards, giving him something to worry about. He tosses his head and ducks against the bit, prepping to go faster. With just one hand on the reins, his weight tips me forward. Thomas takes the advantage and springs into a canter.

"Hey!" I snap, ineffectually trying to get my seat back in the saddle. Thomas hunches up, annoyed with the tiny circle this pen forces him into and for a moment I think he's going to buck. Thomas *never* bucks. Now would not be a good time to start.

"Whoa, whoa, easy, buddy," Landon calls, turning his body quickly so that he's always just ahead of Thomas's shoulder. He holds both arms out, and even though he's not in front of Thomas's path, his body language is enough to slow the horse. Thomas snorts and comes down to a prancing walk, his head bobbing up and down.

I laugh shakily. "How about that lunge line?"

With the line clipped to Thomas's bridle, I feel a little better about my lack of control through the bit. In an ideal world, Thomas would be very attentive to my seat and my reins would be more of a backup system...but that kind of responsiveness takes time to attain, and we aren't even close yet.

Landon turns slowly as Thomas trots around him. I can feel his gaze on me, appraising my position.

"Is there something you want to say?" I demand.

"Lift your chin," he says. "I know your horse is cute, but stop staring down at him."

"Oh, dammit." He's right. For some reason, human brains are hard-wired to look down at our horse's neck and head while we train. And it does no one any good. "Look at the ground and that's where you'll end up," is the old trainer-saying.

Or, alternatively, one I heard at a horse show last year: "It's scientifically proven that if you look down, you're a bad person."

Trainers will resort to almost anything to get their students looking up.

I manage to keep my eyes up for several rounds of the pen; every time my gaze dips, my chin does, too, and Landon calls me out on it. With my head held high, I can see over the walls of the round pen, so when a flash of movement near the end of the barn catches my eye, I stop rising to the trot and sit down to slow Thomas.

"What is it?" Landon asks, reeling in the lunge line as Thomas turns towards him.

"I saw something run into the barn aisle," I say. "It was little. Do we have a small white cat running around here? Smaller than Shadow?

"I guess we might. Not that I've seen, though."

"Huh. Guess it might—" I hold up a hand, startled. "Did you hear that?"

"No." Landon strokes Thomas's nose, and the horse sighs into his palm, utterly relaxed. "Maybe it's—"

Then we both hear it at the same time.

Yap! Yap-yap-yap-yap!

"There's a dog in the barn!" I say, dismayed, just as Landon says, "Sounds like a dog!"

Thomas snorts as if he is also very displeased to know about a stray dog in his home.

"Luckily, it sounds small," Landon observes. The dog is still yapping.

"But maybe not good with horses."

"Want to wait here while I check?"

"Yes, please. I'll be fine."

Landon unsnaps the lunge line and takes it with him as he leaves the round pen, closing the door behind him. The dog keeps yapping and then, abruptly, there is silence.

Thomas walks in a nervous circle, his ears pricked towards the barn. When Landon reappears in the barn door, Thomas can't see him, but I can.

He's holding a small white dog in the crook of one arm.

It's wriggling wildly and doing its best to lick his face.

"Vicious," Landon calls, waving his free arm. "Send help!"

Chapter Twenty-Two

HE CALLS THE dog Sid, after the bad kid in "Toy Story." It doesn't matter how many times I suggest naming a stray dog after a villainous child who disfigures toys might be a bad idea...Landon thinks it suits the little dog. Okay, the dog *does* have a spot over one eye, like Sid's bull terrier. But they're patently not the same breed. Sid is tiny, lithe, and has the smooth, dished face of a hunting beagle. Also, the lust for life and endless energy that you'd expect with a dog of his ilk.

Sid becomes part of our daily life immediately; it's as if he's always lived here. He's not the best behaved dog—I mean, otherwise the name wouldn't stick so easily. He steals polo wraps from the laundry basket and leaves them trailing across the grass lawn outside the barn. He pukes up hoof trimmings after Landon works on hooves. He tears into trash bags and scatters food wrappers around the barn aisle.

But for some reason, we all love him. Even me.

Kayla is crazy about the little hound, to the point where she tries to claim him for herself—"Landon, I know you're too busy for this dog, so why don't I just take him back to the house with me tonight..."—but Landon is adamant. The dog is his.

Well, actually, the dog belongs to a hay farmer whose property neighbors the farm. We find out that morsel in late June, as early firecrackers pop from a hamlet in the distance.

"What?" Landon stares at our vet, who is carelessly peeling off a very dirty disposable glove. "You're kidding."

Dr. Ramsay shakes her head and tosses the glove into the trash can by the tack room door. "I was just down at Vince Funk's place. He says that one of their barn dogs disappeared last week. A hunting beagle, mostly white, kinda runty." She gives Sid an ear-scratch, and the dog leans into her fingers with a contented expression. "But you know, I never saw this dog before."

"You mean, you never saw this dog at Vince's place?" I repeat, confused.

Landon and Dr. Ramsay give me penetrating looks. The vet repeats, "I never saw this dog before."

"Got it." I'm not completely sure I do, but fair enough. We aren't telling the neighbor about Sid.

"Keep him close and Vince'll forget all about it after a while," Dr. Ramsay says to Landon. "He's got a dozen dogs and he won't fix any of them. He's always putting puppies in people's trucks and hoping they won't bring them back. You drop off this mutt with me for a little nip of the old balls, and we won't have a problem."

"Hear that?" Landon asks the hound, who is wagging his tail happily. "We're gonna have to do some family planning if you want to stay here. Sorry. I don't make the rules."

"It's that or back to the cow barn for you," Dr. Ramsay tells Sid. "You won't feel a thing."

Sid licks her hand enthusiastically.

"Oh, Sid prefers my sofa to sleeping in a barn," Landon

assures her. "He'll give up his balls for the right to continue living on cushions."

After the vet leaves, Landon holds an emergency meeting in the tack room. Kayla and Basil don't care for Vince the hay farmer, either, it turns out. I feel lucky I've never met him.

"You are," Kayla says, rolling her eyes. "He thinks we're snobs because we feed our horses alfalfa and orchard grass instead of his hay."

"We kind of are," Basil says. "I mean...aren't we?"

"Maybe." Kayla shrugs. "But he doesn't have to be rude about it."

"One time," Basil tells me, "he cut in front of her at the Winn-Dixie checkout."

"It was the *express* line," Kayla says, backing him up, "and he had *twelve* items. That's two more than what's allowed. He did it on purpose."

"I'm going to ride," Basil announces, standing up. "Come with me?"

Their horses are already tacked up and waiting in the aisle, so I stay in the tack room after they leave, soaking up the last few minutes of air conditioning before I head out to pick the empty stalls. Landon is still leaning over Sid, rubbing the dog's silky white ears like they're lucky amulets.

"You missed having a dog, huh?" I guess. "You've been crazy about him since he showed up."

Landon grins, still stroking Sid's ears. "I sure did. Haven't had a dog in years."

"Maybe, when you said I ought to have a dog, you were talking about yourself."

"You should have one, too." He glances up at me. "Pretty girl like you ought to have a German shepherd at her side. Or a wolf hybrid. I know a guy."

"I am not getting a wolf," I say determinedly, although the idea is a little alluring, the way many bad ideas can be. Also, did he just call me a pretty girl? He's about ten years too late for the *girl*, but it's okay being called pretty once in a while...by a friend.

And yeah, it's becoming apparent to me that Landon is now my friend.

I still have reservations about him, because I know he's hiding something from me and I think I've been pretty open about my history with him. But I'm no longer furious that there's a man living in the barn with me.

He's good company, and he's been good to me.

"I guess you'll forget all about me now that you have Sid in your life," I say, sliding off my chair. I better get out and start mucking. "Well, it was nice while it lasted."

"We had a good run," Landon agrees, but now he's smirking down at his dog. "See you around, I guess."

I head out and pick up a manure fork, toss it into a wheelbarrow, and push them both down to the closest empty stall. Feather was only in her stall for a few hours this morning, and yet it somehow looks as if she's spent several months destroying it. That mare has real talent. I sigh and head in to do battle with the mess.

But despite the less-than-ideal conditions, I have a smile on my face.

And I know it's because the scene I just left in the tack room was so darned cute.

Something about a man and his dog just tugs at my heartstrings. We had a dog when I was a kid. Well, my dad and I had a dog, but Lucy was really all my dad's. The lumbering yellow Lab was uncertain of me throughout my childhood, clearly remembering that when I was a toddler, I pulled tails and yanked on ears. Apparently, more than once when I was learning to walk, I used Lucy's head as a support and hauled myself to my feet with her long-suffering face as my anchor. As a fine, upstanding member of the Labrador retriever nation, she was not about to punish a baby for such behavior...but she was understandably wary of me from that time on.

Lucy went to her doggie reward in the sky when I was twelve, and we didn't get another dog after that. A dog was something else I would have to take care of, and in my teen years, my riding career was the most important thing in my life. I was barely even at home most of the time. I was always at the barn. And maybe Dad didn't want to replace Lucy. Even though my dad never pushed the idea of adopting another dog, he always kept a picture of Lucy on his desk in the home office.

Right next to a picture of me with my first pony.

I sniff, wondering how my dad is doing right now. He was disappointed when I left south Florida. Disappointed, but understanding. Obviously, I didn't want to come home and stay with him, although the invitation had been extended once it was clear Ryan and I were not going to stay together. He split with my mom when I was in my early twenties, and now he's seeing someone else, an energetic real estate agent named Sunny. She makes a good living, and they don't need each other for money, which means they can take things slow and casual... ideal for my dad, who doesn't always remember things like dates, or dinner, or going home from the office before nine at night.

"For the Sunshine State of your dreams, call Sunny!" ads are plastered in high-end magazines all winter, every winter, and who knows...maybe they'll get a dog together. Something tasteful, that won't shed too much on Sunny's power suits. I'd be okay with that. I'd be fine with someone like Sunny taking care of my dad. Since I can't do it anymore.

"You look sad, horse girl," Landon observes, leaning against the door-frame.

I rearrange my face, which must have been teetering on the wistful side of things, and expertly toss manure into the wheelbarrow from across the stall. "How can I be sad when I am living the dream and working with such skill?"

"Beats me. Listen, I gotta run into town tonight and get Sid some stuff. Food and things. I can't feed him hamburgers every night. You want to come with, grab some dinner?"

I turn away so he can't see the surprise on my face. Dinner together, again? It's been two weeks since we went to the diner together. I can't say I'm not tempted, but... "I better not," I say. "Saving money is a hard job, but someone's gotta do it."

"Oh, come on. You have to know it's my treat. I *asked* you."

"You can't buy me dinner," I scoff. "Absolutely not."

"The hell I can't. Have you *seen* what a good farrier I am? I make a very good living, madam. Don't turn down my offer to spoil you."

Now he wants to spoil me? Oh, boy. "Landon, seriously, thank you, but I bought groceries a few days ago and I don't want them to go to waste." I drove to Winn-Dixie and did the shopping after work and riding. It was awfully tedious. I miss grocery delivery.

"You're worried your frozen vegetables will go bad? I've seen your grocery cart, woman. We went shopping together a couple of weeks ago, remember?"

We did. And what an intimate thing that is to do. But it's

not like I had a choice. I couldn't really drive myself, or push a cart with one hand.

And anyway, I had fun. That's more than I can say about the trip I made alone.

"Fine," I sigh. "You wore me down. Are you happy now?"

"Yes," Landon says gleefully. "Very happy."

AFTER THE HORSES have been fed and we're showered and soap-scented, we drive through a hot and steamy evening. Landon points the truck towards Gainesville. The university town is crammed with traffic during the school year, but the parking lots around the shopping malls are weirdly empty in summer, and the big-box pet store Landon leads me to is basically the kingdom of a single cashier and several dozen lizards in terrariums. Sid trots happily beside us, with a lead-rope for a leash and collar combined. The cashier flicks away at his phone while we giggle and paw through the dog aisles.

"This one," I declare, pulling out a crystal-studded leather collar. "Sid looks like a dressage queen to me."

"How dare you, woman," Landon rumbles. "This fine hound-dog wouldn't be caught dead in diamonds. Would you, Sid?" And he takes down a plain leather collar with a dull nickel buckle. "How about this? Nice and understated."

"That's shameful, Landon! At least get him something with brass. He's living on a horse farm, for heaven's sake." I rummage through the collars on display, but there's really nothing as nice as what I'm looking for. "We should order him one from this leather shop in Kentucky that I know. Just get him something cheap for now and I'll send you the website. Or maybe you know it? Bergen's Leather? They're kind of the gold standard for leather work—"

I realize I've been chattering without a single sound from Landon and look over at him.

He's staring at the collars with a weirdly intense look on his face.

Like there's something he'd like to say, and he's doing his best to hold it in.

"Is something wrong?" I ask, putting a cautious hand to my chest, my neck, my hair. All the places where a woman might have something seriously embarrassing going on.

"No," Landon says tightly. Then he grabs a collar with a Hawaiian print—big red flowers, tropical green leaves. "I think Sid would like this one."

"Yeah," I say, watching him closely. Something's up. Something's not right.

"Let's grab him some dog food and go get dinner, okay? I'm starving."

Landon walks away from me, his hound trotting happily at his side, the tacky Hawaiian print collar dangling from his hand like he's already forgotten it's there.

LANDON TAKES ME to dinner at a local brewery with a wide deck overlooking a beautiful round pond. We get fried chicken sandwiches with slaw and fries from a food truck and a couple of beers from the taproom, then sit at a picnic table to eat. An alligator slowly glides across the pond. Beneath the table, Sid chews contentedly on a stuffed plush duck, slowly tugging its fluffy guts out through a pin-sized hole he has made in the toy's back. He smacks his lips to get the fuzz off his tongue and mouth, then goes back in for more, a look of pure contentment on his face.

"Hounds are so destructive," Landon says, watching his

canine companion with a pleased smile on his face.

The weirdness he showed me back in the pet store is gone. But I know I didn't make it up. I said something wrong.

Kentucky? It has to be Kentucky, right? He won't tell me what town, or even what part of the state, he's from. There's something weird going on with this guy and his home.

Well, join the club, mister. We're all just out here running from our past, aren't we? Like Thoroughbreds, we just run and run from our prior lives, looking for our forever homes.

That's downright poetic. Might be the beer, though.

I'd like to bring it up again, but we're almost an hour from home, and I don't want to risk making the truck ride back to the farm a weird, silent ordeal. So I start talking about the Thoroughbred Makeover instead, all my plans for Thomas, and Landon listens with interest.

"It's a pretty big show," he says. "I know you said you're going to take him to some local shows...think that'll be enough to get him ready for the atmosphere there?"

"I have to hope so. It's hard to find a big show in Florida in summer, though."

"There's Legends," Landon says.

"Legends *Equestrian* Center?" I laugh, shaking my head. "I can't take him there. That place is a horse show factory on steroids."

"Most people say it's like Disneyland for horses, but I like your description better."

"Either way. It costs a fortune just to walk in the door with a horse. The show fees are hundreds of dollars, there's stabling fees, office fees—"

"They have a schooling weekend coming up," he says. "Forty bucks to ship in and ride in the arenas for the day. Kayla told me it's packed every time. There are a couple of them this summer. That's what you need. Do an easy local horse show first, then the Legends schooling day a few times, and he'll be ready for anything."

It's a good idea. I don't even have to mull it over to know Landon's figured out the best path for acclimating Thomas to large horse shows this summer. But I'm borderline excited/horrified at the idea of taking Thomas to the three-ring circus that is Legends Equestrian Center. Actually, just to be accurate, it's more like a twelve-ring circus. There are always horse shows going on at Legends—*always*. Horse shows in the indoor arenas, in the outdoor arenas, in the Grand Prix jumping arena that sits like a bowl beneath the towering edifice of the hotel and the grandstands.

But Landon's right...from everything I know about the Thoroughbred Makeover, held at the sprawling Kentucky Horse Park, it will be just as chaotic and busy as a show weekend at Legends.

It's the perfect place to prep him for the Makeover environment. And myself, too.

"Now I just have to figure out getting some weekends off," I say. "That might be the tough one."

"Weekends?" Landon snorts. "How new *are* you to Ocala? There are weekday shows all the time. Look."

And he pulls out his phone, flicking through websites to show me different schooling shows around Ocala. He's right, there are shows on Tuesday, Wednesday, and Thursday every month. "And even more in winter," he says, "not that it matters right now. But if you want to show him this winter without getting on the wrong side of Bas and Kayla's schedule, you'll be able to do it, no problem."

"This is awesome," I say, leaning close to him so that we can both see his phone screen. I look up at him and he smiles down at me, and suddenly I'm intensely aware of his closeness, his warmth, the feel of his muscled arm against mine.

Before I even know what I'm doing, I slide away, putting a good foot of space between us.

Landon's chin hardens. He reaches for the leash wrapped around the picnic table bench and urges Sid to come out from beneath the table. "We should head back," he says.

And just like that, I realize, I've made the drive home weird.

Chapter Twenty-Three

KAYLA LOVES THE idea of taking Thomas to weekday shows for a build-up to a big schooling day outing at Legends. She thinks it's brilliant and tells me so while she's walking Feather out to the mounting block. The mare swishes her tail and wheels around the block. Kayla stands still and lets her pop off. She always says there's no point arguing with Feather—you just have to let the mare get bored with arguing and come around on her own.

I smile weakly and admit the show schedule is Landon's idea.

"He's so great," Kayla gushes. "Honestly, I am *so* glad he's here. All the horses' feet look amazing and he was such a big help when you've had to rest your arm."

I don't bring up that he's the reason I ended up in a sling in the first place. I just nod. Yes, Landon is so, so great. He's great with horses and he's great with dogs. He could be better with people. We drove home in a stony silence last night and it was pretty clear that I upset him by sliding away from him on the picnic table bench. But what did he want from me? We're friends. We work together. I've sworn off men and have no plans to change my mind anytime soon. I'm not sure what he expected, frankly.

"And now he's helping you with Thomas?" Kayla clucks to Feather, who paws at the ground and blows through her nostrils like a bull about to charge a red cape. "Just a match made in heaven."

"Well, I don't know about *match,*" I say uneasily.

She laughs and turns back to her horse. Feather is standing by the mounting block now, looking at Kayla with pure demand in her big brown eyes. "I'm really glad you guys work together so well," she says.

"I'm not dating Landon," I blurt. "We just had dinner two times. As friends."

Kayla is halfway into the saddle, but I can see the stutter in her smooth movement as my idiotic words hit her ears.

Why did I feel the need to say that? She just used the term "match made in heaven" to describe how Landon is helping me with Thomas. She didn't imply we were in love or something.

She settles in the saddle, gathering the reins, before she looks back down at me, a smile on her lips that I refuse to read as pitying. "I didn't mean anything by it," she says. "But Landon's a great guy. If something happens between you two, it wouldn't be a problem for me or for Basil."

I watch Kayla walk her horse away, Feather's red-chestnut hindquarters moving rhythmically beneath her. She lifts a hand from the reins to wave to Basil, who is already riding on the far side of the arena, and Feather dances sideways, swishing her tail. Kayla laughs.

Basil doesn't ride like Kayla, who treats every spook her mare makes like a good joke. With his jaw set and his eyes straight ahead, Basil always looks beyond intense in the saddle. And yet, despite his fierce expression, I can tell he's having a very good ride this morning. His dapple-gray horse looks relaxed yet alert, his strides coming in an even cadence. I watch the two of them trot past, wondering if I'll ever train Thomas to move like that. This horse is younger than Thomas, but he came with less baggage; his whole, short life, he was coddled and prepared for the life of a Grand Prix jumper.

It occurs to me, as I walk back to the barn, that when it comes to horses, I have more in common with Landon than Kayla or Basil. He's not out here hustling horses to sell as quickly as possible. He's just quietly looking for answers, trying to mend broken things with gold.

I have no problem with my employers' choices, but I prefer Landon's.

I've seen enough of big money and fancy horses. Enough to last a lifetime.

Landon is off on calls this morning, shoeing horses in Ocala. It's just me to do barn chores, and it's one of those days when everything seems to take forever. Mentally, I feel like it's kind of a mercy to have Landon gone, since last night ended so quietly and uncomfortably. But then again, the silent barn gives me way too much time to think about the things I said, and to wonder how long he'll stay angry with me.

Not that you could tell Landon was *angry*. I'm not sure he has that emotion as a real, heart-on-sleeve option. And that's probably a good thing, because a man built like a Viking has the potential to be very scary if he loses his temper.

I slip into Crunchy's stall and start flicking through the shavings, looking for manure—he's the type that buries his poop—while my brain begins a comprehensive rehash of last night's events, specifically the moment where I slid away from Landon on that picnic bench, putting space between us for no good reason. It wasn't that hot, so I couldn't act like environmental factors had been a concern. He'd had his hands on me before, helping me with Thomas, so I couldn't pretend like it was shocking to be touched.

But that was the thing.

It *had* shocked me.

I felt the spark between us, like a flash through my entire body, when he sat up against me, so close we might as well have been...well, a *couple.*

And he had done it so thoughtlessly, without any kind of play in mind. He saw me as the kind of person he could slide up against, and be comfortable with.

And I scooted away as quickly as possible.

I find a manure pile, scoop and sift, and toss it towards the wheelbarrow. I am a good shot with two hands. With one, I miss half the time. This is one of those times. With a sigh, I move to scoop up everything that fell before it hit the wheelbarrow. A swing and a miss. Much like my attempt at being friends with my barn neighbor.

I don't want things to go back to the way they were; I know him too well to want to fight with him, or avoid him. At this point, as much as I hate the realization, I miss his company.

I'm going to have to fix things with Landon. I need his friendship.

My answers to myself seem too simple. I'm recently divorced and don't want to get involved with anyone else, and it makes me paranoid. I value his friendship too much to risk it. I am focused one hundred percent on getting this new phase of my life correct and can't be in a relationship with anyone until I have time to work on myself. I have to get Thomas to the Thoroughbred Makeover because that's the sum goal of my entire first year on my own, and if I don't get this right, who knows if I will ever get anything right, in my entire life, ever again?

Okay, maybe the last one has a lot of baggage to pick through. I won't lead with that.

I won't lead with *any* of them, though, because who am I trying to kid here? On what planet would I walk up to Landon and say, "Hey, about last night, sorry I made it awkward but you see, I'm newly divorced and my entire self-worth depends on my proving I can do just one thing on my own, and wrecking my chances by getting into bed with you would be the ultimate act of self-sabotage?"

Not that that isn't a great speech, because it is, and imagine if I could actually put it together like that, what a coup. But no, I couldn't possibly say that to him, because he will then lift an eyebrow and ask, incredulously, "What the hell are you talking about, woman?"

And I'd be like, "Oh, haha, when I moved away from you on the picnic bench last night?"

And he'd ask, still incredulous, "You thought I was hitting on you?"

And then I'd die, so at least the scene would be mercifully over.

I find a wet spot and dig it out, wincing at the strain on my shoulders when I have to lift and dump a forkful of heavy, wet bedding. I'm stronger on one side now; if I don't even it out, I'm going to have a right shoulder like a stone mason's...or a farrier's.

Great, then I'll always be thinking of Landon. Every time I look in the mirror, at my grossly half-farrier physique, I'll be reminded of the friend who got away.

* * *

HE DOESN'T COME back to the farm for lunch.

I give up looking for him around one o'clock, when Kayla and Basil are standing around the tack room eating sandwiches and saying things like "I just really don't know what's going on between Avon's ears anymore," or, "Time to try a donut girth on Crunchy...he's got rubs again."

Kayla offers me a sandwich when I come in. Or rather, the means to make one. "Sandwich fixings in the fridge," she says. "I was getting tired of going back to the house and then making myself come back here after lunch."

The house is a quarter-mile away, but we're having an uncomfortable run of hot, sunny days without clouds or rain to cool us down, so once inside, no one wants to go back out again. I get it.

"Thanks," I say. "Is Landon coming back for lunch, do you know?"

Basil shrugs. "I heard him say he was going to the south side of Ocala, so probably not. Too far if he has a full day of clients."

"Yeah, he won't be back until late," Kayla adds. "So if you need help with anything, like getting on Thomas, we can do that after the last horse."

"That would be great, actually." I pull out the sandwich things, raising my eyebrows at Kayla's choices. "Is this... bologna?"

Basil guffaws. "I told you, Kayla. No one in America eats that stuff. You made it up."

"You Commonwealth boys don't know what you're missing," she retorts, waving her half-eaten sandwich at him. "Baloney is life."

I find myself on Basil's side. "Is everything okay, Kayla? You seem delirious."

"I bought it by accident," she admits, laughing. "And now I'm the only one who will eat it. There's ham underneath."

I tug out the ham and cheese while Basil continues ribbing Kayla for all the disgusting things Americans eat. I guess his background in Hong Kong and the U.K. didn't adequately prepare him for life with Kayla, because I've heard her housekeeping can be somewhat chaotic at times. He has, on several occasions, asked her if she was secretly employing a maid when they met at a house-sitting assignment with Basil's former riding coach.

She always reminded him that of *course* there was a maid, did he really think she kept that mansion sparkling clean when there was a gorgeous barn to occupy all her time and energy?

I like listening to them squabble gently; there's no doubt these two are couple goals. I never had silly little fights with Ryan. Just big ones, not silly at all, and I was rarely allowed to win them.

Settling down on a chair to eat my sandwich, I let my thoughts wander...so naturally, they go looking for Landon. It's only because he isn't here and we had that weird moment last night, I tell myself, that's why I can't stop thinking about him. I got used to having him around.

We wouldn't fight very much, if we were together. Just a few little teasing arguments, like Kayla and Basil have. But every now and then, I'd bet, his temper would show itself. What would that be like? We'd carry on at each other, shouting and stamping, and then, suddenly, we'd realize how ridiculous we were being. We'd kiss and make-up and—

I shake my head and shoulders all over, like a horse after a good roll, to clear those thoughts from my head.

Luckily, no one notices.

"Uh-oh," Kayla says, suddenly interrupting their ribbing. "Is that thunder?"

We all stop chewing and listen.

The barn sounds gently echo around us, horses snorting, horses chewing, one horse peeing with a sound that reminds me of forgetting a hose has been left running.

And then another rumble rolls through, low and forbidding.

"Dammit," Basil sighs. "I have *got* to get on Shakespeare. He's got a sales video due to go out by the end of the week."

"Well, let's go." Kayla jams the rest of her sandwich into her mouth, slaps her hands against her breeches, and grabs a saddle before heading out into the barn aisle.

I can't help but sigh to myself; I would have liked more than five minutes on break before heading back out to groom and tack a horse. Basil hears me and shakes his head.

"Stay here and take a lunch break," he says. "We can manage our horses this time around."

I start to protest, but then I just nod, letting him go. I'm exhausted, doing this entire barn by myself. There's no room for pride now, and I have to take whatever break I can get.

THOMAS'S TRAINING DIARY
June Without End

We had a really nice jumping school with Kayla's help this evening. I told her I want to pay but you know Kayla. She won't take anything from me. Says I work more than she pays me for. Crazy. But I'll take it. She says Thomas is going to be plenty ready for the show jumping division in October, but reminded me to work on transitions within the gait. Even if it doesn't seem like he's shortening or lengthening in the canter yet, if I keep asking then one day he'll be strong enough to show me he's doing it, and then I'll have more control between jumps. Good advice. She also said everything gets perfected at the walk, then bleeds into the other gaits. Good thing, because most of our rides seem to be walking, what with the heat and all.

Landon came out and watched, and took some pictures. He sent them to me for my Instagram, which was really cool of him. He also noticed I was wearing the purple outfit. I guess now he thinks of me as a big important fashion designer. Lol. That'll be the day.

He's gone a lot more now. I miss having his help around the barn, but that's what I signed up for. I guess I was just lucky to get a little help settling in, even if I didn't want it at the time.

Chapter Twenty-Four

THAT SURPRISE THUNDERSTORM ushers the return of daily rain into our summer. As June rushes headlong into July, our life grows very wet. The arena is full of puddles, every hoof-print its own tiny lake. The depressions around the pasture gates, where the sand has been hard-packed from horses hanging around waiting to be brought inside for meals, turn into shin-deep ponds. Mud sucks at my boots as I tramp between the paddocks to check water troughs for algae growth —the rain keeps them overflowing, but they still have to be dumped and scrubbed regularly—and the farm's beautiful, jungle-green grass grows pockmarked with black, muddy patches where hooves and constant rolling have torn up the sod.

A hefty new generation of mosquitoes arrives on the fourth day, and the mornings and evenings become a torment worthy of south Florida, where the Everglades run full-time bloodsucker production.

The more sensitive horses in the barn begin coming in with painful little bumps on their hindquarters and backs, victims of a bacterial infection charmingly known as rain rot, and there's a flurry of panic as I have to start setting aside specific grooming tools for different horses and make sure every saddle pad is washed in hot water. Disinfectant baths become the norm.

"This is why so many trainers don't stay in Florida year-round," Basil says to Kayla, while I'm gently brushing a thin-skinned Thoroughbred with rain rot around his withers. The horse's skin shivers in protest. If I take off too many scabs, he'll bleed and be too sensitive to ride.

"We're not moving up north," Kayla says. "For the millionth time!"

"You want to move north?" I ask, startled. "Where to?"

Basil shakes his head. "Nowhere specific. I happen to think a New York base would be nice for summer. But everyone's against me on it. Even Pete."

"Pete knows if you mention it to Jules, there's a good chance she'll go for it and then be miserable once she gets there. He says Florida girls don't transplant very well."

I snort. "We're not orchids!"

But he's kind of right, at the same time. On every extended vacation I've ever taken, I've missed Florida terribly by the end. Not just home, or my horses. But *Florida*. The wild, dangerous sky. The flat expanses of wetland and prairie. The massive live oaks and the upstart clumps of cabbage palms. The sunsets.

Even the humidity. Dry air feels delightful, but humid air feels like home.

"We're talking about moving north?"

Landon's rumbling voice makes me jump, and the horse I'm rubbing jumps, too. I turn around just as he takes the horse's halter in hand and says a few crooning nonsense words to him. "Where'd you come from?" I ask, trying not to sound excited to have him back. Sid winds around my feet like a cat, wagging his tail.

Landon winks at me. "Have you missed me?"

"Well..." I let my hesitation hang between us, a ghost of a grin on my face. I need it to hide the way I really feel around him.

Which is...confused.

"She doesn't miss you, Landon, because you just cause her more work." Kayla gives me a sidelong smile. "We were all just saying how much easier it is around here when you're actually out doing your job."

"Sheesh, tough crowd." Landon shrugs. "And here I thought I came bearing interesting news, but if no one wants me here..."

"Tell us," Kayla laughs. "What's the word?"

"Well, it's really for Mackenzie, here." His warm smile shines down on me. "There's a horse show at Canterbury this weekend, and I have some free time. Want to take Thomas?"

"Oh, my goodness." The possibilities, big and scary and fun and horrifying all at once, wash over me. I have been hoping to take Thomas to a show—I *need* to take Thomas to a show. It's non-negotiable. We can't go to Kentucky if he isn't acclimated to horse shows.

But damn, it's scary when that first show becomes reality! All at once I feel sick to my stomach, and it's a queasiness I recognize like an old enemy. There's no quiver in your gut quite like show-ring jitters. I might as well be trotting around the warm-up arena right now.

"Are you okay?" Kayla tilts her head at me. "You look green all of a sudden."

"I think I need to sit down."

Landon is the first one to move, grabbing me a chair from in front of the tack room and settling me down into it as if I'm an invalid. "Okay? Do you need water?"

"I'm fine," I say, the queasiness dissolving into acute embarrassment. "I just felt a little light-headed for a minute."

"The heat," Kayla suggests. "It's brutal. Maybe you better go inside and lay down for half an hour."

"It's not the heat," Landon says. "It's the horse show."

I give him a quick glance. How does he know? "I might have gotten a little overheated," I say gamely, not willing to show my nerves in front of Kayla and Basil, two horse show professionals who probably haven't been nervous about the show-ring in years. "But I'll be okay in a second. You know how it goes."

Landon's gaze is knowing, but he leaves it alone.

I appreciate that.

THE QUEASINESS IS back on Saturday morning as we load Thomas into my trailer and Landon joins me in the truck. I didn't really expect him to come along, but now that he's sitting in the passenger seat, I'm so glad he's there. Showing a horse is hard enough without doing everything alone. Sid settles into the backseat and goes to sleep with a sigh. Truck rides are about the only thing that calms Sid's constant motion.

"Thanks for coming," I say, putting the truck into gear. I start to inch down the lane, avoiding any bumps that might upset Thomas. He's a good traveler, but I like to baby him when we're on the road.

"I couldn't let you go alone," Landon says, looking in the rear-view mirror. I know he's watching the trailer, keeping an eye on the way it travels just to be sure everything is perfect before we get out on the main road. I'm the same way.

"Kayla wanted to come, but she had to take that horse to his new barn today. I hope he's happy there." Avon is a nice horse and I'll miss having him around, although I will not miss his terrible stall. Cleaning up after him takes twice as long as a normal stall.

"I'm sure he will be."

There's something absent about the way Landon's speaking. I glance at him, but decide that I can't be worried about him all the time. I have a horse show to worry about. And the drive there to focus on. In the back, Thomas whinnies.

"Missing his friends already," I say.

"Mm-hmm."

Well, this is just great. Annoyed with Landon, I pick up the pace a little. The truck engine growls reassuringly as my foot descends on the pedal, and I let myself enjoy that little thrill of professionalism and self-reliance that I always get when I'm hauling my own horse trailer. Most of the women I rode with in Wellington paid for someone else to move their horses between different stables and show-grounds. Ryan thought it was a ridiculous expense when I bought a shiny new truck and a trailer of my own. As if he didn't make ridiculously expensive purchases all the time—why did he own a boat, for example, when he got so seasick we couldn't even cruise on a mega-ship? He was always just full of hot air. In more ways than one.

I pull out onto the main road with caution and slowly accelerate the truck, watching the RPMs rise and fall with every gear change to make sure I'm not taxing the engine. I'm sure it can handle a lot more than one horse in an aluminum trailer, but I don't have throwaway-money anymore, so I can't afford to abuse things. The live oaks and pastures on either side of the road begin to flash by as I cruise towards fifty miles an hour, and my fingers start to unclench from their death grip on the wheel. I feel less queasy, too. Things are going fine. Today is going to be fine...maybe even fun?

"Pull over up ahead," Landon says.

"What?" I glance at him, confused. "Why would I pull over?"

"The back right tire looks wrong," he says. "There's a wide spot just ahead. Pull over."

The wide spot is actually a delivery entrance to Vince Funk's ranch. I hope Sid doesn't think we're taking him back to his old farm, but the dog just sighs in his sleep. Thomas kicks the trailer wall in anticipation as I slowly angle the truck and trailer into a grassy patch along the road, and Landon's out of the cab and heading for the trailer before I've got it in park.

Trying not to freak out, I unbuckle my seatbelt and head after him.

He's kneeling by that back right tire, shaking his head.

"What's wrong with it?"

"It's traveling unevenly. You're about to have a blow-out."

The words chill me through. I've never had a blow-out on a trailer, but the idea has always terrified me. I see the social media posts from time to time, trainers who are stranded along the interstate with six horses in ninety-degree heat, waiting for roadside assistance to come. Can anyone help with the horses? The thought of unloading Thomas alongside a busy highway and loading him up into someone else's trailer is absolutely horrifying.

"What do you think we should do?" I croak.

Landon looks up at me and his face changes, losing the intense look he's been wearing since we left the farm. "Oh, honey, it's okay," he says soothingly. "I'll change it and we'll be on our way in a few minutes."

That soft drawl I hear occasionally is back in his words, as if the Kentucky side of him he's been hiding from me and everyone else is escaping. I like it. The accent suits him.

"You're sure?" I ask, wishing I could tell him how warm his words make me feel inside.

"Positive." Landon straightens up. "Let's get started."

THE SHOW IS lightly attended, thanks to the summer heat and the constant afternoon storms. When I finally unload Thomas, the mid-morning sun is blazingly hot and I feel terrible about tying him to the trailer in the full sun. There is no shade in the parking area.

"I should have gotten him a stall," I fret, looking at the rows of stabling. Canterbury has beautiful wooden barns, not temporary stabling in tents like so many shows. Luckier horses with more thoughtful horse-parents than me stand in their stall doors, looking over their stall guards at the festivities, enjoying the cool breeze of their fans.

"I'll take care of it," Landon says. "Let me go to the show office and get you checked in, and I'll see about adding a stall."

I really don't have stall-money budgeted for this, but the thing about horses is that it doesn't matter if you can't afford it. If they need something, they get it. And no, the math doesn't always work out. But at least the horse stays happy and healthy. "Thank you," I say gratefully. "We have two walk-trot classes to start and then I want him to be able to hang around and watch everything for a few hours."

"I'll be right back with your number and a stall assignment," Landon promises, leaving me with Thomas.

Now, being alone with Thomas is not feeling like the best idea. I know I can't tack him up like this: he's standing with his head straight up, staring at the arenas a few hundred feet away.

There are maybe a half-dozen horses and ponies in the show-ring, trotting around in a children's hunters class, and half-dozen more in the warm-up. A few other horses are scattered around the grounds between the stabling and the arenas. It's really not terribly busy, but I know what this set-up looks like to Thomas.

A racetrack.

Chapter Twenty-Five

I'D REALLY PREFER to just walk Thomas around today and stay on the ground where it's nice and safe. But before Landon even comes back from the show office, it becomes pretty apparent that I'll have to get on my horse's back. Thomas just seems to get taller with every step. His head is getting higher and higher. If his neck would stretch this long in the stretching circle near the end of the training-level dressage test, we'd be looking at some serious tens on the scoresheet. It's giving me food for thought.

But he's not calming down. He's just getting hotter and huffier.

"You going to get on him?" Landon asks, walking back over with a bridle number and a stall assignment. "I can bring your tack over."

"I have to," I sigh.

He looks at me like I'm crazy. "Don't sound like you're being tortured here, Mackenzie. I thought you *wanted* to show him."

"I did want to, but that doesn't make it any easier when he's acting like this!" I gesture at my fire-breathing dragon.

"You guys will be fine," Landon says firmly, as if he can simply ordain these things. "Walk him around the barn a few times while I get your stuff moved over, and then we'll put him in the stall for a few minutes. He can pee and catch his breath."

Part of me would really like to ask Landon who died and left him in charge, but I'm overruled by the part of me that realizes I'd be the one who is doing the dying, so I just nod and take Thomas on a tour of the shed-row surrounding the barn.

After a few laps, Landon points towards the open stall door and I obediently lead my snorting horse inside. While we've been walking, he has made quite a nice set-up, with shavings and water buckets inside; canvas chairs, a grooming kit, and a saddle rack outside. He puts up the stall guard while I'm still inside with Thomas, so I unsnap the lead-rope and duck out beneath it, leaving my horse to spin around the stall a few times, still blowing like he's just run a race.

"He's being a maniac," I fret, turning the lead-rope around in my hands.

"He'll settle," Landon predicts. "Have a water." And he hands me a bottle of water, dripping with melting ice.

It's too cold for my queasy stomach, though. I put it on a chair and watch Thomas circling. After a few minutes, he puts his nose to the shavings, snorts, and then stretches out to pee.

"Now we're getting somewhere," Landon says. "A tense horse doesn't pee. A relaxed horse does."

"We have a class in like, half an hour," I say. "Think we can make it?"

"We'll tack him up once he's had a sip of water," Landon suggests, and because I feel like my own brain is short-circuiting too much to make my own decisions, I agree.

Ten minutes later, a hydrated Thomas stands remarkably still while I jiggle the lead-rope under his chin and Landon girths up the saddle. My horse lifts his head high and gazes out at the horses in the show rings.

"He's standing awfully still," I say doubtfully. My younger self learned about motionless Thoroughbreds the hard way. They have an explosive way of leaving their trances.

"He thinks he's in the paddock," Landon says.

"What paddock?"

"This is like the saddling shed to him, in the paddock at the track. He thinks you've been walking him around before his race, and now he's here to be saddled. That's why he's standing still. He's sizing up the competition, too. Look at his eyes."

I look up at Thomas's round eyes. There's an expression old horsemen have for Thoroughbreds with their blood up: *the look of eagles.*

"Oh, god," I say. I don't want to ride an eagle. I want to stay on the ground.

"You're okay," Landon says soothingly. "You know your horse."

But, do I? Thomas the Racehorse is taller and scarier than Thomas the Goofus OTTB that I'm used to. This is truly like a different animal.

Landon tosses the reins over his neck as I step aside to make room for him. "You're going to be just fine," he says again, dropping the halter from the crown's buckle and slipping the bridle over the horse's head in one quick movement. Thomas mouths the bit obediently, his eyes still focused on horses in the warm-up arena, his brain still somewhere else. Calculating his strategy, maybe, for beating the rest of the pack in the homestretch.

"You're going to be just fine," Landon keeps repeating as he helps me through all the pre-mounting rituals, walking Thomas out to the mounting block at the end of the barn—maybe it's someone else's, I don't know, but it's here and it's getting used —tightening the girth a few holes on either side, circling the horse around the block as I check my hat, my boots, my gloves, and above all else, my safety vest. I tug at the shoulder pads, already hot and uncomfortable. I've never been big on vests, but when my horse is being this big of a banana-brain, you better believe it goes on.

"Okay," I say, stepping up to the mounting block. "Let's do this thing."

Landon barely halts Thomas before I'm on his back, then he walks on, keeping the horse moving so there's no time for silliness. Thomas tosses his head while I kick my feet into the stirrups and organize my hands on the reins. I wish my heart wouldn't beat so fast. I wish my breath would slow down. I wish my fingers didn't feel like they were trembling. I know of trainers who can slow their own hearts so that they can keep their horses calm. It sounds like witchcraft to me, but at this moment I'd gladly sell my soul for the magic spell that would quiet dancing, dangerous Thomas.

He snorts loudly and digs down at the bit. Landon hauls his head up again and snaps, sternly, "Enough of that!"

Thomas blows again, but he keeps his head up this time.

"I'm gonna let you go at the in-gate to the ring, okay?" Landon calls back to me.

I bite my lower lip, then remind myself not to do that on horseback. A trainer in Wellington told me about a student who bit all the way through their lip once when their horse unseated them. Maybe it was just a scary story to make me stop a nervous tic in the show-ring, but it worked.

"Okay," I say finally.

Landon is looking back at me, his eyes hard to read.

"You're going to be fine," he says.

And he lets Thomas go.

AS SOON AS Thomas's hooves hit the arena footing, he breaks into a trot, and I move with him, rising with the beat. I feel my position shift to accommodate his momentum, my upper body shifting forward slightly, my hands hovering above his withers, not pulling back but just feeling the edges of his mouth. I feel him take a hold and I squeeze my fingers, then release, and for a moment he softens his jaw instead of tugging.

It's a very forward trot and we're really pinging around the arena at a nice clip, passing ponies and swinging around slower, older horses with enough sense to conserve their movements on a hot summer day. Sweat rises on Thomas's neck and foams around the reins almost immediately, as if he's been working for hours. I hear his teeth grind against the bit and know it's all nerves. Squeeze. Release. Soften.

We're going to be fine.

Landon is by the gate, a thumbs-up ready for me. We zip past, still trotting like a Standardbred, and I know instinctively that Thomas could keep up this trot all day if he had to. You can't wear out a Thoroughbred in the warm-up ring. You can only show them the ropes and hope they adjust their energy levels accordingly.

It takes about five minutes for Thomas to decide maybe he can walk.

And another fifteen before he stops looking around with such expectant eyes, wondering where the starting gate is.

At about the thirty-minute mark, he actually comes to a halt and sighs, right in the middle of the warm-up arena.

I rub his neck enthusiastically. "You're such a good boy!

Thomas! I'm so proud of you!"

The halt only lasts a few seconds before he's walking again, but it means something. He takes a breath and lets it out through his nostrils, signaling that he's relaxing.

He's figured out he's not going to race today.

"Think I should take him in our class?" I ask Landon, circling Thomas near his spot on the rail. We hold back a moment to let another horse trot past and Thomas tugs longingly on the bit, but doesn't give chase.

"You've already paid for it," Landon says. "It's just another arena. Might as well."

I tug at the shoulder of my safety vest as I look towards the neighboring show-ring. They'll be calling the walk-trot class next, and I'm soaking with sweat under this thing. It would be nice to appear somewhat tidy and put-together in a show class... "I was thinking of taking my vest off," I say.

Landon's face darkens. "Absolutely not."

We glare at each other for a moment, before Thomas's circle makes me break eye contact. I shake my head. Did spending half an hour on the ground watching me suddenly turn Landon into my trainer? My hand goes to the zipper at my chest—

And then stops abruptly as I see Landon's expression.

He's genuinely worried about me.

I sigh and drop my hand to the reins. "Fine," I tell him. "I'll wear the damn vest."

He smiles. "Thank you."

IT TURNS OUT "just another arena" is maybe not a cut-and-dry concept for Thomas. He's happy enough to leave the warm-up, but he's worried when we join the scrum of other horses waiting to enter the show-ring. And once we're in there, supposedly walking calmly along the rail without getting too close to the other horses, he starts bouncing around, his ears swiveling and his breath huffing loudly.

It doesn't look good. Thomas is hot; I'm hot; we're both dripping with sweat and look like we're ready to collapse. I honestly don't feel great. The heat is getting to me and I'm queasy like a child who has spent her summer morning gorging cotton candy and riding roller coasters. That might have been a superior decision to this horse show. I've dealt with a nervous stomach in the show-ring before, but I've never felt quite like I might make a fool of myself the way I do right now. I swallow nervously.

Again, that magic trick to slow my heart-beat would come in handy right now, for me as well as for calming my horse.

When the announcer breaks in over the loudspeaker to say, "Riders, you are now being judged at the walk," Thomas jumps like a wasp stung his rump. I sway with his movement and bring him back to a jig while he snorts and looks around at the other horses. Something about their slow, hypnotic movement around the arena railing is making him nervous. Maybe he thinks he has stumbled into an equine zombie apocalypse.

The idea makes sense to me. Imagine being a racehorse your entire life, used to horses who are always speeding to the next pole. Then enter a ring where every horse is walking with their head down, no destination or desire in sight. It must be really unsettling to him.

I run my inside hand along his withers and speak soothingly in a soft voice so that I don't bother anyone else. He flicks his ears back and sighs, working the bit in his mouth. After a few more strides, he settles back into a bouncy walk.

I'll take it.

WHEN WE COME out of the arena, I slither out of the saddle and land on shaky legs. Landon is there to take Thomas's reins, but he puts an arm around my shoulder and pulls me close. For a moment, I lean into him.

"You did it," he whispers. "I'm so proud of you guys!"

The words are so sweet, I want to lap them up. No one ever says they're proud of me anymore. That was my dad's job, and Ryan did not take it over.

Then I realize how sweaty we both are, and I step out of Landon's embrace. Affection is great, but in Florida, there are limits to the physical side of things. "Thanks," I say, finally unzipping my safety vest so that some air can get to my squashed chest. "That was a little scary, but we made it."

"And a pink ribbon," he declares. "You got fifth place!"

"I did!" I'm a little embarrassed at how excited I am for that pink ribbon. Grown-ups are supposed to be too sophisticated and mature to compete for a ribbon. We are competing against *our former selves,* we tell ourselves with great pride. We are competing to show *how we have improved.* But blah blah, give me a freaking ribbon and tell me I'm pretty in the saddle, thanks.

"Let's go and pick it up while we walk this guy," Landon says, turning towards the show office. I fall into step beside him, and the three of us walk along the sandy road between the arenas and the stabling, a happy little trio. At the office, he hands me the reins before going inside. When he comes out again, he has the ribbon, two cans of Coke, and a receipt, which he's folding into quarters.

"I settled up your tab," he says, tucking the receipt into his back pocket. "I assumed you weren't doing the second class, but there are no refunds. That's alright. It was only twenty bucks."

"They didn't have my card on file," I say, taking the Coke and tucking the ribbon onto Thomas's brow-band. "I'll have to Venmo you."

"No, no, I got this," Landon says, waving a hand. "I insisted on the stall and all."

Did he? I don't remember it that way, but everything about this morning seems pretty hazy. That's probably the heat stroke talking. I let him take Thomas back to the stable area, drinking my Coke and trying to revive myself. Suddenly everything seems very heavy and dim, as if I've been plunged underwater.

Thomas is getting a shower, so when I finally keel over, Landon isn't there to catch me.

THOMAS THE BIG *Scary Show Horse Training Diary*
July Forever-teenth

Might as well get used to it being July and a million degrees, I suppose. I passed out at the horse show today. The perfect way to get ready for two more months of high summer. Kayla says that September isn't usually like the surface of the sun, unlike south Florida, so I guess we have that to look forward to. But after September comes October—ugh!!!

I think Ryan would ask me why I'm even doing this crazy Makeover if the only reaction I ever have to thinking about is abject terror. But Ryan doesn't know the value of hard work, or doing things on your own, or feeling like you've really cleansed yourself of all the bad juju in your life. (I know juju is neither a technically nor culturally correct term, but this journal isn't for anyone but me, so.) When I have this Makeover under my belt, Thomas and I will have come through fire together—not literally, although I think it's going to feel that way, with the way this summer is roasting me from the outside in. And I'll know that I'm really capable of doing something big and scary on my own.

Of course, Landon seems to think he needs to play a part in all this. What can I do to make him lay off?

Do I really want him to?

Don't answer that, Mackenzie. Just focus on your horse. Right. Well, all I can say is that Thomas tried his little heart out today. I'd write more, but I'm tired and my hand hurts. And really, what else is there to say?

Chapter Twenty-Six

"WHOOPS, ARE YOU going to fall? Don't pass out now!"

I glare at Landon, who is standing before me with his arms wide open. Again. He's been doing this all week and despite what he might think, it wasn't funny six days ago and it's not funny now. "Like you've never had heat stroke," I snap, pushing past him and going into the tack room.

Landon trails after me, so I throw him some leg wraps from the warm dryer—he might as well make himself useful if he's going to be underfoot.

And he has been underfoot, constantly, ever since the horse show.

He's being ridiculous about it. Yes, I passed out, but it was only because of the heat. It meant nothing. The heat index shot up to like one hundred and twelve degrees that day. I was not the only person who passed out. The paramedics eventually just set up a triage tent with ice and bottled water.

Plus, I was only out for maybe half a second. Just enough time to totter to the ground, land uncomfortably, and open my eyes again, wondering what the hell had happened. It was *not* a big deal.

Landon knows it was not a big deal, which is why he's

making it into a huge joke.

Well, it's not that, either, okay? It's nothing. It's better forgotten. Landon isn't letting it be forgotten, though.

"You're being really childish about this whole thing," I inform him, hopping up on a tack trunk so that I can hoist a stack of clean saddle pads onto the top shelf of the storage rack.

"Is that a turnoff for you?"

I look down at him. "A *turn*off? Excuse me?"

Landon grins and shoves the rolled-up leg wraps into their storage bin. "I'm just kidding, Mackenzie. Jeez."

He'd better be. I give him a dark look from on high, then climb down from the tack trunk and start working on the standing wraps, which are all twisted and tangled up from their trip through the tumble dryer. Someone forgot to put them in a laundry bag first. Can't imagine who that might be. (It was me.) I settle down in a chair with the wraps on my lap, and Landon tries to pluck one out of the tangle. He ends up with half the wraps dragged across the floor. Shadow, gifting us with a rare public appearance, paws at one of the wraps with a delicate paw, while Sid glowers from beneath a chair. Shadow let Sid know who was boss on day one at the farm, and he's never questioned her authority again.

"My god, man," I sigh, standing up to help Landon untwist the wraps as Shadow retreats to the top of the washing machine. "You're determined to make my life hard today, aren't you?"

"It was kind of the opposite idea," he mutters, suddenly sounding sheepish. "Sorry about that."

"No, it's fine. They're easier to untangle with two people working on it."

He looks happier and I smile to myself. I'm not sure why he's attached himself to me like this. But it would be pretty ungrateful of me to complain, and the truth is, I like having him around. I'm used to his presence now, and it's lonely when he isn't around. And I know that sounds like I'm going against my entire set of reasons for coming here, which was to learn a new job and be left alone and avoid men at all costs. But maybe, when I was setting those parameters, I didn't recognize just how quiet and isolated this farm would be. Kayla and Basil are an efficient little business of two: they arrive, ride, and leave in coupledom. Pete Morrison comes out a few days a week and rides, then goes back to his farm. No one else comes here. It's not like the busy hustle and bustle of the barns I was used to back in south Florida, where students are constantly in and out, trailers are always pulling up in the driveway, and trainers are stopping by to look at sales horses, share the news on their latest prospects, or just shoot the breeze with some excellent gossip.

In very few instances could I have said any of these people were my friends, or that we even spoke to each other. They were there for my trainers. But their presence filled the barn up with conversation.

This barn is very, very quiet.

Especially when Landon is off shoeing horses, taking away his dog, his chatter, and his warm, easy laughter.

"Here we go," Landon announces, plucking one complete standing wrap from the squirrel's nest of fabric between us. "That's one. How many are there? A hundred?"

"Just four," I laugh, tugging a knot loose. "I really need to remember to use laundry bags. My trainer in Wellington always did."

"Do you miss Wellington?"

"No! Why do you ask?"

"You've mentioned it a few times this morning," he says. "I don't remember you saying anything about it before, though."

"Oh." It probably wasn't a coincidence that Landon was gone Monday through Thursday on shoeing work, and now I was bringing up Wellington constantly. "I guess I've just thought of it a lot lately, because I've been away for so long," I say lamely.

"Sure," he says. "Good thing it doesn't measure up to this farm, or you might be homesick."

"Yeah, I guess it doesn't."

"You *guess*?"

"Well, it was just very busy there," I explain. "Constant hubbub."

"And you miss that?" Landon sounds skeptical.

"I don't miss being busy—I didn't even work there, not really. I helped out, to learn the ropes, so I could do this job." I free a second leg wrap and hold it up triumphantly. "I guess I'm just used to a barn being more like an office. Lots of people in and out all day. Ordering in lunch and having a gossip session in the break room."

"We can do those things," he offers gamely. "I think we can even get Domino's delivered if we call an hour ahead."

"But who will we gossip about?" I ask. "Kayla and Basil? How cute they are when they ride together?"

He shrugs, grinning. "Maybe we gossip about each other. You know, I heard about this girl who left her husband and moved to north Florida to run a barn. Pretty brave, right?"

I shake my head, but I can't deny it's touching. "Nice," I say. "I heard about a really secretive farrier who lives in a barn with that girl but won't tell her anything about his mysterious past."

Landon raises an eyebrow. "His *mysterious* past? Is that what you think of me?"

"See, this is why gossiping about each other isn't going to work."

"Well, what are we supposed to do that makes this place more interesting for you, then?"

Notice that he has already shifted the conversation from his mysterious past. This guy is good.

Also, I really need to know what he doesn't want to tell me. Call it a character flaw. Or else, no, let's call it a safety instinct. After all, he does live across the barn aisle from me on a dark, isolated farm in the middle of nowhere, Florida.

"I know!" Landon announces. "You and me should go on a trail ride."

I look out at the midday sun. It's shining with all its might, and in Florida, that's really saying something. "A trail ride? Are you crazy?"

"There's a full moon tonight," Landon says, like that makes it better. "Just trust me."

AFTER THE AFTERNOON thunderstorm rumbles on through, the evening air is humid and heavy. But it *is* cooler, which isn't always the case. After sunset, with the horses turned out for the night and a blue dusk settling over the farm, I'm preparing to head inside for a late dinner...when Landon intercepts me on the way to my apartment.

"Where are you going?"

"It's almost nine o'clock, so I'm going to eat dinner, shower, and collapse into bed." The long summer days are starting to catch up with me, and I can't help the tart note in my voice. "Why, do you need something?"

"Our trail ride?" Landon reminds me.

"Oh, god, Landon. Not tonight. Not—" He grabs my arms and walks me, puppet style, to the barn door. "What are you—oh!"

A golden disc of moon is rising above the tree line. Not just any moon. The biggest, roundest, most terrifyingly close moon I've ever seen. I am pretty sure that this moon is about to crash-land in the pasture. We should be donning our hard hats and hiding under our beds. "Holy shit, Landon," I breathe.

"Uh-huh. Now go grab your hat, your bridle, and your horse."

I'm not about to argue with him, not when that astonishing moon is rising so quickly I can see it already lifting from the grasp of the dark trees below. But I also grab my saddle, girth, and a pad before I run out to the paddock where Thomas is grazing. I'm not about to ride my ex-racehorse *bareback* under a full moon. I don't have a death-wish, thanks.

In less than ten minutes, I'm mounted and waiting outside of the barn. The moon is already noticeably smaller, much less likely to topple to the earth, but still pretty astonishing. Landon comes out of the barn with one of his previously lame Thoroughbreds, a pigeon-toed bay mare named Bess. He hops on her bareback, grinning at me. "First time she's been ridden in three months," he says.

"Good lord, Landon."

"She's fine." Bess side-steps anxiously as Landon swings his legs alongside her barrel. He lets her move as she pleases. "She just wants to go."

"Well, where are we going?" I ask, letting Thomas sidle alongside the mare. She pins her ears and Thomas accordingly takes two steps to his left to give her space.

"Just along the tree-line. It'll be beautiful. Wait and see." He whistles and Sid comes racing up beside us. We set off down the driveway, Bess snorting as the dog dives in and out of her path. "Just a dog," he tells the mare. "Time to get used to dogs. You're going to have a life again, Miss Formerly Lame Mare."

"Bess is looking really good." I watch her with appreciation. She has a long stride and a bright expression, dark eyes that seem to glow at me through the dusk. "You really turned her around in a month."

"She grew a lot of nice toe," he says contentedly. "And my soaks killed all the bacteria in her hooves. I'm really happy with the results so far."

"What are you going to do with her?"

"This girl?" Landon pats her neck. "I think I might keep her as my riding horse."

"Will you show her?"

"I could," he says. "I haven't thought a lot about it."

The horses walk animatedly along the sand driveway, heading down towards the lights of Kayla and Basil's house. I can see their shapes through the windows, heating up dinner in the kitchen. They'd be so surprised if they looked out and saw us.

"I don't know anyone who doesn't think about what they're going to do next with their horse like, obsessively," I say.

"Oh yeah?" He gives me an appraising look. "Well, what are you going to do with Thomas after the Thoroughbred Makeover?"

"Keep showing, obviously. Take him to Legends Equestrian Center in the winter, if I can afford it. Show him in classes with a Thoroughbred Incentive Program division when I can." The T.I.P. classes have cash prizes for high-placing retired racehorses. I'll take a payday anywhere I can find it. The longer I can manage without touching my investment accounts, the better shot I have at launching my clothing company someday. It takes a lot of money to get a business like that off the ground.

"Where does it all lead?" Landon asks.

"I don't know. As far as it can get me." Surely he knows there's no end-game to horse showing. You just do it.

Landon persists in his questions, though. "Where do you want it to take you? Beyond showing, I mean. Is this for the clothes you design?"

I shrug. When I'm ready to launch my business, then people will know. If I can ever make it happen.

We reach the tree-line at the front of the property and Landon swings his mare onto a trail that runs along the fence. Beneath the oak trees, the moonlight struggles to find its way to the ground, creating bright patches that contrast with dark pools spreading across the trail like bottomless seas. I find it nerve-wracking and want to see where Thomas is going, but he and Bess step without hesitation into the darkness, seeming to step around roots and shallow depressions that I can't see. Sid runs happily ahead of us, his coat shining blue every time he finds a splash of moonlight.

"Bess is making Thomas confident," I say, surprised at how forward he's being, despite the darkness and the strange territory.

"Stallions and geldings will always feel better in the company of a mare," Landon says. "Mares are the leaders of the herd. They make all the decisions about where to graze, when to go to water, where to find shelter."

"Maybe I should hire the two of you to be our companions at horse shows," I joke.

"Maybe that's a pretty good idea."

I glance over at Landon, but the darkness shades his face and I don't know if he's being serious or not.

Suddenly, Sid darts forward, barking furiously. Both horses snort. I feel Thomas draw back as Bess's steps slow. He's watching the mare, taking his cues from her, and she's saying there's something worrisome ahead.

"Ah, shit," Landon mutters. "Did Sid just wriggle through the fence?"

We reach the corner of the property and find that Sid has done just that. His white coat shines in the moonlight as he races across the neighboring hay field, still barking like he's on the hunt.

"What do you want to do?" I ask, letting Thomas circle. The horse is nervous, upset that we've stopped and possibly confused about what set the dog running off, too. "We have to go after him. Is there a gate?"

"There's something down here—" Landon slips down from his mare's back and leads her off the path. "Here," he calls. "There's a narrow gate. Be careful riding through it."

Thomas trots through the gate, a natural reaction to being asked to go through something so skinny, and we have to circle to let Landon mount up again and catch up with us. By now, Sid's barking is in the distance. The hay-field, a vast sea of knee-high grass, stretches out to a distant tree line, and I see lights glinting beyond that—barns, a house. The neighbor's place.

"He's going back to Vince's," I say, dismayed. Why would the dog go back there? He's been living happily with Landon for weeks now. He could have gone back to his old life at any point. The fact that he chose tonight, when we're having such a nice time, makes me irrationally angry. "Ungrateful mutt."

"He probably just caught a scent, and it happens to be leading in that direction," Landon says defensively. "He wouldn't go back there. Come on, let's trot after him so he doesn't feel lost when he changes his mind and wants to come home."

Landon bumps Bess with his heels, and the mare springs into a trot that quickly becomes a canter. Thomas immediately gives chase. I would rather not be galloping across a hay-field with nothing but moonlight to illuminate our way, but it's not like I have a choice. If you have two Thoroughbreds and one of them starts running, then you have two running Thoroughbreds.

Fortunately, even if Vince is a terrible dog owner, he's an excellent hay farmer. The field has been cultivated for years and now, in the height of hay season, the ground beneath the high grass is rolled and smoothed to perfection. There are no holes for hooves to find, no divots or depressions to throw a horse's balance off. And so I can't help but give in to the euphoria bubbling up from within as Thomas's strides lengthen and he gives me a taste of what he really does best.

Galloping.

He stretches out until Landon calls for us to slow, reminding me that he's riding bareback while I have the advantage of saddle and stirrups. I stand up in the stirrups and slow Thomas, bringing him back alongside Bess. Landon is cantering along comfortably.

"You're a very good bareback rider!" I call, raising my voice to be heard over the horse's hard breaths and the rolling thunder of hooves on firm ground.

"Thank you!" he calls back. "I have a lot of practice!"

As usual, his words make me want to know more, but I

know he won't tell me anything.

So annoying.

We pull up the horses at the far end of the hay-field, where a barbed wire fence tells us this is the end of the chase. A few hundred feet away, dogs are barking around a barn lit by a single street-light. Beyond that, there's a house. The front porch-light is on, and the silhouette of a portly man stands in the doorway.

"That's Vince," Landon mutters. "Dammit, Sid!"

"He's going to see us," I say, looking around for somewhere to hide our horses. The trees growing between the field and the barn area are thin and sickly, and there isn't much shade from the moonlight to be found.

"I'm not going back without Sid," Landon says, riding Bess along the fence. I know he's looking for a way in, but horses and barbed wire don't mix.

"Don't ride so close to that fence," I hiss, finding the darkest patch of shadow I can and halting Thomas in it. "Get over here and hand me her reins if you want to go over the fence."

"Okay," he agrees, but it's too late.

"Who's out there?" an angry voice challenges. It's a high-pitched voice with a twangy, country accent, and for some reason, that makes me more nervous. Vince sounds like a guy in a movie who comes out of his trailer with guns blazing. I would have been less afraid of him if he'd shouted with a deep baritone voice and a New Jersey accent. "Whoever's out there, better get out now! I'll set my dogs loose!"

"Okay, we do not need that," I tell Landon urgently. "We need to go."

"If we ride back now, he'll know we came from next door," Landon says, "and that will cause problems for Kayla and Basil.

Also, my dog!"

"He's not *your* dog, Landon!"

As soon as I say it, I know it was a mistake. I don't need full sun or even dusk to see the anger clouding his face. "Then go back," Landon says, his voice a growl. "Go back to the farm alone. I'm not leaving without Sid."

This is a pointless standoff. He has no chance of getting Sid back, and if he goes over that fence, he's going to get himself killed. Vince isn't going to have any tolerance for a huge, hulking Viking of a man suddenly appearing in his yard after dark, demanding dogs.

But what will he do to a woman?

Suddenly I know what to do. And before I can talk myself out of it, I fling myself out of the saddle, throw Thomas's reins to Landon, and run for the barbed wire fence.

Chapter Twenty-Seven

I HOLD UP the top strand of wire and slip between the middle and top without snagging my clothes like I've been doing this all my life. In fact, it *is* a skill I picked up when I was a kid, way back before I started riding ponies. My grandparents used to live adjacent to a cattle ranch where there were always a few horses out on the pasture, and I'd sneak out to pet them on bright, moonlit nights just like this one. Funny, how you never forget some things, like how to get through a barbed wire fence without tearing your shirt, because if you do, Nanna's gonna know you went sneaking off to pet horses again.

With Landon hissing warnings behind me and the dogs barking like crazy ahead of me, I walk steadily towards the house, not bothering to try to hide. I can tell the moment Vince spot me. He put his hands on his hips, clearly perplexed by this trespasser who didn't come off the main road.

"Who the hell are you?" he demands, although I'm still shouting-distance away.

"My dog ran off," I call back. "I'm just out lookin' for him."

I can't help dropping my *g* like that. It just happens when I'm talking to someone with a strong accent. I start picking it up myself.

Luckily, adding a little twang to my voice seems to be just the ticket. Vince drops his hands. "Well, shoot," he says. "He probably came runnin' up here when he heard all mine carryin-on like this. They're always loud on a full moon. You see him anywhere?"

Sid, who has been touching noses with all his friends behind the chain-link fence, chooses that moment to come bounding over to me. I scoop him up in my arms, hoping we're far enough away that Vince can't recognize the dog. He's a pretty ordinary hound dog, anyway. I figure loose hunting dogs are a fact of life around here.

"I got him!" I crow, turning around quickly to hide the dog. Sid is licking my face rapturously. I try not to think about all the disgusting things a farm dog eats in an average day. "Thanks, I'll just be headin' home now!"

"Well, now, wait a minute." Vince's voice lowers, as if he's just thought of something.

I walk faster. Sid wiggles in my arms. "Hold still," I hiss. "Be a good dog!"

"Let me give you a ride home at least," Vince calls.

"No need, thanks so much!" I shout, breaking into a run. I know it looks suspicious, but I have to get moving. This is going far too well. Sid's hindquarters bounce against my thighs. "Do not fall," I whisper. "Do not wiggle, do not bark."

Behind the barbed-wire fence, Landon is staring at me, his mouth round in a silent o. The horses stand behind him, touching noses and nipping at each other. I give Sid a scoot through the fence and pluck up the middle string so I can slide through unassisted. Landon's immobility is a little annoying and a little flattering at the same time.

"You're welcome," I say pointedly, taking Thomas's reins

from him.

"You just went right over there," Landon says, astonished. He looks down at Sid, wiggling around his boots with his tail wagging a mile a minute. "You just picked him up and came back like it was nothing."

"Yeah, I did." It's exhilarating when he puts it like that. I did a thing. A crazy, thoughtless, powerful thing, all on my own. And I saved the freaking day while I was at it. I put my foot in the stirrup and mount. It's finally getting easier, mounting from the ground. I'm getting stronger. This has been a month of muscling up, in more ways than one. I grin to myself, settling my fingers on the reins, in the curve of Thomas's short, dark mane. To Landon, I say, offhandedly, "You gonna get on that horse or what?"

He's still staring at me as he leads Bess over to a tree stump by the fence. The barking dogs are quieting; Vince has gone inside. I can see the blue glow of the television inside the doublewide. "I can't believe you did that," he says.

"Women can get away with stuff men can't," I tell him, suppressing a mischievous smile. "Like trespassing, and stealing dogs."

"Do you live a secret life of crime?" he wonders, riding Bess alongside Thomas. Sid runs along beside us, looking a little worn out from his moonlight run. The horses pull at the reins, happy to be on their way home. I'm just a little annoyed with Landon for implying that I have kept things from him, for overlooking the way he deflects the moment I ask about his life outside of the farm.

"Oh, like I'm the one with the secret life," I snort. "What if I said yes?"

"I'd be really impressed."

"I think you'd be afraid of me," I tease.

"Honestly?" Landon looks at me for a long moment. I feel myself blushing under his gaze; I'm happy the moonlight covers up my pink cheeks. They flush even hotter when he says, "I'm a little afraid of you, anyway, Mackenzie. And I mean that as a compliment."

WHY IS THAT the hottest thing any guy has ever said to me? The words echo in my mind as I scrub off the day in a lukewarm shower (we've reached the part of the summer where hot water is just too much to handle) and towel-dry my hair, noticing that it's past my shoulders now and heading for my chest. I've missed my usual six-week salon appointment and my hair is beginning to curl at the ends, finding the natural wave I haven't seen in years. I look cute, I decide. Cute and, apparently, scary.

I'm a little afraid of you.

Ugh! Devastating!

No one has ever wanted me because I am powerful. No man has ever told me that doing something simply crazy, whether it's getting on a half-ton horse and jumping a four-foot fence, or charging across a redneck's farmyard in the darkness to steal a dog back, makes me desirable. And to be fair, Landon did not outright *say* those things. But his tone, and the way that he looked at me in the moonlight, did say those things.

I'm sure of it.

So now, the thing I was afraid of is now the thing I also want, like a secret that I can't keep any longer. Landon Kincaid, friendly Viking, is definitely attracted to me. And I didn't even want him for a friend, or a helper. Things have definitely spiraled out of control.

I pour a bag of frozen vegetables and chicken into a pan and light the burner underneath. The moonlight shimmers through the kitchen window and dances on the puddle in the sink. This ceiling leak is having a sensational summer, but I've gotten used to the drip. It's almost a friend at this point.

A friend. Right.

I should talk to Casey, before I start telling my troubles to the drip-drip-drip in my sink.

She answers her phone on the first ring. "Where have you been?"

"What?"

"You haven't called me in a week. You haven't texted me in three days. I was beginning to think you had some horrible riding accident."

"Casey! If you thought that why didn't you text me?"

She snorts. "That would make sense, right? I was busy and forgot."

"Well, same here."

"Fair enough. So how are things?"

I take a fork and poke at my slowly thawing dinner. "Pretty interesting, actually."

"Interesting, how?"

"Well, you know Landon...some things are happening." A horde of questions rise up when I say the words out loud. Do I just embrace it? Simply slide into having feelings for him, even though it's the worst idea that I've ever had? Okay, that's not fair. Ryan was clearly the worst idea I ever had.

On the other end of the call, Casey gasps. "Tell me everything! *Brandon*! Turn down the TV! Oh, forget it. I'm going outside." I hear an assortment of noises, televised and otherwise, in the background, and then a slamming door.

"Okay, I'm on the porch. It's a million degrees out here and mosquitoes are launching an assault on the screens, so make this worth the trauma."

"You know, we barely have mosquitoes here? Just at sunset and sunrise. I almost forgot how bad they are all the time down there."

"Mackenzie, if you don't stop boasting about your bug-free life and tell me about Landon—"

"Okay, okay!" I laugh. "You won't believe what happened tonight."

After I relay the story, ending with the line about finding me scary, Casey is quiet. My nerves ramp up to a vibration I can nearly hear, like tinnitus ringing in both ears. "Casey? Hello?"

"I'm here. I'm just...processing."

"Okay, I'll wait." I use the time to fill a glass with water, add some lemon juice, and take down a bowl for my supper. I'm not eating directly from the pan anymore, thank goodness. That little depression passed. I'm not even sure when. Everything over the past month has just slid soundlessly into place, like I am a little twig floating in a stream, carried past reeds and rocks and quiet alligators sunning on muddy banks, and now I am here in the dark, still waters of an oxbow, wondering when the current will pick me up and whip me forward again.

"Here's what I think," Casey says suddenly.

"I'm ready."

"I think he's into you."

I smile. "Me, too."

"But I don't love that he's so silent about his background."

My face slackens, smile fading. "Me, too."

"You need to know more about him before you get involved with him," Casey says. "He could be anybody." She says *anybody* but *serial killer, horse murderer,* and *venture capitalist* are all implied as potential outcomes.

"I didn't say I was going to get involved with him," I point out.

"But you are, right? That goes without saying. He lives across the barn aisle from you. He takes you on moonlit trail rides. He helps you with your horse. He's the *dream.* This is why I had to go outside," she adds. "Imagine if I said that in front of Brandon."

"But *Brandon* is the dream," I remind her. "He learned to ride horses for you. He moved to a farm for you."

"I know. I never forget it. But Landon is another version of the dream. And you need to be careful, because he could break your heart."

I take a breath. It's awful to hear that old line. It's worse to know it's true.

I moved here to get away from a man who broke my heart. But Ryan didn't find me powerful, or scary, either. He thought I was someone to push around, someone to own. A girl on a leash. Landon would never, ever think that.

But if I'm so powerful and scary to him, does that also mean that Landon doesn't think he could break my heart?

How dangerous is that?

THOMAS THE TRAIL Horse's Training Diary
  Midsummer Full Moon

Well I definitely didn't expect to take Thomas on a moonlight ride, and I didn't expect to go chasing after a dog on someone else's farm, either, but I guess that's what living around Landon can be like. It was so silly and childish of him to suggest the ride...but I'm glad he did. We had a lot of fun, even if things got crazy.

And I'm so proud of Thomas! He handled the dark trail and galloping across the field like a total pro. Not exactly conditions we have to prep for in Kentucky, but it just gives him more exposure to problem-solving and keeping his cool in weird situations. Also, he's really fine with barking dogs. That could come in handy. Horse show dogs can be a real menace if they're not properly trained. One less thing we'll have to worry about at the Makeover!

Chapter Twenty-Eight

THE SECOND HORSE show in my Prep Thomas for Kentucky schedule is also at Canterbury, and once again, Florida's climate shows up to make things weird. This time, though, it's not the heat. It's the tropical depression. A big blob of rain rolls in from the Gulf of Mexico on Friday evening and sits there as the horse show tries to go on, intermittently dumping rain on the show-grounds with the subtlety of one of those kid's water parks where a large bucket just tips over on the screaming children beneath every few minutes. Everyone is drenched, everyone is frowning, and everyone just wants to go home.

I definitely feel like a screaming child when a monsoon opens up on us during our hunter under saddle class. It was tough enough convincing Thomas to go around like a hunter, on a nearly loose rein, when I've been trying to teach him to reach for the contact like a dressage horse. When the rain comes down, his ears go flat and his head goes straight up. My fingers are slipping on the soaking-wet reins, and there's not much I can do to convince him that we should trot politely around on the rail.

Luckily, none of the other horses react well to the heavy rain or the whipping wind, either, and we squeak out a fourth place in the class.

Back beneath the stable overhang—once again, Landon has paid for a stall that I did not budget for, and I'm too grateful to protest in this weather—we watch the clouds racing overhead and try to decide if we should stick around for the cross-rails class I've already entered, or just get back to the farm before we all wash away.

"On one hand, fame and glory," I say, wringing water out of my gloves.

"On the other, dry and comfy," Landon says, wiping the water spots off my saddle.

"True."

Rain roars on the roof as the wind picks up, knocking down a few bridles and saddle pads from the large farm stabled next to us. I hear some shrieks from the show-ring and warm-ups. "This is why showing in summer in Florida is a bad idea."

"You get what you pay for," Landon says. "If you wanted to summer in upstate New York, you should have started saving twenty years ago."

He doesn't know that a year ago, I would have had the means to rent a farm in upstate New York and show on the circuits up there for an entire season, and I decide to keep that to myself. "Where would you summer, if you had the choice?"

Landon shrugs. "Florida's fine, but I'm not trying to make a show name for myself."

"Landon! I'm not trying to do that, either, and you know it. I just want to have Thomas ready to go to Kentucky in October."

"Is that worth drowning for?" His tone is oddly sharp.

"My god," I snort. "I don't think it's that serious."

Lightning flashes over the show-grounds, followed by an echoing roar of thunder. He flinches. "Not serious?" he demands.

"That was up in the clouds," I say. "You learn to read Florida storms."

"You shouldn't go back out there."

"I'm going to." It's a struggle to keep my voice light. I don't want to fight with him...but he's also not going to tell me what to do. "What if it's storming in Kentucky? We have to be ready for anything."

"Why?" Landon practically shouts. Then, catching himself, he quietly adds: "Why is Kentucky so important?"

"I feel like we've had this discussion," I say cooly, ducking under Thomas's stall guard and into the shed-row to put some space between us. "The Thoroughbred Makeover is a big deal," I say. "I thought you knew that. I thought I made it clear."

"Training a retired racehorse is a big deal, but I don't know why you have to go to *this* show to prove what you can do. There are shows in Florida, Mackenzie! We're at one, if you haven't noticed."

"I don't have to explain myself to you," I snarl, retreating behind Thomas so that I can't see Landon's injured expression. I *don't*—but even if I did, I'd have a hard time explaining this obsession to him. Maybe Landon doesn't know how it feels to be alone, like I am. There is something to be said for belonging to a tribe. And right now, I don't. When I left Wellington, I wasn't giving up a group of friends who would miss me; I didn't leave a coach who was desperate for me to stay; I certainly didn't have a man in the rear-view mirror who would mourn my disappearance.

But Thomas is my key to a secret society.

The (mostly) women who retrain ex-racehorses in hopes of showing them off at the Thoroughbred Makeover seem like a sisterhood I could be a part of. They post their triumphs and tragedies and stupid horse moves (there are always a lot of those) in their Facebook groups and on their Instagram stories and in their vlogs. They talk about the best ways to sort out their horses' prior training as racers and turn it into valuable experience in their futures as ranch horses or eventers or hunters. They console each other when things go wrong. They congratulate each other for every tiny triumph.

I'm not part of their world yet. I don't post much about Thomas; I don't share his photo constantly in the groups or on my social media. I want to, but I'm afraid. I'm afraid I'm not ready yet, that I'll screw up or I'll do something so obviously wrong that I'll never be allowed into their sisterhood. I'll never be one of those retired racehorse girls, high-fiving at the horse park, showing everyone what I've done with my Thoroughbred.

But maybe, if I keep my head down and work hard enough and watch what they do, things will work out. I'll get to Kentucky and show that I'm worthwhile, that I'm good enough, to be one of the girls.

And then I'll be brave enough to post in the groups and chat with the others and share cute photos of Thomas being the best little ex-racehorse he can be.

After the Makeover, not before. Because once I get through the Makeover, I'll know that I've remade myself, too.

How to explain all that to Landon, though, without seeming insane? He doesn't know that I'm trying to make over my own life. That Thomas isn't just a project horse, he's a second chance for me.

I jumped the gun the first time around. I married a guy who wasn't good enough for me and I let him drag me down. I'm not going to get ahead of myself this time. It's still only late July. In three months, I'll go to Kentucky and I'll be ready.

"We're showing in the cross-rails class," I say, and my tone makes it clear that's final. As I say it, the rain lets up, going abruptly from a full downpour to a piddling drizzle. Typical tropical nonsense.

Landon grunts in agreement, but doesn't say anything in reply

I guess that conversation is over. Good. I don't have anything to say to him about Kentucky, anyway. He's made it clear that he's got some issue with that state. Probably wanted for a crime there or something.

I curl my fingers into Thomas's mane. God, I hope that's not the case.

THERE'S A PATCH of blue sky above us when our number is called for the cross-rails course. I glance up at that little azure spot, glowing through the weeping gray sky, and hope it will stay put long enough for our round in the show-ring. We only need, what, three minutes? We'll trot around this course, maybe canter a few fences if Thomas is feeling super-comfortable in the arena, and then we'll get out. Trot back to the barn. We can stay dry through it all if that blue patch of sky just stays strong and doesn't let the storm clouds muscle it out of the way—

As we trot through the timers and towards the first little jump, the wind picks up again. I don't have to look up to know that the next squall is on the way.

Thomas pricks his ears and lifts his head to look at the cross-rail ahead of us. The standards are cute, all brightly painted flowers with smiley faces, but the poles are what count and they're just basic blue-and-white striped jump poles. Nothing he hasn't seen or hopped over back at the farm. I sink my weight into my heels and give a little cluck of encouragement with my tongue, letting him know that he's free to look, but ultimately there is to be no stopping.

Thomas snorts with each exhalation, letting me know that he's pretty sure the jump has a suspicious air to it.

The sharp, humid wind hits my backs and ruffles his mane, then rattles the jump poles in their cups.

Snort, snort, snort, Thomas says, his head lifting still higher. I'm looking between his ears now.

"Come on, buddy," I encourage him. "We've jumped in bad weather before. You're a Florida horse. You know the drill."

He snorts all the way over the jump and lands in a slow canter, ears already locked onto the next fence. It's five strides away, but the gait he's in right now won't get us there in anything better than five and a half, so I sit and bring him back to a trot. He shakes his head a little in protest, but his strides slacken as I ask. Such a good—

Wham!

The sound comes from behind us, the crash of falling standards and poles rattling to the ground. But I don't have time to think about what the noise might have been; I'm too busy finding out where I'm going. Almost before I hear anything, Thomas is already bolting forward, his head going straight up, foam flicking from his bit to my breeches. Amazingly, we're still heading for the second jump, and he flings himself over it, back hollowed like a deer. I sit tight in the saddle, clinging to his mane with my legs bunched up against his sides, and as he races away from the cross-rail, the next rain squall unleashes itself over the show-grounds.

I'm drenched, instantly; the raindrops are the size of half-dollars and every one of them seems to explode against us like water balloons. Landon cannily added a breastplate to our tack when we came out for this class and I'm thankful for it, because I wrap my fingers around the strap over the withers and it gives me an anchor, a way to keep the slick reins from sliding entirely through my fingers. My gloves were too wet to bother wearing again.

For a moment I don't know what we're going to do next, and then as the end of the arena approaches and the curving rail naturally turns my galloping horse to the left, I realize that we're still technically on course and we hadn't knocked down any poles on that first line.

"Keep going," I mutter, turning Thomas's nose in the direction of the next line. Maybe we'll be fast and messy, but we can still finish the course.

The turn helps me balance him and I bring him back down to a trot, but now we're facing the blowing rain and Thomas shakes his head, upset at the stinging raindrops in his eyes and nostrils. For a moment, I feel bad about asking him to jump, but the fact is, we'd be stuck out in this rain either way, and that jump isn't really big enough to feel guilty over. A dog could jump that cross-rail without putting any effort into it. Thomas will be just fine.

He hops over the fence easily, his mind more on the rain slapping him in the face than spooking at the jumps. And he trots over the second one as well, moving so nicely now that I let him canter over the last two lines. By the time we finish the final fence, the rain is letting up; our two-minute monsoon is moving on.

The hardy few standing by the arena railing applaud as we trot out of the ring, intent on getting back to the stabling. I give them a wave, feeling a little rush of excitement. We did the thing! It was crazy and possibly ill-advised, but we did it, in front of people, and they clapped!

Landon, wearing a clear poncho he must have begged, borrowed, or stolen off someone's golf cart, runs ahead of us to the stabling and waits there with a couple of towels. As I slip off Thomas and let the horse walk into his stall, he throws a towel to me. "Wrap that around yourself and get dry," he says gruffly, following Thomas inside.

I do as I'm told, already feeling chilly now that I'm soaked through for the second time. The wind isn't letting up this time, either, and now the temperature seems to be dropping. I guess the storm is really settling in. "Thank you," I say, as he starts stripping Thomas's soaking-wet tack.

"You should go and get in the truck," he says, not turning around.

"No, I'm not—"

"Then go into the trailer and change clothes." He slides the saddle from Thomas's back. "Get yourself really dry. You're cold. Your lips are blue!" he adds, looking around at me. "You look like you fell into a frozen pond! Go on, now."

I should be annoyed. He's ordering me around.

But something about Landon's gruff commands warms me from the inside instead of ticking me off. And it's only when I'm in the trailer, toweling off my wet hair, I realize that his commands are coming from his heart. For the first time, someone is taking care of me, instead of the other way around.

* * *

THOMAS THE CROSS-Rail Champion's Training Diary
  The Depths of Hurricane Season

Thomas is officially tropical-storm-proof, so that's something. I'm proud of my little monster boy. Today he managed to jump a course while a monsoon blew through the ring. It should have blown his cool, but he managed to get around. I really don't think Kentucky can throw anything this crazy at us. Do they even get hurricanes in Kentucky? If there's a torrential downpour during the Thoroughbred Makeover, we're ready.

Chapter Twenty-Nine

LATE SUMMER IN Florida is a rumbling, dangerous thing. The storms often blow up early and stick around until late, the towering clouds flickering with electricity in otherworldly shades of shiny, dangerous blue and ethereal, bubblegum pink. There is something about those pink and orange-tinted lightning bolts that give me the shivers. They're just a little too beautiful, as if they belong to another planet. As if the Martians have arrived in chariots of literal fire.

It's hard to ride horses in this weather. If the humidity and heat aren't dangerous, the lightning is. Kayla and Basil give their horses a break in August, riding them just enough to keep them from going feral. On these hot, sparking summer days, the horses spend their days dozing or eating hay in their stalls, their faces pressed close to their fans, waiting for sundown and the resumption of somewhat livable temperatures. When there's no lightning around, they can be turned out.

When that means waiting until ten or eleven o'clock, that means it's my job to turn them out in the darkness.

Kayla assures me that no one really expects me to get the horses outside if the weather doesn't clear before ten. She says bedtimes are a boundary that should be respected, and anyway, she knows it's a lot of horses to get out on my own. "If I thought it was the end of the world if they stayed in overnight, I'd get in my truck and come down here to do it myself," she tells me. "I know they need to get out and stretch, so if the weather is awful in the evening, maybe we can just kick them out first thing in the morning, okay?"

But morning turnout is a pain for me, too. Even though they're in light work, horses still need to be clean, tacked up, and ready to go when Kayla and Basil need them. If the horses are outside, I'm the one who has to schlep across the wet, steaming pastures to catch them and drag them back in—while also getting the stalls cleaned and handling the hot horses after their rides. Keeping them in sucks on every level, for the horses as well as for me. It's simply not healthy to keep them inside for extended periods of time. The really fit young horses get difficult to handle when they're cooped up—that's hard on me *and* on the riders. And of course, their stalls are total disasters. That's just hard on me.

And, apparently, it's hard on Landon, who can't seem to stop himself from picking up a manure fork whenever he's in the barn. No matter how many times I tell him it's not his job and to stop coming directly back from his farrier work or from working on his tinctures to do barn work at my side, Landon is there, pitching in. Helping me.

On one hand, the warm, floating feeling of being cared for that I discovered at the rainy horse show hasn't diminished. I can't help feeling content and safe whenever he's in the barn. It's like being cradled while spa music gently tinkles around me. Until I start looking for him, and feeling disappointed and low-energy when he's not around. Landon lights up the barn aisle for me, and it is becoming a serious problem, because, of course, most of the time, he's actually off doing his real job.

"You're into him," Casey says.

It's a stormy evening in late August—like all of them this year, it seems like. I fed the horses alone at five o'clock and came inside, wishing Landon wasn't working in Ocala so late tonight. I want him around so I have someone sympathetic and fun to talk to, maybe even to have dinner with. Our mutual attraction is something separate from this craving for company, or at least, that's what I'm telling myself. It's a suppressed thing, a sparkle beneath every conversation that makes my skin tingle and my fingers tremble if I let myself think about it too much. I steal glances at him; I catch him stealing glances at me. *Are we falling for each other?* I think sometimes, but I can never let myself believe something so foolish. We're friends who are in the midst of a silly little crush. I try to enjoy it; I haven't had a crush on anyone since high school, and those were rarely as satisfying as this one.

Tonight, if he were around, I'd show him I can make real food; he's been making fun of my constant rotation of bagged frozen veggies and chicken. Tonight I planned to cook some actual non-frozen chicken thighs in my tiny oven, surrounded on a sheet pan by summer squash and sliced potatoes, all drizzled with olive oil and rosemary. He'd laugh and call it a girl dinner, but he'd eat it with me, and we'd have a good time.

But he's working late, so I'm talking to Casey instead.

And regretting it, because she doesn't know when to just leave something alone.

"I'm not *into* him," I insist. "We're just having fun. We're just teasing each other." As soon as I say it, I wonder if we are. It's not like I dress seductively—it's hardly my fault all of my clothes are skin-tight. That's how riding clothes work, and it's too hot to wear anything else for barn chores. What am I going to do, wear jeans to muck stalls when it's ninety-eight degrees outside? Hardly. "It's like a little high school crush," I say. "We're just passing notes in class and stuff, because we're always together and it's fun this way."

"We didn't go to high school together," Casey says matter-of-factly, "but if we did, I would have called you out and said this was more than a crush, and I would have been right. I'm always right about these things."

"Okay, and then what would happen?" I ask. "If you were right, which you would not be."

"I'd formulate a plan to find out if he likes you, too."

"You'd formulate a plan? This is starting to sound like a Disney Channel movie."

"Well, they always have happy endings," Casey points out.

She's right. I don't have an answer to that.

"Well, we can figure this out," Casey continues. "I mean, you live together. Practically, that is. It shouldn't be hard to get him into your apartment and find out if he wants to make a few moves on the sofa."

"What are we calling this movie?" I ask sarcastically, because it's such a good idea that I need to deflect immediately.

" 'Barn Crush,' " Casey answers immediately, making me laugh.

"Okay, I like that. Well, we could have begun production tonight, but the leading man is away tonight."

I glance reproachfully at the dark oven, where my chicken should be baking away, giving the apartment a warm, cozy feeling it hasn't yet offered me. Because I haven't used the oven yet. Not once all summer. And if Landon doesn't get home from work soon, it's not getting used tonight, either. I'll microwave something and go to bed.

Lightning flashes, making me blink. Oh, right, and turn out the horses.

Then I can go to bed.

Casey is saying something about forced-proximity romance being one of her favorite tropes, which is when I realize that she's taking this whole thing the wrong way. "Casey," I interrupt, "I don't actually *want* to get together with Landon. You're looking for the wrong ending here."

"What?"

"I am supposed to be getting my life together on my own," I remind her. "Not falling in love with the first guy to be nice to me in my new life."

"First of all, no one was talking about falling in love until right now," she says. "Second of all, what do you *mean* you don't want to get together with him? That's ridiculous. He's nice, he's hot, he likes horses, what's the problem?"

"Aside from what I just told you? Well, we do work together and like you've pointed out, we practically live together, so when we break up, it's going to be awkward as hell and probably get me in a lot of trouble with my bosses—"

"Why are you breaking up with him already?"

"I'm just saying, we will break up eventually, and then—"

"Stop. Wait. No." Casey actually sounds kind of pissed. "I hate it when people say things like that! Don't be like that! You can't be pessimistic about love. It's the worst."

"You're raising your voice at me about this? Seriously?"

"Yes! It's obnoxious when people do that. 'When we break up.' 'He'll make a good first husband.' 'It will be a messy divorce.' All before you're even *dating*. It's so defeatist and it degrades the whole point of falling in love."

"And what's that?" I say, biting back a huffy sigh.

"Giving in," Casey says. "To all of it."

"I don't know what you mean," I say.

"Don't you?" She laughs at me. "Think about how you feel about Thomas, and then tell me you don't know what it means to give in to love."

SHE HAS A point.

Mentally, I concede that to her about an hour later, well after our call is over and she's gone back to her cozy little life with Brandon. I don't know if I'll ever actually tell her that she's right, but damn...loving Thomas really is a great example of going all in and loving without fear of consequences. That horse is all wrapped up in the life I've come here to build, and when I see him, my heart lifts straight into my throat. I feel like I could stare at him for days and not get my fill. He gives me a feeling of warmth, of devotion, of total love.

That warmth he gives me is not unlike the warm, safe feeling I get with Landon around.

I'm almost afraid to analyze that too closely.

I get up, closing my laptop on the training video I've been half-watching, and head to the kitchen.

Rain is still pattering on the roof, although the lightning has let up and the thunder is only occasional, just a distant rumble now. I check the radar on my phone and decide I still have time to make myself some dinner before the rain gives up and I can turn the horses out. It looks like that'll be around nine o'clock, which isn't the worst turnout time I've had in the past week. I can be in bed by ten.

Surely Landon will be home by then? I don't expect him to come knocking on my door, but it would be nice to know he's home and safe, not out driving his huge truck on the dark, wet roads. I already know from past experience that I'll have trouble falling asleep before I hear his truck pulling up to the barn, before I hear his door closing behind him for the night.

Ugh! Must I feel this way? Being a girl is the worst. There's no way Landon is thinking about me right now.

Or...is there?

I turn on the oven to preheat and take out a sheet pan to prep my dinner, even though the microwave is right there, waiting blankly for me to slide in a frozen burrito. Instead, I reach into the fridge. Chicken. Pre-sliced squash and a bag of cubed potatoes. Olive oil, salt, some seasonings. It couldn't be much easier. Why haven't I cooked myself a proper meal before? All summer, I've been using the stovetop and the microwave to heat up frozen food like a graduate student living in a dorm, when with a few minutes of work, I can just—

I sniff, my thoughts arrested. The oven smells odd.

A little smoky, actually.

I blink at the light hanging over the sink. There seems to be a faint cloud hanging around the bulb. Is it...hazy...in here?

"Oh, *shit*," I exclaim, as realization floods over me. I turn off the oven and fling open the door before I have time to remember how dangerous that can be. No flames greet me, thank god, but the gush of smoke belching out in my face gives me a moment of panic that really seems to stop my heart for several milliseconds. I'm pretty sure I've gone into cardiac arrest.

Then the smoke clears and I can see that it's just from something gross on the bottom of the oven which I hadn't noticed before. A patch of oil or grease or burnt dough, who knows what. The important takeaway here is that the barn will not be burning down tonight.

My heart stutters back to life, but there's now a fluttering in my chest which shouldn't be there. I fling open the kitchen window, letting the wet breeze filter in to wash away the charred scent before the smoke detector gets a whiff and starts shrieking about it, then throw myself into a kitchen chair, feeling defeated and a little queasy. The anxious quiver in my chest is no stranger; I used to feel this way every time I got home from a long evening at the barn and knew Ryan was waiting in the condo, ready to be angry with me over something real or imagined. My therapist told me it wasn't a heart attack waiting to happen, but it wasn't a sign of anything good, either. It certainly wasn't an indicator that things were going well in my life.

I hate this feeling. I hate being reminded of Ryan, the way he made me feel. I don't want it to come back, not ever. Not over the fear of fire, and not over the fear of a man who wants to own me.

I *can't* get involved with Landon. That realization is evident, obvious, the easiest decision I've made in years. Even if Casey's right, even if I want to fall in love with him, even if he makes my chest expand and fill—the opposite of this horrible, caving-in feeling I have right now—the same way it does with Thomas, I can't go back to this place. I can't let someone have this much control over me, over how my very heart feels in my chest.

I've been there, I've done that, and I've burned the t-shirt.

"Okay," I murmur. "So, I'll get over him."

The rain is suddenly heavy again, roaring on the roof as if I'm sitting under a freeway overpass. I put my face in my hands, so tired and sad I can hardly think.

And then I hear a knock on the door.

Chapter Thirty

"ARE YOU OKAY?"

I stare up at him. Landon is a big man, but tonight he seems like a giant. Like he could sweep me into his arms and I'd simply disappear.

I don't know if that's good or bad.

Maybe it's neither. Maybe it simply is. Like the way I love Thomas, like the way I've loved horses my entire life with no rhyme or reason or probable cause, maybe whatever is happening with Landon just *is*.

He's looking down at me as if the whole world hinges on my answer, as if he has driven home at a hundred miles an hour so that he can check on me.

"I'm okay," I say, my voice a croak. There are unshed tears in my throat; I was on my way to a full-fledged head-on-the-table sob when he knocked. Like his size, like my disappearing, I don't know if it's good or bad that he's stopped me before I could get rolling on the misery-fest. It simply is.

"It smells like smoke in here," he says, looking past me.

I watch his blue eyes sweep the apartment. If there was a fire, he would put it out, with his bare hands if nothing else would suffice. I know he'd do that for me—and for the horses, too. I know, with an instinct so keen it's like a bolt of pink lightning in my gut, that he'd do anything for me, burn his hands or break his heart. He's been doing so much for me, all summer long, but it's only a drop in the bucket compared to the blood he'd shed for me.

Don't ask me how I know all that; it's just *there*, a realization that takes my breath away.

When I catch it again, he's past me, examining the smoky oven while I put my hand to my chest and realize that the shaking, fluttering anxiety has gone.

"You've never cleaned this oven, have you?" Landon asks, closing it up again. He turns to look at me.

"You know I never cook," I remind him. "You've teased me about it enough." My voice is so natural now. I've always been good at acting calm, normal. Being the woman of the house for an anxious father and a controlling husband can teach you to act. Just one more thing I can do on command to keep the menfolk happy.

"What made you decide to start tonight?" He glances over my prepped sheet pan. It's clearly enough food for two. "Oh. Were you expecting company? In this weather?"

Does he sound disappointed? I can't believe him. "I was going to invite *you*," I say, "but you weren't home yet."

"You were? Well. Why didn't you text me and ask when I was coming?"

And be the pushy one demanding answers? No thanks. I've been warned against that behavior before. "I figured if you wanted me to know, you'd have told me," I say with a little shrug.

Landon cocks his head, and I can see his confusion. "I mean, I would have—if I'd known—"

"It's okay," I say quickly. "I should have asked you ahead of time. I just thought, it would be a fun surprise to prove I can cook...but clearly not."

"Hey, you can still prove you can cook," Landon says, brightening. "I have an oven."

"You want me to cook for you in your apartment?" Somehow, it seems different to take my things to his apartment. Even more so than letting him into my space, eating at my table, is different from our neutral meeting ground in the tack room. I kind of wish there was an oven in there. Then we could do all of this without...I don't know. Expectations. Notions.

Constant vigilance for signals we might read the wrong way.

"All I know is that I'm hungry, and you're probably hungry, and this place smells a bit like someone else's burned dinner," Landon says with a grin. "Wouldn't it be nice to fix this lovely supper and eat it with my charming company? I'll even spare you the most gruesome parts of the hoof resection that kept me out so late tonight."

I actually want to hear all about the hoof resection procedure. That will keep the mood from getting...moody. In case it was heading in that direction. Which it probably is not, anyway. "Okay," I say, giving in. "Let's go cook dinner."

I can only imagine what Casey would say about this.

GOING BACK INTO Landon's apartment gives me an odd sense of déjà vu. I mean, it has been three months since I slipped in here, took a look around, and then stole his coffee. The place hasn't changed much, except for Sid's things: a dog-bed on the floor next to the sofa, where Sid has made a neat pile of plush toys and bones, and his dishes on the floor where the kitchen linoleum takes over for the living room carpet. Sid is on the sofa, wagging his tail madly, when we come inside. He leaps down and runs for me, mouth wide open.

I hold the sheet-pan above my head and carry it to the kitchen before Sid can achieve his heart's desire: knocking me off-balance and stealing my chicken.

"Get down, bad dog!" Landon scolds as Sid flings his front paws onto the kitchen counter, stretching heroically to keep them there. "You had a hamburger two hours ago, for god's sake! You're not starving!"

"A hamburger?" I raise an eyebrow. "Is that on the great farrier's nutrition plan for dogs?"

"Hey, I don't specialize in dogs," he says. "And he stole that hamburger. He got into a bag of McDonald's the farm owner had brought home for dinner."

"Oh, no, Sid! You're going to lose Daddy his livelihood."

Sid pants happily at me and then gallops over to his bowl as Landon pours kibble liberally from a plastic bag. It's a pretty expensive brand. I smile to myself while I switch on the oven. This one doesn't smoke. Fancy times.

"Drink while we wait?" Landon asks.

I nod, expecting a beer, and I'm surprised when a decent brand of Pinot Grigio comes out of a cabinet. "We're being so fancy tonight!" I exclaim and immediately regret how shrill my voice sounds. Like things are proceeding in a direction I'm not comfortable with—and that's just not true.

Is it?

I would like to have a solid take on my own mental state right now, but sadly, that ship seems to have sailed. Landon is pouring us each a healthy measure of wine, an eyebrow still raised in my direction as he tries to read where my thoughts are going, too. Poor man. If only he knew the truth. I'm as confused as he is.

Maybe he's not confused, though.

Maybe he knows exactly where he wants this night to go, and I am just the passenger.

When he hands me the glass of wine, I gaze up at him. I can't quite stop myself; his eyes seem to hold mine in thrall. *It just is,* I think, and I don't let them flutter closed until it's quite clear that he's going to kiss me.

The moment our lips come together sets off a bolt of lightning inside me. I feel like one of those brilliant clouds outside, their billows and curves sparkling from within as electricity snakes through them with hot, insatiable bursts of energy. He makes a soft sound against my mouth, something between relief and anticipation, and I hear myself responding in kind, as if we've both been waiting for this forever.

I think we were. I think I was. But I don't know anything for certain. At this point, I'm not sure of my own name.

Landon trails his fingers down my neck as our lips part. I take a shuddering breath, open my eyes, and meet his gaze. His eyes are so intensely blue, I could drown in them. A cliche, sure, but all the best descriptions are.

"Oh," he says softly, as if I've surprised him. "Was that okay?"

"Yes," I whisper, hardly trusting my voice. "Thanks for asking."

WE HAVE JUST kissed.

This should change everything.

We have just kissed, but we are horse-people and there are horses to turn out.

So, back to work we must go.

I hear a thud in the distance that is certainly a hoof connecting with a wall, and someone whinnies anxiously. "They're dying to get out," I say, stepping back from him regretfully.

"I think the thunder is pretty much past," he replies, a smile twisting his lips. "Why don't we get them turned out first and then come back for another glass of wine while dinner cooks?"

There's nothing I want more than another glass of wine, sipped slowly on his sofa while I pry his life story out of him... and perhaps another kiss or two. Okay, I want the kisses more than the wine or the life story.

"I think it's still raining," I say, glancing out the kitchen window. "Do you mind getting wet?"

Landon takes a jacket down from a hook by the door. "I'll go and get started," he says. "If you go into my bedroom closet, there's another rain jacket on the top shelf. I think it's balled up with some sweaters I never wear anymore."

"Great," I say, watching his broad back as he walks down the aisle. "I'll find it."

Did he just give me permission to rummage through his bedroom closet?

No. It would not be rummaging. I'm just reaching up to the top shelf to get a rain jacket. That's all I'm doing. I turn to his bedroom, catching my lower lip with my teeth. It feels odd to go in there now, as if I might see something I shouldn't... something that will arrest this new scene we've just set into motion. I mean, I can't believe I let him kiss me! More than once! And at the same time, I can't imagine a reality in which I said no, pushed him away, told him it was important to me that we stay just friends. So much for all of my steadfast courage to stay true to myself and be a strong, independent woman who doesn't need a man in her life.

I pause in his bedroom door, apprehensive about what I might do, the way I might behave in his space unchaperoned. His room is just as neat tonight as it was that day in June when I broke into his apartment and stole his coffee, but his closet is a mess, stuffed full of plaid and denim work shirts, with some thin fishing-type shirts jostling for room in the middle. The shelf above the hanging shirts is jammed tightly with sweaters and jackets. I wonder if he remembers it as being neater or something, because this is not the quick, easy mission I expected. With a sigh, I tug at what seems like a rain jacket, and naturally, a selection of wooly sweaters rains down on my head.

"Good grief," I groan, picking up the sweaters and tossing them onto the bed. The rain jacket turns up at last, and I'm trying to decide if I should put away the sweaters or head straight out to help with the horses, when I see something that doesn't belong, mixed in with the jumpers and turtlenecks.

I pick it up and stare at it: a small and filmy shirt that wouldn't fit Landon if he was six years old. I recognize the brand and design immediately; I've seen this shirt on my social media feeds for the past year or so. It's a very fashionable white and black riding shirt in a thin, dimpled technical fabric. It's sleeveless, with a quarter-zipper in front, and a yoke of black over the chest and shoulders, which makes a daring silhouette in the saddle. It's a riding shirt for a certain kind of woman who isn't afraid of making heads turn when she enters the warm-up arena, a woman who doesn't want a single gaze to divert from her while she's performing her round in the show-ring. It's not, in short, a top I would have in my closet. More of an ideal, the woman I'd like to be once I've weaned myself off worrying about other people's judgment.

It certainly doesn't make any sense to find it here, in Landon's closet.

Something inside of me twists, snaps, and I bite back a gasp of pain. It would have been awful to find this shirt half an hour ago, before we kissed. Now it's just agonizing. Whose shirt is this? Does he have a girlfriend back in Kentucky? Or worse, someone in Ocala?

I hear hoofbeats from the aisle, shoes on concrete. The sound spurs me into action and I gather up a handful of sweaters, crushing the riding shirt within their knits and heavy wool. And after I've stuffed it all back into the closet, I throw the rain jacket on top.

I'm not going to wear his clothes. Not now. Not when I don't know who else has been in them.

THE RAIN LETS up as we turn out the last two horses, and Landon turns in the barn aisle, pushing back the hood of his jacket. He gets a look at me, seeing how I'm soaked through, and bursts into startled laughter. "But—could you not find the rain jacket?"

"Couldn't find it," I say, trying to keep my tone light. Suddenly, I'm very tired. Maybe it's the wine. Maybe it's that his secrets are deeper and darker than I realized. Or maybe it's that I've been working since seven this morning and it's now past ten. "Listen, Landon, I'm going to bed. Thanks for your help...and the oven...and the wine. You can keep the dinner for yourself."

He looks disappointed now. "You won't even eat? Can't I tempt you in for a nightcap? I've got some nice fluffy towels you could dry off with, too. Fluffiest towels in town!"

His smile is so entreating, so innocent, that I almost give in. But I know I can't do this again.

And by *this* I mean *men*. I can't do men again. I can't go into his apartment and drink his wine and listen to his jokes and watch his gaze turn hot again. Not when he's got some woman's tiny, elegant riding shirt mixed in with his sweaters. Not when he refuses to tell me a thing about his past. Not when it's increasingly evident that Landon, as sweet as he seems, is at his heart just another man who keeps secrets and lies.

"Goodnight, Landon," I say, forcing a fake smile. I head for my own apartment door, feeling his eyes on my back, and wondering why I feel like I'm the one doing something wrong, when he is the one who refuses to be honest with me.

Chapter Thirty-One

KAYLA TAKES A young horse to the open schooling day at Legends Equestrian Center, and Landon volunteers to stay at the farm and fill in for me while I go with her.

"And Basil can pitch in, too," Kayla adds when she tells me. "It can be a nice boy's day for them." She says this as if they're ten-year-olds who have been studying too hard, and when she adds a wink, I know that's exactly how she sees them.

Kayla's wink goes deeper than just making fun of the boys, though. She's worried about me, and so is Basil. They've noticed that for the past week, I've been avoiding Landon. And it would be impossible to miss the way Landon's eyes follow me when he's around the farm. I've started praying for his long work-days in Ocala to take him away, but wouldn't you know, those lengthy sessions seem to have dried up? He says it's the slow season; with the heat, more trainers are giving their horses time off until mid-September, when they'll put them back into training for the winter season. I just wish our timing could be better. What if I'd discovered that lady's riding shirt in his things in July, when he was still so busy?

I'm keenly aware of his schedule, not just because when he's away working on hooves, I have to do everything around the barn, but also because when he's here, I want to be near him, and when he's away, I miss him.

I hate both of these emotions.

Having him around all the time makes it impossible for me to look at things objectively, to reason with myself that I did the right thing in cutting off our friendship before it went any further. If I could simply stop seeing Landon, I think, I am *sure,* that my days would slip by so smoothly; his brief absences wouldn't feel like a bruise on my heart that magically heals when he walks back into the barn, Sid trotting happily at his heels.

My heart, that should be used to bruises and beatings, which should take his deception and his feints without the slightest deviation in its steady beating, is the biggest co-conspirator in this barn right now. My heart and Landon, dancing in an unwanted lockstep. I feel like the reluctant horse in a pas de deux, a dressage test that can only be perfected if both riders and both horses are in perfect agreement. I just want to be left alone to doze in my stall, but no one will let me wallow when they're sure the alternative is so much nicer.

I just have to wait it out. This will pass—this crush I have on Landon, this crush he has on me. That's all it is, anyway. And on my end, it makes so much sense: a crush on the first guy to be nice to me in a long time. Honestly, I'm lucky Basil is usually so in his head that he hardly remembers to speak to me when we're in the same room, or I'd have a crush on him next. And wouldn't that be awkward?

More awkward, somehow, than what my life already is?

THOMAS ISN'T SURE about Kayla's trailer.

"Come on, buddy," I entreat, tugging gently at his halter. I'm trying to stay next to him, because if I get into the trailer and pull on the lead-rope, Thomas will just back up. This is Horse 101. You pull, and then they pull, too.

And they're stronger, obviously, so that's a match that can't be won.

Kayla clucks encouragingly from inside the trailer. "Do you want me to go back to the barn and get some sweet feed?" she asks when Thomas snorts at the trailer and takes a step backwards. Her horse is already in his slant-load stall, being a little angel.

I sigh at Thomas. He's embarrassing me in front of my boss. Can't I even trust my horse to get me through this summer without looking foolish? "I guess maybe—"

"Here, Mackenzie—take this."

Landon's at my elbow, bucket in hand. My heart lurches in my chest. I swallow, wishing the buzzing in my nerves would stop singing every time he comes close to me, wishing my lips would stop falling open as they remember the night we kissed. That was a *week* ago, lips! It's *over.* Be excited about something else, like peanut butter cups, or the entire bottle of wine we're going to drink after this awful day is over!

Thomas has no such qualms; my unsupportive horse crowds against Landon, nickering his happy food song. The horse on the trailer answers. If the bad horse is getting food, he wants to get food, too!

I want to crowd Landon just like Thomas. Everything in my body pulls towards him.   Rub up against him. Feel his hardened muscles, the way his body softens when I'm pressed against him, the way it did the night we kissed. Ignoring all those impulses, though, I step away in the other direction. The trailer stops me, a sheet of sun-warmed aluminum hot on my back.

Landon notices me edging away from him, and his expression darkens, as it has all week when he's tried to get close to me and I've pulled back from him. But today, evidently, is the day he says something about it. I can see the determination hardening his profile, the way his jaw sets and his lips press firmly together. It kills me that I know what he's going to do with just a simple flex of the muscles in his face. That's intimate knowledge, borne of these hot summer months spent working and laughing side by side, and I can't thrust it all away just by wishing it would disappear.

"I'll just go inside the trailer," Kayla says cheerfully, somehow unaware that Landon has me locked in an emotional death-grip. She shakes the bucket while Thomas leans in after her, desperate for grain without the commitment of stepping into the trailer.

As I stand to one side, my hand still on Thomas's lead, Landon holds my gaze with his endless blue eyes and whispers, "Are you going to tell me why we're not speaking, or are you just going to keep torturing me forever?"

My heart seizes up in my chest. *Torturing?* I'm *torturing* him now?

This would be a perfect moment to remind him that he's been playing games with me all along, masquerading as my best friend but refusing to tell me anything about his life off this farm, or to demand whose beautiful, on-trend riding shirt was mixed in with his sweaters—which presumably haven't been worn since he was in Kentucky, making it quite obvious where the shirt was last with its owner. This would be the right moment, while Kayla is engaged elsewhere and we're alone for the last time this morning, to tell him that I don't have time to play games, that I'm here to put my life back together and there's no room for man-children with mysterious pasts to mess that up for me.

But instead I just stare at him with raw panic—mingled with what feels awfully like anguished longing—surging through my veins. I don't know how to go up against a turn of phrase like *are you going to keep torturing me forever?* I wasn't prepared for this. Nothing in my life with Ryan ever told me that a man could utter a line straight out of a romantic movie with so much conviction, as if those words had never been said before, just to please an audience.

Oh no, he's serious, a voice whispers in my head, a voice on the edge of hysteria, and I can feel that I'm halfway towards reaching for him, muscles twitching as my primitive brain tries to kickstart them to life, halfway towards a reconciliation that my rational mind knows I'll regret, when Thomas shoves against me, knocking me off-balance. I stumble back against the horse trailer, my fingers automatically tightening on the lead, but Thomas pulls it right through my fingers as he clambers into the trailer. I hear him eating from the bucket, Kayla saying "Good boy, you did it!"

Landon turns away from me. The sun is in my eyes as I watch him walk back to the barn, a yellow glare that grows filmy as tears blur my view. It's just the sun, the endless Florida sun, making my eyes well up. It's nothing to do with Landon.

Kayla hops down from the trailer and I move aside to let her close the back door. "Your horse was good!" she says, a little breathless, and shoves home the latch. "Are you ready?"

There's a lunch-bag on my kitchen counter and I want to go and get it, but I'm not walking past Landon. I'll buy something there. If I ever feel hungry again. "Yes," I say, turning away from the barn, where Landon has disappeared into the aisle. "I'm ready to go."

I stare out the window as the truck lurches down the rain-rutted barn lane. But all I can see is Landon, his eyes haunting as he asked if I was going to keep on torturing him. He didn't ask me because he wanted an answer, I'm sure of that. He asked me so that I'd know I am hurting him.

And what am I supposed to do with that knowledge, besides let it eat me up inside?

Chapter Thirty-Two

DESPITE THE HUSTLE and bustle of Legends Equestrian Center, Thomas gets off the trailer with a soft sigh and unconcerned eyes. I know it's all due to our shows over the summer. He's learned that the show-grounds are not the same as a racetrack. Instead of tacking up and going for a gallop, we tack up and go for long walks, followed by some flatwork and jumping in nice, round arenas, surrounded by other horses who are *also* not galloping. Maybe it's not the scene he was hoping for, but he's coming around to the idea.

"My little show-horse," I croon, leading him to the stalls we've booked for the day. The vast, warehouse-style barns spread out around us like airplane hangers, offering enough room to house hundreds and hundreds of horses. In the heat of late summer, the stabling is mostly empty, but in winter I've heard this place turns into a city of show horses, the grounds buzzing from predawn when the braiders arrive to late night when the final holdouts finally head back to their hotels. After that, night watchmen and security cameras take over. The horses are never really alone. They're too valuable for that.

Imagine being too valuable to never be left alone. I would like both, please: to be valuable, and to be left alone. But the world doesn't seem to work that way.

Thomas's hooves pad quietly on the cushioned pavers of the barn aisle. He glances from side to side at the empty stalls, their doors open to reveal the black mats and swept corners within. A few horses nap in stalls near the center of the barn, their heads close to their box fans. He gives each of them a careful look to see if they're acquainted, and snorts when he finds they're not. Thomas must have had so many casual acquaintances in his racing life, the horses he walked past in the shed-row every day, the horses he saw on the track every morning and raced against on occasional afternoons. Does he wonder where all those horses have gone? Do they wonder about him?

What's the shelf life on an equine relationship, anyway? I should read more. There are books on equine sociology. Maybe, instead of closeting myself away each night to pretend I'm watching videos about retired racehorse training, while I'm really sulking about Landon, I should study up on horse relationships. They can't be any worse than human ones.

"You're so brave," I tell him. "The bravest horse in all the world."

"He doesn't have much to be brave about," Kayla jokes, gesturing to an open stall door. We're almost to the end of the barn, and the open doors look out towards a tree-lined path and more warehouses: the indoor arenas. "That one's yours. These stalls are padded, you know. Something called a horse mattress? Thomas is just having a spa day with a little ride in the middle for exercise."

Sure enough, the rubber mats in the stall give with my steps. We have a bag of shavings for each stall, but the horses won't need the bedding for comfort. It'll just absorb any mess they make while they're lounging around, stuffing their faces with hay or napping in the breeze from their fans.

Making several trips with a wheelbarrow, Kayla and I get the horses set up with hay-nets, stall fans, and water buckets. Then she puts out two chairs in front of Thomas's stall and invites me to sit down while she parks the trailer in the lot. "There are drinks in the cooler," she says. "When I get back, we'll just hang out and let the horses get used to the barn before we do anything with them."

"Maybe we should leave them here and have a spa day ourselves," I joke, pulling a couple of Cokes from the cooler. There's something about a horse show atmosphere on a hot day that makes me want a Coke. Something left over from my teenage years.

"It's not a half-bad idea," Kayla muses, accepting a Coke. She cracks it open and sighs, a contented sound. "Maybe we should plan that for ourselves sometime. It's been a busy summer. I owe you a nice massage, at least."

"You don't owe me anything," I laugh, shaking my head. "I'm learning so much from you guys. I just really appreciate the opportunity—"

"Hey," Kayla interrupts. She smiles and shakes her head. "Don't sell yourself short, Mackenzie. You know how to take care of horses already. You just had to learn how to put all the pieces together to keep a barn going all day. Please tell me you know that you're absolutely indispensable, and Basil and I would die if you left us, okay?"

"I doubt that's true," I demure, but Kayla puts her hand on my arm.

"Listen to me," she says. "You're amazing. I want you to know that. Like, really know it. You're good at your job and we don't deserve you."

I smile to myself. "Well, thanks..."

"And this is the part where you say you're never gonna leave us," Kayla prompts.

"I mean, I wasn't planning on it."

And I wasn't. But as I say it, I realize that the situation with Landon is getting worse, and despite all my pep talks to myself that it's just a crush and that one day I'll wake up totally over him, I really don't know if that's true. Without thinking, I say, "How long is Landon staying?"

Kayla takes a long swig from her Coke. She swallows and looks at me, and I get the uneasy feeling she's stalling.

Finally, she says, "Is Landon creating a problem for you?"

"No," I reply, anxious as ever not to complain, not to be the problem child. "He's fine. I just wondered—"

"You guys seemed to be getting along really well," Kayla says. "I know it's not my place to ask, as your boss and all...but hell, I'm not really boss material, right? So I'm just gonna ask...did you guys hook up?"

I choke on my Coke. Bad timing. "No," I splutter, the moment I can speak. "We did *not* hook up."

"Did you want to?"

I can't answer that. Or rather, I *won't* answer that. Kayla's cool, but she's still my boss. I'm pretty sure there should be a line here we don't cross.

Kayla looks at me with an open expression, though. She isn't worried about crossing any lines. "Why'd you change your mind? Did he do something? Oh, dammit, this isn't about your job or being worried about what we'd think, is it? Because I can tell you right now, Basil and I would not be upset—"

"No, it's not about that," I say. "It's just that I don't really know him at all. And since he's not willing to tell me anything about himself, I don't trust him."

Kayla nods slowly. "I see."

There's silence for a few moments. Thomas does a slow circle of his stall, then pees luxuriously. The sound is like a waterfall.

"What do you want to know?"

It's my turn to stare at Kayla. "What?"

"About Landon," she says. "I might know some stuff. What's on your mind?" She holds up a finger. "Think about it. I have to move the trailer."

KAYLA'S OFFER TAKES me by surprise. So much so that when she returns from parking the trailer, ready to answer my questions, I shake my head and turn her down. I say, noble as hell, that it's Landon's place to tell me about his past and no one else's. And so we sit in silence for a little while, all hope of conversation killed off, until she finally suggests that we take our horses around the property and take advantage of the open arenas. Relieved, I leap up from my chair and head into Thomas's stall with my grooming kit.

Thomas is full of piss and vinegar once I'm in the saddle, head straight up and hindquarters swaying as he walks with uncharacteristic vigor. We ride along the lane lining the long rows of stabling, then find our way to the outdoor arenas behind the barns, where the hunter courses and warm-ups are spread out across a wide, tree-studded expanse. The midday sunlight is heavy on the show-grounds, little ripples of heat waving up from the blinding-white footing in the rings. But even late summer heat is not enough to stop the determined riders of Ocala from schooling their horses for the coming winter circuit. There are about a dozen riders scattered in the nearest warm-up arena, and a few are schooling jumps, one horse at a time, in a show-ring set up with a hunter course.

The heat isn't stopping these Hunterland warriors, but I'm not used to riding in the midday sun and it's just about enough to stop me. Already in need of relief, I take Thomas into the shade of some oak trees while Kayla rides her horse into one of the warm-up arenas and joins the fray, trotting him around with about a dozen other horse-and-rider pairs.

Thomas tugs at the bit a few times before he settles and drops his head. I pat him on the neck reassuringly. Learning to stand around and wait is part of being a show-horse, so keeping him here, watching other horses go, is part of his training. He's pretty good at it, actually.

Unfortunately, his standing-still prowess gives me plenty of free mental space, and naturally my brain marches straight back to Landon. *Why* did I tell Kayla I didn't want any answers from her? Why turn down the chance to reassure myself that Landon isn't hiding something huge from me? If the guy has a mad wife locked in an attic somewhere, wouldn't it be better to know now, rather than before I'm fully obsessed with him?

Of course, whatever Kayla knows about him, if there *is* a mad wife, it's pretty unlikely she'll have that information stowed away and has done nothing about it. I'd like to think Kayla would call the police if she came into knowledge that worrisome.

And anyway, Landon doesn't seem like the type. He's more Viking than disturbed and eccentric English gentleman. If he didn't like his wife, he'd just throw her overboard, right?

I don't even chuckle at my own joke. This is serious stuff. I can't make it funny.

Kayla gives up the warm-up arena after about ten minutes

and walks her horse over to meet us. Her face is red with the heat. "I swear it's hotter here than back up at home," she pants.

"We're further south, so it makes sense."

Kayla shrugs, but she's smiling again. "You wanna ride in an indoor?"

"Oh, god yes."

The indoor arenas are air-conditioned. Let me say that again: *the indoor arenas are air-conditioned.* As soon as we enter one of the huge, well-lit spaces, lined on one side with hundreds of empty seats, a delicious chill raises on my skin. This is the way riding in Florida should be all the time. Too bad you'd have to be a billionaire to build an arena like this for home use.

"Okay," I tell Kayla. "Now I will do some work."

"You're so spoiled," she snickers, but she looks happier, too.

Thomas is happy to move into a trot, and he tugs at the reins, squirreling forward with every excuse, until I give up and let him canter. He lopes effortlessly around the arena, his ears flicking back and forth with every stride, his breath coming in happy little snorts. When we pass another horse, he tries to toss his head, and once he comes dangerously close to bucking. I hear the tiny squeal he makes even if no one else can, and it makes me smile. My silly, goofy, lovely horse! He's the reason for all of this work, and the work is the reason for me to keep on going.

Thomas is helping me figure out my purpose in life. Finally, a guy I can rely on.

We're midway through our fourth circuit of the arena when I see him. He walks into the seating and settles down in the third row. Impossible to miss, even if he wasn't the only spectator in a vast and empty grandstand, Landon's red head glows under the bright lights and I can see his head twist to find me, his gaze following me around the arena.

Thomas passes a fat little hunter pony, twists his head to wrench the reins from my hands, and kicks out in exuberance.

I barely know what's happening before I'm spitting out expensive, climate-controlled, state-of-the-art footing, and rubbing it out of my eyes with a damp, sweaty glove.

THOMAS THE NAUGHTIEST *Pony of All's Training Diary*
Humiliation-teenth, August

I honestly can't believe I fell off at Legends today, but the bruise on my elbow says I did. Thomas was naughty...plain and simple. I can't even get mad at him about it. He was excited, he wanted to play, and he kicked out. You can't be mad at a young horse who is having fun under saddle. You can be mad at a dangerous horse, but not a happy one. That's my opinion, anyway. I want Thomas to be excited about his work, and have fun under saddle. And I guess every now and then, that's going to end with me falling off.

I got back on and he was much better, like he was embarrassed about dumping me, and we finished out the day without any more trouble. Good stuff. I feel really confident that he can work in an indoor arena and in a busy warm-up ring.

But why did Landon have to show up? And why did he have to see me fall off?

Chapter Thirty-Three

"EMBARRASSED DOESN'T EVEN begin to describe it," I tell my laptop. Then I take a gulp from a large glass of wine. True to my suspicions this morning, I am indulging in the ultimate exhausted-woman-archetype and going full-tilt at a bottle of Chardonnay while telling my best friend all my troubles. Starting with being told I'm a man-torturer and finishing with falling off a horse in front of that very same man (and a lot of other people).

Casey's expression is sympathetic. She rubs at her dog's ears and shakes her head at me. "I'm sure it wasn't as bad as that," she says gently. "Getting bucked off is a respectable way to part company with your horse. It's not like you just toppled out of the saddle."

"I only did it because *he* was watching me, though!" It's very hard to keep the whine out of my voice. Or maybe it's the wine. Get it? Haha. "He's ruining my life," I say. "And my life was already ruined, so that's like, double-ruined. How unfair is that?"

"A couple weeks ago, it was all about how helpful he was, and you were so lucky to have him," Casey points out, in a way I find very unsympathetic and unsupportive.

"There's no way I said that. Doesn't sound like me at all."

Casey shakes her head. "Girl."

She really doesn't have to say anything else. I know she's got me. It would just be more feminist, in my opinion, if she would pretend to forget our previous conversations and would just accept that Landon is a terrible person who was put on this earth to torment me.

It doesn't have to be true, it just has to make me feel better.

"Well, anyway," I sigh. "I just have to avoid him now."

"That's the plan?" Casey sounds skeptical.

"That's the plan."

IT GETS EASIER to avoid Landon as September begins to limp past, a blend of hot, sunny days and slowly cooling nights. His business picks up again near the end of the month, and when he is around, he keeps to himself. The silences between us grow no less pointed, but at least there are fewer of them to survive. Near the end of the month, Kayla starts putting me on a sales horse called Boris who needs basic flatwork, and a few horses sell to riders looking for winter-season mounts. It changes up my routine; I'm in the barn just a little less. Just enough, it seems, to widen the gap between Landon and me even further.

And it's almost time to pack. I'm going to Kentucky. The Thoroughbred Makeover is in mid-October. I start waking up in the middle of the night, face flushed and body sweating, thinking about the trip.

The one good thing about the steadily waning countdown: I find I barely have any time to even think about Landon, anyway. There's so much to do in getting Thomas ready, making sure I have everything I'll need for the trip, perfecting our test movements. With double entry into dressage and jumpers, he'll be playing to his strengths—showing off with his pretty movement and willing attitude. But I know nothing that we do at home will be as simple once we're in the carnival atmosphere waiting for us in Kentucky. The prep shows were great, and the schooling day was fantastic. The Makeover show itself, spread across a dozen arenas and fields at Kentucky Horse Park, will have all the drama of a hundred young Thoroughbreds in company, with the added pressure of their riders' nerves and competitive spirit.

It's going to be a lot for both of us, but even more for Thomas's green-bean brain. What will it take to send him straight back into racehorse-land, despite the schooling practice shows we've done? On the last weekend in September, I take him to a hunter pace and do the flat course, just jumping an occasional log, so that he can get out and gallop in the company of other horses. The show secretary pairs me up with a twelve-year-old from the local Pony Club, who thinks it's funny every time I go around a jump instead of launching my horse over it. She also knows the course like the back of her hand and gets us in closest to the optimum time, winning Thomas his first blue ribbon.

"He was good," she says, while Thomas tries to eat the ribbon. "Why won't you just jump him over everything?"

"Because I'm old and I'm scared," I tell her impatiently.

She snickers at me. She has no idea what it's like to be over thirty years old. But it's coming for her. She'll see.

At night, unable to fall asleep, I go online constantly, seeking out the groups and message boards where I am reassured, again and again, by veteran makeover participants. "This is the happiest horse show on earth!" more than one person reminds me, making me wonder if the makeover people have actually trademarked the term. "We are all in this together," others say. "Everyone is just trying to make this the best experience possible."

That's definitely not like a normal horse show. I can only hope it's the truth.

"I'm not sure you should go alone."

And then there is Kayla, worrying about me again. She's decided that even though I'm older than her and the veteran of a hefty failed marriage with lots of alone time to show for my past few years, I can't drive Thomas to Kentucky on my own.

"I am not driving straight through," I remind her for the tenth or twelfth or twentieth time. "I am stopping overnight in North Carolina, the way we talked about." It's Kayla's friends who will be our stopover point. Although it requires driving out of our way—the straight shot to Kentucky does not include North Carolina at all—it takes the need to drive through the Smoky Mountains at night out of the equation, as well as giving poor Thomas a break. Trailer rides are exhausting for horses under the best of conditions, and while I intend on driving gently, there's no taking away the strain on his legs from bumps, turns, inclines, and the simple fact that he can't take his midday nap, flat on his side, the way he does every day around one o'clock.

"I know, and the Hendricks are the best, and I trust them to take good care of you guys," Kayla concedes. "But it's still a very long way, and then you have to settle in Thomas all by yourself at the horse park, and it's just a lot. I worry about you."

She's made that very clear. I suppose I shouldn't be annoyed —besides Casey, who else worries about me?—but at this point I don't want to feel like anyone is throwing barriers up in my way. I've spent my entire adult life being thwarted by Ryan. As much as I love Kayla, she can't tell me what to do without raising my hackles. At least, not outside of our employer/employee relationship. And I'm the first to admit that line can get very hazy.

"I'm going alone," I tell her, "and it's going to be fine, and you're just going to have to get used to that."

"Who's going where alone?"

I sigh and edge towards the tack room door. Landon has been in his apartment all morning, supposedly enjoying a rare morning off, but I guess now he wants to get all up in our farm business.

Kayla is grateful for Landon's intervention. She clutches at my sleeve before I can escape under the pretense of cleaning tack. "Our girl here is driving all the way to Lexington by herself, and I do *not* like it."

"Lexington, *Kentucky?*" Landon demands, as if he hasn't been fully aware and an active participant in my plans to get Thomas to the Thoroughbred Makeover all summer. Suddenly, I wonder if the two of them are acting out some elaborate farce for my benefit. And what's the end goal? Why would they—

"Kentucky," Kayla tells him, her eyes wide. She's really going with this little one-act play they've written for me. "Can you imagine? What if she has a flat tire? What if she runs out of gas? What if an insane person runs her off the road? Anything could happen between here and Lex, you know? I worry about her."

"Of course you do." Landon studies me for a moment. I give him my most mutinous glare in return. "Any kind person who thinks about others *would* worry about her."

Was that a dig against me? Because I'm not speaking to him

anymore? Well, he's got a lot of nerve—

"What are we going to do, Landon?" Kayla wails. She's really pouring it on. Shakespeare summer theater would get a lot out of Kayla's raw talents. "Are we going to allow this *dangerous* idea?"

"Absolutely not," Landon rumbles, his voice using every inch of that barrel chest of his. "I will go with her."

My mouth falls open before I can stop it. *This* is the ruse? I look accusingly at Kayla.

She shrugs, as if to say, *you drove me to it.*

She's driving me to something. Around the bend, most likely.

I'M RIDING THOMAS in the relative cool after an evening thunderstorm when Landon comes out to the arena. He hasn't helped me with Thomas since I stopped talking to him, and I've gotten used to working with my horse alone. But when he asks me if I'd like him to move some jumps around, I realize that I could really use some assistance. The jumps are set a little too high for what we need, and I don't want to hop off and change them. Yes, I want to stay in the saddle even more than I want to avoid working with Landon, the man who said I was torturing him.

"Okay," I say.

He raises his eyebrows, as if he fully expected to be turned down.

A perverse part of me hopes he did, and that he didn't actually plan on helping me at all.

"Could you possibly lower the jumps like, three holes?" I ask.

Landon puts his hands on his hips. "I'll tell you what I'm

going to do," he says.

I sigh. Of course, he can't just do what I asked.

"I'm going to make you a little gymnastic right here," he says, hefting a heavy wooden jump standard like it's nothing. "You're going to have to do a gymnastic in the jumper pattern. It's not like you'll just be going around a regular jumper course. You'll be tested on flatwork and trotting into a one-stride before your course."

"How do you know that?" I demand, immediately suspicious. Has he been studying up on the Thoroughbred Makeover? And if so, could he *not*? I really wanted to do this on my own—how many times do I have to tell him that?

And then I wonder if I've ever really told him that. Or if I've just thought it mutinously, over and over, silently seething while he is so kind and helpful.

Gosh.

Maybe I am kind of an awful person?

I'll have to ask Casey later. Ryan would certainly think so, though I should know by now to immediately discount anything that man would agree with.

"You know you're not going with me to Kentucky, right?" I ask as I circle Thomas near him. Thomas's trot is round and forward, exactly the pace I'd like him to display in our dressage test at the Makeover. I give him a quick pat on the neck without disturbing his motion. "I'm going alone."

"I'm going with you," Landon says, grunting slightly as he sets the standard in place. "Kayla said I have to."

"Kayla is not in charge of this."

"She's the boss," Landon replies, as if he works for Kayla, too. As if he *has* to be here, like me, instead of choosing to rent his apartment and stalls from Kayla and Basil when there are a thousand more convenient ones available in Ocala. He sets the first pole into place, then adds another to the adjacent standard, forming a high cross-rail that will require a nice, round jump from Thomas.

"She's not your boss," I say.

Landon gives me a lopsided grin and says, "Who said anything about being my boss? Come on. No one here goes against Kayla. Basil sure can't. Maybe you didn't notice it, because she's so nice about things, but *you've* never said no to her, either."

That's true. I've even taken care of Landon's horses, both before and after our friendship, because Kayla just sort of indicated that they needed to be part of my job, too. I never once complained or asked her why. I just did it. I thought that was part of my annoyingly acquiescent personality, but maybe the real culprit is Kayla's incredibly nice manner of getting people to do whatever she wants.

I wonder if Basil knows about this.

"I will talk to Kayla," I say. "I'll get you off the hook. Trust me."

"She's not going to budge on this. And she's right, too." Landon puts his hands on his hips and faces me. His blank expression makes my heart quiver anxiously. I can't get a read on him anymore. Does he still care about me? Is he over me? Both seem equally terrible. He says, "You shouldn't even consider driving all that way alone. You need a back-up person. And I'm perfectly willing to do it. What's the problem? Is it literally just that since this idea didn't come out of your head, it's not worth exploring?"

"You make it sound like I never listen to anyone," I scoff, putting on the bravest face I can. My chest cavity feels empty again, the space between my ribs sucked-in, as if my heart has fluttered itself to tatters.

"But you *don't,*" Landon says, his tone incredulous in a way that tells me for sure that he's tired of me. He's over my shit. He wants to be done. I wish he'd go inside and leave me alone out here. I'll jump the stupid gymnastic and cool out my horse and be done. With everything. More sharply, Landon says, "You ignore everyone's suggestions, even when people are just trying to help you! Do you really not know that about yourself?"

Anger spikes up, hot and dangerous. My heart comes back to life and starts hammering against my ribcage like it never even left. Thomas sidesteps anxiously, tossing his head. "I don't recall asking you for a personality critique!" I snap. "Or help out here, or, for that matter, *anything,* ever! You can't just show up in someone's life and expect them to take all your unasked-for advice, Landon!"

"That's not what is happening here," he insists, his brows coming together, and suddenly I remember that redheads are famous for foul tempers. There's real heat in his eyes now, the limpid blue pools turning dark and stormy. "We were *friends,* and I was trying to *help* because of that—"

"We weren't friends," I say, and just like that, all the fight falls out of my limbs. I could fall out of the saddle and I wouldn't even be able to pick myself up.

And there's no way Landon would come over to help me.

He was holding a jump pole. But now he drops it at his feet, right in the center of the ring, and with a last, furious glare that sets me slumping in the saddle, he stomps away.

I won! Last word! He finally gets it! Too bad it's not a triumph, not even remotely.

Because that was the meanest thing I've ever said to anyone, ever. And what's more, it was a lie.

My heart seizes up, clenching into a tight little ball, leaving behind a huge vacuum in my chest that threatens to choke me. I can feel heat pressing against my eyes—a whole deluge of tears demanding to be set free. Not tears of rage, like the ones that I shed after fighting with Ryan, when he put me in my place with his quick, evil tongue and I couldn't imagine a life where I wasn't the stupid one in the relationship. These are tears of shame and loss, because I just lied and ruined the one friendship I think I've ever had with a man that wasn't based on power, money, and lies.

Thomas steps carefully over the jump pole Landon has left in the center of the ring. Its awkward angle means it can't be very useful for balance work at the trot and canter, but who has the heart for work like that now?

Chapter Thirty-Four

"YOU HAVE TO apologize, obviously." Casey is cuddling her dog again tonight. The sweet blue-eyed Australian shepherd curled up in her lap keeps his gaze trained worshipfully on her face. Brandon walks past the sofa behind her, pausing to drop a kiss on her head. Her family's sweet intimacy makes my battered heart feel even more bruised. Suddenly, I'm glad Landon has a dog. I'm glad he's not alone over there, on the other side of the aisle, where he is surely over me at last. I don't want him to be hurt and lonely, but also, I don't want him to forget about me? How does this work?

All of a sudden, I care about his feelings, and it's the most life-wrecking series of emotions I've experienced in a long, long time.

"*Mackenzie,*" Casey says. "Do you hear me? You owe the man an apology. I'm sorry to say it, but you were cruel to say you'd never been friends."

"I know I do," I sigh, hugging a pillow to my chest. "I know I was. But I was really hoping you'd surprise me and say something else."

"Like what, that you should just drive around horse country, wrecking men, until you get it out of your system? I mean, in a

313

movie, that might be the best course of action. But this is real life, babe."

She's not wrong about that.

"Okay, but I can't be responsible for Landon's being obsessed with me," I counter, thinking that has been a pretty good point in the past. My only point, actually. Although it's almost certainly outdated at this point.

But, of course, Casey just snort-laughs at me. "Child! You *can* help it! You could have helped it at the beginning of summer by telling him straight that you were not interested in a relationship. And you didn't do that, did you? Did I miss that call? Tell me I'm wrong."

I'm silent.

"Well?"

"Are you saying I led him on?"

"I'm saying you both *like* each other, you dummy," Casey says, stroking her dog's ears contentedly. Is she enjoying this? "And if you'd wanted him to leave you alone two months ago, like really wanted that, you would have said."

She is enjoying this! She likes being right. Well, hell.

"But he's keeping things from me," I remind her. "You're not looking at the whole picture."

"So he doesn't want to tell you his life story yet! He's got shit! We all have shit!"

"What if I can't handle his shit because I'm still trying to figure out mine?"

"Then you need to tell him that," Casey says. "You need to be *honest*."

She can be so reasonable.

Maddeningly so.

"I also think it's an excuse," she says. "But that's just my opinion."

"Okay," I tell her. "Thanks." And I close the laptop lid decisively.

It's good having a friend like Casey, most of the time. But then again, it's annoying to have a friend who has her life so impressively together. Because I'll always feel like I have to take her advice. Even when I really, really don't want to.

IT'S NOT RIDICULOUSLY late, but it's past sunset and the horses are set for the night. So, there's no reason for Landon to be in the tack room right now...but that's where he is, pulling saddle pads out of the dryer and placing them on the shelf. Sid is snoozing at the tack room door. When he sees me, the hound dog stands up, wagging his tail and shaking his ears. Landon turns at the sound, his arms full of horse laundry.

I push back a surge of annoyance that he's out here doing *my* job—I'm still protective of my chore-list, as if Kayla might decide she doesn't need me after all and send me on my way—and focus instead on his face as looks down at me, studying his expression, trying to read how he feels about my presence on this dark summer night. He's been so blank and cool lately; the emotion in the arena earlier was the first time in weeks that he's shown me how he's really felt about us.

"Hey," he says, giving away nothing. He's so practiced at his poker-face. Another reason why I'm so sure he has a secret life he doesn't want me to know about. The sticking point, though he won't recognize it. The line I've drawn, though he won't respect it. If he'd just *tell* me...

"I'm sorry," I say, pushing through my wandering thoughts in a desperate attempt to get the job done. Before I say something else, before I make things complicated all over again.

Landon blinks at me, almost startled. "What are you apologizing for—" he begins, and I cut him off.

"I'm sorry," I repeat. And then, because I simply can't think of anything else to say, I say it a third time for good measure. "I'm sorry."

"Hey," Landon says, keeping the distance between us, still somehow keeping his face clean of expression in a way I'd admire if I didn't feel so ripped up inside, "don't worry about it. You're all keyed up about the show, you got worked up. Things happen."

He doesn't sound like an empathetic friend. He sounds like a robot, repeating a script that's been fed into his system. Like he's doing the job he's been programmed to do, and nothing more. I miss my friend, I miss him so much. My chest squeezes; my throat clenches.

"I'm sorry for before, for the summer," I bleat, half-choking, and for a moment Landon's eyes do widen. I'm reaching him. There's someone in there. I shouldn't keep trying, but I can't stop, either. He has to *know*. "I think I made you think—things —could happen. And they can't. Landon, I don't know anything about you. And I was married, and it went really wrong, and my whole life I took care of my dad because my mom wouldn't take care of us, and I just can't do this anymore. I can't be everyone's keeper, Landon. I need room for *myself*—"

He holds up a hand. Landon's eyes have gone back to their normal shape and size. Only the stormy darkness of them gives away some hint of emotion. Otherwise, his face is still so bland, so unaffected, that I feel a fresh surge of horror lift up from my stomach to my throat, and for a moment I really do believe I might throw up from the sheer shame and disappointment— although I don't think the disappointment has any right to rear its head right now, because if Landon doesn't, didn't, never did want more with me, that's a *good* thing, right? That means we were always just friends, and I never let him believe there might be more, because he wasn't *looking* for more, and the whole thing was just a big, silly misunderstanding. On my part. A misunderstanding with a kiss in the middle that I shouldn't have let break our friendship in two.

I'm the silly one.

Again.

But that storm still darkens his eyes and something absurdly, perversely like hope makes the ground lurch beneath my feet.

"I know you were married to a jerk," Landon says quietly. "I never wanted to make you feel vulnerable like he did."

He's so kind. I feel the tears pricking my eyes again.

Dammit!

I don't want kind. I don't want understanding. A flood of heat rushes beneath my skin as I realize what I really want is an argument. I want shouting and clenched fists and flushed cheeks. I want that storm in his eyes to break and take over this tack room.

I want him to fight for us to have something! I want him to shout that it was never a game to him, or a silly night of wine and loneliness, and that I'm the absolute worst for turning him away and he'll never stop fighting for me. It's so stupid and irrational and not at all what I walked in here for, but that's just me, I guess.

Want what you are.

Want what you deserve.

Accept what you're going to get, because the same, sad ending is barreling towards you, anyway.

Landon is still standing there with saddle pads in his arms, and I feel like a fresh fool all over again.

"Okay," I say, defeated.

I turn to leave.

"Hey," he says.

I whirl around.

"Please let me drive with you to Kentucky," Landon says.

"Okay," I say again. Dull. Flat. Like there was ever even a choice. "Goodnight."

Sid licks my hand on the way out of the tack room.

Chapter Thirty-Five

IT TAKES A day to pack the trailer. Five minutes to load Thomas. And the steel of a lifetime to get into the truck.

Landon clambers into the passenger seat and looks around the cab. I can tell he's impressed.

I keep my truck clean—it's the result of a lifetime spent amongst moneyed horse-people, not normal farm people. We don't have to fill our trucks with hay and grain, and we can take off our dirty riding boots in the tack room and leave them to be cleaned while we slide comfortable loafers on for the drive home. The trucks are our status symbols: *yes, darling, I do have horses!* They are rarely used for their real utility.

I bought this truck to do hard work, but I still keep her clean. It's only fair, right? It's not her fault she didn't get to live out her days in freshly waxed glory amidst the palm trees of Wellington. I gave the cab a good vacuuming two days ago, when I started packing the trailer for the trip, and it hasn't been driven since.

"Your truck is very clean," Landon says eventually, placing his boots just so in the center of the spotless floor-mat. White sand spills gently from their treads. "Sorry about that."

"Relax," I say, amused enough to crack a smile, although the effort makes my skin feel like dried mud splitting. "Old Betty here doesn't get much work. She's clean because she's out of work most of the time."

"Early retirement?" Landon pats the dashboard. "Congrats, old girl. That's the dream."

The engine is already growling; the air conditioning is already ice cold. The early October morning is wreathed in a thin fog that trails through the live oaks lining the pastures. I look around for a moment, taking in the farm as if we are never coming back. Something about this trip feels epochal; it's the closing of one chapter, and an opening on another. My first summer as an independent woman is over. It was messy, and it was hard, but here I am. Now comes the first autumn, then the first winter...but first, the Makeover.

With the man I'm still crazy about, and determined to get over, sitting steadfastly at my side.

Should be good.

THE FIRST SIGN of trouble is the pressure light on one of the tires. We're barely into Georgia, with no more than two hours passed this journey, and a light rain is spitting spitefully onto the windshield, as if to remind me that the Sunshine State is in the rear-view mirror and it's all downhill from here north.

Landon hears the truck's warning ping and looks over at the dashboard. He's been sitting quietly, alternating between looking at his phone and staring out the window, but now I can see he's going to try to take control.

"Go ahead and pull over," he says. "I'll look at the tires."

I give him a skeptical look. "Are you kidding? I'm not pulling over on the interstate. There's a rest area a few miles up. We'll go there."

"You don't want to mess around with this," Landon insists. There's just a touch too much patience in his tone, like he's humoring my delicate temper.

I clench my fingers around the steering wheel, gripping it with everything I've got. This truck goes *nowhere* without my express permission and he is *not* going to take charge. Tightly, I say, "It's just a low pressure sensor. We can check it at a rest area much more safely than along the side of this highway with everyone driving a hundred miles an hour."

A small car races past, as if to punctuate my words.

"I know the traffic is a lot," Landon says, still speaking carefully. "But if we're going to blow a tire—"

Ping! the dashboard reminds us. The warning light flashes helpfully.

"We aren't going to blow a tire," I say, fighting back a rising panic. "These tires are in perfect shape."

"Mackenzie, I am telling you, just pull the truck over—"

"Stop bossing me around!" I shriek, losing my cool so completely that it's a wonder I don't drive right off the road. "For god's sake, Landon, I know how to drive a truck! I know what's going on here!"

I take a breath. Did I just—"I'm sorry," I mutter. "Jeez. I don't know where that came from."

I do, of course. It came from the massive frustration that he causes me, all the time, by simply existing in my space.

"You need to pull over right now," Landon replies tersely, the soft blur gone from his words. Now he's angry, too. Oh, does Landon want to fight?

I feel my heart pumping wildly in my chest, enlivened by a stir of excitement I didn't expect. This isn't like fighting with Ryan. I don't feel small or put down now. I feel up to the challenge, oddly exhilarated.

"I am *not* pulling over," I declare, "and if you don't shut the hell up, I won't pull over at the rest area, either. I won't pull over for gas. I won't pull over for *anything* except Satan himself unless you keep your mouth shut and respect that I'm the driver, I'm in charge, and I make the rules!"

"That's insane!" Landon roars, and I can't believe how excited I am that he feels it's fine to yell back, especially when I just *expressly told him* there would be consequences for his actions if he kept on talking. "You're insane. Did you know that?"

"I'm insane because men *made me insane*!" I holler back, my eyes on the horizon. Georgia sprawls flat around me, the pitiful excuse for a rain shower still speckling the windshield. "*All* women are insane because of men!"

And then Landon starts laughing.

And suddenly, I'm laughing, too. Hysterical, blinding, oh-boy-she's-lost-it-laughter. I grip the steering wheel and thank the interstate gods for a straight road and an upcoming rest area.

We laugh all the way to the exit, until I pull the truck and trailer into a long spot near the long-distance truckers, and then Landon gets out, looks at my tire, and stops laughing.

"NEXT TIME, JUST stop right away, okay?" Landon climbs back into the truck cab and brushes off his hands. The rain has passed, and the sun is peeking out, and sweat has gathered his hair in wet bunches on his neck. In the next parking spot, a tow truck roars back to life and heads off on the next adventure. "We could have died."

"Drop it," I say. "It was a nail. Could have happened to

anyone."

It was unfortunate that we had a bad tire on the trailer back when we went to that first horse show, because now Landon probably thinks my vehicles are rolling time-bombs, but a nail in the tire is hardly my fault. And I don't want to discuss it at all. I enjoyed our earlier argument with an elation I still find bizarre to think about, but now I'm seven hundred dollars poorer and nothing seems very funny. "We made it here just fine, and it's all over now. Replaced the tire. Life is good. Let's go to Kentucky."

"North Carolina," he reminds me, but I ignore him.

There's no time for nitpicking. We're an hour behind schedule and Thomas is already annoyed. He's going to be really pissed in five hours when we finally get him off the trailer for the night, and I don't even want to think about his feeling of betrayal when we walk him out for another trailer ride tomorrow morning. Suddenly, all this work to get to one silly horse show feels like the height of self-indulgence. Why am I doing this to my sweet horse? Why am I doing this with my savings? And when am I going to wise up, *grow up,* and get over this horse show fever? I'm like a twelve-year-old.

"Why are you muttering to yourself?"

I look at Landon, then back at the road. "What? I'm not—"

"You were. Are you okay?"

He spends so much time asking me if I'm okay.

Maybe I should start asking *myself* that question.

"Sorry, yeah. I guess I was just..." I signal to get onto the interstate. A truck driver does not move out of my way and I just manage not to flip him my middle finger before finding a space to merge. "I think I internalized some dumb shit my ex-husband used to say to me. And when I hit a pressure point, that stuff tends to bubble up."

"If shouting at me helps, feel free to do that."

I feel a grin creeping over my face. "Do you think it should help?"

"You seemed pretty in control when you were yelling."

"That's true. I never thought about it that way. Ryan didn't... appreciate it...when I lost my temper with him."

"Well, I appreciate it," Landon says. "You look like a vengeful goddess when you're mad. You can shout at me anytime."

"Thank you, Landon." I feel oddly touched. "I might have to take you up on that. I think vengeful goddess is probably a nice look for me."

"See? It *did* feel good, didn't it?"

"Oh, it absolutely did," I agree. "I guess that's why Ryan didn't let me do it."

"Didn't let you?" I can hear the startled note in his voice.

"We had rules," I say, shrugging. "Not like, written on pillars of stone or anything, but there were certain understandings. One was that I didn't raise my voice to him."

"Did he raise his voice to you?"

I focus on the road. "Not all the time, no."

Landon sighs loudly. I think it's a sign; he wants me to know just how very much he disapproves, without saying anything judgmental out loud. He can, and I wouldn't be mad. The divorce is in the past; I got away.

"I was young when I met him," I say, when the silence stretches over a mile, "and I was looking for someone to take control. I was tired of being the boss. You have to understand I was always in charge. I raised myself."

"Parents were..."

"Busy. Ineffectual. Easily distracted." All nice ways of saying my mother was rarely home and my father was basically a child himself. "Some people aren't natural parents. It wasn't their fault."

"That's very forgiving of you."

"I've had a lot of time to think about it." I feel him glance my way, and shrug away his sympathy, something else I'm practiced at. "I've spent a lot of time alone, Landon. It's fine. What about you? What were your parents like?"

I try not to hold my breath and pretend to focus very hard on the road, but the truth is that we're hanging out in the right-hand lane of a six-lane interstate and there's not a ton going on. All I have to do is keep the truck between the lines. Still, I don't want Landon to see how invested I am in whether he'll answer...or whether he'll deflect, once again, leaving me hanging.

"My parents are wonderful," Landon says.

I let out the breath I was holding. "I'm so, so sorry."

"No, it's...I know what you're thinking. But they're *wonderful.* Like, 1950s-sitcom wonderful. It's impossible to live up to them. I always feel like I'm suffocating when I'm around them, like they're just waiting for me to be as realized and perfect as they are, and I can't get there."

"There's no way they're realized and perfect, though. Right? They just put on a good show."

"Maybe. I don't know. I guess I don't have any perspective that way. An outsider would probably see things differently and wonder why I'm such an ungrateful son."

"They'd probably have said the same thing about me," I reflect. "When's the last time you were home?"

Landon sighs before he replies, "I spent some time there in

May, before I came back to Florida and surprised you. It wasn't actually that long ago. But I can't ever stay there. It's just…a lot. Because I couldn't possibly make the right decisions. I've proven that to them time and time again." Landon's tone turns bitter.

"I guess they didn't want a farrier in the family? That's dumb of them. It's so convenient. You always have someone around to tack on a lost shoe, right?"

"That's what I tell them." Landon exhales a short laugh. I feel good for lightening the mood, like there should be an award or something. "Thank goodness someone gets it."

"So you went home, and they told you, 'My farrier son, you dishonor the family name,' is that it?"

"Something like that. And not marrying the girl they picked out was a problem for them, too. They love her. She's practically a daughter already. I was supposed to make it official and they're disappointed that I didn't."

Now I can't help it. I look over at him, feeling my fingers tighten on the wheel. "Who was she?"

"*She* is Annabelle Harvey Kingsman, if you can believe it," he says. And he gives me the most sheepish smile I've ever seen on his face, because he knows that's a household name. Or at least, a grocery-checkout-tabloid name. Hell, she was on the cover of two gossip rags on the night I went to the grocery store with Landon, all the way back in June.

He's been keeping quite a lot to himself! I knew it!

"The tobacco company heiress?" I ask blankly. Maybe he's kidding.

"And bourbon, and soybean, and a lot of other things that can be farmed to make up for the decline in tobacco. Oh, and wind farms, too. All the farms. Yes. We went to school together. We kind of...went out. When we were kids."

"You're making this up." I know more about Landon now, but this admission has definitely raised more questions than answered any of the ones I had before. What kind of guy is betrothed in grade school to a graceful, willowy blonde who has been showing off her pearly whites in *People* magazine since the early oughts?

"I wish I was," Landon sighs. "The truth is, and I hope you don't hold this against me, but my family is filthy rich. Like, old Kentucky, embarrassing giant house, the works."

"You know I have a poor track record with rich guys," I joke, trying to absorb this without freaking out. In a way, none of his story is surprising, because I knew all along he was hiding some big stuff from me. Now, I just wonder if that's Annabelle Harvey Kingsman's riding shirt hiding in his closet.

She could do better, I think jealously, and I don't mean in terms of men. I'm thinking of that shirt. It's nice, but I've made nicer. I have designs for better shirts, hidden away on my laptop, waiting for the seed money to make them happen.

"Well, I'm not rich," Landon says, "and I don't stand to be, the way things are going. So I'm still eligible if you're exclusively into poor horsemen."

I don't dare glance at him; my heart is too busy doing flips in my chest for me to trust my motor skills to do anything like drive in a straight line while I'm gazing at the man who just implied we should get together. So instead, I just say, "Good to know. I'll keep that in mind."

Landon makes a satisfied little sound, like he's said his piece and done his duty. Leaving everything after up to me.

Chapter Thirty-Six

HE'S A GOOD travel companion, I'll give him that. But then again, I had no real reason to believe Landon would be anything but a pleasure on a trip to Kentucky. After all, he's spent the summer being a perfectly nice, almost aggressively helpful companion—even when I shut him out completely. So sharing a truck cab with him for the better part of a day isn't a trial at all. Unless you count the fact that I'm having way too much fun with him. And I'm trying to ignore that part.

Now that we've both said our piece, things smooth out between us, and it's as if we didn't spend the past month at odds. Landon apparently feels free to entertain me, and I feel free to laugh at his jokes. Before we're halfway through Georgia, I'm having the nicest time I've ever had on a road trip. The fact that things are still unsettled, that he's made it clear he's still interested in me, and that I'm not sure what I'm going to do about that, fades into the background as we travel north.

He's good at pointing out funny billboards, keeping track of where there are gas stations with easy-access diesel, and manning the pump for me while I run in to use the restroom and grab snacks. He's an acceptable DJ with good instincts about when to change the station or just flip on his phone's

Bluetooth for a while. He keeps quiet when traffic gets heavy around Atlanta and my knuckles start to turn white on the steering wheel. And when the road opens again up on the far side of the metropolis and we start nearing the off-interstate route we'll take to get to our overnight farm, he finally obliges my curiosity about his family and his past.

"I came to Florida to get away from them," he says, tracing our upcoming path with one finger on his phone. "The thing is, they convinced me to come home in the spring, then threw Annabelle at my head again. I mean, it was bad. She was staying in the house; she had the bedroom next to mine; my mother was always hustling my father out of the dining room after dinner so we could be alone. My sister was no better. Obviously, I had to leave. I was so glad Basil hadn't rented out my apartment or the other half of the barn."

"So, is Annabelle in on this? Does she *want* to be your arranged bride?"

He shrugs. "She seems just fine with it."

Of course, she would. There's nothing about Landon that might chase away a pretty woman. Some society types might not want to marry a farrier, I guess, but he's such an accomplished farrier. A farrier to the stars. That's something. And the family money wouldn't hurt one bit, either. Despite everything I know I should feel about feminine solidarity, I start to hate Annabelle Harvey Kingsman. Just a little bit. "Maybe she should have her own life and her own opinions about who she should marry," I say rather spitefully.

Landon laughs. "Absolutely, she should. She needs to be able to make her own decisions. Needs to know her own mind."

"Do I know my own mind?" I ask, hardly daring to be coquettish but unable to resist a tiny bit of flirting, anyway.

"The woman who shouted me down over a low-tire pressure warning?" Landon chuckles and taps me on the leg with his open palm. "Yeah, I'd say you are fully in control of your own life and thoughts."

His words—and his touch—warm me like a cozy blanket.

WE ARRIVE AT Pin Oak Farm for our overnight stay as sunset flares behind the low mountains. Kayla's friends are quiet and kind, and Thomas settles into a stall for the night with a bit of snorting but a healthy appreciation for fresh shavings he can roll in. There's a lot of kicking and groaning before he gets up and shakes the shavings from his mane.

"Aww, buddy," I say, smiling through the stall bars. "Feels good, right?"

"Makes me wish I could do the same," Landon says, walking up with a net full of fresh hay from the stash we've brought along. "Let's get this old boy set up with his dinner, and then I think there's something waiting for us in the barn apartment."

It's nice of our hosts to have been so hands-off with us. There's no need to go sit through a dinner with strangers after a full day on the road and another early start tomorrow. They've promised us a heat-up dinner waiting in the apartment just upstairs. I find the staircase around the backside of the barn and lumber up, feeling like even heating up dinner might be too exhausting, but the sight of what's waiting for us wakes me up again.

"Oh my," I say, dropping my bag by the door. "This is not like our barn apartments at all."

This apartment isn't overly large—we've walked into a living room with a kitchen along one wall, and two doors which must lead to the bedrooms—but it's beautiful. Exposed beams overhead and plaid curtains on the windows to either side give it the feel of a luxurious hunting lodge. The space is the width of the barn below, and that alone makes me feel like there are acres and acres of space compared to the tiny apartment where I've spent the summer. Stepping inside, I glance back at Landon, who has taken my place in the doorway. His expression is as impressed as mine must be.

"The Pin Oak people are doing okay," he says after a moment.

"They must have this on Airbnb," I say, running my hand along the plaid blanket covering the back of a fat, comfortable-looking sofa. "No one lives here! It's like a hotel."

"Can you imagine if we had a place like this back at home?" Landon asks.

There's something odd about his phrasing. I turn and look at him, lifting an eyebrow. "We?"

He shrugs and grins. "I mean—you know what I mean."

"If there was a luxury suite like this instead of our two little apartments, then it would be mine, and you'd have to live in your horse trailer or something," I say. "Sorry, it's just the laws of nature. You couldn't possibly be happy living in such splendor while I was slumming it outside in the elements, could you?"

Landon shrugs again. "I mean, I'm willing to try."

I burst into surprised laughter and throw a pillow at him. He catches it and exclaims, "Whoa, princess! We can't be having a pillow fight in our host's living room! What if we break something?"

"Fair enough. This place is full of tchotchkes. But I bet the bedrooms have plenty of pillows." And I run across the living room to the door on the far right. I push it open and find a bathroom. A very nice one, but I stand staring at it for a moment, disconcerted.

"Is everything okay?" Landon asks.

"Yeah, it's just..." I walk across the kitchen and open the other door. There's a lovely bedroom, with a king-sized bed, a large dresser, and a television. The dimensions of the room make it very apparent that this is the whole apartment. "There's only one bedroom," I say, flummoxed. "They didn't say there was only one bedroom!"

He's in the doorway a second later, staring at the king-size bed. Then he glances back at the sofa, and I know what he's thinking. But he's a big guy, and the idea of him sleeping on that sofa is ridiculous. "I'll sleep on the couch," we both say at once, our words running over each other.

He smiles at me. "You're the one showing your horse in a few days. You need that bed. I'm the one who invited myself along, remember? No way I'm taking the bed."

"You'll roll right off that couch and hit your head and die," I argue. "You're taking the bed."

Landon sighs. "What if we just eat dinner and fight about it on a full stomach, instead?"

That seems like the best plan, so I let him heat up the casserole in the fridge while I take a shower. The water pressure is good, the hot water is intense, and the stress of the road falls out of my shoulders while I rub my scalp with a brand of expensive shampoo I remember from my trophy wife years. I almost wish I could steal the bottle and take it with me, but that would be pretty ungracious and I'm sure Kayla would hear about it later. Anyway, I'm not shampoo-stealing destitute yet. If I really wanted this brand, I could splurge and buy it.

Landon sniffs the air elaborately when I walk out of the

steamy bathroom. "Mmm, that's nice," he exclaims. "Lavender?"

This guy is really something. "Yeah. You can smell like it too, if you aren't afraid of seeming less manly in front of me."

"Manly schmanly," he says. "Ten more minutes on dinner. I'm going to drench myself in that soap." And he moves past me into the bathroom.

I laugh to myself as I get dressed in the bedroom. The night is chilly and the apartment's heat isn't on yet, so I pull on soft fleece pants and a long-sleeved shirt. It's actually the most clothing I've worn since last winter, and it's so cozy that I feel like just curling up beneath the covers and eating dinner in bed. Oh, this big gorgeous bed! I run a hand over the duvet with longing, but there's a sense of discomfort as well. Am I really going to sleep in here and leave him to the mercies of that sofa? He makes a good point in that this is my trip and he's just tagging along, but still, there's something truly off-putting about consigning a man of his size to a sofa, especially when he's come along to help me.

"We'll cross that bridge after dinner," I decide. In the kitchen, the oven timer is still three minutes from going off, so I set the little table next to a dormer window with cutlery and water glasses. There are a few bottles of wine above the fridge in a rack forged from horseshoes, and I consider them a moment before shaking my head. I'm not going to take their wine without permission. Although it really seems like if it's here, it's free game...

The kitchen timer beeps at the same moment Landon emerges from the bathroom in his own cloud of fragrant steam, smiling beatifically above his towel. "Now *that* was a shower," he announces happily, picking up his bag from the sofa. I'm too arrested by the sight of his muscular chest to say much in reply, so I just switch off the timer and pop on oven mitts, ready to pull the casserole out of the oven. Landon moves past me, bag in hand, and goes into the bedroom to change. As he walks past, his towel slips to his waist.

Something in me catches and holds for a moment.

I put the casserole on the table between our plates, taking deep breaths to steady myself. My heart is on a crazy, discordant gallop now. Was it just his chest? Maybe it was his massively muscular shoulders, too! I guess I've always known that there's a full set lurking beneath his clothes, since the man's a farrier and all. Horseshoeing builds a pretty serious upper body. But knowing something exists beneath fabric, and actually *seeing* that something, are very different experiences.

With very different results. My hands shake as I put away the oven mitts.

He comes out of the bedroom fully dressed in a plaid shirt and jeans.

"You should have put on something more comfortable," I say, and then blush.

Landon looks down at his jeans. "Were you expecting something lacy?" he asks.

"Oh, sit down and eat." I know I sound scolding now, but I'm embarrassed. I try to hide my pink cheeks with my water glass. "This looks amazing," I add. "Potatoes and cheese and chicken? They're trying to lull us to sleep with comfort food, apparently."

"Perfect for a chilly country night." Landon pulls out his chair. "I don't miss this weather. Not that it doesn't get cold in north Florida, but we've got some time."

"Not a snow kinda man?" I ask, feeling the weather is a

comfortable place for the conversation to land. How long can we discuss the weather? Until bedtime? El Niño is always an interesting subject, right?

"I don't mind seeing a little snow if it's from inside a cabin in the woods, with a roaring fire. There should be a fireplace right there." He points towards the far side of the living room, where an overstuffed chair faces us from beneath a hunting print. "No sense having a fireplace in a barn, though, obviously."

"Obviously," I echo, although it seems funny to think Thomas and ten other horses are just downstairs. It's very easy, back at our farm, to *know* that we are living in a barn. Much harder to tell in this pretty little dreamland of a barn apartment. Where we are going to sleep tonight?

In the same space, not divided by a barn aisle and two steel doors.

"Do you miss Sid?" I ask, and then could kick myself. Now I'm going to make him sad about his dog, who is no doubt happily passed out on Kayla's couch this very minute.

He takes a bite of the casserole and chews thoughtfully, looking at me in a way that makes my cheeks blush pink again. As if he's taking me so, so seriously—something no man has ever done with me. "I guess I miss him a little," he says at last. "But I'd miss him more if I were staying here alone."

"I'm good enough company to replace your dog? I'm honored."

He smiles at me. "You really are," he says. "You always have been."

His words seem to be weighted with meaning, and suddenly I wonder just what we're doing here, dancing around one another, when I feel like it's very obvious what we both want.

What we've both wanted for months.

Maybe I was able to fool myself for a while—I'm good at that—but now I can admit to myself that I've always been drawn to him, attracted to him, and he's spent all our months together, including the ones where I didn't speak to him, attracted to me, too. Waiting for his moment when he could ease himself back into my good graces.

Waiting, maybe, for a night like this, a beautiful space, and only one bed.

"Are you okay? You look deep in thought."

Anxiously, I shove a forkful of casserole into my mouth and promptly choke. It takes more coughing than I'd like to get back in control of the situation, and all the while, Landon watches me with concern in those big blue eyes of his. "I'm fine," I hack, waving a hand at him. "*Fine.*"

"If you say so." He takes a bite and chews, watching me carefully. "But I do know the Heimlich maneuver."

"Of course you do," I rasp. "And I'll bet you've saved lives with it, too."

"I haven't, actually. You'd be my first."

"You're a Heimlich virgin?" I gulp water to ease my sore throat, and hopefully bring down my interior temperature, which is rising dangerously close to the boiling point.

"Unlike some other virginities, this is one I'd like to keep. Maybe, smaller bites?"

"Oh, shut up," I laugh. "How dare you imply I'm a greedy eater?"

"Imply? I'm outright saying it. You eat like a starved broodmare, my delicate angelic flower."

Now I'm heaving with laughter, almost choking on *that*. "I do not—"

"You do, but it's cute. Don't change on my account. You

clean up your dinner while I—" His gaze flicks to the kitchen. "While I open one of those bottles of wine."

"Wait, you can't just steal their wine," I protest, but he shakes his head at me.

"They're here for the guests," he says. "It's a nice gesture. Let's not be gauche and turn them down."

I don't know what I'll do if there's wine involved. I'm tired and already punch-drunk with the stress of the day. I'm deep in the throes of my crush on him. I'm half-ready to lean across the table and kiss him already. As he gets up and walks past me, I reach out one finger and let it trail across the skin on the back of his hand. The soft feel of him sends a shiver shooting up my spine. And the heat in his gaze, as he pauses and looks down at me, sends a rush of blood to every extremity in my body.

This is bad, I think, bizarrely happy about it. *So very very bad.*

And then Landon says, "You take the bedroom, Mackenzie. I mean it."

I bite my lip, start to say something, and then I stop myself.

Not right now, I tell myself. *This is Makeover Week. This is the goal. You cannot get distracted now.*

Chapter Thirty-Seven

THE SECOND DAY of travel is more quiet than the first.

When Landon does begin to speak, just after we set off for Kentucky, I politely shush him. "A wine headache," I say, and pull off the interstate again at the very first Starbucks sign I see. Landon goes in and secures giant coffees for us while I feed Thomas carrots through the trailer window. My tired pony enjoyed his night in the layover barn and was visibly annoyed when I'd presented the trailer ramp to him yet again.

Landon brings him a cookie shaped like a dancing skeleton, which Thomas wolfs down, then licks at his fingers, hoping for more. "He's going to like you better than me," I grumble, and Landon smiles. "One of us gets to be the good cop," he says, "and since you're the rider, that automatically means the role goes to me."

He's right. I can't really complain.

Kentucky is slipping past in green hills and deep forests as a sunny mid-afternoon settles over the interstate, and Landon closes his eyes for a nap. By now it's been quiet for hours and I'm a little disappointed; I thought as the native Kentuckian, he might point out local points of interest, like where he first kissed a girl or got busted by the cops for underage drinking.

338

But he just grunts and shakes his head when I suggest he owes me personal stories of teenage derring-do. "Nothing exciting happened."

"In your entire childhood? But you grew up rich, in horse country! Eccentric bourbon distillers and deranged southern gentlemen going broke in pursuit of the perfect racehorse! Landon, I expected more of you."

"I grew up amongst people who were entirely too concerned with optics and being the high moral standard of the state, even if the way they behaved behind closed doors was not exactly up to the Baptist code."

"Oh, intrigue! Are your parents closeted swingers?"

He gives me a look.

"Jesus, I was only kidding!"

"Some things it's best to simply ignore," Landon says wearily. "My family antics are one of those things. Reminder: I moved to Florida to get *away* from them."

"Do they know you're in the state now?"

"They do not," he says, brightening. "And I am very happy about that fact."

KENTUCKY HORSE PARK seems to go on forever.

I mean, I know it doesn't. But as I peer over the steering-wheel into the golden light of late afternoon, I get the feeling that I'm wandering into an enchanted fairyland just for equestrians. The seating for a vast arena peeps over rolling hills; covered and outdoor rings line up one after another; endless wooden fences march away over vast fields; rows and rows of stabling arrange themselves beneath autumn leaves. Everything is amazing in my eyes, but the trees draw my biggest gasp. They're a riot of fall color, the kind of leaves that I see on social media posts featuring blonde women wearing sweaters and boots, carrying Starbucks cups.

"We don't have anything like *that* in Florida," I sigh, pointing at what must be a maple. It's too flaming red and gorgeous to be anything else.

"But we also don't have snow," Landon reminds me.

"Ugh, I know."

Thomas unloads in front of the stable row with a suspicious glance at me before he looks around, as if he doesn't trust I'll leave him here more than twelve hours. A few horses look through their stall bars and whinny in greeting, and Thomas neighs back, his whole body quivering with the effort. Then he looks down at the ground and paws.

"He wants a place to roll," I say, and Landon jerks his thumb past the barns, where the dirt lane heads between arenas and towards a skyline enveloped in pink clouds.

"Let's take him for a walk down that way," he suggests. "There's grass over there between the show-rings and the cross-country course."

"How well do you know this place?" I ask, falling into step beside him. Thomas tugs at the lead, still anxious to roll, and I draw his head close to my shoulder. "Not here, silly. It's too hard, and there are rocks."

"Pretty well, I guess." Landon shrugs, keeping his eyes on the horizon. "My family's done a few things here."

"Like what?" I ask, but before he can answer, someone calls his name. I watch his face stiffen, his features going still.

"Landon? Landon?" The voice calling him is feminine and southern, as sweet as syrupy iced tea served from a jug at a roadside diner. "Is that you?"

Landon turns with a groan so low that only I can hear him.

Well, and Thomas, who flicks an ear in his direction as he tears at the bluegrass along the side of the road.

"My god, Landon, what are you doing here?" A woman is running to join us now, a platinum-blonde beauty in a maxi dress, sweater, and prim white sneakers. I place her age at a very expensive thirty.

Landon has an expression which tells me he's wishing very hard this coming interaction will not last. I follow Thomas's questing walk as he looks for better grass, allowing a little space to open between Landon and me. The woman walks up to him and opens her arms for a hug, her face expectant. He casts me a despairing look and I smile encouragingly.

I will not be jealous. What is there to be jealous about?

"Big brother!" she sighs, falling into his arms. He wraps her up in a hug, giving in so effortlessly that I can't help but smile.

And she's his sister! That makes it *very* easy to avoid jealousy.

"Wait until I tell Mom and Dad you're here!"

Landon goes rigid all over again. He steps back, holds her at arms-length. "Oh, maybe you'd better not—"

"Landon! No! We aren't doing this anymore! You're coming home and having dinner with us. Tonight."

"No, I'm not. I'm busy, Sara. You see this horse?" He points to Thomas, who is eating with gusto. "I'm grooming for this horse here. He's a client."

I barely avoid a snort. It's true that Landon has done an incredible job on Thomas's hooves, but—

"Right, Mackenzie?"

I sober up quickly. "Yes, that's right. This man is the key to my horse's sensitive hooves. I need him at my side all week."

Sara isn't buying it, maybe because it's the flimsiest excuse ever constructed. She gives me a broad smile and says, "Well, honey, of course you are invited."

"Oh, but we have to settle into our motel—"

Landon shakes his head at me. What? What did I do wrong?

"Motel?" Sara bursts out. "My *word*. Absolutely not! You can come stay with us! We're only ten minutes away."

I should have said hotel. Not motel. One little letter. But it's too late now. Sara is demanding my phone and I'm handing it over so that she can type her address into the map's search bar. "Follow those directions as soon as you're done here. Landon will text when you're leaving—won't you, big brother? And we'll get dinner on the table. Lucky for you, it's Sunday...we always eat fried chicken on Sunday. See you in what, an hour? Perfect. Bye, now!"

Landon stands beside me as Sara sashays away, her maxi dress billowing in the evening breeze.

"I take it you didn't expect her to be here?" I ask.

"She must be volunteering on the horse park board again," he says wearily. "I didn't know, no."

"Fried chicken sounds great, though," I say, trying to keep things light. I feel responsible for all of this. Even though he's the one who insisted on coming in the first place. "I really can't get enough fried chicken in my life."

To my surprise, Landon takes my hand and gives it the tiniest squeeze. It's the first time he's touched me since last night's pause in the doorway, when for the briefest moment I thought we might share the single bed, and the sensation nearly makes my knees buckle. I keep myself upright just so I can ask, "How many guest rooms are there at Maison de Landon's Parents?"

He chuckles and says, "Too many."

Chapter Thirty-Eight

ORIGINALLY, WHEN I said my life needed a makeover, I did not mean that the new version should include a palatial bluegrass mansion sitting proudly atop a hill, but now that we're here, I'm not about to complain, either. The farm lane I've just driven up is lined with blackboard fences, and a herd of yearlings galloped away and over the hills as my truck approached their grazing grounds. It was easy to see, even from a distance, how very well-bred they were.

"How old is this house?" I ask as I pull up in front. It's brick, with a blue door and blue shutters on the many, many windows. The black-shingled roof boasts three chimneys.

"1912," Landon says weakly. "My great-grandfather built it."

"Railroad money?"

"Something like that."

"But it was *not* a plantation...right?"

"Oh! No. The Kincaids were all abolitionists," Landon says. "They just like horses and whiskey a little more than they should."

"Well, thank goodness for that."

Landon looks a little green around the gills as I hand the keys off to a valet and watch my truck be whisked away to an unseen parking spot. "Are you going to be okay?" I ask, standing closer to him than I might have a few days ago. He's spent a lot of time comforting me. I want to return the favor.

"I'm going to be okay," he says. "But just you wait. These people are not normal."

OKAY, SO, THEY'RE not. After being whisked through a marble-tiled hallway—which, it's fine, but I've seen bigger. I am from West Palm Beach, after all—we find ourselves in a lovely library at the back of the house, overlooking pastures and a particularly Kentucky sort of stable: white, with cupolas and wind vanes. Dusk is fading from brilliant blue to tranquil darkness, and lighting set around the stable gives it a dramatic, elegant look. The interior is dark.

"All the horses are out while the weather's so good," Sara explains, pouring me a glass of something bubbly. "Champagne? I thought it would be nice to celebrate with a little fizz, since big brother's finally home."

Landon takes his glass warily. "Where are the parentals?"

"Mother is upstairs changing, Dad is putting the tractor away. She'll make him take a shower before we eat." Sara laughs and shrugs.

I glance at Landon. "The tractor, huh?"

"Dad thinks he's a gentleman farmer," Landon says, and gulps at his glass like he's been wandering the desert.

I give Sara a questioning look and she shrugs again, a little smile playing at her lips. If there's something weird going on, some disconnect between the way Landon sees his family and the way they really act, she's not going to just spell it out. She's going to make me wait and see for myself.

"So," Sara says, taking a seat on an antique lounge that would have looked perfectly at home in Downton Abbey, "you have a horse at the Makeover! That's so exciting. It's my favorite event of the year."

"It's my first time," I admit. "I'm incredibly nervous."

"I can't tell," she assures me. "Tell me all about your horse. I'm not a very good rider, myself, but I try to make up for it in other ways. Like all these boards and foundations I help with."

Landon makes a strangled snorting sound. I glare at him as I sit next to Sara. She wants to hear about my horse? That's no problem at all.

I'm halfway through Thomas's life story when an imposing dowager in a gray dress appears. She stands dramatically in the library doorway for a full minute, giving me plenty of time to take in her beautifully-colored auburn hair, her impressive height, and the very real diamonds sparkling around her neck and in her ears. I smooth a hand over my black trousers, wishing I had packed something just a little dressier than my trot-up clothes, and stand up to greet our hostess.

"My mother," Landon says, waving his empty glass.

The dowager bursts into cackling laughter. "Oh, Landon," she howls, slapping her thigh with abandon that I did not expect. "You would just love it if we were a band of miserable old aristocrats, wouldn't you? Where have you been, son? Come and give your poor mother a hug."

Sara and I exchange glances, and this time, her sparkling eyes give the game away. "Has he just been faking all this blueblood BS for attention?" I whisper. "Because this is *not* what he led me to expect."

"I think he believes it," Sara says with a little sigh. "And if he told you Dad didn't want him to be a farrier, that part is true."

"I guess I can understand that," I say. "It's a tough job that generally doesn't pay a lot. Is your dad like, a businessman?"

Sara nods at the doorway, where a second parent has appeared. With his overalls and with his thick thatch of red beard, the vibe is definitely not white-collar. "He used to be," Sara says, waving to her father. "But now he's a very happy farmer."

I WAYLAY LANDON on the way to the dining room, half an hour later. His father has reappeared, wet hair slicked back and a polo shirt buttoned up to his chin. He looks like a finance guy on vacation, if said finance guy forgot to shave for like, ten years. Landon has avoided him outside of a hug and a few father-son pleasantries, opting to hide behind Sara instead of facing his parents head-on. He looks down at me and shrugs without saying anything.

"I see you couldn't be anything but a redhead," I say. "What happened with Sara?"

"Throwback," he says. "Vikings come in blonde, too. Plus, redheads are going extinct, you know."

"Not if your family can help it," I snicker. We turn into a dining room with French doors which overlook a softly lit stone terrace. The wall to my right is dominated by a massive old portrait of an English Thoroughbred. The oil painting has to be worth a fortune; I pause to admire the brushstrokes, the heavy wooden frame accented with gold. In the light from the chandelier hanging over the long dining table, the horse seems to glance down at me with one rolling eye. "This is gorgeous," I say, appreciative of equine art in general, but this piece in particular. It must have come over the Atlantic—on a steamship, maybe, for the great-grandfather who built this house.

"That's Old Jupiter," Mr. Kincaid says, pausing to admire the horse as though it's the first time he's noticed him there. "Sire of Jupiter, believe it or not." He grins.

"I don't know much about racing," I confess, "aside from occasional days out at Gulfstream Park."

"Don't worry, Jupiter and Old Jupiter didn't do anything in particular for the breed," he says. "I just like the painting. Have a seat! It's fried chicken night. You're gonna want to pop the top button on your pants."

Mrs. Kincaid gives her husband a little swat, but she's smiling.

I can already smell the fried chicken, and my mouth is watering in anticipation. Although it's probably not the best thing before a week spent in my best riding breeches, all of which will pinch if I'm the least bit bloated, I am more than ready to go to town on whatever secret herbs and spices the cook of this homestead puts in her fried chicken. I take a seat between Landon and Mr. Kincaid, who sits at the head of the table like a country squire, and smile across the table at Sara and Mrs. Kincaid.

Landon's hand slides across my thigh, locking my smile in place.

I blink in surprise. My skin burns beneath his palm, sensation singing through my nerves as if the thin layer of my trousers isn't there at all. Sara blinks back at me, confused, and then Landon removes his hand.

I shift and give him a confused look.

He makes a big show of unfolding the napkin on his plate and settling it into his lap.

Sara clears her throat, giving me the impression she knows exactly what just happened, and says, "Annabelle is coming over after dinner tonight. She has to show me some decor samples for the next horse park foundation dinner. Landon, she'll want to say hello."

I swear I can hear the sucking sound as the air leaves the room. Mrs. Kincaid looks at her napkin. Mr. Kincaid looks over his shoulder, as if wondering where the fried chicken is.

Beside me, Landon's agitation rolls off him in waves. "I have to go back to the horse park to check on Thomas," he says after a pause. His voice is husky.

"Oh," I say, surprised into speaking without thinking, "but I paid for the nanny service to check him—"

Landon closes his eyes as I realize my mistake.

"Fried chicken!" A cheerful man's voice rings out, startling everyone. My neck pops as I whip my gaze around to the open door, where a young man in chef's whites has appeared with a huge platter. It's piled high with golden-fried chicken. His eyes are slightly wild as he looks over the chicken at us. "Kincaid family, your dinner is served!"

It's not only chicken, I discover, as a young woman follows him with a dish of mashed potatoes and a tray of biscuits. Butter, gravy, and a casserole dish of cheesy broccoli follows. It's the most unhealthy dinner I've been served in months, and I want to eat until I burst.

"Thank you, Ernie," Mr. Kincaid says fervently, plucking a chicken breast from the platter. "Please tell me again that you'll never, ever leave us."

Ernie and his assistant share a smirk. They leave without promising.

"You're scaring them, Owen," Mrs. Kincaid scolds. "If you keep it up, they'll go downtown and open a restaurant like all the other young people. No one wants to work in homes anymore for this exact reason. Chase them away and we get a divorce. You've been warned."

"Oh, if Ernie and Elle leave, I'm going with them," her husband assures her. "I'm sorry, dear. You know I love you, but this is a matter of life and death." And he bites into his chicken.

Mrs. Kincaid sighs and makes an attempt to pass the biscuits around with an air of weary civility.

I'm starting to see a bit of why Landon thinks his family is insane, but he implied they'd be insane in a bad way. Not in a hilarious, eccentric, who-are-these-crazy-rich-people way. I could only wish for such a warm, outspoken version of family life. As the conversation continues, interrupted only by moans of joy over the food (which is truly amazing), I settle into the family's warm bubble, and eventually, I think even Landon realizes nothing bad is happening, and he relaxes, too.

Dessert is being passed around—strawberry shortcake, with an entire bowl of whipped cream for dolloping on top—when the doorbell rings and Sara hops up. "That'll be Annabelle," she says.

Chapter Thirty-Nine

THE WOMAN WHO joins us for a "teeny-tiny, please" helping of dessert is not the flashy star of a thousand grocery-store tabloids. At first, I don't even place her as Annabelle Harvey Kingsman. She's remarkably good-looking, for sure, but she's also just like any woman dropping by a friend's house to go over a party they're planning: wearing her hair in a ponytail, just the faintest hint of foundation on her face, and dressed in a loose pink top over a pair of black leggings. Heiresses: they're just like us.

I'm used to a little more flash from the daughters and wives of West Palm, so Annabelle's down-to-earth appearance—and her appetite for the slightly larger than teeny-tiny portion of strawberry shortcake that Sara puts in front of her—endear her to me immediately. Even if the entire family thinks she should marry Landon, although I'm not getting that vibe at all. I see no significant glances, no meaningful glares as Landon tries to shrink down in his seat. The poor Viking of a man has no shot of disappearing, though, and finally I give his thigh a squeeze, just to let him know he's going to be okay.

His gaze is on me immediately, burning my cheek as I try to face Sara and answer some question about the horse show scene. By the time I've gotten to the end of the sentence, I've already forgotten what she was asking about. I look at Landon.

His eyes flash like lightning back at me.

I bite my lip.

And when I look back at the table, Sara and Annabelle are both grinning at me.

Well, I can tell one thing.

Annabelle isn't in a hurry to marry Landon, or she wouldn't be giving me that knowing, amused look right now.

After dinner, the other women go off to look at Sara's samples while the rest of us wander into the library. Landon accepts a bourbon from his father, who pours with a heavy hand, and after a moment's hesitation, so do I. His mother pours a glass of wine and opens a book, evidently considering her work as hostess to be complete. She calls over Mr. Kincaid after a moment, and he goes to sit by her on the lounge, looking at something over her shoulder.

"Landon," I say, drawing him over to the windows. The interior lights glare against the glass, hiding the stables and what I suspect is a very starry night out there. "What's the deal, babe? Your family is amazing."

He rubs his beard. "You think?"

"Did you really think I wouldn't like them? These are the people you ran away from? They're incredible!"

"Well, you've never lived with them," he says. "So, take all this with a grain of salt."

But he looks a little confused, like maybe these aren't the people he was picturing back in Florida.

"I can see how they might be overwhelming for someone like you," I concede, taking a small sip of bourbon. The warmth of it spreads in my chest and I place a hand against my skin, pressing into my sternum. "Wow."

He smiles. "That heat? It's called the Kentucky Hug," he says.

I giggle at the name. "That's silly."

"What can I say, Mackenzie? We're a silly race." He fingers his own glass, ragged nails dragging on the cut crystal. "I swear my dad wanted me to join an investment firm, but now I'm realizing he probably just wanted me to buy up old distilleries so he could say he's a bourbon man."

"I wanted my dad to buy me show jumpers so we could be big important horse show people," I admit. "So I guess we all use our powers for evil sometimes."

"Did he buy them?"

"A couple. I had some really nice horses as a teenager. You don't even know how fancy I was." I grin up at him. "Almost as fancy as Annabelle, who is totally over you, by the way."

"I told you, she was never into me," Landon insists. "It was all my parents."

I look over my shoulder. His parents are still sitting on the lounge, flipping through the book together. "*Those* parents?"

"People mellow out when they get older," he says. "It must be out of their system."

"Are you going to mellow out?"

"Me?" He catches my gaze, his blue eyes sparkling. "I'm already as mellow as an old retired plow-horse."

"You're as mellow as a volcano that hasn't erupted in a thousand years," I guess. "The possibility is still there."

"Well," Landon whispers, winking in a way that makes my heart flutter. "I guess you better stick around to find out."

For a long moment, we gaze at each other, and it feels like a dare to see who will look away first. Then there's a click as the library door opens, and Annabelle sashays into the room, followed closely by Sara. They make a beeline for the two of us.

"Uh-oh," Landon murmurs.

Annabelle laughs at him. "First of all," she says, joining us by the window, "I'm engaged." She flutters her hands, and it's true: one of the diamonds on her elegant fingers is indeed a large solitaire. "No one brought it up at the dining table, so I thought I would just put it out there."

"Congrats," Landon says, startled. "That's amazing."

"Yeah," I echo. "Congrats!"

Sara, standing at Annabelle's elbow, gives me a private smile.

"Second of all," Annabelle says, facing me, "Sara tells me *you* designed the shirt you're wearing! And I need you to know I love it, and I want one. No," she decides. "I want three. I need an ecru, black, and a turquoise. Is that something you could do?"

"THIS IS A nightmare," Landon groans.

"I think you're being dramatic."

"Really? Is that what you think? What if your ex-husband showed up suddenly?" And he looks around, wild-eyed, as if he really expects Ryan to burst through the doorway.

"That would be a nightmare," I concede. "But he's a jerk. Annabelle is a sweetheart. And she likes my clothes. She's got a lot of pull, Landon! Maybe this could be a match made in heaven."

"That's what my mother always called us when we were kids," Landon says tragically.

"Well, move over," I tell him, giving him a playful shove. "Because now Annabelle is *all mine.*"

"Can we focus for a moment?" Landon looks around. "Are you taking this room tonight?"

"I guess I am. It's fine." It's more than fine—this bedroom is at least three times the size of the motel room I've booked back in Lexington, and the en-suite bathroom has a huge tub that would be awfully nice to soak in tomorrow night, after spending the day acclimating Thomas. We have three days to get used to the place before competition begins for us on Wednesday, which is a nice long while, but I know with all the other horses and activity going on, we'll need every hour.

Four months ago, I wouldn't have let Landon take me anywhere, let alone back to his parents' house when I have a perfectly acceptable motel room waiting for me...but this guy has grown on me.

He's nothing like Ryan.

"Where are you going to sleep?" I ask him.

He shrugs. "My room is down the hall."

"You want to show it to me?"

"You want to see my room?"

"Doesn't everyone want their friends to see their childhood bedrooms?" I tease.

"Friends, for sure," Landon says. "But..."

"What?" I poke him in the shoulder. "Are you saying we aren't friends?"

"I'm saying...never mind what I was saying." Landon starts to turn. "Come on. I'll show you my room."

But I grab him by the arm. "Landon Kincaid, finish that thought," I command.

"No."

"Do it!"

"Or what?"

"Or I'll...sneak into your room and jump on your bed in the middle of the night."

He grins. "Would you really?"

"Oh, you'd like that, wouldn't you?"

"Hang on," he says. "I'm confused. Are you threatening me with a good time or not?"

I bite my lip, annoyed. Finally, I mutter, "Finish the thought."

"Fine." Landon crosses his arms. "I was thinking maybe we were more than friends. Okay? Is that what you wanted to hear?"

"Yes, actually." Warmth floods through me, and I tug on his arm, dragging him towards the door. "That's exactly what I wanted to hear."

MORE THAN FRIENDS. The thought follows me into sleep, and greets me when I wake up in the morning, so comfortable in the soft, plush mattress of the guest room that I wish I could just stay in bed all day. But Thomas is waiting, so I dress quickly in one of my favorite outfits of dove-blue and gray, and head downstairs to the kitchen. Landon is already there, drinking coffee as he leans on the bar and looks at his phone. The sight of him fills me with an obscene happiness.

"Did you sleep well?" he asks, pushing a mug towards me.

"I did," I sigh, taking the mug and filling it. "Thank you. Did you?"

"No," he says, giving me a meaningful look. "I tossed and turned all night."

"Oh." I look at him over the rim of my mug. "Well. It's probably just that you're not used to the bed being so comfortable. The mattresses back at the farm aren't exactly memory foam."

"That's probably it," Landon drawls, never taking his eyes off my face. "The comfy bed kept me awake. Not the thought of you just down the hall."

A blush begins at my neck and climbs steadily up to my cheeks. I turn slightly, hoping to hide it. But Landon is smiling with such satisfaction, I know he's seen my reaction. And that's alright, actually.

Let him see me. I've got nothing to hide from him.

I wander into the living room and glance around, taking in the squashy sofas and the home theater set-up against one wall. The back windows overlook the pastures, and in the morning gloom I can see horses standing near the stable, waiting to be brought in for breakfast. I sigh, because I should get going; Thomas is waiting for me. But I like this house, these large, airy rooms and the lived-in feeling of the furniture, the equestrian art scattered around the walls and peering up from end-tables. I turn slowly, thinking I'll go back to the kitchen and find my travel mug, and am surprised to see Landon looking gloomily after me. Did I say something wrong?

"Landon?" I ask tentatively.

He sighs. "I'm sorry, Mackenzie. But I just have to ask... before I let myself get all foolish over you again...what happened over the summer? What did I do to get the silent treatment?"

Oh, right.

"There was a shirt," I admit, suddenly feeling foolish. But no —I won't let him make me feel silly about this. I've been lied to before. Deceived and laughed at. I had every reason to believe Landon would be exactly the same as Ryan, didn't I? "In your sweaters, all mixed up...a riding shirt. Ladies' cut, a pretty recent design. I know these things, Landon. I pay attention to riding fashion."

"Oh." He nods slowly, as if he knows exactly what I'm talking about. "I guess that's Annabelle's shirt, after all."

I feel like sinking into the floor. "After all?" I ask, my throat tight.

"She asked me if it got mixed up in my things." Landon looks right at me, his eyes piercing. "She stayed in my room here last winter."

"What?" I blink at him.

"I was in Florida," Landon continues, sighing. "She stayed here for a few weeks, helping with some gala my mom put on back in the barn, having sleepovers with my sister. Sara said they acted like a pair of teenagers and it was great. She must have left that shirt in my closet...I threw all my stuff into a box pretty quickly when I moved out again in June. I didn't notice it."

"Why was she staying in your room, Landon? There are multiple very nice guest rooms in this house." I can't help how thin my voice sounds. This part is weird.

"I don't know. Remember how I said my family is always pushing her on me? This is one of those things I can't explain and I can't deal with."

"I dared her."

We both look up at once. Sara is standing in the kitchen, coffee mug in hand. With her hair up in a bun and flannel pajamas buttoned up to her chin, she looks unreasonably beautiful. The Kincaid family is very pretty, whatever else their faults. "I dared her to sleep in your room, Landon," Sara repeats. She shrugs. "I thought it would set Mother off again, and it did. She read all kinds of crazy into Annabelle staying in your room. It was hilarious."

"For who?" Landon demands.

"For me," Sara says. She sips her coffee elaborately. "You don't think I get bored with them, everyone hanging around this madhouse all the time? We can't all run away to Florida every time we get mad at Mommy."

"You could run away to Florida anytime you wanted," Landon says.

"And who will chair the horse park foundation? And who will organize the Christmas toy drive? And who will run the budgeting for the farm workers' clinic every year? You have no idea how much work I do in this town, Landon." Sara shakes her head. "You just have no idea."

I glance at Landon. "I think you might have misread some things," I say.

Sara cracks a smile. "Yeah, you get it, Mackenzie."

"So the whole Annabelle thing...was just a prank?" Landon croaks. "I moved back to Florida to get away from her!"

"Yeah. I didn't expect that." Sara chuckles. "But it worked out, right?" And she looks right at me.

Chapter Forty

IT'S PRETTY TOUGH to concentrate on Thomas for the first hour or so of my morning at the horse park. I take him for a walk after breakfast, while Landon stays behind to muck out, and his wanderings take him past arenas, along the fences overlooking the cross-country fields, and down to pretty little brooks where clear water tinkles over rocks smoothed by years of erosion. I think about how unfair it is that rocks lose their wrinkles over the years.

I'm pretty sure I acquired some wrinkles via erosion over the past few months of farm life, training Thomas, and navigating my feelings for Landon.

Now they seem more complex than ever. I've let him into my life—something I said I wouldn't do. I've admitted to myself that I'm attracted to him—something else I said I wouldn't do. And I've made it pretty clear to him, as well, that there's something ready to spark between us. All definitely things I said I would not do.

And to find out that the great, looming mystery of his life is just a prank by his socialite sister to stir up life around the family farm? That certainly raises some interesting questions about our future together.

Like, that I think we might have a chance at exploring things.

But first, oh my god, the Makeover.

I'M SO OVERWHELMED, I barely know where to look. Where to stand. How to keep Thomas's attention at least somewhat on me. There are horses everywhere, people everywhere. A chilly wind is whipping up from the west and making the early morning much colder than necessary...in my opinion, anyway. We'd presented to the judges and been formally accepted without too much drama, possibly because Thomas was absolutely fixated on a large trailer unloading horse after horse in the distance. He was too fascinated to bother spooking at the straw bales and mums decorating the arena entrance, or the judges with their flapping coat-tails.

We aren't always going to be that lucky.

Back at the stall, I put Thomas away and slurp down a cooling coffee while I go over the day's schedule. We need to do some acclimation riding. Check out whatever arenas are open. Grazing time. I plan to keep him out of the stall and out moving as much as possible. It'll be good for his brain.

I wish it would just warm up a little.

"Is it always this cold in October?" I ask Landon, who strides up with an empty muck tub and a fresh cup of coffee. "Is this why you moved to Florida?"

"Yes, and partially yes," he says, handing me the fresh cup. He takes the old one and sets it on a tack trunk. "You going to be okay? Do we need to find you some clothes? Sara can lend you something...or Annabelle, probably."

I smile to myself. His tone turns just a little childish when he mentions Annabelle, as if he doesn't want to admit that he's been sadly mistaken about the case of the arranged marriage. "I'll probably manage once I'm riding," I say. "And if the sun stays out."

He glances at the sky and shrugs. "In this part of the country, I can make no guarantees."

HIS LACK OF guarantee proves accurate; a thin skein of clouds layer over the sun while I'm trying to convince Thomas that the cross-country fields are not calling to him for a gallop. We weave in and out of the walking traffic along the rails in a couple of open arenas, but the sheer number of horses makes me nervous. And the wind doesn't let up. I'm shivering by the time I get Thomas back to the barn, and thinking it's time to go find my motel, check-in, and take a long, hot bath instead of grazing my horse through the afternoon.

When I get back, I barely recognize my stall.

It's decorated with ribbon, twine, and those delicate little banners made of triangles. The triangles are lettered with A T O M I C T O M.

"Oh my god!" I put my hand to my mouth.

Landon appears at our side. "Pretty cute, right?"

"Did you do that?"

He laughs. "Woman! As if I could!"

Sara and Annabelle appear next, all smiles. Sara says, "We thought you'd like a cute place to keep your horse all week."

"I love it, so much. I see the kids and some of the other adults doing stuff like this, but I'd never have the time." Or the energy. I blink happily at the decorated stall, feeling tears pricking at my eyes. "You guys, this just makes my day!"

"We're going to be your cheering section," Annabelle says. "Since you don't have anyone else with you in Kentucky."

"What am I?" Landon demands.

"A very nice boy," Sara laughs. "But a girl needs girlfriends."

A few riders walk past as I dismount, and they pause to look at the stall. "Ohmygod," one of them says. "Your stall looks so great!"

"Thanks," I say, startled. "I didn't do it, but..."

"Is this your *horse*?" one of the girls demands, as if she's astonished to see a horse. "Ohmygod, he's so cute. I love him! Brandy, don't you love her horse?"

"I love him," Brandy confirms. "I want him."

I look after the girls as they carry on down the barn lane. "That was nice," I say wonderingly.

"That's the Makeover," Sara says knowingly. "Everyone here is just the best."

DRESSAGE IS THE first up this week. It's drizzling the morning of the dressage competition. I look out the window of my guest-room (his parents never did allow me to check in at my motel) and see that the sun apparently isn't planning on rising this morning. It's still dark, without even a hint of light in the east, and tiny raindrops patter against the glass.

"Oh, please, no," I mutter. Yes, of course I saw the forecast, but obviously I was hoping the weather models were all wrong.

They're not.

And Thomas isn't happy.

One issue that simply did not occur to me: we never ride in the rain. It's too dangerous—in Florida, in summer, anyway. Maybe in other places it's possible to have rain without lightning, but I've never enjoyed such a climate, and neither has my horse. Now we've left behind a season of deadly lightning and plunged ourselves directly into winter (that's how today feels, for sure) and despite all the riding and training and schooling shows, I'm caught unprepared.

Unprepared.

The realization hits me like a kick in the chest. All of that work, all of those shows, and the heat stroke and Landon paying for stalls and even the day we rode in the downpour during the tropical depression—none of that set up Thomas for what I need right now, which is a quiet, forward, attentive horse who can perform a dressage test despite a cold mist of rain that is trickling into his ears and beading on his long eyelashes.

Instead of relaxing into his warm-up, Thomas is getting more upset by the minute. He shakes his head and snorts with increasing frequency as we walk unevenly around the warm-up arena, avoiding other horses who don't seem nearly as concerned by the weather. He lifts his head and flattens his ears instead of relaxing into the bridle or stretching out his back. If we go into the ring like this, our marks are going to be horrible. Bottom of the bunch. Oh, god. I never should have come.

Never should have set my goals so high.

Never should have believed I could do this on my own.

This isn't a game! This is a pro's work and I'm just a thirty-three-year-old former trophy wife who can barely be trusted to feed a barn-full of horses on my own, let alone—

"Mackenzie?"

I glance around and sit to whoa Thomas as I spot Landon standing near the warm-up entrance. Something clenches and unclenches in my stomach, giving me enough room to take a deep breath for the first time since I saw the rain falling this morning.

Landon can help.

I don't know how, but he hasn't failed me yet.

He walks over, a scrap of fabric in one hand, and says, "Ear bonnet might help."

"You think?" I try to rein in my skepticism while Thomas shakes his head again. "I've never put an ear bonnet on him. It might make things worse."

"You never know what contraptions a racehorse has had on his head," Landon says. "He might have worn pompoms in his ears to stop noise, or blinkers, or fleece...you name it. He's been around the block a few times. I doubt a bonnet will upset him."

I know Landon's right. Racehorses experience so much in their short careers. Sometimes it's impossible to give them enough credit for the things they've done, seen, or yeah, worn on their heads. "Okay," I agree, taking a deep breath. "Let's try it."

On goes the bonnet, Landon deftly sweeping Thomas's ears into the fabric sleeves. He smooths the apron of fabric below the ears, pressing it beneath the brow-band of the bridle. It's a fall of deep blue fabric that looks regal and beautiful against Thomas's dark coat. Despite the falling rain and the dull gloss of his damp hair, the bonnet gives him an undeniably distinguished air.

"He looks very fancy now," Landon says approvingly.

"I think he likes it," I say, watching my horse closely. He swivels his ears, feeling out the dry cloth, then lowers his head of his own accord for the first time since I brought him out of his stall. He snorts gently, clearing his nose. It's a welcome sound.

"Of course he likes it," Landon says, satisfaction in his tone. "No more water in his ears. Poor boy just wasn't used to that kind of misery."

"I guess I raised a real hothouse flower," I admit, laughing shakily. "Bringing him inside every day and keeping him inside until it stops storming at night."

"Well, it's Florida." Landon looks up at me, amusement twinkling in his blue eyes. "Maybe we have to do things a little differently there if we want to survive the summer. Now, get back out there and let's see what Thomas has under the hood on a cold day!"

It turns out that Thomas has quite a lot of gas when the weather is chilly. This is the coldest weather we've experienced together, and without the fear of water in his ears, Thomas lets the cold of the morning add zing to his step and zest to his attitude.

All that extra pep carries us through the mud puddles and around the traffic as the warm-up arena fills up with fellow Thoroughbreds, gunned up on chilly air and excitement. When the warm-up ring steward, a fresh-faced volunteer with a clipboard wrapped in a plastic bag, calls our number and "Five minutes to your test!" I wave a hand to acknowledge her, but it's Landon I'm looking for. As if by magic, he reappears by the gate, this time with Sara and Annabelle flanking him. I think confusedly that Annabelle's trench is adorable, and then they're flagging me over.

Thomas buries his muzzle in Sara's cupped hands, accepting the cookie she has palmed there, while Landon runs a dry cloth over the horse's face, brushing away water and muddy grit that has splashed up from the wet arena. Annabelle gives me an encouraging smile. "Know your test?" she asks, like a horse show mom to her nervous child.

I nod. The test might be the only thing I do know right now. I'd be hard-pressed to name the planets of our solar system or even recite the ABCs, because there are alarm bells ringing in my brain that are drowning out all the information I've ever absorbed...except for my test.

Somehow (I assume they lead us over) I find myself and Thomas in the arena, nodding to the judge, and we begin.

"TWELFTH," I SAY, feeling sheepish about how excited I am. "We got twelfth place!"

Ryan would have snorted about not even making it into the top ten. But Ryan isn't here.

Landon is, and he sweeps me up in a tremendous bear-hug that takes my breath away, right there in front of the bulletin board where scores have been posted. We're on the crowded concourse of the indoor arena, surrounded by competitors and their families and shoppers browsing the vendor booths, but in Landon's arms, all of that buzz falls away. I press my head to his shoulder, reveling in the feeling of safety and appreciation. It's so warm here.

"Good job," I hear Sara say, and I shift a little, remembering we aren't actually alone. I make eye contact with Sara and Annabelle, and they smile confidingly, as if we are all in on some little secret.

That Landon and I are really a couple now, probably. Nothing formal has been said, but something about the way they watch us tells me that sometimes words aren't necessary.

THE MIRACLE AND calamity of cold fronts appears the next morning, with a clear, brilliant sunrise that sparkles over grass the texture and color of diamonds. "A frost," I sigh, turning away from the chilly window.

I'm really not made for frosts. And neither are my clothes. I made it through the wet yesterday by wearing my raincoat until it was time for the test, but how am I going to survive the cold on show-jumping day?

Sara joins me as I loiter by the kitchen coffeepot, already dressed in my short shirt and trying not to shiver despite the central heating. "Honey," she says, "That shirt is gorgeous and I do want to know where you got it, but it's not winter-weight."

"It's another one of my designs," I admit, "and it's absolutely for summer riding. That's pretty much the only kind I know."

She surveys me. "You are aware it gets cold in north Florida, right?"

"I—"

"Never mind. We need to get you set for today. And do not let me forget that we need to talk more about your riding clothes. Annabelle and I are both very invested in your style, and how we can make it ours." She laughs. "Let's hit my closet. My show clothes haven't had a workout recently. They won't be as stylish as this, but at least our little Florida orange blossom won't freeze."

AT LAST, SOMETHING we are prepared for! The warm-up ring above the jumping arena is a hairy, scary place full of wide-eyed ex-racehorses wondering where the starting gate has been hidden, but we conquered this madness back during our summer schooling shows. Despite the cold, which gives every horse an extra lift and the Florida horses even more, Thomas is able to keep his cool in the warm-up...unlike a few other characters who are hopping around like kangaroos.

The ring steward at the gate gives Landon a smile and pats Thomas on the neck. "It's good to have a cheering section," she says. "I'll cheer for you guys, too. And so will my ring crew."

She pats my boot familiarly. "You did it! You made it to the Makeover!"

There it is, that heartfelt and genuine kindness that pervades this entire horse park. While it was already obvious from online interactions, it's unmistakable and almost overwhelming in person. Everyone at the Makeover is everyone's cheering section, and we have won already by bringing these befuddled young horses from racehorse to sport horse in less than a year.

Very less than that, in some cases. As the horse on course misses his distance and demolishes a jump, looking astonished at the rails falling around his hooves, the ring steward sighs and applauds, anyway. "He's only been off the track a few months," she says. "He's doing great."

She means it. And when the pair exits the arena and walks past us, the rider blushing under a total of twelve jumping faults, the ring steward pats her boot, then sends another volunteer scurrying after her with a packet of horse cookies and a granola bar.

"She'll be fine," she says. "And now it's your turn!"

Chapter Forty-One

I PLANNED ON going to the celebration party held up in the "Big Barn," a historic barn on the horse park property. But after the day I'd had, and the hours we spent grazing Thomas so that he didn't feel pent up before his trip back to Florida, I decided that an appearance to pick up my ribbons was the best I could do.

Sara stands in my bedroom doorway and watches me pin my hair up in a tidy bun. She's already starting to feel like the sister I never had. "You have the most classic style," she says admiringly. "So simple and elegant."

"I've never really thought of myself as elegant," I laugh. "But I do like to keep things neat and tidy. Does that count?"

"Oh, that's probably the basis of elegance," she says. "Look at your riding shirts! The cut of them, the seams, the colors... you're neat, tidy, and look like a queen in the saddle. They're going to be incredibly popular."

"Going to be?" I turn around, patting my bun to make sure it's centered. "I don't know when that will be. I don't have the cash to get a business started right now, but maybe in a few years..."

"Oh, Annabelle and I are ready to invest," Sara informs me

seriously. She strides over to my closet and takes out a baby-pink shirt with a subtle scattering of tiny rhinestones dotted around the collar. *Bling without screaming bling,* I call that kind of decoration. You can be cute without bearing resemblance to a disco ball. "And I hope you know I'm buying this one from you. I don't even care that it's yours. It's mine now. Say goodbye." She hides it behind her back and fastens me with a sparkling smile.

"You don't have to buy it," I say. "You've been more than generous, and I would love for you to have it. As a gift."

"I'm buying it," she repeats firmly. "And Annabelle and I will be in Florida in a couple of weeks, ready to talk business. I hope you like champagne. We celebrate all our triumphs with bubbly."

"Let's start by celebrating this incredible horse show," I suggest lightly, keeping all my surging feelings beneath my skin, but just barely. If she and Annabelle really want to help me get the clothing business off the ground, I can launch my brand years earlier than I ever anticipated. I imagine sponsoring a class here at The Thoroughbred Makeover next year, adding my own designs to the prizes and seeing horsewomen out in those arenas wearing the show clothes I sketched into life.

And maybe, just maybe, I'll bring another horse here next year, too.

After all, how rare is a horse show where everyone is a winner just for showing up? What a rush of adrenaline to take me into the winter months! This kind of feeling is addicting. I feel like an entirely new person from the woman who drove north from Wellington five months ago.

Like the makeover wasn't just for Thomas, as I'd hoped. It was absolutely for me, too.

* * *

LANDON FOLLOWS ME outside the Big Barn, my goodie bag clutched in one hand. He's been an attentive date all evening, but even with him at my side, exhaustion is catching up with me. The heat and hilarity of the party is just a little too much for me to handle after this week.

At least I showed up, I tell myself. And I have my ribbons. A burst of purple, for seventh place in show jumping, plus a beautiful rosette just for showing up, just for getting here—the biggest win of all, for each of us. That's what makes this show so special. We all won, by getting our Thoroughbreds to this makeover.

They're huge, the kind of rosettes horses take home from A-circuit shows like the ones Basil and Kayla will be frequenting this winter at Legends Equestrian Center, the shows I rode in back in my Wellington days. They'll dwarf the little schooling show ribbons Thomas won this summer. They seem to be a marker, a milestone. A new life that started here.

"You got some real big ribbons in this bag," Landon observes in a country drawl, echoing my thoughts. "These saddle pads are nice, too."

"Landon, I could not have done this without you," I burst out.

He lifts an eyebrow. "Of course you could have."

"No, seriously. You have been the biggest help in the world. And Sara and Annabelle...they're so wonderful. I just feel...I don't know, guilty."

Now Landon raises the other eyebrow. I've confused him. No wonder. I'm pretty confused about what I'm feeling, too.

"All I mean is...I didn't want you around. I was so sure I

could do everything myself, and having a man around would just diminish me. And that wasn't fair of me at all."

"It wasn't," he agrees, "but you didn't know I'd be a help. And you're still wrong, Mackenzie. You could have done this without me. But I hope I made it a little easier."

I think back over the differences Landon made. The help in the riding arena. The stalls and support at the horse shows. The drive up here. The support of his family and the woman he thought wanted him for a prize, not a friend.

"You're right," I realize. "I could have done it alone. It would have been harder, that's all."

"Friends make things easier for each other."

I look at him, weighing his words. "But we're more than friends, aren't we?"

A smile creases his face, something like relief in the slackening of his brow. His blue eyes glitter at me. "I'd like to think we are. We've been circling around it for a little while, haven't we?"

I've been circling it, alright. But I realized it this week...and now I want to say it. "I think I'm in love with you, Landon," I say, dropping each word with feeling. "I think maybe I have been for a while, and I just didn't know how to handle it. After...everything. I didn't come to north Florida to fall in love." I can't help scowling at him. "I still don't really want to be."

He carefully sets down the goodie bag, making sure it doesn't topple over. And then he takes a step forward and tips up my chin. For a moment, I think how much taller he is. It's funny, really. My mouth falls open to laugh, and Landon makes the deepest little growl in his throat, an almost animal sound.

"I love you, Mackenzie," he says with meaning, and then he

kisses me until my knees buckle.

Maybe I don't want to be in love, but Landon is going to make sure I don't regret it.

Chapter Forty-Two

THANKSGIVING IN FLORIDA is not the gray and brown affair people have to suffer through up north, but it does get dark pretty early, which makes holding it outside kind of a rush job...especially when there are still horses to feed and care for. When Kayla decides we should take Thanksgiving Day off from training and just enjoy a barn family holiday together, we put our heads together and plan for a meal around one o'clock in the afternoon. "It gives us time for a nap afterwards," Kayla says wisely. "We never eat that much in the middle of the day. Our bodies won't know what to do."

"My body will know," Landon growls when I give him the news, and I laugh and shove him away, because one thing about workplace romances is that at least one of you has to know where the line is, and that person is occasionally me.

Most of the time, unfortunately, neither of us know where the line is.

But Kayla and Basil are unbothered by the love affair that sprang up in their barn aisle, probably because they got together in a barn, too, and everyone else they know has done the same thing. "Where else would you meet people?" Kayla points out when I sheepishly let her know, after our triumphant return from Kentucky, that I've officially entered into a relationship with Landon. "We don't go anywhere else!"

Anyway, Thanksgiving morning dawns sparkling clear and blue, with a cool breeze playing through the oak trees and rushing along the barn aisle as we feed breakfast and turn the horses out for the day. Landon turns out the two horses he has left on his end of the barn and watches them play a brisk game of chase. I find him leaning on the gate with a nostalgic expression on his face, eyes following the horses as they zig-zag across the paddock.

"Missing the other two?" I ask gently, slipping my hand into his. Landon successfully nursed all four horses back to prime hoof health, and with Basil's help, he sold the two geldings just a week ago. They're at show barns in Ocala, getting ready for their second acts in the hunter ring. Landon has seemed just a little down ever since.

"Yeah," he admits, giving my hand a squeeze. "And I know these two will have new homes soon, too. My end of the barn will be empty."

"There's no shortage of horses who need help with their feet," I remind him. "But you can't get so attached."

"What can I say?" He turns and gives me a smile that sends electricity zipping along my spine. "I'm an emotional guy."

"Some people might say *too* emotional—oh!" I squeal as he tugs me close for a kiss. "Stop that," I splutter afterward, but I don't mean it. There's no line. Who am I kidding? We do whatever we want around this barn. "Come on," I tell him, tugging his calloused hand. "We have tons to do to get the barn ready for Thanksgiving."

CLEAN, SWEPT, AND dusted: the barn aisle makes a

beautiful banquet hall once we've spent two hours sweating over the chores. Kayla brings out the table we ate our June Thanksgiving dinner on, and we cover it with a couple of coolers won at various jumper shows in winters past. They make eclectic tablecloths, and since they've never really been used, they smell like fabric softener, not horse. An important attribute of any barn aisle Thanksgiving, I think, is cutting down on the horsey odors. You don't want anything to interfere with your enjoyment of the flavors to come.

Basil returns from town with two coolers full of food—one hot, one cold—and then the set-up begins. Everything is left in the take-out containers, in deference to flies and the possibility of breaking a china platter or casserole dish, but Kayla and I decorate around the foil and styrofoam with strings of fabric autumn leaves, extra reins that add an equestrian flair, and the occasional snaffle bit for good measure. Landon brings out the folding chairs and adds a unique contribution: colorful saddle towels, numbered and labeled from a variety of stakes races run at Tampa Bay Downs. "Got them from a client last week," he explains, folding a yellow-and-black towel over a chair. "Pretty cool chair cover, right?"

"They're awesome!" I exclaim, claiming a teal-and-black towel for my chair. It has a large number 6 on it, and beneath that, SANDPIPER STAKES in block lettering. "I'm keeping this. It's going to look cool on my couch."

"I know someone who can make pillows out of them," Kayla suggests.

"Oh, yes, *please*."

Landon grins. "Glad I could help you redecorate."

"I think your sister would like them, too," I say. "And Annabelle? They'll be here next week. I'll ask them." Annabelle and Sara have been doing the heavy lifting on getting the Thoroughbred Thread Company in order. That's the name we all decided on for the clothing company we're launching together...with my designs as the primary sale item. I wonder if there's something I could do that brings in these saddle towel designs...

Kayla waves her hand in my face. "I see you designing something new, but it's time to eat! Go wash your hands. And bring back the pilgrims."

"It wouldn't be Thanksgiving in Florida without the pilgrims," I agree, and waltz back to my apartment to clean up and bring the Publix Pilgrims to the table.

Landon sneaks in while I'm drying my hands, closing the door behind him with a sharp click so I won't be horribly surprised by him. I glance over my shoulder and shake my head. "There is not time for anything before we eat. They're in the aisle!"

"That hasn't stopped us before," Landon says, crossing the small apartment in three strides and pulling me up against him.

"Not with dinner on the table," I protest, batting at his hard chest, and he sighs and lets me go.

"Fine."

"Thanksgiving is not a sexy holiday," I say, turning to retrieve the pilgrims from their spot in the cabinet next to the oven, "and yet you are very revved up about something."

"It's our first holiday as a couple," Landon says.

"Adorable." I'm not convinced.

"I'm just so happy that the woman who broke into my apartment and stole my coffee is now my girlfriend." Landon makes a wide-eyed, innocent face at me. "I mean, I should have known that day she wouldn't stop flashing me that she was into me—"

"My shirt got popped open by a very bad horse," I remind him. "Let's not make it more than it was."

"Or was it all part of the plan?"

Outside, I hear a scuffle, followed by Kayla shouting at Sid not to chase the cat.

"Your dog is getting into trouble," I say. "You better get out there and restore order."

"We're going to make this a sexy holiday," Landon warns, turning for the door. "Just you wait and see."

"Later," I say. "After our movie."

"Movie?"

"We're watching *Bambi* later. I want to see you cry at last."

"Oh, no we aren't," Landon says, opening the door. His dog leaps up at him, the picture of innocence. "Right, Sid? No sad deer movies for us."

"Are you guys watching *Bambi* tonight?" Kayla exclaims. "Oh no, I want to, but I don't want to, at the same time. What should we do? Watch it at our house and make margaritas during the sad parts?"

I grin at Landon. "Perfect," I tell her, just to watch him make a face at me. "Thanksgiving dinner, nap, feed horses dinner, watch *Bambi* together. Am I leaving anything out of this amazing holiday?"

Kayla says I have the gist of it and heads into the tack room to get the drinks from the fridge. Landon waits until she's occupied, then scoops me up against him again. This time, I don't try to push him off. I just look up at him, content with life: this place, these people, the work, the play.

I came back from Kentucky feeling like a new person, and that feeling really hasn't gone away. Accomplishing the

Thoroughbred Makeover with Thomas was the reset that my life needed, and doing it with the help of people who cared about me was actually better than doing it all by myself. Now I'm looking forward to a winter season full of horse shows, new personal successes, and the prospect of starting my business with Landon's sister and his old friend...and enjoying this romance with Landon, so funny and full of surprises, wherever it might lead us.

"I think you left out something very important," Landon says, planting a kiss on my mouth.

"I'll let you take a nap with me," I concede. "If you're quiet and stay on your own side of the bed."

"But *tonight*..."

"Skip the sad parts of *Bambi*," I advise, "or else we'll just weep in each other's arms tonight."

"I'm going to do everything in my power to make sure we don't watch that deer movie," he promises. "You shouldn't try to make your boyfriend cry just for laughs. It's not nice."

"Hey, I never said I was nice."

"Oh, you're nice," Landon growls, saying it like it's my biggest fault. "The nicest person I've ever met."

"Stop that."

"And the cutest—" He kisses my neck.

"Enough of that." My knees get weak every time his lips touch my neck. "Landon, stop!"

Kayla emerges with two jugs of iced tea. She takes one look at us and laughs. "We might be skipping movie night tonight," she says.

"Haha!" Landon laughs triumphantly.

"Okay, crazies," Basil announces, and we realize he's been quietly sitting at the table this entire time, watching us misbehaving. "I'm starving over here."

"Let's do this," Kayla urges, pulling out chairs for Landon and me. And as we sit side by side, she leans across the table and pulls the lid off the main entree's foil container. An enticing aroma escapes, pulling me forward like a cartoon character who just spotted a pie cooling on a windowsill.

"Fried chicken for Thanksgiving!" I exclaim. "Oh, this is the best holiday ever."

And everyone around the table agrees...it really is. "I'm thankful we all agree fried chicken is the best," Kayla laughs.

"I'm thankful I thought of it," Basil says comfortably.

Landon gives me a cuddle, pulling me against him, and says, "I'm thankful I came to this barn at just the right time in my life."

I decide then and there that I won't make him watch *Bambi*. Not tonight, anyway. "I'm thankful for the exact same thing," I say, tipping my head against Landon's shoulder. "Just the right time in my life...in all our lives, maybe."

Keep Up with Natalie Keller Reinert

WOULD YOU LIKE to be the first to know about new releases, special sales, book-signing events, and everything going on in the world of Ocala Horse Girls, Briar Hill Farm, and beyond?

Sign up for Natalie Keller Reinert's mailing list and never miss another update.

Visit: https://www.nataliekreinert.com/sign-up/

And for a bonus scene from Landon's point of view, visit nataliekreinert.com/bonus-content.

Acknowledgments

IN 2023, I was lucky enough to volunteer at the Retired Racehorse Project's Thoroughbred Makeover, held at Kentucky Horse Park. And that was enough to convince me this was a pretty magical horse show. Everyone was there to celebrate their personal win: getting their retired racehorse to this landmark event. And everyone was more than happy to share that celebration with their fellow competitors. Of all the shows which claim "just getting there is a triumph," at the Thoroughbred Makeover, that's one hundred percent the truth.

I had the idea to use the Makeover as a goal for one of my Ocala Horse Girls novels and reached out to the team at Retired Racehorse Project for permission to use their name and setting. To my absolute delight, they were in!

So many thanks to Kristen Kovatch Bentley at RRP for taking my idea to the table, for sharing everyone's enthusiasm for the project, and for being as great a cheerleader for a novel about the Thoroughbred Makeover as you are about getting those horses there in real life!

You can learn more about the Thoroughbred Makeover at https://www.therrp.org/ and if you're looking for an awesome way to join the community without a horse, consider volunteering at the event! It's a wonderful time and as I tell everyone on the fence about volunteering at horse shows, it's like having a job where you can't actually get fired if you're not very good at it yet. The advantages of being unpaid help!

Ocala Horse Girls and all of my books are supported by my terrific Patreon and Ream subscribers. Thanks, as always, to all of you for your monthly and annual support of equestrian fiction.

Thanks to: Susan Imhof Wollerton, Amelia Heath-Emmons, Marena, Christine Cavanaugh, TECS, Selina Hornblow, Miranda Mues, Ashley Swing, Eris, Erika Thomas, Shelby Graft, Kellie Halteman, Jennifer Williams, Megan McDonald, Adrienne Brant, Sally Testa, Heidi Schmid, Cathy Luo, Elana Rabinow, Laura, Dörte Voigt, Empathy, Tayla Travella, Gretchen Fieser, JoAnn Flejszar, Nancy Neid, Libby Henderson, Maureen VanDerStad, Leslie Yazurlo, Nicole Beisel, Mel Policicchio, Harry Burgh, Nicole, Kathlynn Angie-Buss, Peggy Dvorsky, Karen Carrubba, Emma Gooden, Katie Lewis, Silvana Ricapito, Sarina Laurin, Di Hannel, Jennifer, Cyndy Searfoss, Kaylee Amons, Kathi Lacasse, Hannah, Diana Aitch, Liz Greene, Zoe Bills, Cheryl Bavister, Sarah Seavey, Tricia Jordan, Brinn Dimmler, Rhonda Lane, C. Sperry, CEB, Andra, Hnnjsmoth, Susan Cover, CHarrison, Karen Wolfsheimer, Rachel, Rtebby, Cat, Agavehurricane, Mary V, Lynne Gevirtz, Michelle Beck, JSF, Megan Devine, SailorEpona, Lisa Leonard Heck, Shauna, Heather Voltz, Susan Lambiris, Alyssa Weihe, Annika, and Renee Knowles.

So many of these names have appeared in my books over the

years, and I see you, appreciate you, and love you so much.
Thank you.

About the Author

NATALIE KELLER REINERT is the author of multiple series including The Eventing Series, Ocala Horse Girls, and Briar Hill Farm. Her novel *The Hidden Horses of New York* is the winner of the America Horse Publications Best Fiction Award and The Equus Film & Literary Festival Best Horse Racing Fiction Award; her novel *Turning for Home* was a finalist for the $10,000 Dr. Tony Ryan Book Award.

Originally from Hagerstown, Maryland, Reinert grew up in Central Florida and now lives in North Florida, where she writes full-time and enjoys the company of her family, horses, and cat. She's always working on at least three new projects, is probably plotting a book festival or a new kind of magazine, and co-hosts the award-winning equestrian humor podcast Adulting With Horses Podcast, along with fellow author Heather Wallace.

In addition to Reinert's interconnected equestrian series (which some fans have nicknamed "the Ocala-verse" since so many series are set in and around the horse-rich town of Ocala,

Florida) she also enjoys writing romantic comedy and literary fiction. Her novel *You Must Be This Tall* explores the world of theme parks and fandom with a richly imagined theme park called America the Beautiful as its setting, while her romantic comedies take readers on swoony journeys through New York City, Palm Springs, and beyond.

Find and follow Reinert on social media:

Instagram: instagram.com/nataliekreinert
Facebook: facebook.com/nataliekellerreinert
Web: nataliekreinert.com